A SUMMER
FOR
WAR

A MALCOLM MACPHAIL
WW1 NOVEL

A Summer for War: a Malcolm MacPhail WW1 novel

By Darrell Duthie

Copyright © 2021 Darrell Duthie

Published in 2021 by Esdorn Editions, the Netherlands

ISBN 978-94-92843-210 (trade paperback edition)
ISBN 978-94-92843-203 (e-book edition)

Cover design by JD Smith Design
Interior design and typesetting by JD Smith Design

Cover photographs acknowledgement: Canada Dept. of National Defence/Library and Archives Canada: A shell bursting in the village of Vimy. France, May 1917 (PA-001289); Canada Dept. of National Defence/Library and Archives Canada: Wounded and prisoners coming in. France, November 1916 (PA-000855)

www.darrellduthie.com

A SUMMER FOR WAR

A MALCOLM MACPHAIL WW1 NOVEL

DARRELL DUTHIE

Esdorn
Editions

Also by Darrell Duthie in the
Malcolm MacPhail WW1 series

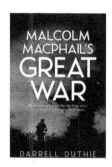   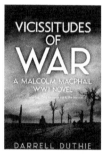

Malcolm MacPhail's Great War – (1917-1918)

My Hundred Days of War – (1918)

A War for King and Empire – (1915-1916)

Vicissitudes of War – (1916-1917)

PART ONE

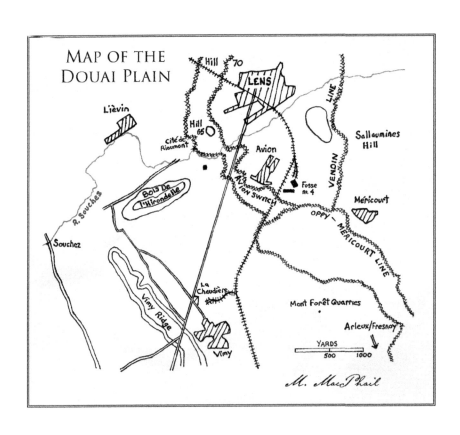

MAP OF THE DOUAI PLAIN

Hill 70

LENS

Liévin

Hill 65

Cité de Riaumont

Avion

Sallaumines Hill

VENOIN LINE

Fosse no. 4

AVION SWITCH

Bois De l'Hirondelle

R. Souchez

Méricourt

OPPY – MÉRICOURT LINE

Souchez

La Chaudière

Vimy Ridge

Mont Forêt Quarries

Arleux/Fresnoy

Vimy

YARDS
500   1000

M. MacPhail

CHAPTER 1

26th of April, 1917
Fort George, northwest of Neuville-Saint-Vaast, France

The general looked up with what might have been annoyance. 'Wait there, MacPhail,' he said curtly.

'Yes, sir,' I mumbled, my head hurriedly retreating through the low, heavily timbered doorway.

As I stood waiting outside his room in the central chamber of the dug-out, I shuffled uneasily from foot to foot. Rarely a day passed that I didn't speak a word or two with him, so on the face of it there was no reason for a dry throat and the terribly awkward leg work. Yet I'd been summoned at a moment's notice. Conscious I had nothing of any importance to report – the division's dispositions had barely changed, and the general was surely aware of that – it left me to speculate uselessly about other explanations for my required presence.

He certainly hadn't called for me to discuss the logistics of a forthcoming operation. If there was to be an operation – although that seemed inconceivable as we'd only just finished bouncing Fritz off Vimy Ridge two weeks before – I would hear about it through the normal chain of command. Which meant it had to be something else. As the junior man on his staff, the possibilities seemed limited. Few of them could be construed as especially positive. I sighed. I'd hear soon enough. Audible through the open doorway, Captain Ferguson of the

3

intelligence section was wrapping up his report.

'Finally, sir, the PPCLI report the Germans blew the tower off the Méricourt church. They say both the steeple and the roof are blown.' The general's reply was too soft to hear, but brief, the news of another Northern European church in ruins so common as to be commonplace. There was some comfort in the fact Ferguson had even bothered to mention it; I wasn't the only one on the staff scraping the bottom of the barrel for something of interest to present to the divisional commander.

While the captain apprised the general on the full extent of the afternoon's damage to ecclesiastical property by our God-fearing adversary, my eyes went in search of the colonel. If there was something nasty awaiting me the presence of the senior staff officer, the GSO1, Lieutenant-Colonel Hayter, was to be expected. He dealt with personnel matters and most things nasty. I was mildly surprised I hadn't spotted him in the room with the general, for he was usually at his side. A quick glance around the chamber now confirmed he was neither there, nor in any of the adjoining alcoves.

At the sound of footsteps I turned my attention again to the open doorway.

Ferguson appeared through it. He acknowledged me with a curt nod. To my questioning look, he responded with an affirmative bob of his head. I smiled politely and stepped through the narrow entranceway, ducking as I did so. Fort George was a sizeable redoubt, but having painfully experienced its low ceilings and profusion of hard wooden beams on more than one occasion, stooping was as much second nature as a matter of survival.

The General Officer Commanding (GOC) of the 3rd Canadian Division, Major-General Louis Lipsett, was seated behind a small, simple wooden table of a kind one saw everywhere behind the lines.

Pulling myself erect I was conscious of him observing me. With as much decorum as I could muster, I stepped forward a couple of paces to the table and came stiffly to attention.

The general's cap lay bottom up on the table. The rest of the tabletop was empty save for a neatly ordered pile of paper and a teapot. 'Lieutenant MacPhail,' said the general evenly. Gingerly he took a sip from his cup, steam still rising from it.

'You called for me, sir?'

'Yes, yes I did. At ease, Lieutenant.' This was followed by a long silence in which he said nothing, engendering in me an opposite reaction.

'I don't have much to report, sir,' I said in a rushed breath. 'The company of the 8th Field Engineers have completed their move, but otherwise the division is as it was.' I hesitated, looking at him for some hint of what he had in mind. There was none. 'Unless there are new orders I should be aware of, sir?'

Lipsett smiled to himself and put down his cup. He knew very well I was on a fishing expedition. Decisively he shook his head. 'No, Lieutenant, the division is remaining where it is. There are no plans at present. However, for you on the other hand –'

I stiffened. 'Sir?'

Lipsett placed his hands on the table, and his expression turned serious. 'I've always thought it important that my officers are well-rounded, prepared for a broad range of duties. General Byng has made no secret of the fact he strongly encourages this. I've no use for an officer if he's not able to adapt to new and changing circumstances. And above all to keep his wits about him.'

'Sir,' I said. In this instance the least said the better.

'With the Vimy show behind us, you'll have noticed a certain lull in the division's operations.'

I nodded.

'Which makes this an excellent moment to expose you to some other aspects of staff work. As it happens an opportunity has come along.' Lipsett rummaged through his papers briefly before extracting what appeared to be a signals sheet. Distractedly he glanced at it. 'The 7th Brigade will be exchanging liaison officers with the 5th Brigade.' He looked up. 'I've decided to send you along.'

A frown formed on my face. I guess I should have been thankful. Half the division were out every day, rain or shine, on working parties building roads over a muddy Vimy Ridge and onto the Douai Plain beyond. That was a backbreaking task I had no particular desire to experience. But contrary to what the general thought, I did have some experience doing liaison work. Beyond several harrowing late night excursions to reconnoitre the enemy wire, I'd ended up liaising between two battalions from two different divisions in the midst of a major attack at the Somme. It had left me holed in two different places; on occasion my shoulder still ached at the memory.

General Lipsett must have sensed something of what I was thinking – he'd recruited me from my hospital bed after all – for he condescended to explain further. 'You won't be at the front, MacPhail, you'll be at headquarters. But as 2nd Division is adjacent to us, as I'm sure you're aware, it's important we keep each other informed. Obviously, the colonel and I are most interested in hearing about anything that might bear on the division's current or future operations.'

Suddenly the whole idea seemed a lot more palatable. Hanging around one of the 2nd Division's brigade headquarters couldn't be that taxing. 'Yes, sir,' I said, with a bounce in my voice.

Had I been just that little bit more alert, I would have realized there was little point in liaising about the state of our joint road-building efforts.

'You may report at the 5th Brigade headquarters at the railway embankment dug-outs near Vimy station,' said the general. 'You're expected tomorrow morning.'

27th of April, 1917
Vimy, France

On the far side of Vimy Ridge, and several hundred yards northeast of the battered remains of the village which gave it its name, were a series of dug-outs whose proprietor had recently changed. These were not the grand German divisional dug-outs we'd found in Farbus. They'd had beer gardens in a Swiss motif, and a porch on which to pass the time, while inside broad staircases led down to the lower levels where high-ceilinged, neatly painted chambers clad in wooden wainscoting and filled with fine leather chairs revealed themselves under an electric light. The railway dug-outs were far simpler. They were dug into the high earthen embankment of the railway to Lens, a whole series of them which had once housed legions of Bavarians tasked with defending the ridge. Having summarily evicted the Bavarians, our sister division had quickly put them to its own use. One of the biggest of these dug-outs – a former medical post I later learned – was in an underpass, not far from the station. It was there, I was told, that the staff of the 5th Brigade had set up camp.

Approaching on a narrow country road early that morning, the blueish-grey mass of Vimy Ridge behind me, and the embankment off my right shoulder, I spotted a rail junction ahead. It was precisely as the map showed it; the line continued northwards to Lens, while a spur branched left to cut across to the west. Before the junction the road dipped as it approached the railway at an angle. Reaching the railway, it jogged sharply to the right, passing through the embankment and underneath the tracks by way of a stone-lined arch.

That would be the spot, I figured. I was pleased I'd made the entire journey with nary a wrong turn. Another man was walking ahead of me and since leaving the village I'd been steadily gaining ground. I could see now that he was wearing a greatcoat and he looked like an officer. He might very well be the other liaison officer from the division, from the 7th Brigade. What our hosts were to make of two of us I don't rightly know.

I hastened my step with the intent of overtaking him when a whirr in the air caught my ear. It didn't so much catch my ear as seized me in a constricting vice, freezing me to the spot, my forehead pulsing. *A shell!*

Instinctively (and wholly unnecessarily) I ducked. I say unnecessarily as I don't think in nearly three years of war there had been a single documented case, nor even a trench rumour, of a man escaping a shell merely by ducking. The shell roared past not far overhead, tearing at the sky as it did so. Only then did I leap away to the side of the road where the blackened remains of a tree beckoned. Where one shell was to be found, others would soon follow – Fritz was wearisomely predictable that way. As I landed in the dirt I heard the shell burst with a deep thud. When finally I turned to look, the telltale black plume was hovering in the air north of Vimy, only a few hundred yards behind.

Then, as if to confirm my fears, another round screeched over very low.

I glanced down the road. The officer ahead of me had also taken shelter, although he probably realized like I did that a few furrows in the earth, or even a tree stump, was shelter barely worthy of the name. While the enemy's efforts were plainly directed at the village, it wouldn't have been the first time a worn-out barrel threw up a short. I stared down the road at the rail bridge, eyeing it carefully. That might stop a shell or two, I thought, noting the thick stonework. A shell whistled over. I glanced again at the overpass. It couldn't have been more than 100 yards away. I could run it in a minute. Less.

I got to my feet and put on a sprint.

Nearing the officer I began to shout: 'C'mon. Run for it!' I was up to him before he reacted. He looked at me in surprise, then began to hoist himself awkwardly upwards. He wasn't the lieutenant from the 7th Brigade I was anticipating but a major I didn't recognize at all. Breathing heavily, I bent at the knees and reached out an arm to help him out of the ditch.

He seized it. Once he was standing firmly on both feet we began to run. The air shrieked as another shell tore overhead.

The weather had softened remarkably these last few days and it was beginning to feel like spring. It had been a long, harsh winter, and not only because of the fighting. Tucked in the crook of my elbow was a trench coat, which somehow I hadn't dropped. The major was still wearing his and probably wished he wasn't. Despite the encumbrances we made good progress.

Winded, more from the excitement than the exercise, we came to a halt in the shadow of the overpass stonework. The shells were coming in rapid succession now, no less terrifying for the many feet of brick, earth and train rails above our heads.

Of average height and lean physique, the major's most remarkable features were his pert little moustache, doleful blue eyes, and sagging dark bags under those eyes. The bags made him look as if someone had taken a few swings at him – either that or he'd been up several nights running. He was scrutinizing me and my tunic sleeve with interest. 'Thanks,' he breathed.

Graciously I bowed my head and followed it up with a smile.

With that the major's demeanour lost some of its seriousness. 'I'm guessing you must be Lieutenant MacPhail, the liaison from the 3rd Division,' he said in a friendly tone. The divisional patch on my sleeve was a sure-fire giveaway, but before I could confirm he added: 'Follow

me.' He led me through a doorway in the embankment I hadn't noticed earlier, and down a long flight of solid wooden stairs. The air was
cool and smelled of damp. I could hear voices below.

'By the way, I'm Clark-Kennedy, the Brigade Major,' he said over
his shoulder. 'Welcome.'

'Thank you, sir. Pleased to meet you,' I called out after him.

We stepped down into a substantial room lit by a whole cathedral's
worth of candles. From the bulbs hanging from the ceiling – approvingly I noted it was possible to stand without fear of whopping my
head against some beam or other protrusion – I could see that the
Bavarians hadn't needed candles. But since their departure no one had
gotten around to re-connecting the electricity. Far more important
than light, the telephones were definitely working. I heard an orderly
speaking into one. '164th R.I.R.,' he was saying, plainly parroting the
person on the other end of the line. 'Yes, sir, I'll be sure to pass it along.'

'Is that news from the patrol?' asked Clark-Kennedy. He'd heard it
as well.

'Yes, sir. They encountered three of the enemy and brought a body
back for identification,' replied the soldier. 'I was to tell you he was
with the 164th Reserve Infantry Regiment, sir.'

The major glanced back at me. 'You've come at a busy moment,
Lieutenant. As it happens, you caught me returning from the brigadier
at Les Tilleuls. We've only just established our advanced headquarters
here, so everything's still a bit rudimentary I'm afraid.'

At this I rubbed at my chin, if only to disguise my surprise. While
I had more or less expected the brigade commander to be on hand to
greet me as General Lipsett's emissary, I certainly hadn't expected to
be reporting at an advanced headquarters. The announcement that I
found myself in one came as somewhat of a shock. Advanced headquarters were invariably for one thing, and one thing alone.

'164th Regiment,' mused Clark-Kennedy, thinking about what the
signaller had said. 'It appears almost certain we'll be up against them.'

'Sir?'

'In the forthcoming operation.'

I coughed uneasily. 'Forthcoming operation, sir?'

'I thought you knew. Why do you think you're here?' He looked
round, then found what he was searching for on a nearby table and

passed me a sheaf of typewritten pages. OPERATION ORDER 141 was printed at the top of the first page.

'"Instructions for attack on Arleux Loop," sir?' I said hesitatingly, reading the title of the order aloud. No one had said anything about an attack being in the works, least of all General Lipsett. Quite the opposite in fact. Lipsett had made it clear our division had no such plans. Or had he? I racked my brains, trying to recall his exact words.

Either way, I was certain he'd said nothing whatsoever about an attack by the 2nd Division. I should have known there was more to it than a simple exchange of officers. Enquiringly I looked at Clark-Kennedy.

'Read on,' said the major. 'It's all explained.' He turned away and began talking to one of the staff.

I sank into an empty chair and started reading. It didn't take me long, although I read carefully.

It was less than three weeks since the Vimy show and the big offensive along the Scarpe began, but it was not to end with those efforts. As was so often the case, GHQ had grander ambitions. It was easy to be ambitious sitting in a château far removed from the objects of your ambition.

Very early tomorrow morning the 1st and 2nd Divisions were to seize the hamlet of Arleux and the trenches surrounding it. It was all part of something much bigger, and I raised an eyebrow when I read that our divisional artillery and machine guns were to play a role in support. Evidently that didn't constitute an operation in General Lipsett's mind.

When the general spoke about the need for his officers to be prepared for the unexpected, he hadn't meant it theoretically. He'd so neatly dropped me in the deep end, I suspect that was his intent all along. It had become a question of "sink or swim" as my childhood swimming coach so quaintly phrased it. Of course, hanging around the 5th Brigade's dug-out and sending an infrequent message was hardly asking the impossible – Boche bombardments notwithstanding.

'Malcolm!' called a voice. I looked up and saw that it was Lieutenant O'Neill. By chance I'd met him only last week. He looked barely twenty, with his rosy cheeks and gleaming eyes. He was fresh from officers' school and an extended stint in England, and was presumably the 7th Brigade's liaison officer. He'd slipped in while I was reading.

We talked for a bit.

'Hey,' he said as we were finishing, 'Captain Walker and I are moving forward to the battalion headquarters at the Mont Forêt Quarries. Are you coming?' O'Neill stared at me expectantly. Over his shoulder the captain in question was watching me.

With an effort I suppressed the groan, if not the sceptical look.

'They have a telephone there,' O'Neill quickly added, 'if that's what's bothering you. You'll be able to send messages without a problem. I figured it'd be easier and quicker to inform our superiors if we're not two steps removed from the action. The captain agreed to take us.'

O'Neill, for all his misplaced zeal, was not entirely incorrect. Although he was obviously unaware of the tendency for German shells to sever telephone lines at inconvenient moments, not to mention the effect they had on eager and unsuspecting liaison officers.

'Do you suppose they'll have pigeons on hand?' I asked, mischievously. 'In case the lines go down.'

He frowned, his eyes blinking as he reflected on this. 'Oh, I expect they will,' he said firmly.

I took a deep breath and sighed. O'Neill was altogether too eager, and too inexperienced; a dangerous combination at the front.

'Sure, I'll go with you,' I said.

Someone had to keep an eye out for him.

CHAPTER 2

Before dawn, 28th of April, 1917
Front line near Arleux-en-Gohelle, France

Cutting through the stilted quiet of the early morning, the cheerful warbling of a single nightingale in a nearby copse sounded down the line. No one paid it any heed. Minds were elsewhere, on matters that had nothing to do with good cheer or song. Somehow the men managed a nervous smile or two. A smile was more than I could muster, especially as some genius at battalion headquarters had suggested we depart the comparative safety of the dug-out to 'observe' the attack going in. I sighed when I heard, for we'd only just arrived. Predictably O'Neill found it a splendid idea.

'Won't be long now,' murmured a lieutenant from the battalion staff, glancing up from his watch. We stood in a small group in the front-line trench peering eastwards towards what was known as the Arleux Loop. The "Loop" was no more than a slight westward bulge in the German line around the modest village of Arleux. GHQ had decided it should be eliminated. It was an old and well-favoured stratagem of the generals, a line of thinking vaguely reminiscent of the training camp non-commissioned officers; except where the NCOs obsessed about straight bed sheets, the generals preoccupied themselves with more important matters like straightening the line. I'd never much understood the need for either.

Two companies, half the battalion, were to lead the attack. They were crouched in wait a couple of hundred yards forward in the middle of No-Man's-Land, packed into a treacherously shallow jumping-off trench that was completed in great haste several hours earlier. It wasn't far from where we were, but yet too far to see. With the creeping approach of dawn the sky was softening to a flint grey, the visibility still no more than 100 yards at best.

The 2nd Division battalion that I was visiting, the 25th out of Nova Scotia, was assigned the left flank of the attack. Three other battalions of the 1st Division, including my old 10th Battalion, were to their right and squared up against the village itself. The enemy was well dug in and in possession of an "unusually large number of machines guns" according to the latest intelligence. While that constituted pretty much the extent of my knowledge and apparently that of the intelligence staff, the brigade captain, Walker, had let something slip. It made me suspect he knew more. As I've never been one content to shuffle along in blissful ignorance, marching to death or worse in some endeavour of which I knew nothing and understood even less, I approached him.

At the sound of me clearing my throat he turned to look. 'You mentioned something earlier about today's offensive, sir,' I began. 'I just wondered what the plan was.'

'Well, 1st Division is to take the village, of course.' I nodded. That I knew. 'And between them and Oppy there's a battalion of Oxford & Bucks from the 2nd Imperial Division on the flank,' he added. Oppy was 1000 yards south of Arleux. There the bulge in the German trenches straightened, and the front line ran southwards until it reached the banks of the River Scarpe.

Expectantly I stared, waiting for him to continue. That the Ox & Bucks were holding our right was not exactly the big picture summary I'd been looking for.

Abruptly the captain looked away – as if there was something to see across the darkened and dishevelled fields. Which there wasn't, so that meant it was a feint. A moment of stilted silence followed. He watched the fields and I watched him. When he spoke again it was with a tone of finality that suggested he was intent on terminating the discussion. 'A half-dozen Imperial divisions will attack all the way south to the Scarpe, Lieutenant,' he muttered out of the corner of his mouth.

Softly I whistled. Only five days earlier Field-Marshal Haig had resumed the offensive east of Arras for the second time this month. Today it appeared he was having another go at it; one clearly didn't become field-marshal without a certain "damn the torpedoes" mindset – cavalry man or not. 'That must be at least six miles of front,' I said thoughtfully. 'So it's another big show, sir?'

'Yes, it's a big show alright, Lieutenant,' Walker replied, but didn't elaborate. Even if I'd wanted to press him, he'd now clamped his field glasses to his eyes. And while they may not have helped in seeing anything, they did help in not seeing me, and I suspect he was looking forward to the barrage when he couldn't hear me either. I think Walker was embarrassed he didn't know more, though instead of simply ad- mitting to his ignorance he resorted to subterfuge. He ought to have realized I didn't expect he was attending the field-marshal's briefings. But some officers were touchy that way. Or perhaps it was the tension.

The soft murmur of conversation died away as the minutes ticked down to 4.25 a.m. and ZERO Hour. We all knew what was coming, but it was unnerving waiting for it to begin, even for those of us present as mere observers. Then, while Lieutenant O'Neill occupied himself with an intense study of his watch's second hand, the guns erupted. A storm of light and thunder followed.

The roar of the barrage was sudden and tumultuous, and it over- whelmed every other sound, including those of the men charging forward and the song of the poor, shell-shocked bird cowering in its tree. It was a sight and a sound some of us soldiers were acclimatized to by this spring of 1917; it was to be hoped the nightingale was as well.

Six hundred yards away, a wall of flashing fire and whirling steel had descended in front of the German trenches. Clouds of dirt and smoke billowed upwards. Towards that the men would be steadily walking, in tune with the barrage, rifles at the high port. Acclimatized or not, I stood gaping like the rest of our little party. Soon sparking flashes, like fireflies, could be seen as the barrage lifted and moved on, and the small-arms fire began. Slightly to the south of our position, where the roofs of Arleux-en-Gohelle and the steeple of a church were lit by shellfire, red and green flares soared into the dark sky above the havoc.

'Fritz hardly needs the S.O.Ss,' I shouted at Captain Walker.

He shook his head. If their comrades in the artillery had slept through the first minutes of the barrage, they weren't likely to spot a red Christmas bulb or two above their heads.

I turned to O'Neill. His helmet was tilted low, the palms of his hands covering his ears, and his eyes fixed on the scene, seemingly enraptured by the sight of what was likely his first-ever barrage. I had trouble even remembering mine. But then I'd been at the front for what seemed half a lifetime, or at least since the beginning of 1915. He positively jumped when I roared his name in his ear.

'I don't want to spoil the show, but if Fritz lobs a Woolly Bear this way…' I shouted.

It was a hint even O'Neill could understand. Captain Walker on the other side of me was already rounding up the others. I feared we'd left our withdrawal a little late.

We only barely exited the trench when a curtain of enemy fire came crashing down in the middle of No-Man's-Land.

'That was close,' said O'Neill, glancing back over his shoulder.

'Not really,' I grunted. At this I saw him frown. 'They must have spotted our jumping-off trenches,' I explained. 'Otherwise that bombardment of theirs would have been falling right about here. Then you and I would have had real worries, O'Neill.'

'But what about the attack? They'll be completely cut up.'

'Don't worry. The boys will be long out of those trenches.'

What I didn't say was that while the first waves had surely escaped the bombardment, and were racing towards the enemy lines, the Germans might keep at it. In which case if men and supplies were needed, they'd first have to dodge a hail of shrapnel and high explosive. Cutting off the attackers from reinforcements then counter-attacking in force was standard procedure for our foe. Even the operation orders had warned about such a scenario. But there was no sense worrying about that now. Time would tell. We hastened towards the Mont Forêt Quarries where the 25th Battalion HQ had set up shop.

However, we didn't remain for long.

That wasn't solely because it was on the crowded side, nor even because a forward ammunition dump was established in close proximity, although I did helpfully point out to O'Neill and Captain Walker the potential implications of a stray German shell. Even bearing in mind the presence of a whole squadron of cooing pigeons to carry messages – O'Neill proved correct about that – there just wasn't much to communicate, let alone liaise about. We decided to return to the brigade, for a better overview.

The captain, O'Neill and me reached the railway dug-out some thirty minutes later. Whereupon O'Neill was informed that the 26th Battalion on the divisional left was in contact with the PPCLI. As the PPCLI was a battalion from the 7th Brigade, *his* brigade, he rushed over to the telephone to report. Captain Walker meanwhile simply rushed off. He seemed relieved at the opportunity.

Having nowhere in particular to rush to, I slumped into an unoccupied chair at the map table and tried not to feel like a leper. Strangely, the brigadier still hadn't shown up. I decided it was best not to ask – besides, everyone except me seemed extremely busy – and applied myself instead to a study of the map. If I was going to enlighten General Lipsett and Colonel Hayter on the progress of the attack, it was probably best I understood something of it.

Sometime past 6 a.m. a few signals trickled in. In the first short despatch the 26th Battalion on the left reported "all correct". Which was hardly surprising as all they had to do was saunter a few hundred yards into No-Man's-Land and dig in. Nevertheless, as a good liaison officer, O'Neill tore off to relay this development. I stayed put, reasoning General Lipsett would have bigger things on his mind. Roughly half an hour later another signal arrived. This time, from the way that Major Clark-Kenney and Captain Walker were studying it, I knew it must be important.

'It appears all three 1st Division battalions have made good their objectives,' I heard Clark-Kennedy say to Walker. Walker grinned. The attack had succeeded, and surprisingly quickly, too. The 10th Battalion, with the 8th to one side and the 5th to the other, were through the trenches that made up the Arleux Loop and had captured the village.

'Anything from the 25th?' asked Walker. Understandably he was anxious to know where their own men where.

'Yes, it's about time we heard something from them,' muttered Clark-Kennedy, and moved over to stand beside me at the map table.

The words were barely out of his mouth when a runner came tumbling down the stairs, missing a step in the gloom, and nearly plunging headlong into the two of us. Quickly I reached out an arm to arrest his progress.

'Careful,' I said. 'It'd be a shame if you knocked out the major before he had the opportunity to read your message.'

'Thank you, sir,' he replied. Straightening himself he turned to the major, fumbled in his satchel for a moment, and handed him a folded sheet of note paper.

Clark-Kennedy glanced at it briefly. Then he pursed his lips somewhat sourly.

'Sir?'

Silently he thrust the note at me. It came from the 25th Battalion, a couple of sentences scrawled in haste.

'They still haven't heard from either their right *or* their left company?' I said incredulously. Seeing as the battalion was attacking on a two-company front, no news was most definitely not good news.

'Not quite,' said the major. 'We received a message earlier that they were held up by machine-gun fire on their left.'

'But what about their right, sir?' I asked anxiously. 'Did you hear anything about their right?' The right was where the 1st and 2nd Divisions bumped shoulders. If the Nova Scotia Rifles hadn't yet made contact with the 5th Battalion as planned, there was a very good chance the 1st Division in Arleux was dangerously exposed. Despite having fought their way into the heavily defended town, the divisional flank would be wide open, a gilt-edged invitation to Fritz that he hardly required – even without prompting he was predisposed to the counter-attack.

Curtly Clark-Kennedy shook his head. He knew what was at stake as well as I did.

'Where's the liaison officer from the 5th Battalion?' I asked, 'Perhaps he knows more.'

'He's at headquarters.'

At this I frowned, thinking, the gears upstairs stuck in neutral. Most days, it must be said, I find the mist seldom clears until well past nine.

'The rear headquarters,' supplied Clark-Kennedy, finally.

'Ah, ha,' I replied.

The major said nothing more.

'The food's probably better in the rear,' I mumbled, but he was already headed to his officers.

An uneasy couple of hours passed. Messages fired back and forth between the brigade major at the railway dug-out, the brigadier in the rear, and Lieutenant-Colonel Bauld, the commander of the 25th, at the quarries. I drank weak coffee and endeavoured to overhear the gist of the story.

Eventually, to sighs of relief from the brigade staff, the 25th reported they had reached the sunken road that was their objective. They were in contact with the 5th Battalion. All was well. It was now a question of mopping up and preparing for the inevitable counter-attacks.

O'Neill called headquarters to report. Feeling I should probably report as well, wary that otherwise the staff rumour mill would conjure up some fanciful tale of me sitting around dry and safe, twiddling my thumbs and drinking coffee all day, I telephoned in what I knew. Most of it they'd probably already heard. None of it was of any crucial significance. But I expect my superiors would want to hear, regardless.

Lunch was frugal. The coffee ran out shortly after. I settled down to what I anticipated would be a long afternoon entrenched at the map table. Nor was I the only one thinking that. O'Neill let rip with a windy yawn that rivalled the blast from a medium howitzer.

'Tedious or not, O'Neill, this beats being up to your knees in mud with Fritz dumping shells on your head,' I said. 'Be thankful you're not in Arleux awaiting the counter-attack.' O'Neill looked unconvinced. 'Here, study the map if you're bored.'

With little to do but take my own advice, I settled down to read through copies of all the operations orders. It was standard army practice that each unit shared its orders with the others involved. There was a whole stack of them; a fairly elaborate one from each division as well as their respective brigades; and shorter, more pointed versions from the various battalions involved. Since General Lipsett had asked me to join his staff, I'd spent many an hour writing the damn things, so I suppose I'd developed a certain professional interest in them.

'Interesting?' said O'Neill, with a mischievous twinkle in his eye, after he saw what I was reading.

'Look, I was a lawyer. I don't get bored quickly.'

Boredom, ironically, proved to be the least of my concerns. After a dozen pages I suddenly sat up erect, completely abandoning my customary slouch, a sense of unease descending over me. As I read on that unease grew progressively. Hurriedly I flipped through the remaining pages. I paused to carefully study the sections entitled "objectives", only skimming the rest. When I was done I did it again to make certain. My mouth was so dry it felt like I was the one preparing to go over the top.

SCREECH.

The legs of the chair grated on the rough planks as I sprang to my feet. Furiously I began laying out the relevant pages one beside the other on the table.

'Malcolm?' said O'Neill.

I didn't spare him a glance. I bent over the map, my finger tracing the coordinates I'd just read. 'Bloody hell,' I whispered.

'What the devil is up with you?' asked O'Neill.

Ignoring him I raised my head. 'Major!' I bellowed.

Seated at his desk in the corner Clark-Kennedy looked up. I think every head in the dug-out looked my way. They weren't accustomed to a subaltern summoning the brigade major from across a room. If O'Neill's eyes bulged any more I would have had to push them back in with my thumbs.

'Sir! You need to look at this.'

With a certain weariness a stalwart Clark-Kennedy got to his feet and slowly made his way over. He looked at me sternly, but said nothing about my manners. 'Here I am, Lieutenant.'

'I'm sorry, sir. But you need to look at this.' I motioned at the first pile in my row of exhibits.

'Yes, those are the brigade orders. I signed them myself... What exactly am I looking for, MacPhail?'

'The final objectives for the brigade are not what is stated there, sir.'

'Yes, yes. I know that,' he sighed. 'That's why there's an appendix where they've been updated.'

'The problem is, sir, what it says in the appendix is not what the 2nd Brigade says in its orders.' I put a finger on both pages so he could see for himself. 'You see, sir, in the brigade's orders the 25th Battalion are to push out patrols to the sunken road from T.30.a to T.24.c. But nowhere does it say that's the final objective. Yet the 2nd Brigade orders state quite categorically that not only do they expect the 25th to occupy that road, but their 5th Battalion will join up with them at that point.'

Clark-Kennedy stared at the passages, then gave a brief nod. 'Yes, I see what you're getting at. It's not pretty I'll admit. But I wouldn't worry overly, MacPhail. As you know, the 25th Battalion has already reported it is on its objectives.'

I gulped. I was going to look like a proper fool if there was an innocent explanation. Or perhaps the barrister in me was nitpicking about some triviality that the men in the field understood perfectly well. This wasn't even my division, and no doubt they had their own ways of doing things. Nevertheless, I couldn't let it go.

'It may be nothing, sir, but what I'm worried about is that the battalion *thinks* they're on their objectives, while in fact they're *not*.' The major looked at me with a start.

'If you'll have a glance at this, sir,' I said. 'Leaving aside the discrepancies, the 25th Battalion doesn't appear to have even seen the appendix. Their orders make no mention of the second sunken road. I'm afraid they believe their final objective is well short of that. They didn't mention any coordinates in their message, did they, sir?'

'No,' said Clark-Kennedy, 'let me have a look.' He bent over and studied Lt.-Col. Bauld's rolling but clear script. 'Damn it,' he muttered to himself. 'I've told him a million times these things need checking.'

I said nothing. I didn't know who *he* was, but some member of the staff was in serious trouble. Not only were the brigade's orders vague and unclear – General Lipsett would have had me staked to a post had I been the one to write them – no one had thought to double check the battalion orders. With only one battalion carrying out the brigade's part in the attack, it was hardly too much to ask.

'Get me the 25th Battalion,' snapped the major.

Across the room there was flurry of activity, a short pause, and then a reply: 'The line's down, sir.'

'Brigade then.'

'Sorry, sir, but all the lines are down.'

'Of all the infernal luck,' he muttered. 'That bloody shelling of theirs. It's neither heavy nor effective, but somehow they managed to hit our telephone lines all the same.'

I nodded understandingly. 'All it takes is a single lucky shell, sir. I'm sure the linesmen will have it patched up forthwith.'

'Yes,' agreed the major sourly, 'but that leaves me in a bit of a spot.'

'Sir?' One of the other men approached waving a signals form. 'A message came in before the lines went down. It's from 2nd Brigade, sir.'

Unspeaking Clark-Kennedy reached out a hand and began to read. When he was finished he cursed. The bags under his eyes were so pronounced they looked like the lip of a shell hole. 'Your fears appear to be confirmed, MacPhail.' He held up the message so I might read it.

"Enemy troops are still reported to be collecting in SUNKEN ROAD T.30.A and T.24.C." was all I could make out before he snatched it away and addressed the signaller: 'As soon as the line's up, copy this immediately to Colonel Bauld.'

It was as I'd feared, the Germans were gathered in the very road the 2nd Brigade men expected to find the Nova Scotians.

Captain Walker joined us. It was a big dug-out, but not nearly big enough to conceal that a serious problem had arisen.

'We need to get this resolved,' said Clark-Kennedy. Then to Walker: 'I'll explain in a minute, Captain, but I'm sending you back to the Quarries. However, first I must contact the brigadier.' His eyes scanned round the dug-out before returning to the captain and me.

'I'll go, sir, if you'd like,' I offered. 'I realize you're short-handed. You could send a runner obviously, but I know the situation. It might save some time and trouble.'

He looked at me appraisingly, then nodded. With hindsight I should have kept my mouth shut.

MAP OF ARLEUX AND FRESNOY

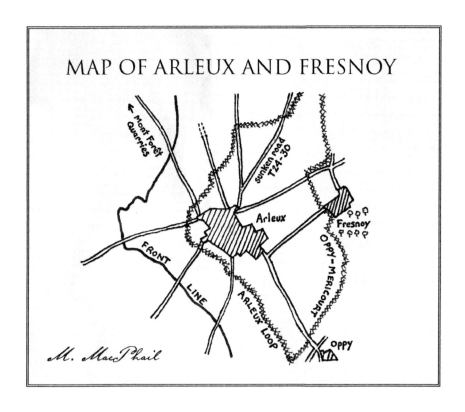

CHAPTER 3

Late afternoon, 28th of April, 1917
Les Tilleuls, France

Crossing up over Vimy Ridge on the Lens-Arras road heading west, one climbs through a bleak, rolling landscape of churned earth and the scattered debris of battle. The pitted blocks of grey concrete from German bunkers and gun emplacements protrude from the earth like so many broken, jagged teeth. Major Clark-Kennedy had somehow corralled a car and a driver for me, for which I was grateful and, after only a couple of miles, Private Billings at the wheel announced that we had arrived.

'This is it, sir. Les Tilleuls.'

Sceptically I peered through the dirt-splattered window to the scene outside. We were close to the backbone of the ridge. Of the hamlet of Les Tilleuls there was little to see, save a muddy and rutted crossroads, which a week of fine weather had yet to dry out completely. Overlooking the junction was a single sentry at a well-flagged guard post opposite. Through some minor miracle the engineers and the working parties had transformed the shell-turned bog into passable roads once again, but the hamlet itself was beyond redemption; heaps of stone, masonry and wood were all that remained. The broken wheel of a limber lay abandoned on the embankment, and the remains of a horse – quite possibly from the limber in question – were submerged in the muck nearby.

The interest of the 5th Brigade in Les Tilleuls lay not in the shattered remains of what they had seized only three weeks earlier, but what lay underneath: Les Tilleuls Cave.

'Wait for me would you?' I said to Billings. 'With any luck, I won't be long.'

He nodded agreeably.

Down a long and winding staircase, the entrance to which was cleverly hidden from sight (and shells), I descended into a remarkably large cavern where the air was cool and damp, but surprisingly fresh. Prior to our attack on Vimy Ridge this cave had been used as a headquarters by no less than two German battalions. I was greeted by a friendly lieutenant and I told him my business.

'The brigadier, you say… You'd best follow me,' he replied. With that we walked further into what turned out to be an astonishing labyrinth of echoing chambers. The flickering of candles danced on the chiseled walls while shadows played on the high arched ceilings above.

'Remarkable,' I said softly, my head twisting round to take it all in. Prior to the Vimy show I'd been in many a tunnel dug in the chalk that underlay this entire region, but this cave had a feeling altogether different than those neatly carved passages. This felt somehow of another age.

'A lieutenant of the division and his corporal captured six officers and a hundred other ranks down here during the attack on the ridge,' said the lieutenant, noting my interest. 'They went down those very stairs you did, just the two of them, armed only with revolvers, and somehow convinced the entire lot to surrender. The lieutenant's been put up for an M.C.'

'He deserves it,' I said, shivering. 'I wouldn't have wanted to be in his shoes.' Nor, I thought, did I want to be in this officer's shoes. Shell-proof it may have been, there was a penetrating chill to the air in Les Tilleuls cave that positively cut through bone and marrow.

'He'll almost certainly be in here,' said the lieutenant, motioning that I should follow him. Before we could squeeze through the narrow entranceway, however, a captain emerged from it. As he turned to face us, the lieutenant stiffened.

'What the dickens do you think you're doing here, Jameson? The general's about to dine.'

'Well, sir,' stuttered the lieutenant.

Quickly I interrupted: 'I'm afraid it's on account of me, sir.' The captain, a short, neat-looking man with thin fair eyebrows, the whisper of a matching moustache and an air of general seriousness about him, shifted his gaze to examine me. Having stared down a Maxim machine gun more than once I didn't find this nearly as intimidating as I suspect he intended. It helped that the crown of his head barely reached my chin. 'My name is MacPhail, sir. I urgently need to speak with the brigadier,' I said gruffly. 'I have an important message for him from Major Clark-Kennedy.'

'The colonel might have called,' he replied, a trifle officiously to my ear.

'And undoubtedly he would have done exactly that, sir, were it not that the line is out.'

'Yes, sir, that's true,' piped up the lieutenant named Jameson. 'It's been down for nearly an hour.'

While the captain pondered this, I pondered the fact that his brigade had an important operation underway and it was curious – to say the least – that he didn't appear to know communications with the front were broken. However, he and I were spared any further need to communicate when an irascible voice called out from the direction of the chamber. More important matters than the brigade attack were at stake.

'Smythe? Is that you that I hear? Where the blazes is my dinner?'

At this my jaw dropped. When I looked questioningly at Lieutenant Jameson, he was studying his feet in a manner that suggested he hadn't heard anything. His reddening cheeks indicated otherwise. The captain meanwhile was paying no attention to either me or him, and had turned abruptly on his heel. Without a word he slipped back through the doorway. Unbidden I followed.

I entered into a small room carved in the rock. 'This isn't the first time that's happened,' I heard the man in the room admonish the captain. If the tone in his voice didn't alert me to who the man was, the crossed baton and sword on his epaulettes sure did. I had found the brigadier.

Brigadier-General Macdonell, not to be confused with his popular cousin, Batty Mac – also a brigadier and commander of the 7th

Brigade – was known as Long Archie. Seated at a table strewn with maps the longest part of Long Archie appeared to be his face. His bushy dark eyebrows were twisted into a deep frown. 'What is so very challenging about serving my dinner on time?' he snarled. 'Can you explain that to me, Captain?'

Captain Smythe began to stutter, much like Jameson had earlier. Fortunately for him his diplomatic skills were saved any further work-out by the appearance of a cook, who bustled in carrying a steaming plate. Appreciatively I breathed in the aromas. It smelled good, and my own lunch suddenly seemed a distant memory. For his part Smythe glowered at the cook who sensibly ignored him, devoting his attentions instead to Long Archie. Judging by the brigadier's expression, he was satisfied with the cook's efforts for he said nothing further.

Noisily I cleared my throat.

The brigadier looked up, his eyes narrowing. What with the privations of a grumbling stomach I don't think he'd actually noticed me skulking behind Captain Smythe.

'I'm terribly sorry to interrupt your dinner, sir, but Major Clark-Kennedy sent me.' I wasn't sorry in the slightest, but it sounded better that way. 'The lines are down and he wanted me to brief you on the latest developments from the attack.'

'I see,' Macdonell replied, and looked wistfully down at his plate. For a big man, with a face whose form reminded me vaguely of a watermelon, he had these curiously narrow slits of eyes. It was as if he was permanently squinting. Presently they were narrower than ever. The pupils had shrunk to hard little beads, and the beads were focused on me.

'Please don't wait on my account, sir,' I said in my very best imitation of a placating minion.

Macdonell dismissed my comment with a wave of his hand. I wouldn't have minded in the slightest if he just began to eat. But amongst a certain generation that was not something one did. Mind you, many of my generation were rushing the trenches at Arleux – without dinner.

'What's your name, Lieutenant?' he grumbled.

'MacPhail, sir. Malcolm MacPhail.'

'What is it you have to tell me, Lieutenant?'

'Unfortunately there's been some confusion with the orders, sir. The 25th Battalion appear to have stopped short of the final objective.'

'They have? How is that possible?'

'If you'd allow me, sir.' I approached and went to stand beside him, carefully laying out copies of the operations orders in a semi-circle around his plate. It was all I could do not to linger – the best I could hope for was cold *Simcoe* pork and beans from a tin. Then I pointed out the discrepancies between the various instructions, much as I had done with the colonel.

'So, you see, sir, I don't believe the 25th Battalion was aware they should advance to the second sunken road. It appears they're somewhere in the vicinity of the first road, some way from where they should be. As a result the 5th Battalion's flank is completely in the air, sir. They sent a message not long ago asking where the battalion is.'

'And you think the brigade orders are to blame?'

'It would appear that way, sir,' I replied. 'They're not terribly clear.' I was more candid than I ought to have been, but I was caught up in the urgency of the moment, and mildly affronted by the mess some idiot on the staff had made.

Long Archie didn't reply. However, it didn't escape my notice that he threw a withering glance in the direction of Smythe. Which was when it occurred to me that Captain Smythe must have been the very man who'd written those orders. Nevertheless, it was Macdonell's brigade I reminded myself. Neither General Lipsett nor any of the brigadiers I knew would ever have allowed such important orders to go out in their names without a careful read themselves. And Captain Smythe was Macdonell's man.

'You'll have to arrange a car to take us to the railway dug-outs,' Macdonell said to Smythe, who began nodding vigorously. The brigadier took up a fork and with another sigh made a listless stab for the meat – no longer steaming – on his plate.

'Sir, the Germans are liable to pounce on this opening,' I said.

'Yes, Lieutenant, I'm very well aware of that,' he snapped.

'Naturally, sir. Only –'

He stared at me. 'Oh, spit it out, Lieutenant, whatever it is you have to say.' Irritably he let the fork fall with a clatter.

'I was just thinking, sir, to clear up the situation it would be helpful to send an officer forward *immediately*.'

Macdonell said nothing.

After a moment I mumbled: 'If the companies in the line were aware of the situation, it might not be too late to do something about it, sir. That's all.' I was conscious the brigadier looked as inclined to stick his fork in me as his dinner.

'Yes, you're probably right,' he said finally. 'But who to send?' He looked to Captain Smythe. Without so much as a second's hesitation Smythe fixed his sights on me – which wasn't entirely surprising as out of the corner of my eye I'd seen him glaring at me uninterruptedly for several minutes – and Macdonell's gaze followed his.

'Of course. MacPhail wasn't it?'

I could have said I wasn't even from the 2nd Division; that I was only here in Les Tilleuls as the result of an officer exchange and a shortage of men at the advanced headquarters; and that my duties included sending regular reports back to my headquarters, something I couldn't very well do trudging through the front-line trenches. I'm not sure my protestations would have mattered though. They certainly wouldn't have mattered in my own mind. I would have felt like the very fool or shirker (the two often being synonymous, at least amongst the headquarters staff) I was always railing on about. On top of which it was undeniably my own dumb idea. Not for the first time this war my mouth was proving to be my own worst enemy.

'Yes, sir,' I replied.

'Good. Well, at least that's settled then.' A smug grin came to the captain. The glimmer of a smile also appeared on Long Archie's face, though it soon disappeared as he took up contemplating his ice-cold dinner.

Thinking back on it during the ride towards the front, I rued not having asked for a posting to the Q side of the staff when I had the chance. While it would have meant a military career dedicated to se-curing adequate supplies of replacement puttees, among other things, at least it would have spared me the hazards of liaising with testy brigadiers and their bumbling adjutants. Another positive aspect of the logistics of puttees was that it seldom required a trip to the front. In my four months on General Lipsett's staff I'd seemingly done little else.

CHAPTER 4

28th of April, 1917, early evening
Arleux Loop, Arleux-en-Gohelle, France

There was still a decent light when Billings dropped me at the Mont
Forêt Quarries and the 25th Battalion. It was a little past 5 p.m., and the
sun had a few good hours left in it. From across the shell-turned fields
to the east, where wispy columns of smoke loitered on the horizon,
came the sound of scattered small-arms fire. At intervals this relative
quiet was punctuated by the thump of a shell from a heavy howitzer
going off. Quickly I turned away and climbed down into the dug-out;
a report to the battalion officers and I was heading that way myself.

'MacPhail!' exclaimed the Officer Commanding, Lieutenant-
Colonel Bauld.

With little warning, save the clatter of my boots on the steps of the
wooden stairs leading below, I'd appeared before him. But without me
saying a word he seemed to know why I'd come, even if this clearly
puzzled him. 'Somehow, I didn't anticipate you'd be the officer Brigade
would send,' he said, looking at me quizzically.

I shrugged. 'It was as much of a surprise to me, sir, as it is to you.'
In my mind's eye I could still picture the scheming captain from the
brigade staff as he fingered me for the job – but I don't expect Bauld
wanted to hear my thoughts on either the brigadier's dinner practices,
or the qualities of the staff he kept. Besides, it *was* perplexing that I

29

was the one expected to pull the 2nd Division's chestnuts out of the fire. Lesser minds would be mightily amused when they heard the story.

'Very curious,' murmured the colonel to himself, his dark eyebrows curling into a frown. Uncurling them he looked at me again. 'But it's fortunate you arrived when you did. I've just instructed Fisher here to go forward and clear up the situation.' He indicated a lieutenant with hazel eyes and light hair, about my age, at his side. 'You can accompany him to the line if you'd like.' While I was at brigade headquarters, not only had the colonel been briefed in person, apparently all the telephone lines were repaired. Consequently, there was no need for me to explain anything at all. Much like my trek to Les Tilleuls this visit to battalion headquarters bore all the hallmarks of an exercise in futility – by no means the first such endeavour this war, nor likely the last, I thought sourly.

The worst of it was the only thing I'd truly accomplished was to antagonize the brigadier and his adjutant. So instead of observing the attack at safe distance, here I was about to saunter into the thick of it. To think all this had come about as the result of a mundane exchange of officers between divisions. For an instant I wondered what my counterpart at 3rd Division headquarters was doing; until my stomach piped up with an answer in the form of a fierce growl. Which reminded me – I was famished. I nodded my agreement at Colonel Bauld.

'Thank you, sir. I'd be happy to go with Lieutenant Fisher. There's just one small thing, sir.'

'Oh? And what would that be, MacPhail?'

'Well, sir, you wouldn't happen to have an extra rifle I could borrow?'

I don't know what surprised him more, that the brigadier had detailed me – a stranger to the battalion, brigade, and division – to sort out the confusion, or that I required a Lee-Enfield to accomplish the task. But I'd been in scraps enough to know that the six-shooter in my holster didn't command a whole lot of respect from our foe, and the two lieutenant's pips on my shoulders not at all. On the other hand, when dealing with either friend or foe, a short Lee-Enfield with a foot-long bayonet leading the way can sometimes provide the very leverage you need.

Lieutenant Thomas Fisher of B Company proved to be a personable fellow, even if it's tricky to get the true measure of a man when half your being is focused on avoiding a lightning barrage from the Boche. The front was at least a mile off, but the enemy had thus far concentrated his fire in this rear area hoping to hit something of importance. Both Fisher and I were determined it not be us.

We followed the Saskatchewan Road in a southeasterly direction towards Arleux. Reaching a spot some 1000 yards from the village, the land crested. Ahead, the gravel road and the earthen fields to either side fell away ever so gradually, affording us an excellent view for miles. The skeletal wooden frames and tumbling brick walls of the hamlet were plainly visible. A white line in the dirt in advance of the village marked out where the German trenches had been dug down to the strata of chalk. In the village itself where fires still blazed, dense pillars of smoke billowed forth, spiralling upwards into a sky painted in shades of a soft pastel blue; the sort of sky that on a languorous spring day you might gaze at for hours, lying on your back with a blade of grass between your teeth, and nary a thought to disturb you. Today, not only was there no grass to lie on – let alone to chew upon – there were far too many things flying around to feel anything like dreaminess, let alone lethargy.

A final glance at Arleux and we veered off the road. We went due east, heading towards the left flank where somewhere the 25th Battalion would be found. After some minutes there were a series of bangs, at intervals of every half-minute or so, each more akin to the crack from a large firecracker than the reverberating boom of a heavy shell. A half-mile in front of us the fall of the shells was plain to see; greyish-white puffs appeared without warning high in the air, followed by a fleeting sight of what looked like flies swarming in their millions. I felt a panging in my gut.

'Shrapnel,' remarked Fisher, stepping forward again with no visible sign of hesitation in his pace. 'From their field guns I reckon.' For all his twenty-four years, Fisher was an old campaigner, having signed up around the time I had in 1914 – so he knew his business.

'Very likely.' I agreed, willing myself to keep step with him.

The air to the north of the village was momentarily thick with deadly, whirring maelstroms of steel fragments. A single Woolly Bear could tear a man or a platoon to shreds before you registered the sound of it exploding. We trudged on in their direction.

After a dozen-odd rounds the shelling petered out. Anyone not already hit was likely well sheltered, some Fritz had rightfully concluded. With two-and-a-half years of war behind them, the German ammunition stockpiles required careful husbanding these days, and that was fortunate for the two of us. Moreover, with the lull in the firing we were keen to step up our gait. Not long after we encountered the first elements of the Nova Scotians. They were dug in at a sunken road.

This was when I discovered the true extent of the problem. Where the orders had spoken of two sunken roads, there were in fact three of them, not including the one we had just walked along, which would have been the fourth. All of them angled north out of Arleux. We'd been told to take the road with young trees planted on the right, but had now seen two of that description. For a small and patently unimportant place in the middle of nowhere, otherwise known as the French Artois, Arleux had the transport network of a metropolis.

'How many bloody roads do a few hundred farmers need?' I muttered. 'No wonder your boys are confused about where they're supposed to be.'

Fisher took it up with the first soldier we encountered.

'One of the officers, he thought this was our objective, sir,' the soldier explained, when Fisher pressed him on what he and the others were doing there.

Fisher groaned. Meaningfully I looked over at him. I'd already explained in considerable detail the muddled orders. I hadn't reckoned on this further complication however. These lads were not just one, but two roads back of where the 5th Battalion was anxiously awaiting them. In fact, even a cartographic middleweight like myself could tell them they hadn't even reached the German front-line trench. The fog of war had been as thick as pea soup this morning.

'Where is he then, your officer?' I demanded of the man. 'Can we speak with him?'

'Fraid not, sir. He's dead.' The soldier motioned up the road where a handful of khaki-clad bodies could be seen. Coming across the fields we'd seen several already, horrifically mutilated by a shell, or cut down by a burst of the machine-gun fire that the early reports had complained about. 'We haven't been able to bury him yet,' he added, a hand tapping nervously on his thigh. 'Heinie's been shelling us on and off all day.' It was obvious he expected a dressing down for having left an officer face down in the dirt.

When my own time came, I held out some hope that someone would look for a decent hole for me. But the middle of an attack was hardly the moment to worry about a proper burial. 'That's all right,' I said. 'Do it when you have a chance. Is the rest of the company forward now?'

The man nodded.

In relief I sighed. At least they'd had the good sense to recognize their mistake. I looked over at Fisher. He was gawking up the road at the corpses. Quite likely he knew the fellow in question. It appeared that his battalion hadn't had an easy time of it. Gently I nudged him with an elbow. He nodded in response and we moved on.

Roughly 500 yards further east we encountered the enemy line, labelled on the trench map in neat blue capitals as the Arleux Loop North. Ominously much of the wire in front of the trench was uncut, bodies strewn about, mercifully few on the wire itself. It was all too easy to imagine the chaos in the early morning twilight as the Germans lined the parapet, laying down a withering rifle fire while our men looked about frantically, searching for the elusive opening as the smoke cleared and the sun rose. But they had eventually found one for I saw a path through the coils that was cleared and marked. Tin hats could be seen at several points moving along the trench. The Arleux Loop North was ours.

I had just passed a lone battered fence post that was listing like a drunken sailor on shore leave, hot on Fisher's heels and almost at the gap in the wire, when I heard the faintest of whistles overhead.

The thunderclap – it must have been almost directly above me – was followed by a loud whirring noise as if I'd thrust my head into an angry beehive. In a twenty-foot radius invisible pickaxes chipped furiously at the ground, releasing puffs of dirt into the air. Air and something else raced past my head and, in a reflex, I turned. A red-hot splinter of steel, the size and shape of a door hinge, was lodged, smouldering in the wooden post behind me. For a moment I just stared at it. Then recollecting the whirlwind of debris that had blown past, I glanced warily down at my body, uncertain what horror I might discover. But everything appeared as it ought to. Relieved, I sighed, and looked up again.

'Malcolm!'

Fisher was eyeing me, grinning exuberantly. He too was unharmed.

I grinned back, matching him tooth for tooth, conscious that my heart was beating wildly and that I felt mildly nauseous. Which puzzled me as I'd been through more close scrapes than I could remember; Christ, the lads in my old battalion had called me 'old timer' to my back when they thought I wasn't close enough to hear.

Fisher threw a hand up over his shoulder, a perky wave to say "follow me". So giving it no further thought I scampered on through the wire after him, before springing down into the German trench with a loud clatter.

'Damn, that was close,' I breathed.

'You're telling me,' said Fisher. 'I don't know you how you ducked that one, MacPhail, but you may be the luckiest buck in the entire Corps!'

I was about to respond with some witticism of my own when his smile evaporated, an uneasy frown taking its place. 'You're bleeding,' he said.

'I am?' Suddenly I could feel a wet trickle down my neck.

'Here. Let me have a look.' With both hands he grasped my head and gently twisted it to one side so he might make an assessment of the damage. He whistled.

'That bad?' My heart was thumping so heavily I wouldn't have noticed if an Ypres Express had landed an arm's length away.

Fisher shook his head. 'Flesh wound. Nicked your ear,' he said. 'And you have a few other scratches here and there. You're bleeding like a stuck pig, Malcolm, but it's my firm conviction you'll survive. The seraphim appear to be firmly on your side today.'

'That's wonderful to hear, although talk of angels would be a little more credible if I wasn't haemorrhaging blood,' I grunted. Gingerly I probed with my fingertips at the back of my head. Thankfully the wound was nowhere that I could see it; I've always tended to be unusually sensitive to the sight of an appendage of mine bleeding out

34

– particularly one as indispensable as my head. Following a similar occasion last fall at the Somme, when some Fritz gunner merrily nailed me in shoulder and thigh, I'd became even more set in my ways.

'Here, take your helmet.' Fisher thrust it into my hands, and began insouciantly wrapping a length of gauze under my chin and up around the ear in question. He did this several times. 'Hold still,' he muttered. With a decisive yank he tightened the cloth and I winced. He proceeded to tie the loose ends in a bowtie under my chin, then stepped back to admire his handiwork.

'You really need to work on your bedside manner, Fisher. But thanks.'

Only after this operation was complete, and deemed a success, did I regain the composure to glance around to better see where I was. The trench was a bit rudimentary compared to what I was accustomed to; German trenches more often than not being loosely modelled on the Palace of Versailles. However, from the spots where the trench wall was stove-in it was evident our artillery had roughed things up a bit. Furthermore, there were numerous men crumpled on the ground alongside the duckboards. I couldn't help noticing that almost all of them wore field grey greatcoats.

Down the trench five soldiers, also clad in field grey, were not prone on the duckboards. Rather they stood circumspectly around two of ours with mud-caked *Stahlhelms* parked unevenly on their heads, prissy little black moustaches adorning their faces. A sergeant from the battalion was flipping through the papers of one of them. As I watched he reached over to the man at his side who held open a large burlap sack and dropped the German's billfold into it. Then he held out his hand impatiently for the next.

'Prussians, eh?' I said to him, as we approached.

At this the sergeant looked up, quickly looked at me again, his eyes bulging for a moment. Like all well trained NCOs in the presence of a superior officer, he sensibly refrained from a smirk or a comment. It was a skill I hadn't yet mastered in my time in the army.

'The 164th Regiment,' I said pointing at the insignia of the man he was questioning, 'they're part of the 20th Division from Hannover and region. Prussian in other words. Did they put up much of a fight?'

'Yes, sir, they are,' agreed the sergeant. 'And yes they did.'

'How on earth did you know that?' whispered Fisher in my ear – the functioning one. 'That they're Prussian?'

I turned to him. 'You'd never guess, but theoretically I'm attached to a divisional staff. Shuffling papers all day, you know. It's quite astonishing the information one picks up...'

'Hmm,' said Fisher, doubtfully. There was no need to add that I'd gone looking for more information after Clark-Kennedy mentioned the regiment back at the railway dug-out. At the time I'd had nothing better to do.

However, more important than impressing Fisher with my knowledge of the German battle order was determining the current whereabouts of the leading elements of the 25th Battalion. A couple of hundred feet east of the trench we were standing in was the sunken road, the first of two. And that road was also a key objective for the day. In fact, regardless which set of orders you chose to consult, the consensus was unanimous that it was meant to be in battalion hands.

Unfortunately, on that score the sergeant was downcast. He shook his head in response to Fisher's question. 'Lieutenant Lewis had our party forward in the road for a time. It was great sport. We bombed out some dug-outs, and pegged a few Fritzs firing a trench mortar, but had to fall back soon after when they came at us with half a battalion. There was nothing more we could do, sir.'

'So the road's still in enemy hands?' said Fisher.

'Yes, sir.'

'No wonder the 5th Battalion had to refuse their flank,' I said sourly. 'Where's this Lewis now?'

The sergeant shrugged.

Fisher was all set to go out in search of the good lieutenant when the man himself limped in with a bayonet wound in the back. Which quickly put paid to any thoughts of accosting him about the battalion's failure to secure the left of the attack. But Lewis was able to confirm the sergeant's story in graphic and convincing detail. 'After we retired we had a bit of a fight up the trench here, but I got the men to place a block,' he said, throwing his arm casually in the direction of where the trench crossed the road. 'Fritz can't get behind us anymore. But I don't think there's a hope in hell of taking that road.'

He was looking pale and we advised him that he should head to the rear. Before he left, though, I couldn't let it rest: 'You may not have heard, but Arleux is ours. For the moment at least. However, without the battalion getting ahead the question is whether it'll remain that way. So there must be *some* chance…?'

Before I could finish my sentence he began vehemently shaking his head. It was because of the MGs and the entrenched positions of the Boche, he explained. No, capturing the objectives was completely out of the question in his opinion. 'I don't think I could even muster the men,' he concluded.

It was only after Lieutenant Lewis was on his way, crawling back towards the rear and a casualty station that we heard the crackling of sniper fire. I realized then what he'd been getting at. Digging in for the night was going to be a challenge for the Nova Scotians, let alone charging two roads in the open.

An hour or two later, around 8.30 p.m., a shout came which made the whole idea of capturing the sunken roads entirely fantastical. Much like burials, taking the objectives was something that would have to wait.

'Lieutenant! They're forming up, sir,' the sentry called out to Fisher.

The two of us sped to the spot where he stood guard and peered ever so cautiously over the new parapet – until the early morning change in ownership it had served as the parados, although beyond an extra sandbag or two I think the new name was the only real change. Either way, it faced east. And even with a furtive glance it wasn't difficult to see what was bothering the man.

'Christ,' I moaned. 'The buggers are assembling to counter-attack.'

'As you feared,' said Fisher.

'There are times I hate being right almost as much as I hate being wrong.' Grimly I unshouldered the Lee-Enfield. 'If they cut through here, Fisher, there's a good chance Arleux is lost,' I said.

With a grimace he went to pull out his revolver. Firearms in hand we stared eastwards.

We were torn from our reverie by a *pop* and the sizzle of a flare going up. The sergeant who was busy questioning the German prisoners, stood with a flare gun in his hand, watching it arc into the sky where it went off in a blaze of light. Far off to our right another flare went shooting skywards.

It didn't take the artillery more than a minute or two to respond. The relative peace was shattered by the crash of many guns. All along the interdictory line, the one so carefully planned and charted by the staff, and entirely forgotten about by me, geysers of dirt and wreathes of smoke shrouded the massing Germans.

'That'll do them,' I heard someone say.

I turned to the sergeant. 'Fine thinking,' I said. 'Where would we be without the NCOs?'

He smiled. 'That's what I keep saying, sir, but no one listens.'

Shortly after Fisher set off to organize the battalion outposts. I offered to stay to help with the defences, but he resolutely waved my protestations aside. So I left them and went in the direction of the Mont Forêt Quarries to report. I had seen the battalion move forward in the first teasing rays of light early this morning. As the last rays dove for cover, I left them. It had been another sanguinary day on the Western Front.

As to my report, it was not as warmly received as I'd hoped.

CHAPTER 5

28th of April, 1917, late evening
Railway dug-outs, Vimy, France

The railway dug-out was much as I remembered it, although more crowded and considerably less congenial with the highly visible presence of Brigadier-General Macdonell and entourage. Regardless, the advantages of two feet of reinforced German concrete overhead had seldom seemed so self-evident, even when compared with the circumstances of my first visit. If truth be told I was still a little shaken from the "scratch" on my head. That was the funny thing about war – right when you thought it couldn't get any worse, invariably it did.

Colonel Bauld back at the Quarries had been most gracious about my efforts, grateful I'd brought word about the state of his battalion, and reassured their progress was acceptable, if not exactly as originally prescribed. I heard the relief in his voice when I concluded by telling him that in my opinion the doughty Lieutenant Fisher had the situation well in hand. Carrying on to brigade headquarters, others saw matters very differently.

'Lieutenant, the sole reason the brigadier sent you forward was to spur the 25th on to take their objectives,' said Captain Smythe, when I completed my account. 'Now you tell me that not only have they not done so, they require a barrage to finish the job?'

Those who had seen me step down into the central chamber all stared, obviously bemused by Fisher's handiwork with a length of gauze and my head. The captain showed neither bemusement nor concern, or even a flicker of acknowledgement I'd been wounded; although that may have been due to the speed with which he reacted. It took him all of two breaths to intercept me en route to Brigadier Macdonell and Major Clark-Kennedy in conference at the corner table. Some men view information as currency, and for Smythe I dare say it was his lifeblood. I would have let it pass were it not for his thinly veiled suggestion I hadn't done what I was sent to do.

'Begging your pardon, Captain,' I said, my words loud and strangely stilted; I was keenly aware this was a performance with an audience. 'The reason the brigadier sent me forward was to clear up the confusion... the confusion that resulted from dangerously shoddy staff work. And that's exactly what I did.' Then realizing I'd omitted a key word, I spat out, 'Sir.' I was tired, hungry, and probably short a few pints of blood in vital organs like the brain, but audience or not, it was not a moment to neglect military form.

My words hit their mark. Smythe recoiled, gritting his teeth, his eyes on a low boil.

Like any semi-accomplished staff man he deftly regrouped from this verbal setback. 'I understand you were a barrister, Lieutenant, but spare me the convoluted arguments. However you wish to paint it, MacPhail, the battalion is not ahead, and the flank is still wide open.'

I couldn't fault him that. The left flank at Arleux was an open sore. I'd said as much to anyone who would listen, including to him and his commanding officer, which is likely how he came to hear of it. But even I had to admit my efforts to set things straight had accomplished little. 'I'm sorry, sir, that's just the way it is. I wish it were otherwise.' My bluster from a moment earlier had gone missing. I bowed my head.

Smythe sighed noisily. 'So, there's no chance...'

'No, sir, there's no chance of the battalion getting forward, not without some guns in support. Hopefully they'll be able to hold off the Boche in the interim.'

'The brigadier will not be pleased,' he said, shaking his head. 'Not pleased at all.'

'I could explain,' I offered. 'I saw the situation myself. There's really nothing that can be done at present, not without a barrage.'

'No, not pleased at all,' muttered Smythe, completely ignoring me. Then he looked up and caught my eye. In a waspish tone he said: 'Don't you think you've done quite *enough* today, Lieutenant MacPhail?' He shook his head again. Then, wearily, to himself: 'No, the brigadier will not be pleased.' After his blunder with the orders I suspected he was frantically trying to come up with a means to redeem himself. My news wouldn't help.

'I'm not much pleased myself, Captain,' I snapped, my ill temper returning. 'Unlike some I've been dodging snipers and Woolly Bears for hours… on an empty stomach to boot.' I don't expect Smythe grasped the allusion with his brigadier, although that was surely for the best. Nevertheless, it may not have been pure coincidence that less than thirty minutes after my arrival, Smythe bluntly informed me I was required immediately at 3rd Divisional Headquarters.

It was going on 10 p.m. by that time. There was no car available. Nor a horse. Not even a single scrawny mule with a lame foot. 'Terribly sorry, MacPhail,' mumbled Smythe, looking anything but. That left me and my sore feet contemplating a four-mile journey, traversing the ridge in darkness. Although with the flashing of the guns – both ours and theirs – it was unlikely to be as dark as I might have wished.

With a smirk Smythe tossed me a can of *Fray Bentos*. 'Enjoy the dinner, MacPhail.'

29th of April, 1917
Fort George, northwest of Neuville-Saint-Vaast, France

It was approaching midnight when the tumbledown forms of the buildings at the village and cross-roads of Neuville-Saint-Vaast edged into view, and well past it when a half mile later I reached a modest sign painted in large white letters on a dark background that announced Fort George. Beyond the sign and the road I caught a glimpse of the battalion camps and bivouacs that had sprung up in the vicinity. I made my way towards them, following a twisting path, intent on reaching the fort and headquarters as soon as possible. Two years earlier this ground had been the scene of desperate fighting between Germans and French, and gruesome reminders were everywhere, so I took care to keep to the path.

The first part of my journey passed remarkably quickly. My thoughts were consumed by Smythe and his self-serving ways, which predictably did wonders for my walking pace. Nevertheless, by the time I'd marched in quick step to the summit of the ridge rethinking all the wittily biting retorts I might have made to the captain had begun to lose its appeal. I was all in. It didn't help that Fritz kept the roads over the ridge under a sporadic but heavy shellfire, particularly at night; so tired or not it was advisable to stay alert. Furthermore, even with wits about you, a moment of absent-minded distraction was all it took to slip or trip and land in one of the sizeable mud-filled holes that pockmarked the road. With nightfall, and in the absence of a greatcoat – my optimism a few days earlier about the coming of spring manifestly premature – the air had a distinct chill. The last thing I wanted was to treat myself to a cold bath on top of it.

Eventually I spotted the breastworks, sandbags and timbers of the Fort George headquarters. All I could think of then was diving into a warm bunk. But it was not to be.

'What the devil do you think you're doing, chum?' growled a voice in protest. In the gloom of the dug-out, the faint flickering of a candle further off, I'd slipped into the chamber where I was accustomed to sleeping and sat down on the bed, bending to untie my boots. Then I felt the bed move underneath me, and heard the voice. Startled, I sprang to my feet.

'Oh, sorry,' I mumbled. 'Didn't realize it was occupied.' Possessed of more presence of mind I would have inquired who it was sleeping in my bed; though the army being the army it didn't particularly matter. The man probably outranked me, even if his breath was reminiscent of the trenches. But then I'd met colonels of whom that was also true, so that was hardly definitive. The man's vocabulary in any event was several shades less colourful than what passed for conversation in the trenches, which suggested a certain seniority. Abjectly I shuffled off. I winced as a stabbing pain shot through my ear.

In the corridor outside I pondered where else I might claim a bed at this late hour. The problem was that the clerks and most everyone else at headquarters went to bed just past 11 p.m., leaving few bunks to spare. I turned in the direction of the candle light down the passageway and followed it. Someone would have a suggestion. While I didn't relish the thought of subjecting myself to the questionable humour of my colleagues, there was little choice.

I entered a large room with half a dozen desks normally reserved for the general staff, a scene not unfamiliar to me as it was there I spent my days when not out on exchange with our sister divisions. Manning the telephone in the far corner I recognized Corporal Timmins. Unusually, the telephone was not in operation. I nodded at him when he looked over at me. Then I spotted the officer in the other corner, where a clerk normally stood churning out duplicate orders on a mimeograph all day. I headed his way, the makings of a grin on my face, droll words on my lips. Both disappeared rather abruptly when I realized who it was.

Seated behind a desk of unpainted deal, the top of which was buried in maps and plans, was the GOC himself. Hearing the scuffle of my boots on the rough planks he cautiously lifted first his eyes, then his whole head when he saw it was me.

'Lieutenant,' said General Lipsett, with a tone of puzzlement.

Stiffly, I straightened up to my full length. 'Sir. I didn't expect to see you here. Not at this hour.'

He put down the pen he was holding and sat back in his chair. 'And imagine my surprise at seeing you, MacPhail, at this hour. You were with 2nd Division the last I recall?' It wasn't much of a question. He'd sent me there himself, and he wasn't the sort of officer to forget it.

In the long pause that followed I made a game attempt to gather my senses.

'Or has something happened I should know about?' Lipsett asked.

Flummoxed I replied: 'Oh, no, sir.'

The general frowned.

'I was told I was required back at headquarters.'

The general frowned again.

'Colonel, do you know anything about this?'

'No, General, I can't say I do,' said a voice behind me. There was no need to strain my neck; the mid-Atlantic accent (stuck somewhere between Canada where he was born and raised, and England where he'd studied) was well known to me. I'd been neatly outmanoeuvred, caught mercilessly in the rear like the French in '14, only on this occasion by the GSO1.

Lipsett returned his gaze to me. 'We did wonder when you might grace us with a report, MacPhail. Although the telephone would have sufficed nicely.'

I coughed uneasily. The general was not one for excuses. But it was difficult to know where to start.

'What's that on your head?' he said suddenly, staring at the dressing that covered all of my right ear and half my head. A medic at the railway dug-out had kindly applied it. Medically speaking it may not have mattered much, but at least it rid me of the ridiculous gauze bow tie Fisher came up with. 'Are you wounded?' the general asked.

'Yes, sir,' I replied. 'Grazed by a shell.'

'But you're fine? You're not seriously wounded?' His voiced had softened and his expression too. Lulled by this expression of concern I didn't think overly of what I said next. After all it had been a long and difficult day.

'Oh no, sir. They tell me it's only a scratch.'

Lipsett pursed his lips. A dark cloud swept across his features. Too late I cottoned on to what he was thinking.

'I see,' he said. His words were as hard as Sheffield steel.

'Sir,' I began. 'You misunderstand…' I wanted to explain that it was not because of my wound that I had returned to Fort George. That I had been ordered to do so, and that my lack of reports was not due to laxity, but for the very same reason that my ear was in shreds – because I'd been in the front line, helping out the 2nd Division. But it was to no avail, for suddenly an officer made an appearance, demanding the general's attention.

There was a symphony of awkward clicks and clacks, accompanied by much heavy breathing. The general peered over my shoulder. 'They're back?'

'Yes, sir. Just arrived.'

'Very well, I'll come. Gentlemen, if you'll excuse me. One of the evening's patrols has returned.' With that he was gone and I was facing down the twin barrels of Lieutenant-Colonel Hayter's glowering eyes.

'We didn't expect you for at least a day, MacPhail,' Hayter said smoothly, having slipped around to take up the general's position.

'No, sir,' I said. 'I didn't exactly expect it myself.'

'Yet here you are.'

'Yes, sir. It's a long story, sir, but it's not what the general thinks,' I said.

The colonel was looking at me dubiously when I heard another voice. It was General Lipsett's.

'Ross, are you coming? It might be best if you did.'

'Yes, sir,' he replied.

'We'll resume this at another moment. You might as well find your bunk.' With that, he too was gone.

I groaned. Rather loudly as it turned out for Corporal Timmins by the telephone asked if I was feeling all right.

CHAPTER 6

29th of April, 1917
Souchez, France

'So what it comes down to,' I said morosely, 'is that I'm in the dog-house with the general. Worse than that, actually. He's convinced I'm a coward; that I picked up a scratch behind my ear from a stray shell and fled to headquarters the first opportunity I had.'

'*Non*, Mac. You're making a fuss about nothing again. *Un tempête dans un verre d'eau… y*ou know?' Lieutenant Benoît DuBois of the divisional field artillery staff looked at me questioningly.

'Yeah, I know the expression. A tempest in a teapot is what we generally say. A whirlwind in a wine bottle you might even call it.' Demonstratively I held up the half-full bottle by its neck.

'Listen, you're one of the few men on the staff who's done any fighting,' he lectured. 'General Lipsett knows that. For Pete's sake he asked you onto his staff when you were on your backside with a Blighty in a hospital ward. Remember? I was the no luck fellow beside you. And on top of everything you've got that pretty little decoration the King gave you,' he continued, referring to my Military Cross. Benoît had listened with infinite patience while I related the lengthy and somewhat twisty tale of my adventures in a theoretically cushy but not altogether bomb-proof exchange job with the 5th Brigade. To my great surprise he hadn't interrupted once. But the time for restraint had evidently come to an end.

'The general must think you had your wind up, that's all.' Then seeing the dismissive look on my face he added: 'Come on, Mac, don't tell me you didn't have your wind up?'

'Of course, I did,' I said. 'Only a fool or a liar would say otherwise. You and I have been through some scraps before, Benoît, so I don't mind telling you; I was scared stiff that whole walk towards the front line. For some reason – I'm beginning to think I've seen a little too much of this war – I've become a real nervous Nelly ever since Vimy. Anyhow, when the Boche put the barrage across...' I shuddered. 'But you know how it is. You get over it. Or try to. At least you put on a face that's no different than anyone else's. I certainly wasn't quaking in my boots when I reached the brigade dug-out, if that's what you think. But the point is, it wasn't my idea to return to divisional headquarters – wind up or not. Nevertheless, that's precisely what Colonel Hayter and the general believe.'

'Take a big breath,' said Benoît calmly, in his best stentorian baritone. 'And a drink, too, while you're at it. A big one.' He motioned at the bottle of France's finest – although at best it was a one franc bottle, rough-on-the-tongue approximation thereof that left you thinking they'd forgotten a teabag somewhere. 'And hurry up about it. It's thirsty work listening to you.'

I did as I was told then silently passed it over.

Despite everything I couldn't help but be amused. Benoît was French-Canadian. So partly it was his accent, but mostly it was just him. There wasn't a pretence about him. I liked that. While his girth could appear intimidating to some – if our side ever built a cannon the size of a *Big Bertha*, I dare say I know whose name would replace Bertha's – his manner was anything but: gay and spontaneous, a breath of fresh air on a Western Front where air, let alone the fresh stuff, was sorely absent.

It was no great surprise he'd become a good friend. He was someone with whom I could share confidences I shared with no one else, not to mention a bottle; someone to rely upon. Why he appeared to feel the same about me was a question best left unasked.

Benoît winked at me. Then held the wine to his lips for considerably longer than is considered polite in civilized parts of the world. But as we hailed from the colonies, something the Imperials helpfully liked to remind us of, those rules didn't really apply. With a generous wiping motion from elbow to wrist he dried his moustache and mouth on his tunic sleeve. He sighed contentedly.

'You *were* thirsty,' I said.

'You should just ask to see him, Mac, and explain it,' he said, ignoring me. 'Lipsett's a reasonable sort... for a general. He'll understand.'

Resolutely I shook my head. 'A junior officer? March in, demand the GOC's time, and explain to him I wasn't *really* afraid...? Oh, no. Not only would it not work, it'd simply confirm in his mind what he already thinks. And that's bad enough, trust me. Surely you must have heard that little speech he likes to give to new officers.'

Benoît looked doubtful.

'No? He probably doesn't think it's worth the bother giving it to the likes of the field artillery.'

Benoît sighed.

'Gentlemen,' I intoned, 'there is a tradition in the 3rd Division that no officer in it shows under any circumstances any sign of fear. Should he do so, he would cease at that moment to be an officer of the 3rd Division.'

'Ring a bell?' I asked.

He shook his head.

'Well, that's how General Lipsett thinks about me: the fearful fellow. I'm on the wire for good this time, Benoît.'

'Hmm,' said Benoît, thoughtfully. 'Pity.'

For a brief moment I actually thought he was referring to my predicament, until I caught him eyeing low tide in the bottle of wine.

I grabbed it and slugged back the remaining inch or so – burped, then tossed him the empty.

'I hope you came prepared,' I said.

Benoît laughed dismissively at this, already turning towards the backseat of the large open-topped Crossley parked nearby. It was quite a car for a junior officer to have to drive a few miles. I was beginning to see what attracted him to the field artillery.

That morning I turned up in the staff room after an abbreviated and uneasy night's sleep in a decidedly cold and damp corner of the dug-out. There was no sign of either the general or Colonel Hayter. The former's small office was empty. For that I breathed a sigh of relief. There was however news. The message came from young Lieutenant O'Neill who, in my absence, had diligently assumed my tasks as well as his own.

Around 4 a.m., while I was shifting restlessly from side to back, and back again, on a few slats of wood without so much as a blanket under or over me, the Germans had attempted another counter-attack to pierce the 25th Battalion line north of Arleux. According to O'Neill's signal the attack was promptly spotted. Once again it was beaten back by the artillery. The village was still safely in our hands.

As the morning and then the afternoon passed, I could feel my unease growing, as did the pangs of guilt at not being there. They may not have been from the 3rd Division but I'd spent enough hours with the boys of the 25th Battalion to increasingly side with General Lipsett's view – that I was derelict in my duties at not being with them. It was only too easy to imagine the Boche decapitating our small salient around the village, trampling all over the Arleux Loop North, and the men who held it in the process.

Later on the signals officer reported that gas shells were falling between the divisional front and support lines near Bois de la Chaudière, and that a large fire had broken out in the outskirts of Lens at Méricourt as the result of our shelling. Then, one of our aeroplanes was seen to fall behind the Fosse no. 4 of the Compagnie des mines de Courrières, also up near Lens. A "red" had engaged it all the way to the ground. None of this particularly interested me.

Finally the relieving message arrived. After a heavy bombardment of the German line the Nova Scotians had advanced and occupied their final objective. I reread it twice to make certain, but the wording was quite unambiguous. The left flank of the attack was secure. I smiled, as did the others, though unlike them I knew the faces involved so mine had a real glow to it.

Shortly thereafter Benoît, on an errand, arrived at headquarters. That was another nice thing about being in the artillery; Fort George was long miles from the front, but apparently the arties considered this an *advanced* headquarters. I was delighted to see him and pro-posed a drink that evening, to which he was more than amenable.

This suggestion however led to a lengthy debate, the likes of which explained why the front had barely moved in nearly three years of war – too much needless discussion, and too little reflection.

'What about Sains-en-Gohelle?' I suggested. 'There's a nice little estaminet there I've heard about, run by a young lady: Marie something. Perfect for an evening out in the Artois. You said you had a car?'

Benoît snorted. 'Mac, that's almost an hour's drive! It's on the road north to Béthune. With the road and the traffic it might even be longer. If you actually knew the girl that might be different –'

He countered with a fine establishment he knew well in Cambligneul. 'You'll love it, Mac,' he said, which sounded jake to me, and proceeded to lavish praise on the place, although he'd already long won me over.

As he blathered on I began to contemplate the logistics involved. That's one thing a spell on the staff will teach you, if nothing else, and that is that logistics trump everything. With that in mind, I proffered the information that getting to Cambligneul required a drive of several miles from Neuville-Saint-Vaast west down the la Targette plank road to Mont-St.Eloi, followed by a jaunt of at least as many miles again, but then to the northwest.

'You said it yourself, Mac. I have a car,' sighed Benoit. 'We'll be there in no time.'

When I pointed out that regardless whether you drove, walked or crawled – or perhaps he had an aeroplane at his disposal? – Camblain-l'Abbé was unavoidable, he gritted his teeth and conceded the point. The quaint hamlet of Camblain-l'Abbé was long home to Lieutenant-General Byng, and headquarters to the Canadian Corps. Neither of us had much stomach for running a gauntlet of military police on our unofficially-sanctioned evening out, let alone generals – me least of all.

Which went a long way to explaining why we were sitting by the Souchez River, in the middle of what remained of the village of the same name, not more than a mile or two from Fort George, nary a military policeman, general, or a single soul in sight. It was what passed for wilderness in present-day France.

Unfortunately, an attempt at locating the Coquelet Vert that someone had suggested was aborted when it turned out the estaminet was closed long before due to a Moaning Minnie having fallen through the roof. We settled for sitting on the remains of the little stone bridge that spanned the narrow, slow-moving rivulet of the Souchez. If one didn't think too much about what had transpired along its banks these past years, it was almost peaceful.

'We took Vimy,' I was saying. 'We smashed them from the ridge. But I'm increasingly of the opinion it probably doesn't matter one iota. I can't envisage the war ending anytime soon.'

'But the war is going our way, Mac.'

Vehemently I shook my head.

'The French attack...' he began. 'The Chemin des Dames...'

'Nivelles and his offensive are a bleeding disaster, Benoît. Read between the lines. Even the papers barely bother to disguise it. What do you think this is all about here in the Artois, what we're doing? Even our bonny Douglas Haig doesn't believe in victory this time. For all the men involved, we're little more than a red cape to wave at the Huns to distract them from skewering the French any more than they've done already.'

Even a seasoned campaigner like Benoît seemed mildly shocked by my tone. It was either that or what I was saying. Few spoke of the war or our commander-in-chief that way. Quite a few believed about Haig what they wanted to believe, despite considerable evidence to the contrary. Quite a few also believed what they wanted to believe about the war. Characteristically those types were well removed from it, preferring to pontificate from safe havens like London. But well into bottle two I was letting fly. They were feelings that had been building for some time, I guess.

'We took Arleux,' said Benoît.

'Sure. But did you realize that on the day of our attack the British Army attacked along six miles of front? Six miles! And do you know what the *only* tangible success of that six-mile long attack by two entire armies was?'

DuBois looked pensive.

'Arleux,' I said. 'Arleux-en-Gohelle. One small village and it cost the Corps nearly a thousand men to pull it off. Personally, I wonder if it was worth it. And if even the victory was arguably not worth the cost, what then to think about the rest of it? The generals talk of wearing down the enemy, Benoît, but the way things are going, surely they must realize we're being worn down just as fast?'

He took a pull at the bottle with uncharacteristically little enthusiasm. 'You're not going to like this, Mac. We've been told to prepare for another offensive.'

I grunted. 'Where?'

'Fresnoy.'

I nodded. Of course. I'd seen the red-tiled roofs in the distance beyond Arleux. Fresnoy was the next village to the east. A mile further. Maybe even less.

From the north – perhaps even from the estaminet at Sains-en-Gohelle I thought sourly – the coughing rumble of an approaching motorcycle on the road caught my attention. The rider throttled back as he entered the village, but the motor still clattered noisily as it passed between the tumbledown walls and shell-battered remains of the village. We both got to our feet to watch.

It was a strange place for a despatch rider to be. Even stranger, the rider had his headlight on, poking a way forward. Amongst the abandoned ruins it gave an eerie effect. A month earlier that light would have made the rider fair game for both the Germans and the field police. Of course that was before we'd taken the ridge. Now there wasn't a German for miles that could see him. Benoît stepped forward and raised an arm in greeting. Even without the headlight you would have had to be several shades past blind not to spot Benoît.

The motorbike came to rest in a cloud of dust billowing up from behind in the moonlight, the motor still grumbling, a pungent smell of raw gasoline wafting in from the rear. Large saddlebags hung beside the rider.

'Evening chaps,' said a voice. 'I'm heading to Thélus. This is the right road, isn't it?'

'Yes,' replied Benoît with a smile.

'Three miles,' I added. 'It's a straight shot to Neuville. Then take a left up the ridge. It's the second road at the village. It's a little bumpy, but you can't miss Thélus. There's a puddle at the crossroads there about the size of Lake Superior.'

'MacPhail?'

The rider lifted his goggles, and turned to face us, allowing me to place where I'd last heard that particular voice.

'I thought it was you,' said the rider.

'Captain Smythe,' I replied stiffly. 'I didn't expect to see you in these parts.'

I was considering following up by asking him how things were at brigade headquarters and Arleux, when Smythe turned almost imperceptibly. I knew from the way his lips pursed together he'd spotted the bottle Benoit was holding.

'Who's your well-lubricated acquaintance?' he asked.

'Lieutenant DuBois, sir,' said DuBois.

'I can see, gentlemen, the 3rd Division is taking the war very seriously.'

I was on the verge of responding when Smythe said: 'Thanks for the directions, MacPhail.' He threw the throttle wide open, leaving us coughing in a thick smoke screen of dusk and flying gravel.

'Friend of yours?' inquired Benoît.

'Not exactly,' I mumbled.

Benoît arched an eyebrow.

'I'm fairly sure Smythe's the one that was responsible for the mix-up with the operations orders during the Arleux attack. Only he works for that brigadier I was telling you about, so he's probably off the hook. They're both still peeved I even bothered to mention it, I think.'

'Oh, *mon Dieu*,' sighed Benoît. 'Don't tell me. In two days' time you've aggravated not one general, but two!?'

I shrugged. It was not the moment to expound on the brigadier's dinner habits. 'Well, I don't expect Macdonell will be putting me up for a DSO anytime soon.' I looked at him. His head was slowly shaking back and forth.

'You're acting as if it's somehow *my* fault.'

Benoît crossed himself.

CHAPTER 7

2nd of May, 1917
La Chaudière, France

The t's were being crossed and the i's were being dotted, and as a small part of that effort I was to ensure that one of the new forward supply dumps was in fact operating as it ought to.

As the orders I'd written were quite plain, blatantly obvious really, I had no reason to expect that wouldn't be the case. Consequently, one might have construed my expedition as yet another example of mindless army bureaucracy at work. Nevertheless, Colonel Hayter was always keen to lecture eager young subalterns on the staff that while it was one thing to write an order, it was quite another ensuring it was carried out as intended. The colonel had some experience in these matters. I on the other hand, as I was discovering, was still learning.

'For Christ's sake,' I exploded. 'Do we need to erect a billboard with a red arrow pointing the way!? Have any of these clods ever looked at a map in their lives? It's not so terribly complicated.'

The corporal looked at me anxiously.

'Look, why do you suppose I want the mules lined up in that sunken stretch while they wait their turn to be loaded, and not on the road itself?'

'Well, sir, I expect you don't want the Heinie artillery to spot them. In the sunken part of the road they're reasonably out of sight.'

'Bingo!' I shouted. 'So why is it that they insist on milling about in a herd?'

'Well I imagine, sir, they don't want to go to the trouble. That part of the road you suggest is quite narrow, even to turn a limber in. And it's well past the dump.'

'Trouble? The whole point of having a dump forward is that it reduces the trouble. Otherwise we'd simply send every man, mule and limber on a return journey across the ridge to the Ariane Dump. *That* would be trouble. They'd be walking day and night. Regardless, if they keep bunching up this way they're going to encounter more trouble than they could dream of.'

'We could string some netting along the far side of the road, sir?' said the corporal, ignoring most of what I'd said. 'As a screen.'

I gritted my teeth, but considered his words all the same. The sunken part of the road past the dump was not exactly ideal as an assembly area. Nor was my plan of painting a red arrow to get them there; the men would still first spot the sign DUMP, stop, and then josh amongst themselves about how illiterate the staff was these days. Furthermore, I could see that where the small road from the east turned northwards towards us the ground rose. As it did, there was a stretch of at least fifty feet without a tree or other obstruction. A sharp-eyed observer hovering in a balloon above enemy territory could probably see everything that came our way.

'Yes, you might have something with that, corporal,' I said slowly. 'All this movement up the road also risks drawing some unwanted attention. The netting might help.'

'Exactly, sir,' he replied. 'And this way the drivers and their mules can stay where they are.'

So much for my attempt to get the best of a bunch of mules, I thought grumpily. To the corporal I said: 'Good thinking.' At the last moment I remembered to punctuate it with a smile.

'Thank you, sir,' said the man. He was beaming broadly when he raced off to see it done.

After the rigours of law school, I naively presumed I could henceforth think my way out of any predicament that came my way. But there were a disconcerting number of factors to consider when establishing an advanced dump. Was it sheltered, or at the very least concealed from enemy fire? Could it be readily supplied by road or light rail, preferably both? Was it close enough to the battalions in the field that they could quickly replenish their stocks of ammunition, food, and other gear, yet not too close to the enemy line as to attract attention? The list was endless. To that I could now add the requirement that it be mule-proof.

The choice of La Chaudière, in any event, had been an inspired one. It was not so much a village as cluster of old and damaged mine buildings, the small villages of Vimy and Petit Vimy roughly a mile to the south of it. The divisional front line was not much further to the northeast, and many of the gun batteries closer than that. In fact it was the presence of an 8th Field Artillery Brigade ammunition dump that first caught my eye. That and a spur of the rail line I saw marked on the map.

While it would be some time before it was possible for a full-fledged train to make use of the track, there was a rail cart of the wide-gauge variety being pulled along into a position where the large pyramid of shells it was carrying (18-pounders by the look of them) could be offloaded. After the enemy scored three direct hits on the divisional dump at La Folie Farm yesterday there was a certain urgency.

Moving closer up the embankment, I was curious how five men were ever going to get that pile down to the long waist-high rows of the dump a hundred feet away. Eighteen pounders are rather small as shells go, but as heavy as the name implies, and there were a lot of them. It was not as if you could tuck one under each arm and another in your breast pocket.

But the crew had it neatly worked out. They threw a plank against one side of the rail cart and lay the other end on the bed of a small two-wheeled limber parked beside the embankment. The two on the rail cart took turns lifting a shell, putting it on the narrow ramp where another man rapidly rolled it down into the hands of a fourth man who saw that it was neatly stacked. The fifth man was either an overseer or relief; he just stood to one side with his hands on hips. He reminded me of myself.

'That's a smooth operation you've got going,' I said to him.

'Yes, sir,' he replied.

'I came to see if the supplies dump was progressing.'

'Up and running, sir.'

'Yes, I saw. They managed it in less than a day. They were quick.'

The man shrugged. If given the chance he'd undoubtedly have told me the field artillery could have done it in half the time.

At the sound of shells crashing down not far to our rear, we both turned to look. Vimy was getting laced again. The daily barrage. Regular as clockwork. Clockwork was a particularly German virtue and, since they'd taken to using a high-velocity naval gun, it paid to pay close attention to their schedule. Especially as they were fond of dropping gas shells in our rear.

'High explosive,' I said casually to the private, who nodded, before returning his attentions to the men of the loading fatigue.

I was about to do likewise when closer to hand I spotted a motorcycle roar into the supplies dump. For convenience the dump had been positioned beside that of the artillery brigade, so I could see it easily enough from my vantage point. Whatever their merits motorcycles are not ideal to transport anything of more than modest bulk or weight, and it was therefore an odd place for one to turn up.

Suddenly my heart began to pulse – perhaps an urgent message had come for me? But then, just as quickly, I dismissed the thought. Who was I kidding? On the other hand, perhaps I did know the rider. I watched him dismount.

While there was absolutely no reason to think it would be him, the image of a certain captain of my recent acquaintance crept into mind. Sternly I reminded myself: Smythe was 2nd Division. He wouldn't very likely be dropping by one of our supply dumps. Come to that, while the brigade HQ in the railway dug-out wasn't more than a ten-minute ride from where I stood, Smythe had proven himself a man wholly uninterested in operational trifles, let alone those involving logistics.

The rider slowly straightened up and I could make out the act of him removing his helmet with both hands. I strained my eyes, but it was simply impossible to see anything else in more detail. I cursed myself for not having brought field glasses. Shortly thereafter, however, a soldier approached him and made what was a very characteristic gesture. It was a motion that had not come easily to me. Which is likely why I recognized it at eighty yards. It was a salute. The motorcyclist was an officer.

Intrigued I watched as the officer spoke with the soldier briefly before the two of them began to tour the various corners of the dump. The newcomer didn't appear in the slightest interested in the crates of grenades or small arms ammunition. The petrol tins were apparently also not worthy of dalliance, though they were filled with water, so this was understandable. Nor did he pause at the boxes containing tins of victuals like *Huntley Palmer* hardtack, *Batger's* plum and apple jelly and the thin witches' broth of turnips and potatoes known as *Maconochie* stew. Instead he disappeared behind a wall of wooden boxes in the furthest extremity of the dump. For the life of me I couldn't recall the corporal telling me about anything more thrilling than water bottles and other such miscellanea kept there.

After a minute or so, the two finally re-emerged, and I could have sworn they shook hands. It struck me as odd at the time.

Likely I would have reflected on it more, except for the shouted warning immediately behind me. This was followed by noises of an indeterminate nature, capped by a scream that positively curdled the spring air and my blood along with it. I whirled round in alarm.

The man who'd been deftly rolling the shells down the plank lay writhing on the ground, grasping at a leg. Beside him lay the shell responsible.

By the time I'd gotten close he was already surrounded by the artillerymen. The fellow I'd been speaking with earlier had knelt on a knee to help, and the others were giving well-meaning advice of a kind that probably made him wish they wouldn't trouble themselves, or him. Over the shoulder of one of the loading crew I saw the laces of a boot being cut away and an attempt made to remove it. It hardly seemed worth the effort as the sole was coming loose of its own accord. A barely-controlled moan of pain cut short the attempt.

Away from the obvious dangers of life in the line, it was all too easy to let down one's guard. From a height, and with weight and momentum, the ankle hadn't stood a chance. There were more reasons to be wary of an 18-pound shell than I could have imagined.

Soon a stretcher was located and we set off down the road to collect the only transportation suitable to carry him to the dressing station at Vimy: my little staff car.

'Lucky bugger,' I heard one of the man's comrades say as we left. 'A good Blighty.'

The others laughed.

All I could think of was the gruesomely twisted foot hanging from his right leg, and the white pallor that consumed his face. I'd seen worse wounds than this, far worse, but they had always come from the things you expected when at war. I guess I never really considered until that moment that this, too, was war. Certainly the casualty toll kept climbing. Although I had a feeling that with good luck (or bad, depending on how this fellow viewed it) he was soon destined to rejoin us.

When we passed the dump the motorcycle rider was gone. At least I don't recall seeing the wheel he'd come in on. I must confess to not having really looked though; I'd forgotten clean about him in the excitement. In fact, it was not until later that evening, once I was long back at Fort George, that I recalled the peculiar scene at the dump. I remember thinking it was unfortunate I hadn't remembered it earlier. Had I done so, I might have returned to the dump and enquired around about who the man was.

Then I ran into Benoît in a great tear.

CHAPTER 8

2nd of May, 1917
Neuville-Saint-Vaast, France

'ZERO Hour's at 3.45 a.m. you told me. There's no rush. We've got plenty of time,' I said to him.

It was going on 10 p.m. and Benoît was behind the wheel of the very Crossley we'd been in a few days earlier. It was a beautiful clear evening, an almost full moon stroked the slopes of Vimy Ridge on our left with its rays of silver. I had my arm resting on the door, a hand outstretched to catch the wind, trying to assume a nonchalance I didn't feel as DuBois wrenched the car to one side and revved the motor to overtake one of the Whites from the divisional supply column.

An arm went out in greeting from the lorry as we sped past and I waved back. It was either that or duck, and hope they hadn't seen me.

'I told you, already, the S.O.S. barrage table was changed,' said Benoît. 'Our artillery is supporting the 1st and 2nd Divisions, so we can't let them down.'

'I'm quite certain they telephoned it ahead,' I replied.

'They did. But they've been unable to reach one of the batteries.'

'Well why doesn't Pete from Battery A simply amble down the road to John at Battery B, and tell him? That's what we'd do in the infantry. Common sense was what we used to call it.'

Benoît sighed irritably. 'You keep forgetting you're not in the infantry, Mac. You're on the staff. But that's not how it works. And the batteries aren't lettered, they're numbered.'

'I know that,' I said. 'I was just seeing if you did.'

A loud groan erupted beside me.

'Seems odd, that's all. It's a lot of effort merely to deliver a message.'

Benoît didn't reply. We bumped along for another minute, un-speaking. He'd been jumpy ever since he nearly ran me down coming through a dug-out entrance. This tenseness wasn't like him at all, and I had the feeling something was going on. I wouldn't have suggested accompanying him otherwise, but I thought I could draw him out. My duties for the day were done. Hopefully he'd have me back at Fort George before dawn.

We were on the Arras road heading south from headquarters. Ahead I could see Neuville-Saint-Vaast looming into sight.

'Slow down, or you'll miss the turn.'

'MAC!'

'Shhh, listen,' I hissed.

'What? I don't hear anything.'

'If you stop gabbing and take your lead foot off the pedal for a minute–'

I stuck my head out the car window and stared up into the night. There was no mistaking the nature of the droning noise, approaching fast. Then I saw it. Beside me a building flashed by and I knew that we'd reached the village.

'Benoît!' I shouted, pulling my head onboard.

But it was too late. The droning intensified, now reinforced by a loud, coughing staccato. *TUF-TUF-TUF.* With a sinking feeling in my gut I saw the flashes and watched as a machine gun stitched a seam across the road in front.

DuBois didn't hesitate. Resolutely he pressed the pedal down further, while my brain screamed that he should be applying it to the brake rather than the gas. But this time I kept my own counsel. As it transpired, it was fortunate he was the one driving.

The aeroplane buzzed low overhead in a turbulence of wind and noise, a much larger dark shadow of itself following menacingly in its wake. Vaguely I was conscious of something falling from the machine as it passed over.

KABOOM!

The blast blew out the rear window, nearly taking the entire canvas rooftop with it. Instinctively I reached up to prevent it from collapsing on our heads.

'*Merde*,' I heard Benoît mumble, with some feeling for understatement.

The big Type J Crossley swerved back and forth, but Benoît kept it on the road until we rolled to a stop in the lee of a house.

'I hope you didn't promise to bring it back in intact,' I said, and we both got out to examine the damage. Somehow, beyond the torn rooftop which I was intending to rip off and leave by the wayside until Benoît insisted we stuff it in the back seat, the car was little worse for wear. Although I did hope for his sake that the brigadier in command of the artillery wasn't looking to use it anytime soon.

'This unresponsive battery of yours. Where is it?' I asked.

'Near Fosse no. 1. In La Chaudière.'

'Well, what the hell, Bill, what the hell?'

I pounded my thigh with a hand and began to laugh. Miraculous escapes from Fritz laying a 10-pound egg on my head sometimes leave a sensation of light headedness, I find.

Benoit was eyeing me as if I if I'd gone completely bugsy. 'You'll never believe this but I was at La Chaudière a few hours ago. It's a bit of a dump,' I said, then paused for him to catch this flash of wit. Benoît stared back at me blankly. 'Here, let me,' I continued. 'I'll drive. I could find it blindfolded.'

Dumbly he nodded his approval. I think he was relieved. He settled into the passenger seat and took a long nip at his water bottle.

In keeping with my frayed nerves, and a gentlemanly tempo appropriate for two promising, if prematurely greying, young officers of the Canadian Corps we reached the battery of 4.5-inch howitzers. A couple of miles over the ridge, and down the other side, and we were there.

As I'd suspected it proved a wild-goose chase. The officer in charge had the map coordinates down pat, and was mildly bewildered why we'd come. Should one of the battalions in the line call for help he knew precisely where he was to direct the interdictory fire, he assured us.

'All right, what's going on?' I said to Benoît, when we were alone.

For a moment he met my glance, then his head sagged and he studied his boots. 'They gave Patterson the job as counter-battery liaison.'

'That's the position you wanted, wasn't it?'

He nodded. For some reason Benoît had taken it in his head that he was the man destined to neutralize the enemy guns opposite. The newfangled position of counter-battery officer was popping up everywhere, including in the 3rd Division, and ever since he'd spent some time with our prickly gunner-genius, Lieutenant-Colonel McNaughton at Corps headquarters, he was determined to become one himself.

'I'm sorry to hear that, Benoît,' I said. I realized full well that was why he'd raced off this way, trying in some tortuous and ultimately pointless fashion to prove to his superiors they had made a mistake. But I didn't have the heart to say it. 'Look –,' I began.

'Forget about it.'

'No. Don't give up hope. You and I have seen a lot. Well, me considerably more than you…' He rolled his eyes elaborately at this. 'So trust me when I say your time will come Benoît.'

As mollifications go it possessed all the effectiveness of a Lee-Enfield duelling it out against a low flying Fokker. But I think he knew I meant well. He clapped me on the shoulder.

3rd of May, 1917
West of Fresnoy-en-Gohelle, France

Benoît's rationale for dashing off to the batteries in the middle of the night may have been a few rounds short of a full clip, but his intelligence about the forthcoming attack was spot on the mark. While we tooled from battery to battery on an improvised tour of inspection – he felt it might be useful, and uncharacteristically I didn't quibble – I quizzed him about what he knew. All I knew was that something was going on, and that an officer other than me was sent out on exchange duties with the 2nd Division. I suppose I should have felt pleased.

The gist of what Benoît told me was that once again we of the 3rd

Division were holding the 2nd Division's left flank. Once again the 2nd Division was supporting the 1st Division. And both were once again involved in a big offensive. I would have inquired about it earlier at headquarters had I not been trying to keep a low profile. Despite that, General Lipsett had spotted me on a couple of occasions. There was absolutely nothing to be discerned from his even-toned greetings; though his friendly tone meant little if he counted me amongst the milksops, as I was convinced was the case.

'So our entire divisional artillery is firing in support?'

Benoît nodded. 'Feints mainly. A deception so the Boche won't think it's the real attack when it comes. You must have heard the creeping barrages the past few mornings.' I hadn't, largely on account of being dead to the world in the security of the Fort George dugouts. At that hour, and at six miles distant, they could have shot off the entire combined artillery of the Entente and I would have simply rolled to my other side. But I understood what he was getting at. 'We'll be ready if they try something,' he growled.

His feelings about the Hun were familiar to me, though the sheer ferociousness accompanying this last remark brought a smile to my face. I still hadn't figured out what the Germans had done to produce such blatant animosity – well, other than overrun Belgium and half of France, and try to poison or shoot us whenever the opportunity presented itself – although this being war the latter grudge seemed par for the course. 'That will be a great relief to all concerned,' I said jauntily.

Benoît grunted.

I applied myself with extra devotion to keeping the Crossley on the road.

'It's all about Fresnoy, eh? And Oppy to the south?'

'*Non*, it's much bigger, Mac. Fresnoy and Oppy are the main objectives of the First Army. But the 3rd and the 5th Armies are also involved,' he said, his voice rising with excitement. '*Fourteen* miles of front.'

'What's this,' I asked, 'the third attack in a month the British Army has made astride the Scarpe? In view of the overwhelming success of the last, I can easily understand why the field-marshal is keen to try his luck again.'

'Fresnoy is on high ground,' protested Benoît. 'We need to gain a good defensive line, Mac.'

'That's rich,' I muttered, falling momentarily silent as I battled a rut in the narrow road. 'First we're sent into action. At great cost a few acres of French mud change hands. Only then it turns out the acres gained aren't ideal to defend. So what do we do? We send in three armies to gain a few acres more at the cost of Lord knows how many men. Just so as not to need defend the ground which cost thousands their lives and their limbs a week before!? The more I see of it, the more this strategy of attrition puzzles the hell out of me.'

Benoît shrugged.

'Or does anyone at GHQ even give a damn about the casualties?' I mumbled.

Sensibly he also let this pass. It may have been that I'd asked him before.

We were keeping low at a forward observation post as ZERO Hour approached. The signallers had strung a telephone line across the open fields so that the two observers in our cavernous shell hole could report back immediately on the fall of the shells and any targets of opportunity.

Benoît and I took turns peering through the constricted but clear sights of Benoît's field glasses as the moon's brilliant glow silhouetted the troops assembling in their jumping-off trenches on the open ground east of Arleux. It was around three in the morning. Nevertheless, we were not the only ones to spot them for the preparations drew an immediate and heavy fire from the enemy. The casualties must have been considerable. It seemed a disturbing portent.

When the time came, the assembled guns hidden all along the railway embankment roared in anger, the heavens thundered and the sky coloured from their flashes, while the very ground rumbled and shook. A conflagration consumed Fresnoy Wood to the south of the village, transforming it into a glowing pyre of red and orange – a useful beacon for the battalions who were to force their way into Fresnoy. I felt my spirits rising.

Despite the threat from the German shells, which came in sudden rushes overhead, we lay on the lip of the crater and watched in wonder. Flares soared into the air all along the German line from Méricourt in the north to far south of Oppy, the small arms fire popping incessantly. The pungent smell of the fighting drifted over us. Before long, dawn was in the offing and I needed to urgently return to Fort George. I had no desire to explain to Lt.-Col. Hayter why I was not present and taking care of my duties; with the current thick cloud of aspersion that lay over me that was a discussion best avoided. Yet I also desperately wanted to hear whether the attack had succeeded.

'Gentlemen?' The artillery observer was calling to us from the opposite side of the crater. 'I thought you'd like to know. 1st Division reports Fresnoy is taken. They're holding the switch on the other side of town.'

We both smiled, and so did the observer. The daunting task of holding the village against the forceful and immediate counter-attacks that the German manuals prescribed was still to come. But somehow, having taken it, I didn't worry that we would.

CHAPTER 9

9th of May, 1917
Fort George, northwest of Neuville-Saint-Vaast, France

"The 1st Canadian Division is the pride and the wonder of the British Army," our Army commander General Horne had cabled in his congratulatory message to General Currie in the aftermath of the attack; Fresnoy the third victory in a month. Or so said the knowing tongues at headquarters who generally knew such things. Having come from the 1st Division and fought in it for all but the past few months, I confess to a welling of pride at this most unusual and effusive praise. The sensation disappeared when I recalled that my own contribution to the attack had been to keep my head down in a shell hole a mile to the rear.

On the other extremity of the offensive, to the right and well south of Arras, the Australians breached the German line at Bullecourt, and were holding the village against concerted counter-attack. But Fresnoy was the only real highlight on a day which had seen bitter few; by all accounts one of the more dismal in the long history of British arms.

The 1st Division went into relief a few days thereafter. The British 5th Division replaced them as guardians of Fresnoy. Then yesterday morning, preceded by two days of heavy shelling and abundantly ample evidence of their intentions, the 5th Bavarians proceeded to knock the 5th Imperials soundly about the ears, and even more soundly out of the village. The Imperial's flustered general, a fellow by the name of Sir Reginald Byng Stephens, finally mustered the counter-attack. It went in at 2.30 a.m. this morning.

When Fotheringham entered the staff room the assembled faces looked up, staring at him expectantly. He shook his head.

'Isn't that the damnedest thing,' said someone, after the worst was confirmed. The sombre details were more disheartening than I'd feared. The commanding position of Fresnoy was lost. We were back where we'd started. 'The entire show was fucking pointless in other words,' growled another.

Generally the staff refrained from such language, but no one present felt it at all inappropriate. Going on 1300 men had fallen to take Fresnoy. A foundation stone in the German defences had been neatly removed – but no longer. The stone was back in place.

'The really sad thing is they could have retaken Fresnoy, if only Sir Reginald hadn't taken the better part of a day to get his checkers neatly lined up,' I offered. I was throwing unnecessary kindling on what had the potential to be a real bonfire. More voices piled on with their own sharply-worded opinions.

Only with the appearance of a sombre looking Lt.-Col. Hayter did we settle down and return to the pressing affairs of the division. Four companies were to be employed tomorrow by the pioneer battalion on La Folie Road; the signals company required an additional 250 men to bury cable; and the divisional boundaries were to shift leftwards. Orders needed to be written, arrangements made. In addition to which, the colonel had a rather pleasant surprise in store for me.

10th of May, 1917
Paris, France

'Have you ever been, Malcolm?' asked the well-starched officer opposite. He came from an Imperial regiment hitherto unbeknownst to me, the South Staffordshires; and it was only when I heard they belonged to the 46th Division, which I was quite certain was the division that came after the 45th and before the 47th – and more importantly held the ground to the north of us – did a small bell tinkle. His question was predictable enough. I might have asked the same of him if my nose hadn't been pressed against the pane of the carriage window in anxious anticipation. I felt like a small boy standing outside the window display of the candy store staring inwards.

It had taken the better part of the trip, ever since we entrained at Arras in fact, to coax a single word out of the taciturn Lieutenant Hollace Bennett (as of yet no word what his friends were invited to call him – Holly?). Now I couldn't shut him up, and just as the view started to become more interesting.

Judging from the procession of low-slung warehouses rolling slowly past, followed by one large yellow-grey limestone building after another, each with a dozen or more small balconies demarcated in wrought iron and adorned with white washing, we'd reached what must be the outlying districts of France's legendary capital city.

'No, it's the first time,' I replied. 'What about you?'

'Not yet,' he said. 'How do you say that in French?'

'*Pas encore.*'

'Paz en core,' he enunciated loudly and slowly, following my example – the brakes tenaciously applied as an Englishman of a certain class and background is wont to do facing down a word or a situation of foreign character.

'You see?' I said. 'Add a little southern temperament, Bennett, and in another day or two you'll be speaking it like a native.'

'Hardly,' he chuckled. 'What do you say we join forces and conquer the city together?'

Bennett with his lean hooky features, long, slightly effeminate fingers, and piercing hazel eyes, was not exactly the twentieth century's answer to the conqueror Hannibal. Far from it. In fact, I would have said his polite manners were learned in the previous century, were it not that he would have been about four at the time. There was also the matter of his neat little brown moustache. It positively cried out for a stiff breeze to set things right, preferably to blow it away altogether. None of this suggested that Bennett would be of much use conquering anything. Nevertheless, I gave the idea some thought. Although I wasn't entirely certain I wanted my first leave in a very long time – in Paris no less – dictated by the company I kept. On the other hand, I didn't know a soul in the city so this was a purely theoretical consideration. As company goes, Bennett seemed a friendly fellow, at least once you cut through all the conventions and pretences that Imperial officers wore so heavily.

Fortunately, Bennett had cast those aside and afforded me the benefit of the doubt. Which was flattering considering that our ties were measured in mere hours, not generations. In turn I might even be able to help the poor fellow find a barber. I'd have to think about the best way to say, 'shave it all off', in French.

'All right,' I replied. 'But the first thing we're going to do is reconnoitre one of these famous cafés everyone talks about. I'd like nothing better than to sit on my butt and watch life pass me by for a change. Usually, I'm eyeing it though a rifle sight. Worse, it's eyeing me.'

Bennett was amenable. I think he was as thirsty as I was after the trip. We found precisely what I was looking for directly opposite the station. Later I kicked myself as I'd chosen the most expensive location in the city.

We sat balanced on two frail-looking yet sturdy metal-frame chairs, each with a hand outstretched to hold our drinks upright; the tiny round table was far from stable. For the longest time I said nothing, taking in the sounds and sights of Paris playing out around us. Bennett seemed as awestruck as me.

'Seeing this you'd hardly think there was a war on,' he remarked at length.

I grunted. 'I'm not sure I'd go that far,' I said, jutting my chin at the surrounding sea of tables, all occupied by men in uniform. As far as I could see there wasn't a single table the military hadn't seized.

'What about another?' I asked. Pressed, Bennett drained the last of his glass in a gulp, leaving his moustache flecked with foam.

He nodded eagerly. 'It may be a wait, though,' he said, looking around.

The elderly waiter outfitted in a black jacket, black vest, and black bowtie, with an elegant long white apron that fell so low it risked tripping him up, was clearly overwhelmed by the thirsty mob that had descended. Furiously, hands were being waved in the air, anxious voices raised. The Australians two tables over were whistling loudly and cursing. But the waiter came from a nation that had held the Germans at Verdun.

I looked over at him and caught his eye, then raised a finger. The old fellow disappeared inside, eliciting a chorus of loud groans from those assembled. Then within a minute he magically reappeared and came tottering towards us at speed, tray extended. I wasn't the only one to catch my breath as he stumbled briefly, navigating the cobblestones and the many tables, but he was more dextrous than age suggested. The beers were still upright. I greeted him with a broad grin and a friendly '*Merci, monsieur*,' while he wiped down the table, collected our empty glasses and deposited two overfilling ones in their place.

The Australians were gaping. The table of British staff officers – a captain, two majors, and a full colonel no less – simply looked sour.

'Cheers!' I said to Bennett, raising my glass. 'Damn, that tastes good.'

'How the devil did you manage that?' he asked.

'Oh, it's simply a question of asking nicely,' I said. 'It's a shame no one tried it back in '14, or we might not have been in this mess –'

There was no need to mention I'd slipped the old geezer five francs when he brought us to the table. At Benoît's favourite watering hole at Cambligneul five francs would have bought us an entire evening out – but I'd reckoned with Parisian prices.

Meanwhile the Australians and the staff officers were throwing increasingly nasty looks in our general direction. On the premise that the Australians were the more formidable of the two parties, I waved the waiter off towards them, and was rewarded by an ebullient, 'Thanks, mate!'

'One thing about the Aussies, at least they can fight,' I mused to Bennett. 'I'm not sure I can say that about that other lot.'

'Oh, God,' said Bennett, shrinking into himself. Alarmed, I turned to look at him. He appeared ill.

'What's the matter?' I asked. 'You're not sick, are you?'

'No. No. It's nothing like that,' he murmured.

'Well then?'

'Don't you know who *they* are?' He had lowered his head – there was something furtive about the gesture, as if he was hiding. I get that sometimes so I wasn't immediately alarmed; not every drinking companion is happy to be seen with me. But from his expression I could see he was referring to the "other lot".

'Rabbits of the rear,' I said breezily. His eyes widened at this blasphemy. 'The red tabs and the arrogant looks are a sure giveaway.'

'He's from GHQ,' he whispered. 'That's Colonel Whatley-Wigham, Malcolm.'

'Oh?' The name meant nothing to me. Having met a few generals in my time I was not in awe of a mere colonel. I glanced over at the officer in question. Pencil-necked. Well-dressed. Somewhat pompous. GHQ sounded plausible. 'What the hell is this Wigham character doing drinking beer in Paris if he's from GHQ? There's an offensive on, man. Or at least I can't recall the last time there wasn't.'

Bennett was spared the necessity of responding by the arrival of the waiter at the officers' table, whereupon bad French was spoken and smiles returned at this sudden turn of their fortunes, and he was able to once again sit upright without fear of being branded a troublemaker. I figured Wigham was likely some sort of acquaintance of his father's.

Paris was everything I expected and more. From dawn 'til dusk we toured the sights, many known to me for their names, and from well-studied photographs in books. As a young boy I was always fascinated by the sights of the Old World, never thinking I'd mature to an age where I would see some of them myself – those that weren't already transformed into rubble.

Most days I accompanied Bennett on an outing on the right bank, or the left bank, or both banks if we were feeling ambitious or in search of that elusive small restaurant we'd heard spoken of. And steadily Bennett threw off his shackles. By the third day – not long after we ascended Gustave Eiffel's famous tower to a majestic view of the city by the Seine – he insisted I call him Hollace. I don't think he'd ever been so uninhibited.

Hollace was most interested in the ladies of Paris, and I can't say I blamed him, though it did cause me to think of my young wife who had passed away three years earlier. Nevertheless, if ever there was a time to forgot the war, or her, it was when a dark-haired beauty came strutting down the *trottoir* with Gallic imperturbability and front lines as curvy as those of the Ypres Salient, wearing a rare hobble skirt, and looking as if she'd stepped from the pages of *La Vie Parisienne*; which is surely how the publisher struck upon the illuminous idea of such a magazine.

On such occasions Bennett took on the appearance of someone who'd caught an ice hockey puck in the teeth he was unable to dislodge. I grew accustomed to waving off his frequent pleas that I intercede in French on his behalf. Still, the idea of being shot down in flames representing him didn't hold the same petrifying fear than if I were the suitor. I was prepared to do my best, too. But Bennett called off the horses before they were even saddled up. All as a result of my innocent inquiry about which language he planned on using should I succeed; or was his plan that I accompany them?

On the next to last day of leave we climbed the hill of Montmartre to the all-but-completed, white-domed basilica where I bought a postcard for my parents. I still hadn't thanked them for the tins of Pacific salmon they'd sent more than a month earlier. I knew my mother would appreciate the card for the picture of a city she'd always longed to visit, and for my words; my father grateful for the fact it was from me. Both were accustomed to the traffic over the North Atlantic being of a decidedly one-directional nature.

As evening approached we took what was nearly a straight line downhill, southwards, heading in the direction of the Opéra where a bistro of our recent but fond acquaintance beckoned. We were walking down the rue Laffitte – I recall looking up and seeing the street sign – when I spotted a face I knew emerge from a doorway ahead, on the opposite side of the road.

'A friend of yours?' asked Bennett, who must have noticed my reaction.

'Not altogether…' I replied. 'It's a captain I know by the name of Smythe. He's with our 2nd Division.'

I hesitated, but then decided there was no reason not to and raised a hand in greeting. Smythe wasn't looking my way, however. With an abundance of caution I cast a glance over one shoulder to ensure we weren't done in by one of the famous Parisian taxis barreling along at the speed of a whizz-bang, then skipped across the cobblestones in a few hasty strides just in case. 'Come along, I'll introduce you, Hollace,' I called after me. 'Don't worry, it won't take long.'

I made for Smythe, who was standing outside a pair of heavy wooden doors of a model that were used to secure hilltop forts in centuries past. They were set in a long façade of grey stone so typical of a Parisian street, and consequently easy to miss walking by. Unusually these doors were flung wide open. Smythe, oblivious to our approach, was completely absorbed by a thick manila envelope he held in both hands, the contents of which he was examining. Thirty feet from him I realized my mistake. To all appearances it was Smythe. Only it wasn't him. For one thing the officer was wearing the crown of a major. The army being the army I suppose a quick promotion was possible, Smythe's recent incompetence notwithstanding. There was certainly nothing unusual in the army about incompetents being elevated to senior ranks; how else were a sufficient number of generals to be found? I saw now however that the man was distinctly older than Smythe, his uniform that of an Imperial formation.

Slowing my pace, I turned to Bennett and shook my head. 'It's not him.' For some reason I felt mildly disappointed. Perhaps it was a question of a familiar face and all that.

'Happens, sometimes,' Bennett said, coming abreast of me.

'It's the oddest thing. I could have sworn it was him.' Bennett looked sympathetic. 'No matter,' I continued. 'It's probably for the best.'

I glanced to my right as we walked towards the officer and past the wooden doors, and was astonished to see an elaborate courtyard beyond, a very distinguished-looking building at the far end. A discreet sign on the wall outside read: de Rothschild Frères. My forehead creased in a frown. It was a bank.

Then we were upon the major and we saluted; I observed him with interest, noting his features. At the last moment he noticed. He thrust the envelope hurriedly into a pocket, returned our looks, and made a cursory movement of his arm to acknowledge us. 'Gentlemen,' he mumbled.

No. It was most definitely not Smythe, but the likeness was quite extraordinary.

20th of May, 1917

Leave ended as quickly as it came. Where I'd spent most of the trip to Paris giddily contemplating the delights that awaited, on the return trip to the division I felt about as deflated as one of the observation balloons after some Fokker let out half the gas.

Nearing Arras the train slowed to a painful crawl, which is not to say that the journey had passed particularly quickly (not even in the carriage reserved for officers), only that as the city approached I began to wonder if we were going to be asked to get out and push. Back home getting out and pushing was a common enough request – mind you, that was usually after a snowstorm.

But of snowstorms in May there was naturally no question. Not that there was much visible of the verdure of a French spring, either. It had faded away miles before; shell holes, lines of wire and trenches – both old and new – and other ravages of war began to appear with regularity. The Boche artillery must have once reached this point. Or maybe it still did, I thought, suddenly concerned about our creeping tempo. There was a perceptible weariness to the countryside, the same I'd seen in many a French *Poilu*.

Paris had been a glorious respite, but with the windows open the thumping sounds of the guns could be heard. In my absence the war had plunged on relentlessly. In this frame of mind I had no desire to chat mindlessly with Hollace Bennett. While I liked him, and even considered him a friend after the adventures we'd had, I preferred to peer gloomily through the window. I think he felt similarly; he wore the glumness on his face.

Rolling past what looked to be a very sizeable dump, I perked up. Netting was cleverly hung overhead, and it was only as the train moved alongside that I could see row upon row of materiel, and the sheer scale of the place became evident. Something else piqued my attention and I bolted upright.

A motorcycle was leaning lazily on its stand on the road nearby. A lorry was parked further on. Beside the lorry a man, most definitely an officer, stood in animated conversation with one of the other ranks. Both men turned and looked towards the train as we puffed past at two miles per hour. This time there was no mistake possible. I looked him square in the face.

The officer was Captain Smythe.

PART TWO

CHAPTER 10

21st of May, 1917
Fort George, northwest of Neuville-Saint-Vaast, France

Gazing north and east from divisional headquarters towards the front lines, and past the dark blueish-grey etching of Vimy Ridge that dominated the view close at hand, the skies were dull and sombre. Far above, a veil of dense, endless cloud concealed the heavens and the sun, the wind slight from the southeast. And floating between heaven and earth was the reason for all the consternation amongst the staff.

'I count fourteen!' I cried. It was hard not to marvel. Not even at the Somme had I seen so many.

Sausages, we liked to call them, but the thing the kite balloons resembled most were the fin-tailed bombs the aeroplanes carried. In fact their bulbous form was nearly identical to that of the egg some goggled-eyed Boche ace in an Albatross, abetted by his evil twin in the rear seat, nearly cracked over my head a few weeks before. Worse, it had nearly cracked Benoît's borrowed automobile. He still hadn't forgiven them for it.

The balloons, while infinitely larger than bombs, were only specks at this distance. On the ground they dwarfed a line of lorries, and even whole buildings, requiring a dozen men or more to ready them for flight. Underneath the broad expanse of captive hydrogen hung neat little wicker baskets, with just enough room for a couple of observers

– assuming the observers skipped breakfast, lunch, and maybe even dinner. The size of the balloons aside I didn't envy those doughty sorts, holding tight to their field glasses, cameras, wireless sets and, absolutely not to forget, their parachutes.

In the event enemy aeroplanes approached, the balloons were rapidly reeled in by means of guide wires strung between them and motorized winches on the ground. But sometimes they were caught unawares, or were too slow to react, or simply too brazen. Then, if they were lucky, the observers were able to spring out at 3000 feet amidst a rift of machine-gun bullets through the air. Assuming church parade had passed successfully, they would then swing down to earth like a star shell.

It was not something I could ever imagine doing. But then I'd been absent without leave from church parade a little too often to have any delusions about my own chances in such circumstances. That being said, these were enemy balloons I was looking at. Which meant the boot was firmly on the other foot.

'Where the hell are our aeroplanes?' I asked. 'It'd be like shooting ducks at a granary.'

There were casual shrugs. No need to get worked up about something you can't do anything about. That was the way of the army, and I ought to have known. I think they appreciated my rants and raves for the entertainment value, if nothing else. Recently some clown had the temerity to suggest I apply to the Dumbells, a divisional concert party that was being formed.

'Christ,' I continued. 'Half you guys thought it would be a lark to join the Royal Flying Corps. So where are our flying brethren now, I ask you?'

'Maybe the wind's wrong?' offered someone.

'Well, I'll grant you it's wrong enough that if it doesn't shift soon we're going to have a gas alarm on,' I said. 'Which might be a good thing. Most of you look a sight better wearing a mask.'

'I wouldn't worry excessively about gas, Lieutenant,' said an even-toned voice approaching from the rear. 'The enemy is concentrating his shells on Vimy again today.'

I turned as Lt.-Col. Hayter came striding up, halting beside me. He'd left the dug-out to come and see the excitement for himself.

Straightening, I plucked at my tie, which seemed once again to be exhibiting a will of its own. My cap I'd inconveniently forgotten on my desk. Being on the staff brought with it challenges I never envisaged back in the trenches.

'Yes, sir,' I said. Then quickly shifting gears I passed him the field glasses and pointed out the intruders in the sky. When you're heading straight for a lee shore it's best to tack as quickly as possible. It was something I'd once read, and the wisdom stuck with me. I never thought it would prove so useful in practice, especially as it was a naval term.

'When do you expect our attack will be mounted, sir?'

I'd risen early as had the entire staff. The final touches to Operation Order no. 101 needed to be made; a scheme involving the 3rd and 4th Divisions, with the 1st Corps on our left along the Souchez. Having been on leave the heavy lifting was already done by the others. But I was taken aback that yet another attack was planned so soon, literally on the heels of the previous two. And this one involved my division.

Hayter grunted, his face noncommittal, field glasses still surveying the eastern skies. 'The enemy will be able to observe for their guns shooting along the entire divisional front,' he mused.

'Yes, sir. That's what we thought, too.'

Hayter put down the glasses and looked me in the eye. 'As to the attack. You read the orders, Lieutenant. The date will be communicated later. However, as you're asking, the date depends to some extent on what we learn tomorrow.'

'Sir?'

Momentarily the colonel looked irritated, but quickly resumed his countenance of unflappability. Since my return he'd appeared weary and drawn; General Lipsett could be a demanding taskmaster, and not only with lieutenants. 'What you're dying to ask is what happens tomorrow, is it not?'

Like a schoolboy I bobbed my chin up and down.

'This may surprise you, but I'm actually going to tell you, MacPhail,' he said. 'The foremost reason is because you're the man I'm sending to gather the intelligence. Major Lindsey leaves for London today, and Captain Ferguson is still indisposed, so I'm a little short-handed at present. But what happens tomorrow depends to some extent on what you come up with. What do you think of that?' He raised a bemused eyebrow.

'I see, sir.' I didn't see much of anything at that stage, but it appeared to be the response he was looking for. Fortunately, he followed up with an explanation.

22nd and 23rd of May, 1917
Front line, 1700 yards south of Avion, France

'There's some concern the Germans are engaged in a general withdrawal,' Hayter had said. 'We're sending out some patrols to see if there's any truth to it.'

Which is how I found myself at 58th Battalion headquarters at Bois de la Chaudière, where I could have easily remained. But when the officer responsible, the acting adjutant, a Major Greary, suggested I might like to accompany him I jumped at the invitation. His was an earnest face, bespectacled and clean shaven. And boy, could the man talk. Afterwards I learned he was mayor of Toronto before the war. Later still I heard they sent him on a mission to sweeten up the famously taciturn Swiss about the living conditions of the Canadians interned there – so glad-handing me proved no grand feat.

Besides, I already knew from the daily intelligence summaries that the German artillery had a grouch on about Bois de la Chaudière and the battalion headquarters quartered in the vicinity, so staying put had its dangers too. As such, Greary had the advantage of rolling a stone downhill. I was beginning to think this rumour of headquarter jobs being bomb proof was dreamt up by our foe as a means to lure us staff men to our deaths.

Nevertheless, I figured I had a reasonable hope of avoiding that fate. Greary led me to an advanced bombing post 700 yards north of the battalion dug-out and immediately west of the Arras-Lens railway, the east side of which was carved up by several German trenches. Ironically these were a continuation of the very trenches we occupied on the other side of the embankment. They ambled northwards to their main line, part of the stiff Oppy-Méricourt defences. Avion, one of Len's outlying villages and home to the trench of the same name, was less than a mile further north. Which is not particularly far, spitting distance really for an MG 08, or one of their 77mm field guns. But in the trenches, so long that Fritz was busy elsewhere it was far enough. I was counting on it this would again be the case. Tonight's action, in any event, was supposed to occur further along the railway embankment.

It was believed the Germans had built a post there in advance of our front line at Blue Nose Trench. With an eye to the forthcoming attack, and a desire to secure the right flank, the division had ordered this be set straight immediately.

The order was passed down to the 9th Brigade. After further consideration they passed it down to the 58th Battalion. There it landed with the major and his OC for execution. And somehow I stood in the middle of what they'd come up with – though thankfully not assigned to one of the working parties who were to dig a communication trench to our lines when it was done. Lt.-Col. Hayter hadn't sent me here to dig trenches.

'What about the patrols, sir?' I inquired. 'Will they be leaving at the same time as the others?'

Greary was understandably preoccupied with the final details of the operation. In a couple of hours he had four parties going out to secure the thorn in our side. While he was much too gentlemanly to say so, a tapping finger gave me the impression he was silently bemoaning the thorn in his other side. The patrols were the least of his concerns.

'Don't fret, Lieutenant, they'll be leaving shortly.'

'Would it be possible to speak with them before they do?'

Greary sighed. 'If you think it's necessary.'

I did. The whole exercise he and the battalion were engaged in tonight was pointless should the patrols report back as Colonel Hayter expected they might. And we had to know. I tried to be diplomatic about it.

Several minutes later he introduced me to the most junior, cherub-faced officer I'd ever seen. Apparently he was leading one of the patrols. Seeing him I was glad I insisted on a personal briefing.

After Greary left, Lieutenant James ('call me Jimmy') Haines turned to me and asked: 'What's it all about, s –?' There was a brief awkwardness, accompanied by a gulping for air as he swallowed the inadvertent "sir". It didn't take a genius to conclude that Jimmy's commission was of a very recent nature.

'I'm not entirely certain, but I'm told there are reports of various signs of an enemy withdrawal…' Enquiringly, I looked at him. While the colonel hadn't explicitly said so, many of those reports must surely have originated with the 58th Battalion.

If they had, Jimmy wasn't in the know. He shrugged.

'But if the Boche retreat, that would be wonderful news,' he said enthusiastically.

I forced a smile. 'Yes and no,' I replied. 'It's not the first time they've pulled that stunt. Not long before our show at Vimy the Germans did the same all along the front near Arras. Took up and disappeared behind their fortifications miles to the rear. The ground they surrendered wasn't worth much. And less so after they mined the roads, levelled the villages and poisoned the wells. No one noticed what they were doing until it was too late.

'It took the Brits more than a week to close the gap. Only the sad thing was, by that point there was little advantage to doing so; the Boche positions were stronger than they were before. So yes, Jimmy. It would be good news, provided we're ready to follow up. In fact, it would be very good news, but only if we can nip at their heels, and maybe force a break in the line. That's where you come in. General Lipsett is most anxious to know whether the Boche are up to something.'

I laid it on as thick as maple syrup in January. His eyes widened at the namedropping, and he began to nod vigorously. Then he asked a couple of surprisingly sensible questions about what he should look for. He was young, eager, and inexperienced, but he wasn't dumb, and I answered them as best I could.

A handful of men were to accompany Jimmy and they were casually loitering outside, awaiting orders. After days of unseasonably warm weather, it had rained today and the air was damp and cool; the conversation lively all the same. Jimmy may have been a rookie but the others were audibly not.

'I've seen some tussles before, but you should have seen this one,' remarked a man to his mate. The gears upstairs began to crank over. It didn't take me long before I realized they were referring to yesterday's air duel; four Germans had gone up against four of ours. Slowly but inexorably the air war in this corner of France was turning in our favour. It was about time. Even if that wasn't how it turned out on this occasion.

'I only watched the first period, mind,' said the soldier. 'But we were down by one. They drove our machine down out of control behind their lines. Then off they raced.'

'Do you think we evened it out?' said the other. 'The score?'

'Count on it.'

Not wishing to dampen morale with the real story, I said nothing, and went off to brief the other patrols.

Twenty minutes to midnight Jimmy and the men went over, crawling out through the wire into an unusually dark night. The darkness was on account of the low-hanging clouds and I hoped they'd be able to see something when they arrived at the German line. It wasn't as if you could take out your trench torch and start waving it around in No-Man's-Land.

The other patrols followed shortly thereafter. All headed north in the direction of Avion. If the Germans were truly withdrawing the proof would be in the pudding at the Oppy-Méricourt line. I found an empty funk hole in a nearby trench and settled down to wait.

Waiting is a big part of the life of a soldier. But it's not something I'll ever become accustomed to. Unless I'm sleeping, and in that case nothing less than the detonation of a Flying Pig wakens me, I generally find myself confounded by too little to do, a lot to think about, and too much time to do it in. Fretting was what Benoît called it. I rued having taught him the word.

Briefly I debated how Jimmy Haines would conduct his patrol. But that's one thing I *had* learned in my years of war; there was no profit in second-guessing these things. Either way you'd eventually hear. In the interim there was nothing you could do to alter the outcome.

So naturally my thoughts wandered on down the trench system of my mind. At the first traverse they arrived at another topic I'd been contemplating: Captain Smythe. Spotting him twice at a dump in the space of two weeks was mystifying – particularly as the Arras depot was miles south of our dispositions. Consequently, it was impossible to imagine it had anything to do with us. Unless of course he was simply visiting someone he knew, however unlikely I felt that to be. And what to make of his nocturnal travels through Souchez, when Benoît and I were out that evening? No, there was more to Captain Smythe of the 5th Infantry Brigade than met the eye. I was quite certain of that.

These musings were interrupted by the loud screech of a shell.

Nervously my hand went in search of my helmet. It turned out to be positioned much as I'd left it – square on my head. The sad thing was, if the shell did have my name on it, the helmet would have counted for little anyhow. Once that brand of common sense had been instinctive to me, but that's what a few months on the staff will do. Regardless, I should have recognized that the shell was underway to the nearby battery of field artillery that had been taking it on the head all day.

Round about two-thirty in the morning, three hours after they set out, the first patrol returned. Shadowy figures loomed menacingly out of the darkness. I stood waiting, shuffling on my feet to keep the limbs moving, hands deep in my trouser pockets.

Eagerly I descended upon them.

The lieutenant commanding wore an expressionless mask and at the sight of this I felt a shudder go through me, presuming the worst. I racked my brain but couldn't recall hearing anything worrisome. The sporadic patter of small arms fire and the sound of an occasional shell going off was certainly no reason for alarm. Nor was the commotion over by the railway embankment. That was foreseen. Anxiously I looked past the lieutenant's group to see if the other patrols were following, but they weren't. Briefly I thought of young Jimmy Haines.

Thankfully he came straight to the point. 'All quiet,' he said, halting in front of me.

It was never entirely quiet on the Western Front, so I was uncertain if I correctly understood his meaning. And if it was quiet, was that because the Germans were already gone?

'Really?' I said.

'You sound surprised?'

I took him by the arm and pulled him aside while the men filed past in single file. They were in good spirits and I soon heard from their lieutenant why. They hadn't encountered a single enemy soldier, all had returned without a scratch, and I expect they felt they'd cocked a snook at Fritz. As the Fritzs I'd known were generally unaccommodating to late-night intruders, none of this allayed my concern that our foe had indeed surreptitiously withdrawn. The lawyer in me surfaced.

'Oh, no,' the lieutenant protested when I confronted him about it. 'Their trenches were well manned. We could hear them from 30 feet away. Talking amongst themselves. Even smelled their tobacco.'

I took him at his word, but it was only when the other patrols returned with similar stories did I feel somewhat reassured. Ironically it was Jimmy Haines who sealed the case.

'You know I'd never have imagined it, Malcolm, but lying out by the wire and listening to them all going about their business, you would have thought it was our trench.'

I might have laughed at this, or shook my head in derision. Instead, the picture that formed in my mind was so vivid that all I could do was nod agreeably. Whatever they were planning, the Germans were not pulling back. Our plans for an attack could move forward.

Dawn's bright fingers were creeping over the ridge when I reached Fort George and proceeded to report to the colonel. I found him with the other staff, who themselves were only just appearing from their bunks. He accepted my report with a discouraging equanimity; discouraging because he appeared oddly disinterested. He didn't ask a single question and left little doubt he had no tolerance for one of mine. I had the suspicion I'd told him nothing he didn't already know.

General Lipsett stuck his head through the doorway. He cast his eyes on me for a fleeting second. Was I imagining the frown? Then he shifted his gaze to the colonel. Hayter left immediately.

With a groan I sank down into my chair, leaned back as far as was possible, and closed my eyes.

'So, no withdrawal after all?' said someone.

'No,' I replied, 'How –'

'Oh, the brigade telephoned an hour ago.'

'You may not have heard,' added someone else. 'They reported their operation went well.'

'Yes, thank you, I know,' I mumbled. There was little to be gained from mentioning I was with them two hours before.

CHAPTER 11

5th of June, 1917
1500 yards southwest of Méricourt, France

There are few things I relish less than being woken early, especially as it's almost always a precursor of worse to come. It never fails. When not deprived of sleep my memory is usually fairly good. Even now, rubbing at my eyes, I couldn't think of a single instance since round about the autumn of 1914 when an abrupt wakening had led to anything good. Coincidence or not, that's when I'd signed up for the army.

'Sir,' pleaded the private, bending over as far as he dared, reticent about shaking my shoulder as the situation clearly demanded. 'Captain Ferguson asked if you would hurry, sir.'

'Let me guess… I'm to be knighted and I've got the first appointment of the day –'

The poor private looked befuddled at this.

'Or is headquarters under attack?'

'Sir?' The man looked even more befuddled. 'No, sir.'

'What time is it?'

'A little past 4.00 a.m., sir.'

'Dandy,' I muttered, 'just dandy.'

Captain Ferguson saw it rather differently when he spotted me entering what was otherwise a largely deserted general staff room. 'Ah, great,' he enthused, an irritating perkiness to his voice. He followed it up with a breezy, 'Good morning, MacPhail.'

'Morning, Captain,' I said, unwilling quite yet to preface it with "good" – not until I'd learned more. Ferguson was all right, though. There was no sign of General Lipsett, and the colonel was absent too. There wasn't even a major present. I didn't imagine I'd been woken on a lark, but it was evidently not terribly serious.

'There's been some activity overnight,' said Ferguson.

'Oh?' I felt like telling him that there was activity every night, and so long as it wasn't Fritz in a tear I didn't much worry. But Ferguson was in the "I" section, so he might have thought I was infringing on his terrain.

On the other hand, I recalled a battalion of the 4th Division was to go after the electricity generating station near the Souchez River, on our left. They'd taken it two nights before, but were cut off from reinforcements by a fierce barrage and forced back. Perhaps the new attempt tonight hadn't gone well, either, and there was a serious threat on our flank. So I asked.

'No, no,' he replied. 'A message came in not long ago stating they were successful in recapturing the plant. I meant something else. The Boche raided our line tonight.' He paused.

I said nothing.

'Luckily we caught them out both times. They sent over nearly a hundred men in the first party.'

I grunted.

'The second raid was smaller…' He smiled. '*However*, the 4th CMR report they took a prisoner.'

'Good for them,' I mumbled.

'Would you hop over and pick him up?'

Ferguson was clearly mistaking me for a Montreal taxi.

His family had a place up on Mount Royal which, despite not having been there, I gathered was one of the better neighbourhoods in the city. Ferguson was likely accustomed to using a taxi now and again. But the roads on Mount Royal were probably less conducive to breaking an axle than those of the ridge, or the Douai Plain. The air was also undoubtedly better in Mount Royal; if nothing else the chance of being enveloped in a poisonous fog was minimal.

He took my silence for wavering. To his credit he might have ignored me altogether, reflecting the age-old army principle of seniority, and simply added an imperative note to his request. But I think he wanted to convince me of the importance of the mission. 'I was going to send the corporal and a couple of men, but then I thought, MacPhail has the gift of the gab.' I raised an eyebrow. 'You might get a few words out of him on the way back. Corps intelligence would like to see him as soon as possible, so we won't have him for long, which is why I didn't want to sleep on it. It might be important. I'll send a man with you to drive.'

'Thank you, sir.' I didn't mention that this last detail pleased me enormously. At least now I'd have an opportunity to fully waken without fear of an unseen pothole ending the venture prematurely.

'Oh, and remember MacPhail: ask for Captain Scott. He's the man you need.'

'Captain Scott?' repeated the soldier, tentatively. His face was streaked with dirt, huge bags under his eyes. He'd been up all night from the looks of him. At the sight I felt drowsy all over again.

'Yes,' I replied, hanging half out of the window of the battered, small Ford and speaking loudly so as to be heard above the chugging of the motor. The skies were lightening and I was relieved to find someone who might help before they lightened too much. At battalion headquarters – they were camped out in the very tunnel under the railway embankment that the 5th Brigade had occupied weeks before – they simply pointed us in the direction of the front line.

'Tall feller?' asked the soldier.

'I wouldn't know. All I know is that he's with the 4th Mounted Rifles, and that he's a captain.'

The man thought about this.

'Which company, sir?'

I looked pensive. 'If I was a gambling man I'd say one of A, B, C or D.'

There was the beginnings of a frown. Then the lightbulb went off and he grinned.

'Surely the battalion can't have that many Captain Scotts on the roll?' I added.

'No, sir,' he replied. 'I was just thinking, though… you might want to travel on foot from here. The Hun would get a kick out of strafing a staff car like yours.'

The headlights were out, and I hardly would have gone so far as to describe this small jalopy as a staff car. But the soldier's admonition, wrapped up nicely as a piece of advice, was not out of place.

A short time later the driver and I set off on foot down a dirt road. *'Why don't you just hop over and pick him up?'* I grumbled to myself.

'What's that, sir?' inquired Ainsley, my erstwhile driver.

I shook my head. 'Oh, nothing.'

I began thinking about what I remembered of the map. Méricourt was to the north, the next village over from Avion. It was not very far up this road from what I could recollect. And Méricourt was most assuredly in enemy hands. While I assumed we would encounter some trenches (I was counting on them to be ours, not theirs) prior to arriving in the centre of the village, stranger things had happened this war. I felt for the Webley in the side holster, glad I'd brought it. The heft of a Webley revolver can be oddly reassuring when uncertainty strikes.

As it happened, we located Captain Scott in a stand of trees up the Quarry Road, only 500 yards from the Mont Forêt Quarries where we'd left the car. He had a section of men with him, and one sorry looking specimen who fit the description of the individual I was to pick up. Other than mentioning the battalion name in passing, and that of Captain Scott, Ferguson hadn't actually thought to furnish me with any other details, let alone directions, or a description. But as the fellow I had my eye on was decked out in a field-grey tunic and a *Stahlhelm* parked at an unsoldierly angle, it stood to reason he was the man.

'Am I glad to find you, Captain,' I said. 'Division is rather anxious to meet this trophy of yours.'

He eyed me coolly.

Belatedly I saluted. 'I'm Lieutenant MacPhail, sir, of the divisional staff. I was ordered to collect him.'

'Division, eh?'

'Yes, sir. Everyone is very pleased how you repelled the Boche raid, sir. There's a lot of interest in what this lad has to say.'

There was no harm buttering him up. Though when I heard the full details of the raid shortly after, I felt a little guilty at my guile. A small group of them manning the post down the road had beaten off a much larger group. Scott swiftly organized two parties to harass the retreating Germans from in front and behind, and captured the prisoner in the process. 'Is there anything I should pass along to the intelligence staff, sir?'

'You can report back, Lieutenant, that the enemy is very alert and active.'

'No indications of a withdrawal then?' Every time the topic came up the answer was always a resounding no. But it never hurt to keep repeating the question. Some had their doubts. Fritz was not so set in his ways that one day he might not try to surprise us.

'No,' he replied, 'but speaking of trophies, you'll want to take this before you leave.'

He motioned to the group of soldiers beside the nearest tree. One of them had a boot off and was humorously demonstrating to his mate the inadequacy of his footwear by flapping the toe away from the sole, as if it were the mouth of a puppet. The third man noticed the captain. Quickly he made for us, cradling what appeared to be a machine gun in his arms.

When I was able to better see I whistled. Long, black, an elongated thick tube-like barrel similar to that of a Lewis gun, it had a sharply-curved walnut stock designed to fit tightly against the shoulder, and a matching walnut hand grip by the trigger guard. It made for an intimidating sight. 'That must be one of their new, light machine guns we've heard about. Never seen one before.' I reached out to take it.

It was heavy, half again as heavy as the thirty-odd pounds of a Lewis gun, but much lighter than the large MG 08 to which it bore a certain resemblance, and wherein lay its attraction.

'The Boche have long wanted their own Lewis gun…' said Scott.

'… and heaven help us, now they have it.'

Back at the car, the prisoner recoiled in alarm at the sight of me getting in beside him in the back seat, the muzzle end of the machine gun leading the way. It was entirely unintentional; the Ford was simply not terribly roomy, and the machine gun not terribly small. To get it to fit eventually I had to stick the end out the window. But the overall impression left by these antics was not at all unsatisfactory for my purposes.

'Watch your speed,' I said loudly to Ainsley, doubling down on the strategy. 'And try to avoid the ruts. I wouldn't want to napoo some innocent Fritz by accident with this thing.'

'No, sir,' laughed Ainsley. 'That wouldn't do at all.'

Out of the corner of one eye I noticed the prisoner nodding. Which was interesting. He understood at least a few words of English.

This conclusion quickly proved as overoptimistic as the predictions two years ago that the war would be over by Christmas. Nevertheless, we quickly established that he was from the 1st Battalion, 93rd R.I.R., which I knew was a regiment of the 4th Guards. While this revelation was in German, if there was anything I'd learned in that language it was military terminology: unit names and numbers foremost of all. Furthermore, the revelation was anything but revelatory as the 4th Guards Division had been in and out of the line near here since April. They had a reputation second to none, but this information was not going to set Ferguson's, or anyone else's, ears flapping.

I glanced over at the prisoner, suddenly keen to keep him talking – even if it was in German.

'Quick, Ainsley, give me your cigarettes!'

Ainsley reached into his tunic and without a word passed the pack over his shoulder. *Woodbines* I noted grimly. *Wouldn't you know it?* Here I was trying to get this fellow to spill all he knew and I was offering him the cheapest tobacco ever to come out of the British Isles. I'd have to hope the thing didn't spontaneously combust.

Through it all I kept up a big grin, radiating what I hoped was good cheer and comradeship. 'Have one,' I said, passing it over.

He hesitated, but only briefly. I flicked a match into flame for him – quite an effort with the MG on my lap – and he took a deep puff. The bloody Woodbine shrank by a third. But the man seemed content.

'*Danke*,' he said softly, plucking a shred of tobacco from his tongue.

I smiled again. Joviality was a poor substitute for being able to speak the language, but I was running out of cards to play. 'You were telling me about the 93rd Regiment,' I said. I looked at him quizzically while I enunciated his unit number vowel-by-vowel in my best German.

A wisp of a smile appeared underneath the dust-caked moustache, and the weary blue eyes sparkled into life for an instant. Then he repeated my words back slowly and distinctly. Even I could hear the difference.

'*Danke*,' I said, curtly bowing my head in a manner I could picture a Prussian doing. As a rule of thumb most of the low numbered divisions in the German Army (including the 4th Guards) were Prussian – I wasn't certain whether this meant they were sent first into the fight, although that wouldn't have been inappropriate given that Prussian generals were the ones most intent on this war. However, this was no budding General Hindenburg sitting beside me.

Then I asked the question again. And once again. Until it became a pattern. Short sentences. Ever simpler words. I would have employed mime had I thought acting out 'What are your orders?' was remotely possible.

At each effort, no matter how valiant, the soldier shook his head. The automobile rattled on.

Then inspired I said: '*der Befehl?*' I'd read the word somewhere and remembered it meant "an order". The plural version would have been better, whatever that was – German was exasperatingly unpredictable. Better yet would have been to know whether this word bore any resemblance to what I wanted to know. In the absence of better I was back to employing the discredited tactics of the Somme of attacking in wave after wave in the hope something might work.

While not endowed with the gift of languages, the prisoner was not a dull man, nor an insensitive one. Digesting what I'd just said, the clouds suddenly cleared as I watched.

'Ah!' he exclaimed. Ostensibly he was as relieved as I was that he understood. Whereupon he rattled off what I guessed was a decent approximation of my question. He stared at me, awaiting a response.

Vigorously I nodded my head, not wanting to waste the moment, or this flash of mutual comprehension.

He began to speak.

'*Langsam.*'

Another glimmer of a smile, and he was off, more slowly than at first. He just kept talking, and I kept listening, straining every bone in my body to comprehend his words. I think he felt it was easier to tell me his story than to endure another round of painful questions. Regardless, his war was over.

His apparent candour made it doubly unfortunate that I understood perhaps a tenth of what he said. But I like to think I picked up on the most important part.

That came when he mentioned the *Vizefeldwebel*. This was the equivalent of a sergeant-major, likely his platoon or section commander. From what I could gather this fellow had seen an order that indicated they were to pull back within days. When he named the very line they were to withdraw to, one which anyone who had studied our front knew well, I could restrain myself no longer.

'*Und Lens?*'

At Méricourt the German defences split in two. One line, the Avion Switch, went west towards Avion and the Souchez River where it then curved northwards around the town and up towards Belgium. The other line, the Oppy-Méricourt-Vendin line, the very one he'd named, took a short cut and headed straight north with Lens to the west. If they planned on decamping to there, there was no question they were planning to abandon Lens.

'*Minen,*' he said.

'*Minen?*'

He made the sound of an explosion and his clenched hands blew apart in demonstration.

'My God,' I whispered, as the realization sunk in. We were wrong. They were going to retreat, and when we followed up and occupied the town, they would detonate the charges. It would be a disaster!

'Step on it, Ainsley,' I shouted.

Back at Fort George, an automobile and a party of soldiers was waiting on the nearby road when we arrived. It was under command of a corporal. He was there to collect the prisoner for transport to the Corps cage he informed me.

'Tell them,' I said, 'that all the evidence to the contrary, the Germans *are* planning on withdrawing. They intend to blow Lens when we enter it!'

With little ado and a commendable efficiency, though this was surely how they always worked, they hustled the prisoner towards the car.

'Wait,' I shouted when they reached it. I fumbled in my pocket, my hand emerging with the pack of Woodbines. I tossed it at the German soldier. He missed the catch and had to kneel to retrieve them.

When he got to his feet again he knuckled his forehead. I nodded in return. With a slamming of doors and a roar of the motor they were gone.

'Sir?'

I glanced over my shoulder. Ainsley stood there half apologetically.

'I was just wondering, sir… but what should I do about the machine gun?'

CHAPTER 12

5th of June, 1917
Fort George, northwest of Neuville-Saint-Vaast, France

'Withdraw *entirely* from Lens you say?' said General Lipsett when I was done.

'Yes, sir, that's what he told me. They plan to abandon the town and the salient around it, and consolidate in more defensible positions.' That last bit I'd invented, but trying to think like a German it seemed the most plausible explanation. It sort of flopped out of its own accord.

'I never realized you spoke German, MacPhail?' said Lt.-Col. Hayter, in a conversational tone.

In my head someone began clanging noisily on an empty shell casing. This interview was heading into dangerous territory. I could sense it already. 'Not exactly, sir.'

He frowned. 'Well do you, or don't you?'

'No, sir. Only a few words.'

'But on the basis of a conversation you had in German – which you don't speak – with a private soldier privy to the orders of his army group no less, you would have us believe the enemy is intending to withdraw, booby-trap the town, and subsequently set off mines as we enter?'

The way he said it sounded ludicrous even to me.

Captain Ferguson, who was watching, looked as if he wanted to crawl under the table posthaste – anywhere so long as he could escape any association with me.

Wearily I sighed. 'Sir, I'm only the messenger in this. I may be a little woozy having been up all night, but I didn't imagine it.'

'Forgive me for saying so, MacPhail… but you were a lawyer, you'll understand. If you were on the other side of this table, how would you rate the credibility of your testimony?'

I knew now what it was to be a young steer, being corralled in a direction it had no inclination of going. The irony was that earlier I'd dismissed this whole withdrawal scenario as a pipe dream dreamt up by some eager staff officer anxious to make a name for himself. Hayter had done to me what in my short career I'd only ever dreamed of doing to an adversary in court; he'd used my own words to hang me. Only this wasn't a courtroom. And I was damned if I was going to hang for it.

'Put like that it sounds incredible, sir, but I'm only relating what I was told. I grant you I don't know much of the language. But I am certain that's what he told me,' I said obstinately.

From his expression I could see Hayter's rebuttal was already being pushed into the chamber. Until General Lipsett forestalled him – with a wave of a raised hand – followed closely by a question.

'What I'd like to know, Ross. Do you think it's possible what the Lieutenant suggests?'

Hayter chewed on his lip for a moment. 'Naturally it is *possible*, General, but I'm not convinced. I certainly can't fathom why they'd pull back from Lens. Their defences in the town are at least as strong as those of the Méricourt-Vendin Line. More so, really.' He shook his head. 'They'd be crazy to retreat.'

Under my breath I cursed. The plausibility of my entire account was undermined simply because my big mouth didn't know when to call a halt.

Lipsett nodded. 'What about the line in question? Is it ready for occupation should the Boche retreat? I recall a great deal of talk earlier about them withdrawing to the Wotan Stellung. As you'll remember, Ross, we learned soon after that their Russian prisoners of war were still hard at work on it.'

'Yes, sir, I remember. But it would seem this line is prepared. Corps intelligence reports that prisoners say the trenches are two metres deep, the dug-outs are in good order, and there's five to six metres of wire out in front.'

In any other company I would have whistled. *If that wasn't ready for occupation, what was?*

'So it is possible?' said Lipsett.

'Yes it is, General,' agreed Hayter. 'Although as Lieutenant MacPhail knows full well we've been unable to find much evidence of a withdrawal being prepared. I certainly see no reason not to continue with our plans.'

Ferguson didn't commit himself either way. In fairness no one even asked him.

But I was already all in. And it irked that I'd spent the night traversing the front, only to have my report dismissed out of hand, for reasons I could do nothing about. There was one consolation; I'd missed the bombs from an enemy airship that caused several casualties over the ridge last night. I coughed.

Lipsett swung his head in my direction. 'Lieutenant? You had something to add?'

'I was thinking, sir, the interrogators at the Corps cage will report on their preliminary findings from the prisoner before long. I expect they'll confirm – or not – the veracity of my account. I may not be a trained interrogator, but I thought it best to tell you what I knew, as soon as possible.'

Lipsett nodded.

'There was one other thing, sir. Something I know both of you would wish to see. In fact it speaks quite eloquently for itself.' Conscious a bitter tone had crept into my voice, I went silent.

Neither Lipsett nor Hayter appeared to notice. 'Very true, the interrogators will get to the bottom of this,' Lipsett said. 'And you were right to mention it, MacPhail. Now what's this you have to show us?'

I turned and called out to Ainsley. At my orders he was standing outside the room, waiting nervously for his premiere with the divisional commander and his second-in-command.

Unspeaking, Lipsett and Hayter tracked his progress as poor Ainsley marched self-consciously across a squeaking plank floor. I wanted to shout out and tell him to keep breathing, though his reddening features may also have owed something to the weight he was straining under. With a heavy *clunk* he laid the spanking-new MG 08/15 on the table, took a step back, and with a gaze fixed firmly forward, smartly saluted the wall. By then neither Lipsett nor Hayter was paying him, or me, the slightest heed. They were both staring at the machine gun.

7th of June, 1917
Vimy, France

'Did you 'ear it last night?' enquired Benoît.

'Hear what?' I said, frowning.

'The explosion.'

'You'll have to do better than that, Benoît. Unless there's some risk of a follow-up detonation that may involve me, I usually ignore them. So, no. Otherwise I'd never get any sleep in this place.'

'*Non*!? You didn't hear? It was a little past three. One big roar that kept roaring, far to the north. *Mon Dieu*, Mac, you must have heard! The windows in our hut shook for a whole minute.'

'That's one advantage to sleeping in a dug-out.'

Benoît grinned. 'Underground you mean?'

'No. No windows.'

'They blew up Messines Ridge.'

'They did what!?' Messines Ridge was a landmark wearily familiar to the both of us. We'd met there. Many months we'd spent in the trenches up in the Salient, with water to our knees, staring at that damned ridge in front every morning when we stood-to. In fact, much of the water we were standing in had probably drained off the ridge with its honeycomb of German trenches.

'The British mined all underneath it. Blew the Boche to Kingdom Come.'

'Did they now? Wow!' It was hard to imagine what that looked like, yet at the same time believable enough. I'd seen what mines could do. 'Well, good riddance, I'd say. I was never very fond of that ridge.'

It was a fine day in June and we were standing beside what had once been the main crossroads in the village of Vimy – still was, in fact. The village was a weary dustbowl of finely broken masonry slowly baking in the unseasonably warm June air. Piles of brick and stone and protruding timbers lined the streets, the lone brick façade of a large two-storey building the only structure of any significance still standing. Down the main road in a northerly direction was the timber skeleton of another, its chimney stiffly erect but strangely naked for lack of walls. Across the road from it a solitary tree had survived the shells and, inappropriate to the surroundings, was wearing all the green finery of spring come summer. The road was the best thing about Vimy, straight and level. While Fritz did his utmost each day and every night to raze the village and dishevel the road, the engineers were having none of it – so far as the road went; the village was beyond repair. They'd sensibly abandoned it to its fate.

Whichever route I chose when I went to leave this spot, and I'd taken all of them at one time or another this past month, each in its own way had a significance for me. To the north one came upon the dumps of La Chaudière first, before reaching the Arras-Lens road, and finally the front line near Avion: beyond it Lens. In the opposite direction lay the legendary ridge we had wrenched from the clutches of Wilhelm and consort, on the other side of whose back were sprawled the rear areas with their billets, their headquarters, and the estaminets and other victuallers that had sprung up to service them. To the west one might head to the hamlet of Petit Vimy, or the Souchez River several miles distant. East, whence I'd come, was the railway and the dug-outs, and further east still the front line at Arleux and the Quarry area. The 7th Brigade was to relieve the 8th this night and the necessary preparations explained my presence here. My rendezvous with Benoît had come about due to a fortunate congruence of tasks and locations.

'So tomorrow, eh?

My head shot up, momentarily taken aback that he knew. The plans were floated nearly two weeks before, but I had only just heard the date for Z Day. *That* secret was not well known at all. Someone must have let something slip.

Sharply I said: 'The orders and the date were only issued yesterday.'

'What did you think I'm doing here, Mac? A little *tête-à-tête* with you is lovely, *mon ami*, but we have an entire barrage plus some wire cutting to prepare. It helps to know the date.'

'Of course,' I mumbled, and at that Benoît began to enlighten me in great detail what a barrage plus some wire cutting entailed.

After several minutes of this, I chose my moment carefully and interrupted. 'What I wonder, Benoît, is whether it's worth all the effort?'

Puzzlement settled over Benoît's face. He'd heard my cynical take on the prosecution of the war on plenty of occasions, but this bordered on outright defeatism, a word unfamiliar to him in either French or English.

'I interrogated a prisoner a couple of days ago,' I hastened to explain. 'He told me that they were leaving Lens any day. If they're leaving anyhow, I don't see why we're bothering to attack.'

At this new information his puzzled expression gave way to scepticism.

'I can see you're as open minded about this as General Lipsett and Colonel Hayter were,' I said.

Now he was simply amused.

'What's tickling you?' I grumbled. 'The officers at the Corps cage interrogated him as well and confirmed my version of the story. Fritz is planning on withdrawing.'

'Don't tell me… You told the general and the colonel to pipe down and to listen to you.'

'No, of course not,' I mumbled. 'I respect Lipsett and Hayter. But the colonel refused to listen to a word I said.'

'Perhaps he did, Mac. Maybe it was you who was not listening. The colonel has a lot of things he must weigh on his scale. A single prisoner is not much to go on. You know what the Boche are like. They say anything if they think it will help their cause.'

'Yeah, sure, but that prisoner was pretty damned specific in what he said. They're getting the hell out of Lens.'

'*On verra.*'

'We'll see? So you don't believe it either, Benoît?'

For a moment there was silence. I could see he was trying to think how to let me down diplomatically. Finally he just shook his head.

'The Boche are feeling the pain,' he said. 'They want to believe any trench rumour that will get them out of here.'

I'd never considered it like that. It was true that while Fritz was continually shelling, bombing and shooting us, the traffic in the other direction was a sight worse. It had only been several days since the 4th Division used 600 projectors to bombard the German positions between the river and the small village of La Coulotte with gas. In the days that followed intelligence suggested more than 150 of them were dead or incapacitated as a result.

'Look. I accept that your average Fritz may want to escape to the hills,' I said, 'but they follow orders. It wasn't exactly a rumour this fellow was repeating.'

'Maybe. Maybe not,' he replied. 'Actually, I hope your man is right. Have you ever seen Lens, Mac?'

It was my turn to shake my head.

'If they order us to take Lens that will be…' He paused, visibly ruminating over the appropriate word to use. 'Tough,' he said eventually. Knowing Benoît, tough was a euphemism for a bloody, bare-knuckle scrap – in other words a little too similar for comfort to other battles I'd experienced.

'So the way I see it, it's not a bad thing we're knocking at the Boche door with our attack,' he added. 'Maybe they will withdraw then, as you think they will.' Then, before I could put in my one franc's worth. 'That reminds me. I saw your friend a few days ago. He was in a big hurry.'

'Friend?'

'*Le gars*, the guy with the motorcycle. The captain.'

The connection was easily made. The vision of him at the supply dump near Arras flashed again in my mind. 'Smythe, you mean? Where exactly did you see him?'

'Oh, in that estaminet in Cambligneul where I wanted to take you. He must have been late. He almost ran me down when he arrived. He was with the DAQMG and a couple of others I didn't recognize.'

'Fredericks… He was with Fredericks? Our DAQMG?'

'*Oui.*'

Before I could properly quiz him on what precisely the 3rd Division's Deputy Assistant Quartermaster General was doing with a staff officer from an infantry brigade from our sister division, there was a *BOOM* and the ground shook. A hundred yards down the road a cloud of white smoke appeared. A moment later there was another bang, and a veil of smoke cloaked the skeleton of the building no more than 100 feet from us. Smoke and dust clogged my nostrils. I didn't wait around to see where the next would fall.

'*A bientôt*, Mac!' shouted Benoît, who was already sprinting to his transport. I'd noticed earlier he was driving the big Crossley again. I piled into the backseat of the small Ford with no regard for dignity. From the floorboards I shouted to the driver to put a little effort into it.

CHAPTER 13

8th and 9th of June, 1917
Trenches south of Avion, France

The day had been cloudy and unsettled, the latter not solely because of the former, even if the clouds were serving up regular rain showers every few hours. Three battalions of the 7th Brigade were girding themselves for battle. At long last the attack was going ahead.

While those in the eight companies involved (going on 1800 men) did their best not to show it, it was impossible to completely overcome one's nerves. No matter the four hours of training every day the past week, the good meals, and the sport and relaxation in between, the hours before ZERO Hour were anxious ones. I was wound up and all I had to do was report back.

'I'd like to go, sir, if I may?' I'd said to Colonel Hayter, not because I wanted to, but because it was the only way I could think of to overcome any lingering misimpressions he or the general might have regarding my courage. Not that keeping my head low so as not to bump it on the beams of a dug-out a mile to the rear was going to require Herculean fortitude. The Boche artillery was the only thing that might drop a fly into that particular ointment.

Approaching the Brigade Report Centre down Blue Nose Trench, I was challenged by a sentry. He stepped suddenly from the shadows of a traverse, sending my heart thumping. 'Who goes there?' he demanded in a voice straining to overcome its adolescence.

It was indisputably evening, but still not dark enough to be night, and certainly not dark enough to conceal the fact I was wearing an officer's uniform of the kind the entire BEF wore. A young fellow like him, barely out of high school, and with fine eyes; he must have spotted the rectangular French grey patch of the 3rd Division on my shoulder – not to be confused with the darker field-grey shade our foe was fond of – long before. Yet he persisted in asking the question all the same. And having me jump out of my skin. But orders were orders. I was quite sure I was never going to reconcile myself with army practices, even if I spent the next five years trying.

'Highball,' I grunted in response.

'Pass friend,' said the sentry, and he came smartly to attention.

'What would you have done if I'd said, "schnapps"?' I enquired mischievously.

'Sir?' His face was screwed up in a terrible tangle of crooked eyebrows, bulging eyes and open mouth that I had no hope of untangling.

'Never mind,' I said. 'Carry on.'

'Oh,' said a deadpan voice from ahead. 'I think in such circumstances I would have stuck a bayonet in you. Maybe two. Just to make certain.'

Peering forward the form of a figure emerging from a dug-out could be seen. He stepped out of the shadow to greet me. As he did so, I made out his face.

'Sir!'

'What's wrong, MacPhail? Is the pomp and circumstance of headquarters boring you to death?'

It was Major Meredith. Once of the divisional staff before he'd been shipped off, a promotion it must be added, to become the brigade major of the 7th Brigade. He and I were well acquainted. As it was his brigade's show tonight his presence was not in the least remarkable.

'I'm a little bewildered as well, sir, to see myself here.' Friendly face or not, this wasn't entirely true. But there was no need to volunteer more; I'd done enough volunteering for a single day. 'But it's nice to see you, Major. Colonel Hayter sent me.'

Meredith nodded, and didn't enquire further. I didn't think he would. After all, orders are orders. And on this night he had orders of far more importance on his mind.

'What's with the reference to my favourite beverage?' I asked.

He frowned.

'The password,' I prompted.

'Ah, yes, Highball. Well, it's not the only relevant drink tonight. In your honour, MacPhail; Cream, Scotch, and Sherry are the key words to remember. Just don't ask me straight away which is for what. Listen, if you're here to pass along the progress of the raid to the general and the colonel, you'd best come down into the dug-out.' He turned and motioned that I should follow.

The report centre was in the "test" dug-out, a large but fairly standard affair, fifteen steps deep, whose original tenants had been evicted after liberal use of various implements of an explosive nature. I never did discover why it was so named. At the time it seemed better not to pursue it. The number of steps though required neither guesswork nor testing; German dug-outs were nothing if not predictable.

Meredith introduced me to the others who mostly consisted of a handful of staff of the Royal Canadian Regiment (RCR) whose headquarters this was, including their commander, Lieutenant-Colonel Hill, a dependable-looking sort with a friendly manner who'd only just returned from leave in England. Hill had replaced Long Archie Macdonell as OC when the latter was given the 5th Brigade, so I was predisposed to feeling favourably towards him. Also present was Meredith's adjutant, and a couple of signallers at a table manning a field telephone attached to a well-buried cable and surrounded by an array of other equipment whose general purpose I could surmise, even if I was still pondering what use a Lucas signalling lamp might possibly be underground. There were also a couple of runners, relaxing with few apparent worries in the world judging by their demeanour, and a startlingly young lad flitting about with all the worries of the world etched on his face, tasked as he was with manning the teapot for his superiors. He offered me a cupful and I accepted.

I shuffled over to talk to the signallers. Meredith, I noted, was still scanning the dug-out. 'Hasn't he arrived yet?' I heard him mutter darkly.

I stuck my head in the proverbial sandbank, and listened to the signaller's elaborate explanation of the workings of a Fullerphone. That was always a useful tactic to stay out of jams. Ask someone a detailed question and stand back and feign fascination. If only I could remember to employ it more often.

Soon the initial frisson of excitement ebbed away. The troops were assembled. The orders were long given. And there being not much to do awaiting ZERO Hour at 11.45 p.m., Meredith drifted back over to me. I'd claimed an empty chair beside the Lucas lamp. We'd once shared a laugh or two, and Meredith wasn't so awestruck with his current position that he forgot. For ten minutes or so we cheerfully reminisced about old times at Divisional HQ, and about some of the fellows of our mutual acquaintance. Until I referred in passing to one of the recent reinforcements we'd received. The boy was as green as the grass of Ireland.

'What was that, you said?' he interrupted.

'You mean about eagerness being no substitute for experience?' It was one of my recurring nuggets of wisdom. These days I had few opportunities to hold forth on the topic. My colleagues were well versed in the theory, and typically began groaning when I trotted it out.

Meredith nodded. It appeared to jog a memory.

'Blast,' he said, looking around. 'Where could he be?'

This time there was no sandbank available. And I was curious. 'Who?' I asked.

'O'Neill. He's supposed to be here.'

'Lieutenant O'Neill?' I said, a half-smile creeping onto my face.

'You know him?'

'Oh, yes,' I replied. 'I think O'Neill's wasting away on the brigade staff, however. He's dying to be in the action.'

'Yes, well, I'll put him there directly if he's not careful,' growled Meredith. 'O'Neill's supposed to be here, assisting me. Where is he?'

One of the signallers appeared to hear, for he got up from his chair and came and explained to Meredith that his assistant had left an hour before, to head to the battalion reporting centre at the junction of Dartmouth Trench and the railway embankment.

Meredith sighed irritably. 'What's he doing there, for heaven's sake?'

'He thought he'd be of more use closer to the action,' replied the man.

'Sounds familiar,' I muttered, a picture springing to life of O'Neill and me standing behind the front-line trench at Arleux as the barrage roared. Then as now he was attracted to the fireworks as a moth is to a flame. Evidently my warning at the time that this would eventually lead to a painful singeing had not left much of an impression.

'Well he's dead WRONG,' barked Meredith. 'He's of no use there at all.'

The signaller shrugged and quickly retreated to find a sandbank of his own.

'I could go and get him,' I offered. 'There's still more than an hour before it begins. It can't be far.'

'Would you?' said Meredith. 'It's only a thousand yards, north along the railway. A dug-out in the trench. You can't miss it. I'd see it as a big favour.'

While it was a dark night, overcast without a glimmer of moonlight, I'd walked this exact area only two weeks before with the 58th Battalion. The railway running north to Lens was a landmark even I couldn't miss.

Hours after sunset it was still warm despite the rain, a sultry, clammy heat that lay heavy in the air. Down below in the crowded and stuffy dug-out the rivulets of sweat had coursed down my face uncontrollably. A little fresh air and a walk couldn't hurt, I figured. I welcomed it in fact, which is why I didn't suggest simply calling by telephone. Furthermore, Dartmouth Trench was far removed from the front line – or so I believed at the time – therefore it wasn't as if I was running much of a risk.

With barely a breeze to speak of, the hot air topside was sadly only moderately fresher than the stuff below, and it clung to me and my woollen tunic like an invisible wet blanket. With the exertion of walking, I was soon sweating profusely, my boots and the belt around my midriff chaffing irritably as a result. I loosened my tie and began to regret what I'd gotten myself into.

When I reached the battalion reporting centre I began mentally counting back how long it would take to retrace my steps. Only O'Neill wasn't there.

'The lieutenant?' said a Major Willoughby of the RCR, staring distractingly at my tie, which I then went to tighten. 'I sent him forward. He wasn't of any use here.' In that assessment the two majors, Meredith and Willoughby, were in complete agreement. It didn't look good for O'Neill.

My protestations that he was with the brigade staff, and was required in the rear, made little visible impression on Willoughby. In
fact, after a spell, I had the distinct idea he was eyeing me up for similar
duties. I pleaded a need to return to the brigade reporting centre, and
ducked out into the trench, intending to do just that. However, before
I did, I got to thinking.

As far as I could tell O'Neill lacked the most important asset you
need in combat: experience. He was one of those clever officer cadets,
fresh from university, and desperately anxious to go overseas. As the
war dragged on such sentiment was increasingly rare, and consequently the number of recruits as well. It wasn't just in the trenches that
enthusiasm for the war had waned rather markedly. 'He's going to get
himself killed,' I muttered to myself. Then, in a quick riposte, a voice in
my head countered that was precisely why we were here, so what was
I getting myself in a lather about.

But that was cynicism talking, I knew. O'Neill was a good lad,
friendly and competent. I could picture his face before me. How
many young men… boys, really… had I met in the past two years who
wouldn't be making the voyage home? The lieutenant just needed a
tight leash for a bit, or at the least a good sergeant to take him under
his tutelage until he learned the necessary skills for himself. He'd have
a chance then. It was hard not to think of myself, and many others,
after we first arrived. Then there was what Meredith had said about it
being a 'big' favour. I'd look like a proper fool if I couldn't manage this.

Sighing, I removed the boot from the rung of the ladder, crossed to
the other side of the trench, and took hold of another ladder. Major
Willoughby told me D Company had a jumping-off trench less than
a couple of hundred yards north of Dartmouth; it appeared I'd landed
at the front, for all intents and purposes. This was precisely the kind
of spot, not far behind the fire-trench, where the Germans could be
counted upon to lay down a counter-barrage. With a certain urgency
I began to climb the rungs.

As Willoughby promised I encountered the company, roughly 200
strong, shortly thereafter. I moved along the ranks of soldiers stooped
and crouching against the earthen walls of the shallow ditch. They
held their rifles casually by the stock with the butts resting in the dirt,
but their features were alert, and nearly all glanced at me as I passed.

In none of those faces did I recognize O'Neill. Nor could I find anyone who'd heard or seen anything of him, and the men I asked all shook their heads. Eventually I located the company commander, Captain Thompson. He too looked mystified and shrugged his shoulders when I inquired about the lieutenant. 'Perhaps he's with C Company,' he offered.

'Where is C Company, sir?'

Distractedly he pointed an arm. C Company was apparently on the far side of the railway embankment – the German side. Despairingly I looked from the trench to the high gravel embankment on our right, which appeared to be the only avenue to get there. I wasn't very keen on climbing that and possibly being silhouetted for an enemy sniper. For a moment I debated returning to the dug-out in Dartmouth Trench and asking Major Willoughby to send a message to Meredith to inform him of my whereabouts. Or even abandoning this wild goose chase for what it was and heading back. But then in a raucous storm of noise and light the barrage intervened. Orders were shouted. Whistles blew shrilly. Around me the men were all on their feet, climbing out of the trench and moving forward.

Shocked, I raised a wrist to check the luminous dials of my watch, certain there was some terrible mistake for it couldn't possibly be so late. But there was no mistake. It was precisely fifteen minutes to midnight.

The raid was on.

It hadn't been a raid when I first read the orders. I remembered the day well. It was the day after my leave in Paris, and even with many languorously perfect ones behind me – or perhaps because of them – the very thought of another attack had led to a vicious thumping in my forehead. It was a headache of the kind I usually only encounter after a night out with Benoît. But in the intervening two weeks the operations orders changed.

Our corps commander, Lieutenant-General Byng, had concluded that with much of the Corps artillery sent north to help out with the new offensive in the Salient, there was insufficient firepower to smother the German guns; even if to my ear the barrage sounded superb. Consequently, holding any territory gained was asking too much. Many generals – most of the general staff I daresay – wouldn't have noticed. They certainly wouldn't have cared. But Sir Julian did. And for that the boys loved him, doughty English noble or not; and it must be said *a priori* this wasn't a species I or anyone else took a great shine to. Nevertheless, the men of the Canadian Corps didn't call themselves the Byng Boys by chance, even if a review of a similar name was playing in London. The result of General Byng's observations to General Horne was that the attack became a raid – a very big one. A sizeable force from the 3rd and 4th Divisions were to break into the enemy trenches in front of Avion, beat the garrisons on the head with everything they had, and withdraw.

The night sky flashed unremittingly. One couldn't hear oneself breathe for the bang of the guns and the succession of explosions, all blending into a single deafening roar. As I moved toward the embankment I picked up the higher-pitched rattle of the machine guns. I needed to move fast if I was going to find O'Neill, but first I had to make it over the embankment.

With a grunt I clawed my way out of the trench, then on all fours scrambled up the loose gravel bank, and over the rail tracks, before sliding ignominiously down the far side. Only to discover that in those frantic few minutes most of C Company had disappeared. They'd filed up the communication trench that led northward along the embankment. Quickly I went to follow.

The raid was to be carried out on a leap-frog system. Individual groups of men would move forward and seek cover and consolidate, while other groups close behind went past to continue the momentum. It was one of the new platoon tactics we began using after the Somme. Unfortunately, my adaptation of the system was imperfect due to the employment of only a single frog. This had its drawbacks, not least the limited endurance of the frog's legs and lungs.

Despite the madness of noise that could reasonably have been expected to drown out all else, I was conscious that I was puffing loudly after several minutes running along the trench. I put it down to the excitement. It wasn't very long before I encountered a group of RCR men establishing a block at the intersection with the German front line, Alcove Trench. Fritz's barrage came down at that very moment. It must have taken them nearly ten minutes to arrange and, not only was it late, it was falling hundreds of yards to the rear. After the initial startled glances no one paid it any further notice. I asked around for O'Neill.

'Try Amble, sir,' said a corporal, taking his eyes off the Lewis-gun position they were fashioning only long enough to address me.

'That's their support trench isn't it?'

He nodded. With that I continued up the communication trench for roughly 75 yards until I came upon the trench of that name. It jutted off to my right and then curved northeast where I knew it eventually intersected the main switch near Avion. There wasn't a sign to announce it. But with another group of soldiers present, also establishing a block, it didn't require one.

Then any thought of O'Neill went up in a spiral of smoke – even though the round in question was from a Gewehr 98, which is practically smokeless.

A soldier on the parapet who'd been manhandling a troublesome sandbag into position for another block – the trench was badly knocked about by our artillery – dropped the bag, which somersaulted down into the trench, and clutched his side. There were shouts. The men with shovels dropped them, snatching for their rifles. With alacrity I yanked out the Webley revolver, the only weapon I'd brought. While I'm not the fastest draw on the front, it was good I did.

In an instant the German appeared at the crest of the parapet, and I squeezed at the trigger without even taking care to aim; but that way neither could he. Although the Gewehr 98 is a fine rifle and highly accurate, its sheer length makes it cumbersome at close quarters; unless of course you're charging down upon someone with a bayonet fixed and the intent to stick it in him. But this fellow was stuck in No-Man's-Land, too close to aim effectively and too far to charge. I got him with my second shot. Only by then there were three others beside him and I was pulling the trigger as fast as I could. Until a soft *click* reverberated back, and my heart skipped a beat. My fingers fumbled awkwardly in my tunic pocket in search of another clip.

However, the rifles were already in action. When I heard the throaty cough of a Lewis gun I dared to breathe again. It took a few clipped bursts of the machine gun before a voice shouted, 'that's the last of them,' and a section of C Company showed off its dental work. The moon had peeked out from the clouds for the occasion.

'They must have come from the shell holes in front,' I shouted at the officer in charge. 'I'm going to run forward and warn the others.'

He waved his approval and I set off down Amble Trench at a fast gait, but wary. I'd since found my spare clip – in my *other* pocket. At the third traverse I came upon a half-dozen soldiers cloistered together in a semi-circle.

One of them turned to me. Seeing my uniform he said: 'Stand back, sir. We've cornered some Huns.'

The Huns were nowhere to be seen. The entrance to a dug-out was, however.

'How many?' I asked.

'Four or five we think, maybe more. We heard them.'

I didn't ask if they were given the option to surrender; they may have been before I arrived. On the other hand, they may not have been. The brigadier (Long Archie's capable cousin, Batty Mac) had let it be known he didn't want to be bothered with too many prisoners on a dark night.

The fellow with a Stokes bomb in his hands was making his final preparations before tossing it down. Stokes ammunition was originally designed for the trench mortar of same name, but it had garnered itself a reputation as a useful tool to blow dug-outs.

This one went up in a dull *clap*. An impressive geyser of dirt spewed upwards out of the dug-out entrance. I was glad I'd taken the private's advice to stand back.

I never did find anyone to warn, although I did hear there were some casualties from snipers out in the shell holes towards Avion. But there were no further counter-attacks, or even rushes. The Germans in the trench were for the most part dead, the ones in the many dug-outs were being bombed mercilessly, and the ones to their rear were unprepared and unable to do anything to help.

Encountering a lieutenant of the company I asked, 'Did you capture any prisoners?'

'Not many,' he replied. 'We got a couple when we arrived.'

'They might prove useful, you know. In case the Boche are thinking of withdrawing.'

The lieutenant shrugged. 'Look at it this way, we've saved them the trouble of having to pack their things.' To which I merely nodded.

At ZERO plus ninety a succession of gold and silver rain rockets signalled the withdrawal, and I withdrew with the others. The group behind me got caught in a trench mortar bombardment in the communication trench, but I heard that most made it through. Only when we reached our own front line did I think of O'Neill again. I was here because of him, and I'd forgotten him.

I couldn't help but feel extremely stupid.

CHAPTER 14

9th of June, 1917
Fort George, northwest of Neuville-Saint-Vaast, France

Colonel Hayter saw it similarly, albeit for different reasons.

'It's a matter of judgement. I sent you there in order to keep us informed,' he snapped, 'not to go cavorting around the battlefield. Or whatever it was you say you were doing…' He looked at me sharply. 'This isn't the first instance I can recall. If you'd prefer to be in an infantry battalion, MacPhail, just say the word.'

'No, sir,' I said quickly. 'And yes, sir, it was the battlefield where I was.' I didn't like the way he'd insinuated I was doing something other than plucking an inexperienced man back from the brink – or attempting to. Granted it wasn't much of a story set against his fairly explicit instructions, not in the hard light of day after what had been a hard winter, and an even harder spring. Furthermore, there was every sign it was shaping up to be a summer for war, no different from last year, or the year before that, or even the year before that when it all began.

New men were expected to use their heads and take their chances. So were experienced men when it came down to it. That was where it got tricky. Convincing the colonel I'd used my head was a cause as hopeless as Belgium's in August 1914. But so long as he and the general didn't question my motives or my fortitude, there was always another day.

Later that day my mood was temporarily buoyed. Congratulations were pouring into headquarters at the success of the raid. General Lipsett had the air of someone who was pleased (he was not the sort to make a big show of it), and well he ought to have been. The enemy's line fronting Avion was in a shambles, in total disarray – their casualties reported as very heavy where ours were said to be light. The 7th Brigade alone submitted a tally of an estimated 722 enemy casualties, versus less than half that themselves, and the vast majority of those were only walking cases. There was also a message from General Plumer of the Second Army up in the Ypres Salient. In part it read:

Much appreciate all you did to help us before, during, and since our operation to draw off enemy's attention. Hope you will let the troops concerned know how much I appreciate their efforts. Your raids last night must have been splendid.

I would have felt more splendid myself had I not spoken with Major Meredith. It was not that Meredith held anything against me for my sudden disappearance – quite the opposite; he thanked me for my efforts on behalf of his brigade. Partly his graciousness was due to what he had to say next. For in addition to formally relaying the casualty figures – a full report would follow – he informed me that Lieutenant O'Neill was killed near the railway embankment during the withdrawal. He was shot once in the head, most likely by a sniper, he said. A few men from the RCR had carried him back.

Sitting at my desk it was all I could do to keep up pretences, when all I wanted to do was to slump down into a heap in the corner, with a blanket over my head and my eyes closed.

Fortunately three pieces of news arrived to break my stupor. Not for the first time I was reminded that the war paused for nothing, and for no one. I think that's what kept us all going; the knowledge that no matter what happened, you still had to put one foot in front of the other lest a day come when you weren't able to do that.

The first piece of news was in the form of a telephoned report from the Corps cage. A prisoner of the 156th Regiment had been brought in. In response to questioning he said that he had heard talk of a withdrawal. While he couldn't be sure when it would occur, he was convinced it would be soon. I clenched my fist. I may even have banged the table.

I brought the message to the colonel. He glanced at it, but beyond raising a sceptical eyebrow, he was silent. It was obvious he put more faith in the Corps intelligence summary which concluded: "unlikely there was any intention of withdrawal". Nevertheless, the message served to get my blood flowing again, if not that of the colonel. The second announcement sent it coursing.

The mood in the general staff room was one of incredulity. General Byng was leaving us. He was passing over command of the Corps. 'But why?' went up a cry. It was the question every man in the room had.

Fotheringham, who'd broken the news, had an answer. 'Sir Douglas has given him the Third Army, that's why. He's been promoted to full general. What did you think? He'd turn down a job like that to stay with an uncouth mob like this?'

We all grinned, although I think deep down there were a few who thought Byng ought to have done precisely that. My theory on generals, and dregs rising to the top, was wobbling. But then, I quickly reasoned, this was evidently the exception that proved the rule.

Before I could go too far down that hole, or share my conclusions with the others, a handwritten note arrived by way of a despatch rider. I recognized the illiterate scrawl that passed as handwriting in the nether regions of Quebec's eastern townships. It was Benoît's. He was being sent to Corps Headquarters at Camblain l'Abbé tomorrow and inquired in the most flowery language if I would join him for dinner at his favourite estaminet. There was no need to respond. "Come if you can, and *tant pis* if you can't," it read.

The *tant pis* bit was his way of saying it was "too bad" if I couldn't make it. Between the lines he was rubbing it in, a not so gentle re-minder that I'd regret it if I didn't come. Cambligneul was no Paris, but knowing Benoît's gastronomical bent I was inclined to take him at his word. I gritted my teeth. Someone in the division must have an unwanted chore I could assume that would bring me that way...

10th of June, 1917
Cambligneul, France

'You what?'

'I transported a half dozen of the new German machine-guns and a fair-sized *Minenwerfer* to Corps headquarters. Had to give the fellow whose job it was a bottle of rum, too. So I hope this is worth it, Benoît.'

He was staring at me with an easy grin. Even with wheels, the large trench mortars Fritz employed were weighty devices. 'What I most want to know, Mac, did you push or did you pull?' He chuckled loudly.

I shifted in the simple wooden chair, trying to find a cool spot. After only a minute on my rear I was already stuck to it like a piece of chewing gum. 'I didn't do it by myself, that's for sure. We pulled it behind the lorry. A tricky operation, though.'

'Hmm. And then?'

'Well, once we arrived at Camblain L'Abbé, I was able to hand off the whole lot to some wide-eyed lieutenant fresh off the boat from England. Did you know they've got a whole waggon park of German trophies at HQ? Looks good for the visitors I expect. And after that, well, it was a walk of only a couple of miles,' I said casually, wiping at my brow. The sweat on it was streaming down as fast as any current in the Souchez River, a tributary of which had seeped into my left eye. I rubbed at it furiously. 'It's a bleeding furnace out there,' I muttered.

Benoît had positioned himself strategically in the coolest part of the long room. He was in the corner, away from the open windows through which the sun's last rays shone with unexpected vigour, but close enough to catch the breeze that was rising with the onset of evening. From his vantage point, behind the table for two, he had a perfect view of the entire room. More importantly he had a platoon-sized mug of beer in front of him. The mug was perspiring a good deal more than he was. 'I'll never understand you,' he rumbled between sips. 'Why didn't you just borrow a car from the staff pool?'

'Are you going to offer me one of those?' I said, pointing at the beer. 'Or shall I beg?'

Benoît lifted an arm and circled a finger the size of a rifle barrel in the air. A white sleeve at the end of the room promptly signalled back.

In Paris an immaculately clad waiter would eventually have come to see what it was you wanted; in Cambligneul they just got on with it. It was that kind of place.

'Thanks. Yeah, well, Hayter's not in a frame of mind that I could simply say: "Colonel, I've had a difficult few days. I was thinking of making an evening out of it with a good meal and a few drinks. Shall I take the general's car?"'

'Mac?' Benoît put down his glass, something he was rarely known to do. He eyed me. 'Tell me.'

'What!?'

The arrival of a frosted mug on the burly arm of a pug-faced, middleweight boxer in a blue-striped apron, otherwise known as the farmer's wife, intervened. And it was good that she did for I had no particular interest in reliving my latest fumble at headquarters.

'*Merci*,' I said with enthusiasm, and reached for it greedily.

The woman grunted. Taciturn or not, the corners of her mouth had turned upwards, even if the emerging smile turned out to be a dud.

'She likes you,' said Benoît, when she was gone.

I ignored him, too busy chugging at the amber-coloured liquid. French beer was usually a weak concoction, but this was perhaps the best I'd ever had, cold and refreshing, with the rich malty taste I adored yet seldom tasted, and a refreshing bitterness at the end to quench the thirst. Already I felt better. I drank again.

When I first arrived I'd almost turned away in confusion. The long, narrow, single-story farm building was crudely built with big bricks painted white, and a steeply sloped red roof – snow was common in these parts. About the snow I knew; Christ, it had snowed for two days straight over Easter when we attacked Vimy Ridge. But what puzzled me were the sounds and the smells. For it sounded and smelled precisely like a farm, as far as I'd ever thought about a farm having lived in a city my entire life. Which of course was exactly what it was. Though somehow a farm didn't seem the kind of place that might serve a meal, let alone a meal to satisfy Benoît. Despite years of iron rations, he was not a man to surrender his taste-buds to the questionable tastes (or budgets) of some functionary in a non-descript ministry in London. Not that I was prepared to sound the retreat immediately, not having walked a couple of miles in the blazing heat on the hard *pavé*. Having helped wrestle an assortment of the German Empire's newest munitions onto and off a lorry I was hungry and thirsty. Then I noticed the small white sign jutting out from the corner of the building, like a street marker. Estaminet, it read in crudely-drawn black letters. The wind shifted as I looked at it, and I caught the whiff of something delicious. I bounded to the door.

'So, General Currie's getting the Corps with General Byng gone,' said Benoît conversationally.

'Yes, I heard,' I said, still eyeing my beer, which was showing signs of requiring precipitous resupply.

'A good choice, *non*?'

'Yeah, I'm beginning to wonder what the hell is happening with the army. Suddenly it's not only the nincompoops getting promoted.'

'Don't tell me, Mac, you made captain?'

I grimaced. 'You know what I mean. First Byng, and now Currie. Who's getting 1st Division with Currie promoted, anyhow?'

'Brigadier Macdonell.'

'They're giving Long Archie a division!?'

Benoît sighed. 'Of course, not. Mac. What's wrong with you?'

I didn't reply, gulping at the dregs of my beer instead.

'Batty Mac of the 7th Brigade, he's promoted to major-general,' he said. 'Not sure who's getting his command.'

My theory, like the contents of my mug, was in poor condition. Although I'd seen too much of the British Empire at war to think this was anything but a temporary setback. And Benoît did his thing with the finger to alleviate the more pressing concerns.

'But speaking of the other Macdonell,' said Benoît conspiratorially, glancing around. 'He's planning to shoot someone,' he said softly.

'I sure hope he is,' I said. 'Otherwise this war is going to last a very long time.'

'One of ours.'

I frowned.

'They sentenced a fellow, Gaudy, from the Royal 22ieme. He was absent without leave. Macdonell confirmed it. They're going to shoot the poor bugger.'

'For being absent without leave?'

Benoît nodded fervently. 'They want to make an example of him.'

Poor Gaudy aside, I couldn't help but think of myself. I wasn't exactly on leave. But I was absent, and I'd kept that fact close to my vest. I hadn't seen any particular reason why I should inform Colonel Hayter what I was doing in my precious few hours off duty. He might see it differently.

'I'm surprised Macdonell found the time for the paperwork,' I said. 'Or perhaps he was simply grouchy because dinner hadn't arrived on time.'

This time Benoît was the one frowning.

At which point I was forced to relive the experience, still fresh in my memory, of a brigadier sheltering in his cave and bemoaning his tardy meal, while his boys rushed the German trenches. I didn't spare him any details.

'They should shoot the bastard,' growled Benoît when I was finished.

To which thought there was nothing I could usefully add.

Around dinner time the room suddenly filled up with khaki green, and it was not a small room, so even though the evening air was cooling it was heating up in the farmhouse with fifty-odd men packed in, imbibing, conversing and singing until the military police would put an end to it. However, when the *plat du jour* arrived, to a thunderclap of joy from Benoît's thick hands, and a background accompaniment from what sounded like my stomach, I realized I was famished. *Andouillette à la moutarde* the dish was called: a thick sausage smothered in a creamy sauce accompanied by a big fistful of spring beans artfully wrapped in a strip of bacon. A large dish of sweet young potatoes with lacings of fresh parsley was also laid out before us.

'What is this?' I asked Benoît. It smelled wonderful.

'Sausage with mustard sauce. The brown specks… those are seeds. *Moutarde à l'ancienne.*'

'Yes, but what's the meat?' I persisted. 'I hope it's not too *ancienne?*'

'*Ça, c'est mieux de ne pas demander,*' he replied cryptically, methodically applying himself to cutting a piece of the sausage before shovelling a generous forkful into his mouth, after smothering it first in the sauce. The French were famous for their sauces I was told, even if I wasn't supposed to ask about the meat.

In normal circumstances I would have been wary having been

warned off discussing what kind of meat had gone into dinner, but fearlessly I followed his example and went over the top. 'Hmm,' I said, chewing. It was probably the best bite I'd had in months, including those in Paris. When it came to eating there was no one I would sooner follow through No-Man's-Land than Benoît. That I'd worked my way through several very large beers, didn't hurt.

'That'll put a little meat on those skinny bones,' he said, licking his lips, seemingly oblivious to the fact I was 200 pounds – even on army food.

After dinner there was no rest for the weary as another beer was dropped unceremoniously onto our table, unasked for. I wouldn't have asked further. All around us beer was arriving at every table in the room. But Benoit did: of the young girl who served us.

She smiled at him – he was a regular here, after all; either that or she was amused at his Québécois accent – and pointed a thin finger at our patron saint. He was one of the large group sitting at a table in the corner directly opposite, thirty feet away. We raised our glasses and bobbed our heads in gratitude. Someone waved. With this unexpected bonanza the noise level in the place cranked up a notch.

'Who are they?' I asked Benoît, as I turned around to face him again. 'Do you recognize any of them?'

He hesitated, still observing the group over my shoulder. 'I think I've seen one before. They all look to be NCOs,' he said.

'NCOs,' I mused. 'I've treated a few fellows to a drink in my day. And when I got my first stripes I may have treated a few more, but there's an entire platoon in here. How the blazes can one of them, or even all of them, afford that on an extra 40 cents a day?'

Benoît said nothing; he was likely reflecting on how he'd ever managed to get by on a private's wage of a dollar a day. Had my belly been empty I probably wouldn't have given it a second's extra thought. But it wasn't – I was sated – and I was consumed by curiosity.

Taking a parting sip of the man's offering, I stood. Squeezing my way past the other tables I headed toward the far end of the low-ceilinged hall. The tables were set so close together the backs of the chairs rubbed against those behind. I had to tap on more than a few shoulders in order to pass. Seeing me approach, one of the soldiers at the corner table leapt to his feet, donning a smile. It was a corporal, and other than sharing the same divisional patch as me, he seemed vaguely familiar. I'm not always greeted with a smile, and being offered a drink other than tea was even more of a rarity, so I was inclined to be friendly.

'Is it to you we owe our gratitude?' I asked cheerfully, looking at him more closely. 'Do we know each other?'

'No, sir, it was one of the others,' the man replied. 'And yes, sir, we do know each other.'

I made an attempt at focussing, always difficult after a few hours out with Benoît, but gave up the effort when recognition evaded me.

The man seemed to recognize my difficulty. 'If you'll recall, sir, we spoke at the munitions dump at La Chaudière.' A star shell burst into light upstairs, piercing through the mental fog that had grown ever more impenetrable as the evening progressed. I'd spoken with the fellow only a couple of weeks before.

'Of course,' I said. 'It's just that it's terribly dark in here. You were the bright spark who had the idea of putting up the netting, so Fritz couldn't see what we were up to?'

He nodded and beamed. I remembered him doing exactly the same when I complimented him then. Which was obviously why he'd jumped to his feet at the sight of me.

'Who are your benevolent friends?' I asked. 'I'm at a bit of a loss. I'm quite certain I don't recognize any of them. I rather expected I might, as one of them just bought me and my friend a drink.'

'That would be Cuthbert, sir,' he replied. 'He's 2nd Division, from the divisional train, so I don't imagine you've seen him before. The others are acquaintances of his. They all have family roots in England, in the Midlands. Actually I'm one of the few from our division. But this buddy of mine knows Cuthbert and he invited me along. They're celebrating.'

'Celebrating? So they thought they'd lighten things up and buy everyone a drink? Not that I don't appreciate it. I do.' I grinned. 'But how is it that a sergeant from the divisional train can afford that?'

'Beats me, sir,' he replied. 'They've been throwing money around all night. All I know is that one of them said they'd found themselves a benefactor.'

'A benefactor?'

'Yes, sir. That's what he said. I reckon it's a wealthy uncle or something.'

'Probably,' I said.

After chatting for a minute more, I thanked them, excused myself, and went back to the table.

'*Alors?*' said Benoît. 'Who are they?'

'Supply column, divisional train, quartermasters…'

The very words seemed to provoke in Benoît an all-too predictable reaction; he yawned. 'See, I could have told you that before you went tearing off. They're bored. You'd be bored too, Mac, if you were driving a lorry filled with mess tins back and forth to a railhead twice a day.'

'I don't think mess tins is all that they carry, Benoît.'

'Of course not. But the boys are having their evening off. Let them be. And be thankful.' He frowned.

I grunted. 'What now?'

'Your beer. It's getting warm. And flat.'

With that we returned to more serious business. But later as Benoît drove me back to Fort George, I couldn't help thinking about it, while I gazed out the window. It wouldn't have been the first time something was purloined from army stores. Although there wasn't much of a black market in 60-pound shells, nor even in bicycles, for all the shenanigans that went on. Iron rations weren't worth a pot of gold. Some would have paid just to be rid of them. Perhaps it was as simple as the corporal's speculation that a well-to-do relative had stepped forward. Benoît always accused me of overcomplicating things.

CHAPTER 15

25th of June, 1917
North bank of the Souchez River, near Lièvin, France

The morning dawned warm and muggy as the clouds that had shifted over during the night trapped the heat and the moisture, as the lid on a simmering pan will do. I was barely on my feet and already my shirt was clinging to me like a second skin. Mingled with the sweat, there was also a tenseness to the staff as we assembled at our desks. The mood was not a result of the weather, nor even the early hour.

The day before had seen our neighbours on the left, the 4th Division, and their neighbours further left, the Imperial 46th Division, successfully push out some posts into enemy territory astride the Souchez. It was anyone's guess what the German reaction overnight was. Although it wasn't much of a guess to think the retaliation was probably heavy. Heavy enough and there was a good chance we'd find ourselves embroiled in the brawl today, maybe we were already involved and didn't know it – thus the edginess. My friend from Paris, Hollace Bennett, came to mind, and I wondered how he was faring. The 46th was his division. However, the morning reports were soothing: beyond a heavy shelling in the vicinity of the Electricity Generation Station near La Coulotte, the night had been quiet.

'That's a relief, Malcolm,' cracked Fotheringham when he also heard. 'Looks like you'll have time for that horse show after all.'

For some the day's highlight was the First Army Horse Show being held at Château de la Haie. It required an equine bent, or an invitation; preferably both. I had neither, and avoided the creatures if given half a chance. Despite their usefulness, they and I had what was known as a mutually wary relationship. Even assured of a safe distance in between, I preferred my desk to dodging the piles of dung now artfully decorating the château grounds. I hadn't made any secret of my feelings.

On the other hand, I would have been interested in attending the day's second event – a visit to Vimy Ridge by an advance delegation of the American army, the first troops of which were to arrive any day. But that too required an invitation. Had someone considered giving me one – improbable I grant – they were likely warned off by the thought my diplomatic skills might scare our southern cousins into turning their troopships round mid-ocean and returning home. There weren't many these days who still believed in the war's resolution by Christmas. The Americans were most welcome.

In the absence of more glamorous undertakings there was plenty of staff work. A profusion of orders needed to be arranged, written, and distributed. Colonel Hayter assigned me to coordinate orders with the 9th Brigade who were soon to push out the line towards Avion. It beat drawing up march tables for our forthcoming relief. Ever since I sent a battalion marching off to the wrong village it was a chore I ducked, whenever possible.

The afternoon passed slowly. Until, going on four o'clock, a message was received. Like all the others that came by telephone or by wire it was first transcribed onto a signals sheet and duly passed to the duty officer for perusal. This one landed promptly on Colonel Hayter's desk.

Then things moved very rapidly indeed.

'1st Corps report the enemy appear to be withdrawing,' I heard Hayter say to Majors Festing and McAvity as they came to his side. A discussion ensued.

Captain Ferguson was waved over. My ears flapping, I attempted to overhear something of the conversation. In vain. Then I saw how Ferguson nodded his head and left, reaching out to snatch his helmet before slipping away. Dollars to doughnuts he was heading to our brigade in the line. Hayter would be anxious to gather all the intelligence possible.

'I knew there was something to that withdrawal,' I muttered, more loudly than intended.

Fotheringham heard me. 'Just goes to show, Mac. Spin your wheels in the mud long enough, and eventually you get out.'

'Don't you have a few thousand billets to arrange by tonight?' I snarled. He smirked, and turned away. Much as with the horse show, my thoughts about the withdrawal were well known.

Others were summoned, one by one, and given their marching orders. Major Festing went to the telephone and called what I presumed was 8th Brigade headquarters. He would be asking if they could send out patrols as soon as possible along our entire frontage, to assess the situation.

I returned to my papers. When I looked up several minutes later, Colonel Hayter was staring pensively in my direction. As he caught my glance he motioned with his finger that I should come to him.

'You heard?' he asked, without preamble.

'Yes, sir. The Boche are withdrawing.'

'That remains to be seen, Lieutenant. But once we know more we can assess what steps are required. However, you realize how difficult it is for the front-line battalions to liaise across the Souchez?'

I nodded. The British held the northern bank and the Canadians the southern, and a little more than a loud bellow was required to overcome the barrier of the river. A message from a unit a thousand yards away typically took hours to arrive, first being shunted around various headquarters in the rear before it reached the neighbouring unit. Anything could happen in the interim.

This was apparently the colonel's concern. 'I'm sending you to 1st Corps,' he said. Seeing my bewildered expression he continued. 'No, not the headquarters, the front line near Fosse no. 3, the coal works. You'll find the 46th Division there. They're on our flank. I want to hear the moment they think the situation is changing.'

My eyes bulged. A 4th Division battalion was at the boundary with the Imperials. Some might view this as us tramping over our sister division's turf, and I had no desire to explain otherwise to Lieutenant-Colonel Ironside, the intimidating GSO1 of that division.

'Yes, I realize this is a little unorthodox, MacPhail. But I thought that might appeal to you. Otherwise it's all rather straight forward.'

'Sir?'

'Find the 46th Division, determine the situation as accurately as possible, and report back. And don't forget to inform 4th Division about what you learn.'

For something so 'straight forward' it seemed anything but. For one thing, it wasn't clear how I was supposed to trot back and forth across the watery barrier of the Souchez. Hayter had refrained from asking whether I could swim. Nor did he offer any pigeons as an alternative. One thing I did know was that crossing on a tight rope was likely to be child's play compared to navigating the various personalities and sensibilities involved. It made me wonder if this was Hayter's way of testing my mettle after letting him down during the raid two weeks earlier. That would have been just like him.

Impatiently he cleared his throat. 'You'd best be on your way, MacPhail. Time is pressing. And I need to speak with the general.'

Within thirty minutes I was deposited on a deserted road, the remains of the generating station to the east and, according to the despatch rider, the Souchez River dead north down the dusty path. It had been a terrifying, if mildly exhilarating ride, clutching firmly to him as we raced up and over the Ridge and down on to the Douai Plain, while he threw the throttle wide open and did his level best to swerve around every hole or depression, of which there were many. I regretted telling him that my mission was urgent. But now the last leg appeared to be up to me.

'I'm sorry, sir, I'd like to take you, but I have strict instructions to remain away from the front,' he said. 'The despatches, you understand?'

I doubted he was carrying anything of import, but he wasn't wrong about the front. As a soldier you soon develop a sense for these things; the scattered gunfire was an indication, but mainly it was the unnerving absence of anyone moving, or anyone at all. I waved the rider on his way. Then I took out a small map to consult, of the kind so lacking in detail that no one would fear were it or I to be taken.

A couple of soldiers from the 46th South Saskatchewan Battalion spotted me. They invited me into their support trench, which I now noticed ran parallel with the road. When I explained where I was headed they nodded their heads. 'Yes, sir, there's a bridge across the river a couple of minutes further. If you stick to the road it'll take you through the marshes.'

'Marshes?' I began to mumble. No one had mentioned marshes earlier, least of all my little map.

'Watch yourself, sir. The Hun have a few snipers and machine guns on the high ground further east. The South Staffs tried for Hill 65 yesterday, but I don't think they made it.'

'Course they didn't make it,' said one of his mates caustically. 'Where do you think that blasted MG is that keeps firing?'

I frowned. 'The South Staffs… the Staffordshire Regiment, you mean?'

'Yes, sir. We're in touch with them.'

I groaned. Not because I didn't want to run into the South Staffordshires – I did – rather that the whole pretext for me coming here was to summon a rabbit out of a bag. Apparently, the rabbit was already hopping around at his leisure, marshes, snipers and MGs notwithstanding. Then I thought of Colonel Hayter's last penetrating look. Hurriedly I took my leave.

As promised the road north and west led to a stone bridge. I crossed it, keeping low. A few steps later I passed through the underpass of the rail spur that went towards Fosse no. 3. Exiting the underpass, the towering shaft of the coal mine loomed prominently in the distance, with its characteristic steel frame construction, topped by a platform, and a second beam which abutted the tower at an angle and made it look as if it were keeping the entire construction from toppling over. Maybe it was.

Ahead was the Cité de Riaumont. There were long rows of small brick dwellings, most in a condition similar to other buildings one saw at the front. Closer to hand I noted the narrow causeway, a pond and a veritable swamp reaching out to either side. Remembering the soldier's warning I paused here and took careful stock. That was when I caught sight of the unmistakeable furrow of a trench parapet off my right shoulder. Gambling the South Staffs would be manning it I headed that way. It was either that or risk sprinting down Sniper Alley. I moved quickly all the same.

Coming from behind I caught the three men bending over a cooker unawares. Not often this war had the surprise been so complete. But then High Command had more often than not preferred a more measured pace and a well-advertised parade down Main Street.

'Relax, fellows,' I said, as they sprang to their feet, flinging perfectly good mess tins filled with dinner to one side for the belated security of a short Lee-Enfield. I sensed that it was an inauspicious beginning of my visit to the Staffordshires. But then I hadn't eaten either, and wasn't likely to anytime soon.

'Sorry about that. But battalion headquarters; can you point me the way? I'm in a bit of a hurry as you may have guessed.'

Following their instructions, I set off in the direction of the mine shaft through a warren of trenches, water above my boots in places, hoping I wasn't about to round a bend and discover where the advance of the South Staffordshires had come to an unceremonious end.

'Malcolm!'

Having at last exited the trenches, I'd come to the mine buildings, and was moving down a street of bleakly uniform and uniformly battered miners' houses, when I encountered a party of soldiers forming up. Someone in the party had spotted me. And I had an excellent idea who that was.

'Lieutenant Bennett,' I enthused, as I approached him. 'It's not exactly the Champs Élysées, but I was hoping I might run into you in these parts.' I thrust my hand in his, and he shook it warmly.

'Can't do anything about the surrounds I'm afraid. It's not Paris I'll grant you.' He grinned. 'We're being relieved, shortly.'

'That's definitely a reason to smile,' I said. 'Almost as good as a leave pass.'

'Not quite, but good enough.' He smiled again. 'What the blazes are you doing here?'

'Actually, I'm in search of your headquarters. Or any headquarters, really.'

'Oh?'

I explained. 'So, you see, Hollace, there's a lot of consternation about whether Fritz is indeed pulling back. I need to hear what the situation truly is. No one wants a repeat of the winter.'

'When they slipped away and nobody noticed.'

'Right.'

'No chance of that here. We're locked in a dance step; they move and we follow.'

'So which way is the tango progressing? Forward or back?'

'Forward. We're most definitely moving forward. I don't know what you've heard, but the rumours are true. Today there's every sign they're retiring. You can go looking for our OC, Colonel Llewwellyn, if you like, although he's likely in the rear by now. But you won't hear it any differently from him. Most of what I know he told me himself.'

'Well, so long as you're certain, Hollace,' I said, hesitating. Dallying around the front in an unfamiliar area as evening approached was far from ideal. And Colonel Hayter had impressed upon me the importance of haste. On the other hand I had to be sure. I had no intention of becoming legendary in the division as the fellow who cried wolf, followed by a hasty posting to the trenches.

'Oh, I'm quite certain,' said Bennett, drawing himself up, his features keen and most serious. 'You see, we're in Adept and Admiral Trenches…' he continued as he extracted his own map, a better version of the one I possessed, and proceeded to describe the enemy's dispositions in considerable detail. It didn't take long to convince me.

Then we spoke the words you speak when parting from a meeting with a friend after a long interval, and resolved to meet again soon in more uplifting surroundings. We shook hands.

'The road. That's the fastest way to the other side of the river, I suppose?' I asked, already moving.

He nodded.

'Yes, I was afraid of that.'

I made for it. It would be dusk soon, and finding my way, let alone finding that single bridge that crossed the river, would become steadily more difficult. It was impossible that I could reverse my circuitous route through streets and trenches, around buildings and the marsh, without a landmark such as the mine shaft to orient by, all while keeping my head down. The road was the only option. Fortunately, I had a plan of sorts.

Where the road left the shelter of the buildings, I went to the far (western) embankment and got down on my knees. Very slowly I began crawling along it. For much of the time one leg was submerged in water where the pond lapped against the gravel. This way, any Fritz on high ground looking west with a rifle or a machine gun wouldn't notice. I didn't give much for my chances if I tried to rush the 300-yard long causeway, silhouetted, with the sun setting to the right, and the Germans to the left. As tactics go it was uninspired but successful, though it left my trousers a mess, while my boots fared arguably worse.

Across the river I located some of the boys from south Saskatchewan – Moose Jaw to be precise – settled down in a post near the bank with a Lewis gun: a flank guard. After first marvelling at the unofficerly state of my dress, they took me under their wing, sketching carefully on my map to indicate where I could find their battalion headquarters, then supplemented it with a whole battery of spoken instructions. They even gave me a tin of bully beef when I explained I hadn't eaten.

Thanks to them I found the dug-out. But unsurprisingly the only telephone they had was connected with their brigade headquarters, and possibly the 4th Division – I didn't ask. Either way, I had no wish risking an encounter with the fearsome Colonel Ironside, not even at the end of several miles of coiled wire buried a few feet deep. I neatly sidestepped the hazard by informing the officers present of what I knew, with few explanations how I knew it, and asked for directions to the 3rd Division.

That night the wind gusted fiercely and a torrential rain came driving down. Thunder rumbled ominously, and for a change it was not the thunder of the guns, though the sky flashed every so often as one erupted in anger. The storm caught me about half way to La Coulotte, which was half way too soon. My boots were not the only things soaked through when eventually I washed into the headquarters of the 43rd Battalion, the Cameron Highlanders. They'd only just arrived themselves.

The Camerons were preoccupied, for they were in the midst of relieving another battalion, but they did have a telephone. This one was connected with the next best thing to divisional headquarters: brigade headquarters. I spoke with a major whose name I've since forgotten, and probably didn't hear properly the first time. Big talkers are terrible listeners my mother liked to say; although she was usually referring to my father when he had the audacity to interrupt. I was simply in a hurry to tell my story.

'Yes, sir. There seems little doubt about it,' I replied. The major's cross-examination was a mild one by most standards. Thankfully he was no Ironside. Above all he wanted reassurance that what I was telling him was accurate. 'I was at the front with the Staffordshire Regiment. Prior to their relief tonight they were holding the line near Fosse no. 3. According to them, the Boche are pulling back to their defences nearer Lens. They're going to make another attempt for Hill 65 shortly. The 4th Division are also nipping at the Germans' heels.'

The line crackled. The major spoke at length but his words ran together in an unintelligible garble. I could guess however at what was being asked. Or so I thought. On reflection, the strategic insights of a junior officer were probably not what he was looking for.

'My advice? My advice is that we push forward some strong patrols towards Avion, sir. This may be the very chance we've been waiting for. We could pierce their line as they retreat.'

There was a muffled reply. Then a few words emerged from the static, including, 'Colonel Hayter'. Then the line went dead. Between the Boche shelling, and the rain that sounded as if it was going to batter a hole in the galvanised metal roof of the dug-out, it was a wonder the thing worked at all.

Shortly thereafter I followed the example of the telephone line. Someone graciously pointed out a corner I might fall into.

CHAPTER 16

26th of June, 1917
Front line east of La Coulotte, France

The next morning it appeared as if my advice was being put immediately into action, although it only appeared that way, for the scheme of attack being employed was largely determined two weeks previous, and I don't think my missives had much effect at all. On our left the 4th Division was moving against the trenches north and west of the tiny village of La Coulotte. It was another step towards Lens.

The enemy was jittery. Before dawn he sent up multiple parachute flares near Victoria Road, slightly to the east of battalion headquarters, and was nervously firing off white rockets and split-red and orange cluster flares to the west – much as if he suspected what our sister division had planned. The 3rd Division's Camerons and 58th Battalion were tasked with the trenches on this side of the village. These consisted of the primary fire-line and a support trench behind. They were Fritz's final defences before the main Avion line, the settlement immediately beyond, and Lens looming like an irresistible beacon due North.

Initially it went swimmingly.

'Finally, the 43rd have a company on their objectives in Acorn Trench and are moving forward,' I told Lt.-Col. Hayter, not far past 10 a.m. After the report came in I walked two miles down the tree-lined road to brigade headquarters at Petit Vimy to find a direct line to the division. Fortunately my call found Hayter at Fort George, and fortunately the fellow who answered the call didn't fob me off on Major Festing or one of the others. If I was ever going to convince Hayter I wasn't the misfit of divisional headquarters, it was best I spoke with him myself.

'I see,' said the colonel, when I came to the end of my account. I was disappointed at the blandness of his reaction given the effort I'd gone to, not to mention what the Camerons put into it. But I suppose in his position, after all that the Corps and the 3rd Division had been through these past years, he found little extraordinary in what I said, even if my point of view was coloured by being in the midst of it.

'Just so you know, Lieutenant, the 4th Division also report they're on their objectives,' he added. 'Encountered little opposition, they said.'

'Indeed, sir! Perhaps this is the moment we've been waiting for?'

A silence followed, one that somehow didn't invite further commentary on my part. It was relieved by a loud crackle, followed by: 'Was there anything else?'

'No, sir. But what are my orders, sir? Would you like me to return?'

The line went all fuzzy. Briefly I thought it had been cut. Then like the British line in 1914 in the Salient it suddenly crackled back into life. Through some quirk a signaller might better be able to explain, the colonel's voice was booming in my ear: 'No, best stay with the battalion, MacPhail. Keep me informed.' There was a loud click. Now the line was most definitely dead; the example of the first battle of Ypres relegated to history.

Taking my leave of the brigade staff a few faces looked puzzled, first by my abrupt arrival, and now by my equally abrupt departure. I headed up the road towards La Coulotte again. On the way I overtook a pant-less formation marching in double file with shouldered rifles going the same direction I was. I had a fair idea where they were headed. It was a platoon from the Cameron Highlanders.

For the first time ever the idea of a kilt actually held some attraction for me. While cooler after the overnight rain it was plenty hot tromping up and down this accursed road, being enveloped in a fine but all-encompassing dust whenever a lorry or an animal train rolled past. A little breeze around the knees might help, and I did have my Scottish genes to consider. But then I spotted their officer, a lieutenant.

'You fellows must be the reinforcements,' I said, falling into step beside him.

He looked at me puzzled, unable to place my features but recognizing the divisional patch. The same one he wore.

'I'm MacPhail with the divisional staff,' I explained, 'temporarily attached to the battalion.'

'Anderson, D Company,' he said. 'To answer your question, I have no idea. All I was told was that we were to move forward.'

'Hmm. That sounds about right for the army. To where we do not know, but so long as everyone is in step... And heaven forbid that the buttons aren't polished –'

'Dang,' he said, smiling. 'I knew I forgot something.' He glanced at his chest, and for the show ran his fingers down a row of brass buttons in dire need of some polish. 'What's it all about, anyhow?'

'Well it appears our dear friend, Fritz, may finally have had his fill of holding the line in this backwater. I'm told on good authority he's showing every inclination of pulling back. Which means of course we're moving forward in lockstep – or at least that's what I keep advising headquarters. In fact, some of the lads in your battalion already captured a couple of his trenches early this morning. So if you ask me, I'd guess you boys were heading Avion way in the not too distant future.'

'I see,' he replied. 'I figured it'd be something like that.'

'If it was up to me it'd be sooner rather than later, too,' I muttered, a little too loudly for polite company. Too late I realized that I sounded like some cantankerous old relic who'd been on the staff since the Crimean expedition.

Anderson pulled a face. I'm not entirely certain why I was so fired up about pressing the attack, only that it was likely my way of driving home the message I'd been right all along about this withdrawal. The taunts and scepticism of certain characters at Fort George stuck in my craw. Certainly it seemed more sensible to take it to the Germans when they were in no mood for a fight than when they were bristling with self-confidence, fortified behind ten feet of angle irons and wire, in a trench at least as deep.

Unfortunately there was little evidence GHQ shared my viewpoint. Which was maybe why, when I reached the battalion dug-out and discovered there weren't any further plans for the day, I rushed to the Camerons' OC. 'But, sir, we need to keep pressing,' I said to Lieutenant-Colonel Grassie.

Grassie, a distinguished, well-groomed man with a paucity of hair on the fore half of his polished head, excepting a neatly groomed banker's moustache, nodded patiently. He appeared to be mustering a response when a signaller's voice sounded above the murmur of the others in the small chamber. 'Sir!' The colonel was required on the telephone.

And subsequently other matters intervened, and we never did continue our discussion.

An hour later the situation at the front had settled down. The trenches taken this morning were occupied, and the battalion was in touch with those on both left and right. A series of heavy explosions was reported in Avion. I whipped off a signal to Lt.-Col. Hayter about these latest developments, rounding off my message with the boldly worded suggestion that at the very least we should push out some patrols towards Avion Trench. Then I waited impatiently as the signaller tapped out my words. He paused once or twice to ask what I'd scrawled.

Later that afternoon Lt.-Col. Grassie appeared before me. He was wearing a suitably wry expression as he handed me a copy of his latest orders. 'It appears you got your wish, Lieutenant,' he said. 'I intend to send two large patrols tonight to occupy Avion Trench.'

I nodded dispassionately. Nothing riled a superior officer more than the thought that a junior officer had somehow subverted him. 'It wasn't exactly my wish, sir, but the patrols sound like a fine idea.'

He raised an eyebrow, the glint in his eyes either bemusement, or irritation.

'I imagine you're keen to accompany them?' he said.

I swallowed. Contrary to what Grassie believed I had no such ambitions. Lt.-Col. Hayter had been unusually frank in his views the last time I was caught up in the action to the detriment of my liaison duties. 'A question of judgement' was the phrase he used.

It was one thing to come up with a course of action after carefully marshalling the facts and weighing the factors involved, and quite another to carry it out. I raised my chin and met the colonel's searching look. I'd gained a certain measure of respect I could see. Nor was it difficult to imagine how ephemeral that would be when I excused myself, scorn and derision to take its place.

'Naturally, sir,' I replied. 'I couldn't very well miss it, could I?'

At precisely 10.30 p.m. two platoons from B and D Companies, some 90 men in total, augmented by one circumspect lieutenant of the divisional staff equipped with a borrowed Lee-Enfield, departed down the warren of trenches in the direction of Agent Trench. Until this morning Agent Trench had been the German reserve line. Barring any nasty surprises from enemy soldiers not yet rooted out, we would assemble there before moving on to penetrate Avion Trench.

'Lieutenant MacPhail! My, my! This *is* a surprise,' said Lieutenant Anderson when he saw me, several minutes before the stunt began.

'Staff you mean? Yet here?'

He shrugged. 'We don't see many staff in the flesh round these parts.'

'No, I suppose not. That's more or less exactly what I used to think, too – before they put me on the staff. And truth be told there are a few of the staff who rarely see the light of day, let alone a trench. However, I can assure you from experience that it's not everything it's cracked up to be. There are a lot more hazards than dying from a paper cut.'

'Hmm,' said Anderson, dubiously. 'Well, you've got some pluck coming here, I'll grant you that.'

I didn't respond. I was hoping I wouldn't be needing that pluck, but there was no way to say that and still appear that I had any. However, if the Germans had packed away their mess tins and departed for more hospitable climes, as I expected, it would be a walkover. Not having ever experienced a walkover in my years at the front, some healthy caution was still only prudent.

Agent Trench was weakly manned. As I'd hoped it was a khaki-clad bunch from Manitoba doing the manning and not a platoon of stocky Bavarians reared on sausage, beer and alpine climbing, with a predilection for Maxim machine guns. The platoon from B Company under a Lieutenant Fowler was awaiting us. Anderson went off to confer with Fowler, and I let them be. As an equal in rank, albeit not in command of anything, I could have blustered myself an invite. But I was here strictly as an observer. It was their show; let them decide. You didn't become a good platoon commander with someone hovering over your shoulder muttering hints.

I occupied myself by checking first the magazine, and then the action on the Lee-Enfield. But the magazine had ten rounds in it, and I chambered one of them. Otherwise, it was in good working order. That couldn't be said of the boot one of the men had off and was furiously berating.

'If the sole's letting go, you should've asked for some new ones,' advised his mate.

'These are new! And I did ask, at the quartermaster's. But they're fresh out.'

'Fresh out of boots?'

'I wished I'd stuck with the old ones,' growled the soldier.

Then Anderson appeared and began moving down the line of his waiting platoon, giving instructions.

'All set?' I asked as he came up to me.

'As set as we'll ever be. What time do you have it?'

I glanced down. 'A quarter to midnight. Not quite. 11.44 p.m.'

He looked at his own watch and nodded. 'Good.' Then he told me the plan.

A minute later we clambered up the trench walls, and over a few newly placed sandbags that formed the new parapet. Our patrol veered to the right, and that of B Company to the left, but otherwise the approach was identical. We split into three well-spaced files of roughly fifteen men each, and I took up the rear position of the middle column. Slowly but deliberately we began walking across the open ground in a north-easterly direction, towards what Anderson had told me were some gaps in the wire.

Here in No-Man's-Land an oppressive silence reigned. It was often so. On its periphery, off near Méricourt, a field gun barked out, and to the left the cracking echo of a rifle, several rifles, could be heard. But nearby there was only the soft rustle of gear and of feet crunching forward to disturb the calm. Miles to the north, the horizon pulsed with a yellow glow, a distant rumbling as another barrage from the heavy howitzers came down upon Lens.

The ground was flat and unencumbered by obstacles, a farmer's field. While it bore the mark of shellfire, the fighting here was too recent and of too short a duration for the terrain to resemble the apocalyptic landscapes of the Somme, where every yard of earth had been churned and re-churned by high explosive. With clouds sailing overhead the night was reasonably dark. It took some time for my eyes to adjust. When they did, I peered forward, alert for signs of the enemy.

Suddenly I turned, for I thought I'd heard something, and there was a thump on my helmet. The feeling of it reverberated down through my body in a flash, the dull sound arriving only later. For an excruciating moment my stomach hung there. But when my heartbeat eased, and I concluded I was still standing, my hand traced over the rounded form of the tin bowl on my head. Encountering nothing untoward, I breathed out.

'A bird, sir,' hissed a man to my right. 'Startled.'

I inhaled deeply of the damp night air. Slowly I let it seep out of me, grateful for the fact I was still on my feet. The need to keep moving and thinking distracting me from thoughts better not thought.

After roughly 300 yards, with no visible sign of Avion Trench or the coiled barbs that preceded it, Anderson signalled a halt. Whereupon, as had been decided by the two lieutenants, the files melted away and the men adopted what was known as an attack formation. The long unwavering lines of men that had offered their machine guns such endless targets at the Somme were abandoned early this year, thanks in no small measure to our new corps commander, Lieutenant-General Currie. We remained there in the middle of nowhere, crouching in position – waiting upon the tick of a watch hand that would signal that the advance could continue.

Then Anderson's arm waved. One of the sergeant's repeated it, and we were off.

Avion Trench was almost precisely 500 yards northeast of Agent Trench. We had already walked two thirds of that distance, which meant that in a hundred yards we might expect to encounter an outpost, a man in a forward shell hole, or even a glimpse of the line itself. I'd left the planning to Fowler and Anderson, but beforehand I'd studied the map with considerable care. Preparation was key – that was the watchword we lived by these days.

After a hundred yards, or as close to it as I was able to estimate – neither the pace nor the ground being conducive to exactitude – I still saw nothing.

The men, relieved of such concerns by the presence of the NCOs and the lieutenant, carried on.

Through the gloom the first fence line appeared. Just behind those wire entanglements would be Avion Trench. The trench itself ran along what had once been the southernmost street in the village, houses to either side. The intelligence reports noted that the houses were shadows of their former selves, destroyed by shells or raised by our adversary – machine-gun positions in their stead. But the enemy was withdrawing, so with some luck they'd be gone, too.

Somewhere above us in the inky sky – no stars tonight – there was a pop. An altogether different sound than a Woolly-Bear prior to it hailing down shrapnel, but potentially lethal in its own way. It was a flare. Fritz was feeling antsy.

We maintained our progress and covered another ten feet.

Two more flares popped. These burst almost directly above the first group of men, individual figures easily visible to the eye as the sterile bluish-white lights glared down from above. A rifle cracked. More flares fizzed into life, one after the other. Twenty yards to either side the scene was lit up like an evening baseball game. It was at that moment that I realized that I'd terribly misjudged it. The trench was packed.

A machine gun began to rattle. A thousand fireflies began winking along the length of Avion Trench. Another MG was pounding. The sound of it ripped across a hundred yards of French countryside. A stray bullet zipped past, and I was thankful I'd sunk to my knees. Behind me I heard a gasp.

'The lieutenant is down,' came a shout from the group in front. That sent me off in a wild scrambling race to locate him. He'd be in one of the holes where the men were sheltering. Decisions had to be made. Half a battalion had us under fire.

Instead, I found Lieutenant Fowler. 'I'm MacPhail. Anderson's been hit,' I said by way of introduction.

'Christ,' he said. He looked anything but pleased. 'I don't know which idiot thought this up. Thinking that Avion Trench wouldn't be heavily garrisoned… they must have a hundred rifles there, if not more.'

'Very likely,' I replied. I remember thinking he'd underestimated it. 'So what now?' I asked.

'I don't see much choice, MacPhail. There's no way on Earth two platoons are going to take that trench.'

'No,' I agreed. 'No, they're not. We need to withdraw. I'll get D Company going. Good luck.'

I held the Lee-Enfield in one arm as I ran, although I might as well have been holding a crutch or a cane for all the good it was. There was nothing I or any of us could do against this storm of fire. In so many words that was what I told the first NCO I came to, before I again went in search of Anderson.

He was in pretty bad shape. It was all I could do to keep him upright and moving. Not that there was any choice. Quite a few men were down and those that weren't had their hands full. When at last we reached Adept Trench going on 2 a.m. I handed him over to two waiting stretcher bearers.

At the battalion dug-out they informed me I was summoned to headquarters. Before I left, I sat at the only table they possessed and condensed the night's action into a few routine and, because of that, utterly unsatisfying sentences. But no one was interested in more.

'Sir, there's something on your cheek,' said the corporal, when I passed it to him to be sent. With a sigh I went through the motions of rubbing. 'No, sir, it's still there.'

Whetting a finger I rubbed again. 'Better?'

He nodded.

Turning, I glanced cursorily at the finger. It was stained a deep crimson.

Well past dawn I reached Fort George, and only then because I was able to hitch a ride with a lorry from Petit Vimy all the way to Neuville. From there it had been less than a half-hour walk.

Colonel Hayter noted my arrival and approached. I drew myself up straight.

'I received your message, Lieutenant,' he said without preamble, his face divulging little. 'So it didn't work out?'

Thirteen men had fallen and Avion Trench was ever so firmly in enemy hands. To make matters worse, the result of the 58th Battalion's patrols on the Camerons' right was equally dismal. Fritz may have been withdrawing elsewhere – on our frontage he was obstinately dug in. It had been an exercise in futility. No wonder Hayter was questioning my judgement.

'No, sir,' I replied. 'It didn't work out.'

Hayter simply nodded.

CHAPTER 17

27th and 28th of June, 1917
Fort George, near Neuville-Saint-Vaast, France

To my surprise the colonel said nothing more about the failure of the patrols. Nor was I summoned by General Lipsett to explain myself, as I thought I might be. Even the other staff refrained from needless comment, something I found truly extraordinary. Although there was a perfectly obvious explanation for this last good fortune; they were busy with the preparations for a larger and more thorough assault. While I was prancing around No-Man's-Land on the erroneous assumption that the Germans were half way out the door, orders had already been drawn up to deal with the eventuality they were not. In case I hadn't grasped it earlier, there was a good reason why Hayter was the colonel, Lipsett the general, and MacPhail the subaltern.

During the long hours of the bone-weary day that followed – I'd missed a night's sleep and in the circumstances it didn't seem appropriate or seemly to mention that – the staff room was a busy place. The telephone buzzed incessantly. Mostly a succession of majors and captains calling to confirm some trivial detail, and occasionally someone from Corps headquarters with new, though hardly vital, information.

Nevertheless, I would have gladly occupied myself fielding their calls had I not already been assigned to a backwater, double-checking the numerous orders for errors and inconsistencies; 'You were the lawyer, MacPhail.' And when that was done the task of arranging the relief and billeting of the battalions following the attack found its way to my desk. Compared to early morning sentry duty, standing in frigid water up to my shins, I had few reasons for complaint. Still, I uttered a couple of foul ones in my head for good measure. Fotheringham, meanwhile, was returning from a quick word with the general, and terribly anxious to spread the news.

'General Lipsett would like to see me exposed to other aspects of staff work,' he said, all puffed up.

'But the latrines are in perfect working order,' I protested.

There was a derisive snort.

Naturally, I recognized the turn of phrase the general used immediately. He'd said something similar to me, almost verbatim, months earlier.

Fotheringham was convinced Lipsett's words were a precursor of greater and grander things to come. 'You know, I think he must be considering me for promotion,' he mused. Eyes rolled, mine barely stayed in my scalp, and someone guffawed loudly. The stupid thing was, no matter how ludicrous the notion would have sounded a month or two earlier, I wouldn't have bet against him – not anymore.

Then with helmet firmly in hand – helpfully I'd advised Fotheringham that an untimely piece of shrapnel might otherwise endanger his chances for promotion – he went forward to the 9th Brigade to serve as the exchange officer. With that distraction removed, I was able to return to a tricky problem involving a burnt down barn in Villers-Châtel, and the resulting shortage of near fifty beds. The number of beds required being a direct function of the success of the attack, I couldn't help wondering if my efforts were like so much surplus; although having come from the infantry that's not the sort of thing I like to speculate on.

Later at dinner time, while the others tromped noisily off to the mess, I snatched a few hours of sleep. It would probably be another sleepless night tonight and keeping my eyes open was already proving a challenge.

'You must have been tired, MacPhail,' marvelled Captain Ferguson, when I returned. 'Sacrificing a meal in favour of sleep!'

'And, oh, what a meal it was!' supplemented a second wit.

As one day passed into the next, and the hours added up until they came to 2.30 a.m., the first phase of the attack was launched. From a point north of the Souchez River to a penciled boundary two miles to the southeast, three divisions sent forth their soldiers. Stationed behind a telephone, as the duty-officer in the room, I didn't see or hear the barrage. Not directly. Telephone duty did allow me to experience it vicariously.

'I'm sorry, sir,' I said, talking much louder than normal, 'You'll have to speak up. I'm afraid I didn't hear the last thing you said.'

'The men are off nicely,' said a disembodied voice, followed by a further burst of words that were all but lost in a burst of shellfire in the background. Had he not coughed I probably would have wondered if the dug-out was still there.

'Yes, sir. And the enemy barrage?' I prompted. 'You mentioned the barrage, sir?'

'Desultory,' replied the battalion major. Even through miles of telephone wire that single word was infused with a quality that made the meaning entirely clear. The next time I was caught in a barrage I hoped I'd be able to describe it likewise.

'Thank you, sir, for your report. I'll pass it along to the general and Colonel Hayter.'

More details were not long in coming. On the heels of a stiff barrage it took the three battalions of the division less than an hour before they were on their objectives. The officer of the 9th Brigade who called in a report shortly thereafter noted that although the trench was securely in our hands, a number of the 5th Guard Grenadiers were obstinately refusing to leave their dug-outs. Fotheringham, when he called shortly thereafter, said they were being 'dealt with' – no explanation provided, and none asked for.

An hour before dawn, with the battalions digging in, Major Festing took pity and sent me to my bunk. However, after what seemed like no time at all, I was startled into consciousness by a gas alarm, a god-awful clanging in my head.

It turned out to be past noon and there was no gas alarm at all. With shell casing in hand, the dubious characters of my acquaintance had decided I couldn't possibly survive missing a third meal in twenty-four hours. When I finished thanking them trench style, I tagged along; there was some truth to what they'd said.

That evening ominous dark formations swept rapidly over the ridge, flashes of light rippled through the clouds like electric veins. The air was rumbling angrily as thunder rolled across. At round about the same time, or more precisely at 7.10 p.m., a whole assortment of naval guns, howitzers, field guns and trench mortars joined in the storm and the skies above the Douai Plain took on a most menacing appearance and sound. As the rain came pouring down in sheets, the second part of the operation got underway. Hurriedly, together with a couple of others, I ducked back into the Fort George dug-out.

Bennett's division, the Imperial 46th, was to occupy the remaining high ground of Hill 65 north of the river, while to the south the 4th Division was moving on Avion and Eleu dit Leauvette, the latter a strongpoint on the south bank and only a half mile from Lens. The 3rd Division's task was to work forward on the flank in concert. People were calling it a "push" operation. The noose was being tightened around Lens.

Whether Lens was of great strategic import was difficult to say and, while it was easy to say that little of what we did was "strategic" in nature, that applied to almost everything in a war of this magnitude. Personally, I had the impression it was a bit of a show, a very deadly show but a show nonetheless, to distract the German High Command from Field-Marshal Haig's huge offensive in the Salient. Having experienced the greater part of Messines Ridge blown up under their feet, I couldn't help thinking we would need one heck of a performance to distract the Germans from that.

Back from corps headquarters and a performance of his own, General Lipsett poked his head through the doorway. He was one of a high ranking delegation invited to greet His Royal Highness the Duke of Connaught this afternoon – the division had provided the band and the honour guard. I had little experience (recent or otherwise) with royalty. I had, however, spent a considerable portion of my time of late traipsing around the front line – providing a useful reminder about the importance of paying attention to your senses. It was the sandy rasp of the general's leather soles on the planks that made me look up.

Taken aback, his presence so sudden and unexpected, I just kept gawking like some recruit who'd spotted his very first Hun in the flesh. Lipsett noticed my glance – his gaze not unfriendly, neutral rather – but then even more disconcertingly, he looked straight through me.

'Ross,' he said, lifting a hand to command attention. There was a clatter behind me.

'Ah, General. Yes, I'm coming.'

'The work is on your desk, MacPhail,' hissed Hayter, as he brushed past.

While it would be well into the next day before all the details were gathered and known, it was soon evident that our attack had come as a surprise (one of the few benefits of a thunderstorm). The stream of messages arriving were uniformly positive. Step by step the enemy was being forced back on Lens.

At a certain moment, Lipsett came to the telephone himself and spoke with Lieutenant Fotheringham, which I'm sure sent Fotheringham aflutter.

I was more interested in what the colonel said to Lipsett afterwards.

'Yes, he did fine,' I heard Hayter say. Unfortunately I was unable to hear what the general said. But such words from the colonel were definitely high praise. Although for the life of me I couldn't figure out how, or why, Fotheringham deserved them. Maybe it was simply a question of surpassing low expectations – he had after all found his way to Petit Vimy without getting lost.

Sourly I screwed up my mouth and went back to my papers.

CHAPTER 18

1st of July, 1917
Fort George, near Neuville-Saint-Vaast, France

Dominion Day began like any other day; first there was a hurried appraisal of the night's actions, then everyone scrambled to do what had to be done before the day could truly begin. Because all the divisions save the 2nd were in the line, the traditional festivities were to be low-key. Even the annual games didn't carry the frisson of excitement they ought to have; there were too few men taking part to make it much of an Olympiad. The only real fireworks were those planned for noon. It was therefore with a certain feeling of anticipation that all who could assembled on the grassy ground near the battalion huts north of Neuville-Saint-Vaast, under a brilliant blue sky, to watch the honours being paid to our national day. And to think longingly of home.

At the designated hour guns from the entire Corps went off. From behind walls, ensconced in sunken roads, mounted on rail cars, and hidden in small copses and on the reverse slopes of small hills, they fired their salvoes in unison. It was a hearty, blustering roar that did each of us good and resonated for twenty miles or more in every direction. Heaven knows what the army bean counters would later make of this wanton spillage of ammunition – we were forever using more than our share, being ticked on the fingers for our extravagance as a consequence. Benoît had told me. Strangely, one never heard the same outrage when the casualties proved excessive. However, as General Currie was fond of saying – or something approximating it – avoiding the latter necessitated the former; shells versus casualties. It made sense to me. Newly promoted, and newly knighted, I was nevertheless sceptical he'd found any converts to this revolutionary way of thinking.

'Well, that was that, eh,' said a soldier when it was over.

'Happy Dominion Day,' pronounced another. 'Nothing like a good holiday.' There was a smattering of laughter.

In contrast to the stereotype, there are some who say Germans have a good sense of humour. I doubt however they were aware of the existence of national holidays in the British Empire's nether regions, let alone the precise dates, and a holiday celebrated with a few pops of a gun wouldn't have sent them grasping at their bellies in laughter. Still, they were awfully quiet. In the wake of the midday hullabaloo Fritz was more bashful than most church mice of my acquaintance.

I'd recently gone on record predicting our enemy would scramble to fire a retaliatory strafe in response to the fireworks, my confidence based on their previous weeks' jitteriness. Yet like so many of my predictions of late this too appeared to be a misfire. But perhaps their intelligence section was better than I realized. More likely they were so baffled how to respond to guns firing from every which way they simply kept their heads down; when in doubt duck, as my old sergeant-major wisely instructed.

An hour later a message arrived that caused some nervous flutters of excitement. The Major-General General Staff (MGGS) of the First Army had informed Corps Headquarters that the 46th Division was being counter-attacked. He ordered a battalion of ours be sent north to act in reserve, in case matters got out of hand. While it was one of the 2nd Division's battalions that got the call, it was yet another nail in the coffin of Dominion Day.

Fortunately, the counter-attack was of little consequence. The war carried on with the usual patrols, the local shelling, and the tussling over sections of trench. On our front there was also a relief or two. By far the most remarkable development occurred within spitting range of me, and at a fork's length from dinner time. Captain Ferguson and Major McAvity were in a real flap about it.

'They knew when our attack was to come!?' asked McAvity of

Ferguson. Excepting the choice of a word or two, this was the second time he'd asked the exact same thing. Patiently, Ferguson nodded again. I'd heard Ferguson perfectly the first time he spoke – at twenty paces.

But witnessing Major McAvity in a tizzy had a curious appeal, and what Ferguson had said was actually rather shocking. So my ears perked up and I raised myself out of a slouch. Temporarily my protesting stomach was assigned a position in the rear, where it could growl at will without distracting.

'Yes, sir,' said Ferguson. He'd evidently concluded there was a need for further elaboration. 'One of their larger Ah Rent stations behind the lines has been intercepting our telephone communications.' Naturally he muddled the German; not that I could have done better. But he meant an *Ahrendtstation*, a listening post to intercept communications. 'They're using one of the large sets, according to the prisoner. His friend who works there told him they overhear much of our communications, from as far back as the telephone lines between division and brigade.'

'My God,' whispered McAvity. 'Do you realize what that means, Captain?'

Ferguson bobbed his head up and down.

'Did he say anything else?'

'Only that he thinks they're using their old telephone wires to tap our calls. He said it was certain they were aware of our intent to attack on 28th, and even knew that it was to come in the evening. Apparently the information was disseminated as far down as the company commanders.'

'Good Lord. I need to inform the Colonel and General Lipsett,' said McAvity.

If I'd been in McAvity's boots, I would have immediately asked why our attack came as such a surprise if the Germans knew all along. I suspect McAvity would think of that eventually. But before he could ask, a man loomed up in front of me –a full solar eclipse. He stood there, five foot ten with the broad shoulders and thick arms of a labourer, shuffling from foot to foot, blocking my line of sight and utterly spoiling my hearing.

Usually I have a weak spot for the soldier who goes up against the enemy without a second thought, but lapses into an embarrassed muddle when presented with an officer. This fellow I was ready to send packing. Finally he spoke: 'Lieutenant MacPhail?' I nodded. 'Lieutenant DuBois sent me.'

I looked at him with surprise. For a frightfully long time he paused, mulling over what to say next.

My patience broke. 'Yes, yes,' I snapped. 'But what does he want?'

'He asked if you would join him in his quarters, sir.'

'In his quarters? I'm busy as it happens. And when I'm done I was intending to find something to eat.'

'He said it was important, sir.'

Wearily I sighed. Knowing Benoît he'd made the acquaintance of some local farm girl, far too young and far too fetching, and wanted to describe her dress in endless detail while I attempted to translate the finer points of country fashion, and perhaps more, from French into English.

'*Very* important, sir,' stressed the private, seeing my reaction, and now suddenly sure of his business. It made me wonder what Benoît had promised him. Something consumable I'd guess.

'Oh, alright... Where the blazes is the good lieutenant?'

Once the man had told me, completed an awkward about-face on the planks and marched off, I lifted my head to retune the wireless to McAvity and Ferguson.

Only McAvity had disappeared. And Ferguson was furiously scribbling on a message pad. Asking the captain what had been said was asking altogether too much. The last time I'd enquired about some relatively innocuous detail, he'd looked furtively both ways and replied: 'I'm sorry, Mac. I'd love to tell you, but it's secret.'

I went in search of Benoît. The private said he was presently billeted in one of the many huts in the grounds behind Fort George – news to me – but fortunately he knew a number and a letter for the row, and then it was child's play. A trifle grumpy from the heat, and not having eaten, the walk gave me some time to think about what I'd heard.

The telephone was instrumental to our communications. More so every day as the war progressed. No one chose to send a written cable anymore, not if they could speak through a headpiece to the very person they wanted to communicate with and get an instant reply.

Most everything of any importance was said through a telephone, and barely a word of it was coded. So if a German listening station was able to hear what was spoken through a line fully two miles from the front, it was a serious matter. Battles could be lost.

A signalman had once explained a bit of the theory. Field telephones require a closed electric circuit, one line connecting sender to receiver, and a return line which completed the circuit. That added up to two separate lines – math even a lawyer could understand – and where a single line was a bleeding headache to lay, bury and keep active, two lines doubled the trouble. Ingeniously a solution had been found. Rather than laying that extra line, some genius had discovered that the earth itself was a wonderful conductor. Thus the second line, attached to a bayonet and spiked into the earth, carried the current back to the sender, completing the circuit.

But an electric current is a fickle thing. Much like my wilful Labrador on the scent of something wonderful, it never followed the direct path you laid out, but went bounding off in all directions – all 360 degrees to be precise. Which was where the old German telephone lines and this clever apparatus of theirs came into use. The lines were used to pick up the currents and relay them back to a listening station. There they were amplified, the currents turned into sound, and the sound meticulously transcribed.

The British had done it first, but the Germans were quick learners. McAvity's concern was all too real. Even if it remained strange that the enemy, forewarned, had been so woefully unprepared that blustery Thursday, the 28th of June. It had been one hell of a thunderstorm, admittedly.

Benoît was uncharacteristically somber when I reached him. Sober, too, but that was soon explained.

'Hi Mac.'

A terse smile.

A broad grin from me.

'Hi Benoît,' I said, offering him a hand. 'So what's the urgent summons all about?' He stiffened. A little friendly jesting and parrying was part of our age-old routine, but this evening I sensed something was wrong. So I didn't pursue it and kept my peace.

'I've been confined to quarters,' he said.

'You have?' "Why?" and "By whom?" were the first two questions that sprang to mind, and I could easily have thought of a half dozen others. But I didn't ask and pulled up a chair instead. He'd tell me in his own good time.

'You see I was at Château de la Haie. We're moving our headquarters there in a few days and I was supposed to make some arrangements.' I nodded. Château de la Haie was a small hamlet in the hinterland behind Vimy Ridge. 'And when I was done, I decided to take a *petit promenade* to see the sights. Maybe even find a new *estimanet*.'

'And? Were there any?'

He shook his head. Whether he meant there were no sights or no estaminets was unclear. Neither probably. Château de la Haie was not the kind of place rich in diversions. 'But then I kept seeing these children everywhere, playing. That's not so strange, of course. But every one of them was wearing army boots. Can you imagine? Some of them were so little the boots came to their knees.'

'Army boots? Are you sure about that?'

'C'mon, Mac, I've seen plenty of army boots. They were army boots, alright. Brand new too. So I went over to the children. Gave them some sweets and began to talk. I asked where the boots came from. At first they were shy, until I said I was from the army, so they could tell me. But I don't think they really knew much. One of the older ones said that a man from the army had given them to them.'

'Not from the army I'm familiar with,' I mumbled.

'*Non*, that's what I thought. And I was going to ask more, but then a staff car pulled up. It came up real sudden, and your friend Captain Smythe got out.'

'He's not my friend,' I interrupted quickly.

Benoît shrugged. 'Anyhow, he started to ask me all sorts of questions. He was very aggressive. Why I was there with the children? What business did I have meddling with them, asking questions? Did my commanding officer know I was slacking off? That sort of thing.'

'What did you say?'

'I tried to explain but he kept demanding answers, and I'm afraid I lost my temper.' Forlornly he looked at his feet. 'I said a few things,' he mumbled. 'Then the captain said I was drunk and he intended to put me up on charges.'

'Were you?'

'Mac!'

I caught his look and held it.

'I had a small taste from the canteen. But that's all, Mac! You have to believe me.'

'Well thankfully he didn't catch you breaking into a brewery,' I laughed. I remembered precisely such an occurrence, the soldier's thirst getting the better of him, somehow unaware production had ceased back in 1914 due to unforeseen circumstances.

Unusually, DuBois didn't join in the merriment. 'They'll take my commission,' he said glumly.

'What happened then?'

'I was too shocked to say anything. The captain told me he would discuss my case with the authorities. I was to return to quarters and stay there until I heard from him.'

'He can't confine you to quarters!'

'Maybe not, but he suggested it would be better for me if I did as he told me.'

'Ridiculous,' I bristled. 'If he wants to lay charges that's a different matter. However, not only is he from another division, he's just a captain. Who does he think he is? And charges for what? It isn't as if you refused orders to go over the top. Half the army is walking around with a drink inside of them, and you weren't even drunk. In addition to which you were miles from the front. Frankly, Smythe doesn't stand a chance. This is ludicrous.'

Benoît looked a little uneasy.

'There's something else, isn't there?'

'The brigadier was with him in the car.'

'I see. The brigadier? You mean Long Archie Macdonell of the 5th Brigade.'

'*Oui.*'

I grimaced. 'So you think Smythe will bring him into it?'

Benoît nodded. He was the biggest soldier I'd ever seen, but his eyes were those of a child reprimanded and told to stand in the corner. The injustice of it made me livid.

'Alright. I'll see what I can do.'

'Thanks, Mac. I knew you'd help.'

CHAPTER 19

3rd of July, 1917
Lièvin, France

'Captain, this is preposterous, sir,' I said, raising my voice. 'Not only was Lieutenant DuBois not drunk, he was on duty as ordered. Might I remind you, sir, those duties are determined by his commanding officer in the 3rd Divisional Artillery, not by officers of the 5th Brigade staff.'

'You were a barrister before the war, weren't you MacPhail?' said Captain Smythe. I stood in front of him, while he sat relaxed on a chair, nonchalantly ignoring everything I said. He didn't deign to explain or even argue, but repeated 'No, Lieutenant MacPhail' at intervals, accompanied by dismissive waves of his hand. For the occasion of my visit he had pushed his chair well away from the desk, crossed one leg over the other and was leaning slightly backwards, as if relaxing at some gentleman's club. What I wouldn't have given to have provided a firm shove.

I smiled thinly. 'Yes, sir, that's correct. I was a lawyer.'

'Hmm. I thought so. You sound like one. Although don't think that will help you here, MacPhail. Besides, it's out of my hands. Brigadier Macdonell will decide whether or not to press charges. But I must add, Lieutenant, it looks rather grim for your man. The brigadier witnessed the events himself.'

'He was sitting in the back of a staff car!'

Smythe shrugged.

'I'd like to speak with the brigadier, sir.'

He frowned. Then glancing up, a bemused look came sailing across.

'That's possible, Lieutenant,' said an even-keeled voice behind me. It was a voice I didn't immediately recognize, and in my experience that's typically not a good sign.

Being outflanked is one of the worst fears any infantry officer can have. This was worse. I'd been caught in the rear, with no hope of withdrawal, or even of digging in. The infantry had several pithy words to describe the predicament, none of which required any particular imagination.

Brigadier-General Macdonell's eyes warily took in my appearance as I came to attention. At first glance I don't think he recognized me. But I sure recognized him.

'Well, sir,' I began to stutter. Then I recovered sufficiently to go on to make what I thought was a decent case for DuBois's innocence. 'It was after all, only a small nip he took, sir,' I concluded. 'No harm done.'

'Oh, there's much more to it than a small nip,' observed Long Archie. He looked to Smythe who had also gotten to his feet at the sight of him, and had started to nod. 'Remind us please what the charges are that are being contemplated, Captain Smythe.'

Smythe plucked a piece of paper from a pile on his desk, cleared his throat, and began to read: 'Drunk when on active service, one charge; conduct to prejudice of good order and military discipline, one charge; insubordination, one charge; hesitation to obey an order, one charge; threatening a superior officer, one charge.'

I stood there, my mouth agape. At home the young lawyers I'd known had an expression for it when the Crown came down hard on a suspect – an expression which soon became a verb. We called it being "wallpapered", in reference to the multi-page, heavily-bound criminal code. Outside of a court of law the tome would have made a fine implement in a trench fight, though unfortunately I'd forgotten to bring mine overseas. In contrast to its civilian counterpart, military code was surprisingly concise, but no less onerous for its brevity. Benoît was being wallpapered with no less than five articles of it.

Military courts were usually provisional affairs, the members scraped together at the last minute from officers in the field, few of whom possessed the time or the expertise to properly weigh a case. In fact I suspected there'd be even less weighing of facts or arguments when the charges were brought by a brigadier-general. An artillery lieutenant from an out-of-the-way backwater like Trois-Rivières didn't stand much of a chance.

'Sir!' I sputtered. 'There must be some mistake. Lieutenant DuBois is a loyal and conscientious officer, and a heck of a fighter. I can't imagine for a minute him doing any of those things.'

Long Archie sighed, bored with the turn the conversation was taking, and maybe even a little irritated at the demands I was making on his time. 'He most certainly did, Lieutenant. Captain Smythe has assured me of all of it. Now if you'll excuse me, I have other business.'

It was too early for dinner, and somehow I couldn't picture the brigadier bending over a map for hours on end with only a dixie of tea at his side as I'd seen General Lipsett do, so that left me puzzling. What business could he possibly be referring to? Having his boots polished, perhaps? While I puzzled, he stomped off. Smythe gave me a smug "I told you so" look.

Demonstrating my better side, I clamped firmly down on my tongue. Politely, I thanked Smythe and his Brigadier for their time, and told him how certain I was they would soon realize their 'honest mistake'. Then I left. The other option had been to run for it, and lob a Mill's bomb over my shoulder on the way out.

Only yesterday the staff of the 5th Brigade had moved to Liévin, establishing their headquarters in the cellar of a brick building in the centre of the small town, not far from the station. The ground floor had long since been rendered unusable, and it was only by way of comparison that the dank crumbling walls of the cellar looked better. Like most everything in Liévin, the railway no longer worked, had I wished to use that. Meanwhile the use of a staff car had been out of the question for this mildly clandestine activity; I had no desire to draw attention to Benoît's plight – that would do his career no good whatsoever. So I'd just slipped away. But at five miles and a bit from Fort George, I was reconsidering the wisdom of my tactics. The day was blistering hot, breaths of air too short and too warm to provide any relief. Had I been the bearer of good news, I might have looked upon the return journey with different eyes, but my visit was nothing short of disastrous.

Tired, with rivulets of dust-filled sweat pouring down my face, and my feet aching, I reached Fort George. There was no point postponing it and I immediately sought out Benoît. He'd taken my advice and resumed his duties. I caught him outside the artillery hut.

He took the news surprisingly well. In fact, he'd recovered surprisingly well from his lack of composure two days earlier. If anything, he seemed less surprised than me at the profusion of charges levelled against him.

'You'd better tell me everything,' I said firmly. 'Smythe is a two-bit nobody out for himself, but he barely knows you, Benoît. Why is he so determined to see you in a military jail?'

There was a long moment of silence. 'I told you I lost my temper.'

I nodded. 'And?'

'Look, Mac, I said a few words. I may even have waved a hand in front of his face.'

A groan came bubbling up. 'Oh, dear.'

'It's not as bad as you think. I didn't touch him.'

'Thank God for small mercies.' I could picture easily enough how it had gone. Benoît affronted by Smythe's superior tone, and irritated by the sheer obdurateness of the questioning; a few choice words from the trenches spoken in response; Smythe arrogantly unrepentant; then a confrontational step forward underscoring the massive difference in height and weight between the two men; and finally a fist shook in the air for emphasis, perhaps under Smythe's nose. Some officers might have waved off the incident. Most officers would have. But apparently not Smythe. From Benoît's mouth it all sounded innocent enough. But that's not what Long Archie would have heard. Or what a court of senior officers would surely hear. Benoît had good reason to worry.

Naturally I didn't say that. Instead I said: 'For the life of me I don't understand how it got so out of hand –' I was, however, beginning to form some theories of my own.

Benoît shrugged.

'One thing in your favour. I don't think the brigadier actually saw or heard anything himself. He seems to be relying completely on Smythe's account of events. So somehow we're going to have get Smythe to recant or, more likely, find something to cast him in an unreliable light. That won't be easy, Benoît, seeing as he outranks us both.'

'Mac, they shot two men this morning at dawn.'

'Who did?'

'The brigadier.'

Puzzled I just stared.

'They were executed this morning. Comté and LaLancette from le Vingt-Deuxième.' The 22nd Battalion was one of four in Long Archie's Brigade, and of course Benoît knew I would know that.

'Why?'

'Desertion.'

'Oh. That's completely different, Benoît. I wouldn't read too much into it. They're trying to set an example. And, remember, Long Archie probably had nothing to do with those charges.'

'*Non*, but he did approve the sentences.'

It was a valid point. I made certain to keep my face studiously neutral.

There was something about this whole affair which simply didn't add up. For all Benoît had done, it amounted to nothing. It was a joke, a farce. Yet Benoît was facing the possibility of imprisonment and, if not imprisonment, he most certainly risked losing his commission. What I couldn't understand was why. Why had Smythe singled him out? Or was it simply an unhappy coincidence like the German army taking a wrong turn across the Belgian frontier in 1914? I didn't much believe in coincidences.

There was more to Captain Smythe than met the eye. For Benoît's sake it appeared that I would need to make it my business to find out a lot more about the man.

In the meantime, I was expected in the staff room.

Colonel Hayter raised his head abruptly and watched me as I squeaked through the doorway on a plank that seemed designed to keep the chief of staff aware of any untoward comings and goings. Noticing Hayter's reaction I walked straight to my desk, as if I'd only popped out for a moment. To my relief he resumed the study of whatever he'd been studying.

Captain Ferguson of the "I" section caught my eye. And I got up and walked over to him.

Fotheringham was observing me even while he pretended not to. Not long ago I'd made the mistake of telling him I thought the future was in the intelligence section. Whether that was true or not – it certainly interested me more than the mundane, albeit important, details I was usually preoccupied with – I regretted telling him. Of late I saw him as Hayter's pet (it was as yet unclear what General Lipsett's view on the subject of pets was), and as such the first in line for a new position in the section.

'Captain.' I nodded to Ferguson.

'Ah, there you are, Malcolm. If you have a moment, I wondered if you might help out with the intelligence summary. It's in my hands today, and I'm afraid I left it a little late. The colonel will be looking for it soon.'

'Sure,' I replied. While I had my own tasks, there was no harm in having at least one ally at headquarters. A further advantage to compiling an intelligence summary was that you learned what was actually going on. Which made me think of something.

'One thing,' I said. 'I've been wondering about it.'

Ferguson looked at me quizzically.

'I still don't understand how our attack on the 28th was a surprise when the Boche knew the date and time from intercepting our telephone calls?'

His eyes widened. 'How did you know about that?' he asked sharply. 'About the telephone calls?'

I shrugged. 'Heard it from a Fritz, I think.'

Even Ferguson saw the silliness in pursuing this line of questioning and smiled wanly. 'I don't know,' he replied. 'My theory is it must have been because of the thunderstorm.'

'Yes,' I agreed. 'It must have been that. I do hope people are watching what they say on the telephone in future, though.'

Ferguson nodded.

Drawing up the intelligence summary turned out to be a straightforward undertaking, only the usual patrols and artillery bombardments to report. The single thing I did learn was from the wireless news – that the Manchu Dynasty had been restored – and while Chinese politics were undoubtedly fascinating, I'd been hoping to hear about more local developments. With the conclusion of last month's operations, we'd entered the lull before the storm. It couldn't be otherwise. You didn't have to be on the front for long to know that storms never took long in coming.

'No word what they have in mind for us?' I asked Ferguson.

'No, not that I've heard.'

'And Lens?'

'What about it?'

'We're already parked on the doorstep. It seems a logical objective, don't you think?'

'I don't know anything about that. But you might be right, Mac. You might very well be right.'

For all the talk of withdrawal the Germans were still firmly entrenched in the town. Which meant that if we were asked to dislodge them it would be a furious scrap, most likely from house to house. Nothing we'd done previously had prepared us for that. It was a worrisome prospect.

CHAPTER 20

8th of July, 1917
Bois de l'Hirondelle, southeast of Lièvin, France

Following the example that General Lipsett had drilled into me this past year, I'd decided it was time to make a reconnaissance of my own. Other than doing it in my own hours (not that the army is a believer in "own" hours) there was no harm to come from it, and something useful might.

Hill 65 had been my initial choice of a vantage spot. Known in the time before trench maps as Reservoir Hill due to the two water reservoirs on its summit – presumably there to slake the thirst of nearby Lièvin and the many surrounding coal mining settlements – it was steep sided, 65 metres in elevation (thus explaining its name), and less than a mile southwest of Lens. It was captured only weeks before by Hollace Bennett's 46th Division and afforded an excellent view of the entirety of the town and surroundings. These latter characteristics were explained to me by a forward artillery observer when I solicited his opinion on where I should go.

'Don't forget to make some notes, MacPhail,' said Major McAvity when I told him what I intended to do, and where. 'They may come in handy. But keep your wits about you. There's a new observation post on that hill, and the Boche are well aware of it. Also I'm told they occasionally use the water reservoirs as targets to calibrate their guns.'

Which is when I decided to look for alternatives. Fortunately there were some, and the Bois de l'Hirondelle was the helpful suggestion of another artillery man.

With this blessing (of sorts) from McAvity, I was able to inveigle the loan of a small Ford from the divisional pool, with driver no less. How different it had been for my trip to Lièvin days earlier. Then I'd puzzled over the maps beforehand, trying to calculate the optimal route in terms of distance, the height of the hills I would need to climb, and the overall degree of perilousness. My careful planning hadn't proved an overwhelming success – even discounting the encounter with Captain Smythe and Long Archie. A car and driver was sheer luxury.

Today my driver, a shy, curly-haired lad from the Fraser Valley with two red apples for cheeks, assured me that not only did he know the place, he knew the very quickest way. I assured him that was of far less importance than getting there in one piece – the new fellows were terribly keen. Ultimately he chose the plank road over Vimy Ridge, then turned to the northwest and followed the path along the northern side of the ridge through Petit Vimy, until Givenchy. There we turned right. 'The Hamilton Road, sir,' he announced.

'Sounds about right,' I replied. He could have told me it was the Champs Elysée and I would have fallen for it, but there was no need to advertise my ignorance. Following this bumpy track for another ten minutes heading northeastwards, we soon rolled to a halt.

The first thing that struck me about the Bois de l'Hirondelle was that it was not as advertised. My French was known to leave me in the lurch on occasion, but I was quite positive that *bois* implied a forest somewhere. Yet there was barely a tree to be seen, certainly not one you'd readily recognize as such. With the arrival of war, the nomenclature of many a French landmark needed an overhaul; churches and entire villages were reduced to piles of stone and plaster, and forests to muddy fields. Muddy fields for the most part were unchanged.

However, nature was fiercely resilient. A coarse yellow grass blanketed the slopes of the hill, denser near the top and swaying in the breeze like ripe wheat on the prairies back home. Despite the absence of much spring rain the grass had grown almost to knee height. In the absence of trees, I initially feared I would need to conceal myself in some water-filled shell hole, so the grass was welcome. Furthermore the weather had turned wet this morning. The heavy showers would have transformed the dry earth into a morass were it not for the grass. Puffing more than I should have at my age I reached the viewpoint; it turned out to be a fair climb, 90 metres at its peak. At that juncture another deluge began.

The drops beat down in a terrific frenzy on my helmet, soaking my shoulders and the back of my tunic. For a moment I debated returning to the car and waiting it out. But then it might not pass. The tale of me wiling away precious hours in a staff car so as to avoid a little precipitation was better not told. If Fotheringham did get the promotion it wasn't going to be because MacPhail wilted under a little rain. Besides, lying in some wet grass beat doing it under a blazing sun dressed in thick wool, and with two-and-a-half pounds of tin on my head to soak up the heat.

Once the shower passed, I endeavoured to find a suitable spot in the grass. I sneezed as the sun re-emerged, with a renewed ferocity, the smell of fresh hay filling my nostrils. Then I clamped the borrowed field glasses to my eyes and gazed out.

There was no denying the view was glorious. A panorama that began to my left with the massive spindly shaft and ruins of Fosse no. 3 visible to the northwest. Completing a long sweeping turn to the right, Avion, Méricourt, Arleux and Vimy Ridge all passed into sight; all names where the fighting had been hard, most now belonging to the history books, or so one hoped.

Directly in front of me at a distance I guessed to be roughly a mile, lines of crumpled masonry and brick marked out Lens. Through the glasses the details were astonishing, the streets and buildings startling in their proximity. There were rows of miners' quarters in the many suburbs that ringed the town: Cité du Moulin, Cité St. Antoine, Cité St. Elisabeth, Cité St. Émile, and others. Beyond them was the town centre. And everywhere in the surrounds were larger structures such as factories, mine installations, and administrative centres – most built in red brick, some in steel girders, the grander ones in white stone. They were equally battered by shellfire, all save the lone church on a hill near Lens with an imposing girth and a large cross at its peak. It was seemingly unperturbed by war, standing vigilant watch; even if that notion seemed superfluous given that the Germans had moved in two years before.

It was no secret that the boys were stiff with tension and impatience, anxious to get on with the next show. Our creeping, inexorable advance on Lens was becoming a siege, yet even in such conditions the casualties mounted rapidly: hostile shelling, sniping, raids, simple accidents that turned fatal. Every day brought its own toll. They would mount further if the siege became an assault, as I suspected it would.

Then, from a most improbable quarter, my suspicions about our objective were confirmed in a way that I could never have predicted.

Lying there, studying the ground, I heard a sudden rustling of the grass behind me. Alarmed, I turned and reached for my revolver. We were well behind our lines, and in complete safety from a Boche raid, but instinct is a powerful thing. I was in time to see a soldier coming in fast in the final approaches of an ungainly landing. Before I could say or do anything, he landed next to me with a heady *thump*. A sizeable swath of grass and a number of poppies were flattened.

He was a big man, by any definition. He was also an officer, for he wore a shiny Sam Browne belt and calf-length leather boots of a quality appreciated by earls and similar types. Tightly wound round his upper arm was a red-striped band that marked him out as belonging to the corps staff. There was no question at all who it was. He was not a man to lurk in the shadows, least of all because no shadow would have covered him.

'Sweet Jesus', I murmured to myself.

Having established himself in the wet grass to his apparent satisfaction, he glanced my way. His jaw appeared to drop when he saw who it was. The new commander of the Canadian Corps, Lieutenant-General Arthur Currie, solemnly straightened his helmet, retrieved his jaw, and took careful stock.

To all appearances the general was completely on his own. There wasn't another soul in sight.

'Good morning,' he said in a hoarse voice, as if his morning had been anything but. 'I hope you don't mind me joining you, Lieutenant? I see you've found yourself an excellent vantage point.'

'Morning, sir.' I was too flummoxed by his arrival to think of something more original.

'It would appear the two of us are engaged in a similar activity.' He looked at me amiably, and I smiled in return. His eyes widened a touch. 'MacPhail, isn't it?'

'Yes, sir. That's right.' The last time he'd spoken with me was as GOC of my old division, long before the promotion that made him corps commander. Encounters with generals were still rare enough in my experience as to remember the event, although I hadn't expected he would.

'Yes,' he mused, 'I thought it must be you.' From under his tunic he extracted a pair of the finest field glasses I'd ever seen and began to survey the scene.

I followed his example. The Souchez River was virtually at our doorstep, flowing in the direction of Lens where its extension, the Canal de Lens, delineated the southern boundary of town with the rail yards to the left, and Fosse no. 5 and Cité St. Antoine to the right. Sallaumines Hill was clearly visible further to the east of the canal. There, the wrecked headframes of two mine shafts protruded from the hill's rounded top, like watch towers of medieval times. It was between that hill and the town that the Germans had constructed the extension of their Oppy-Méricourt-Vendin Line, to which I and others had once supposed they would withdraw. In light of recent events the very thought seemed lunacy.

To the northwest of Lens was Hill 70. It was better described as an extended ridge, rather than a hill proper. Its highest point, from which it drew its name, loomed over the town below like the battlements of a castle.

'What explains your interest here, MacPhail?' asked General Currie. No less than ten minutes had passed. During that time neither he nor I had said anything. Even now he was speaking out of the side of his mouth, his glasses still jutting forward.

I put mine down and peered towards him through the grass. 'Well, sir, it's like this. Unless we're sent north to the Salient – and somehow that doesn't strike me as likely – I was thinking that the only other alternative was that we'd have to take Lens. So I figured I'd come here and take a closer look; see what we'd be up against. Should General Lipsett ask in future, this way I'd have something to tell him.'

There was no profit in adding that neither Lipsett nor Hayter were apt to consult me. But on the off chance my suspicions about our next objective were on the mark, at least I wouldn't be chewing on teeth like Fotheringham if they did ask. On top of which, this kept my mind off Benoît, whose predicament was increasingly preoccupying me. These last few days I had the impression I was more worried about the muddle he was in than he was himself.

Currie lowered his glasses. 'You've seen the lay of the land, MacPhail. Supposing the Corps *was* asked to take the town, what would you tell General Lipsett about your reconnaissance?'

Suddenly all my bravado and bold ideas felt a little thin on the ground. It's one thing pontificating to the divisional staff over morning coffee, even with a captain or two looking on. This was the Corps commander asking. I took a deep breath.

'The first thing I'd tell him, sir, was that it would be a very costly operation. I imagine every cellar in Lens has a Boche in it waiting to come up and greet us. Although I hardly think I'd need to explain that. I'm sure he knows it already. However, the second thing –'

Currie cocked an eyebrow.

I hesitated.

'Go on, Lieutenant.'

'The second thing is more of a question, sir. I would ask him whether attacking and consolidating the town might not put us in a veritable hornets' nest, sir. At least as long as the Germans hold those two hills.' Helpfully I pointed at them, although it was patently obvious which bumps on the horizon I was referring to – nervousness I expect. For someone expected to respond with 'how high?' when told to jump, this was uncharted territory.

The general however didn't appear bothered in the slightest at this incursion into grand strategy. Nevertheless, he kept his own views to himself, and merely nodded thoughtfully. 'What would you say if the objective was not the town, but rather one of those hills? Say, Hill 70.'

Momentarily I frowned. Then as I mulled over the consequences, my mind began to race. 'That would put the boot firmly on the other foot, sir,' I grinned. 'We could direct our artillery fire from the hill. We'd see their movements for miles. They wouldn't like that one bit, sir. No, they wouldn't like that at all.' Then I frowned. 'In fact I can't imagine them standing for it at all, when I think about it. Their entire position in Lens would be under threat. They'd feel obliged to throw everything they had at us.'

'Yes, I imagine they would, Lieutenant.'

Then another thought bubbled up, and this one, too, I felt compelled to share. 'Of course, sir, if Fritz was *so* worked up about it, that might provide us with an opportunity of sorts –'

It was Currie's turn to frown. But then the dime stopped spinning and fell over to reveal itself. 'Ah,' he said, softly. 'Yes, I see your point, Lieutenant. Employ their Verdun strategy against them.'

'Indeed, sir. Bleed them white, so to speak.' There was no pulling the wool over the general's eyes. He was far too quick-witted for that; in no time he'd grasped the essence of the idea. I hadn't considered the parallel with Verdun in 1916, though it did bear a curious resemblance. Falkenhayn, the German commander, had based his plans on the notion that the French would feel compelled by history and by sentiment to throw in their reserves *en masse* to defend Verdun; reserves that the German heavy guns and defensive positions would then annihilate. In the end it didn't work out that way, and Hindenburg was given Falkenhayn's job in the aftermath. But I didn't need to remind the general of any of that. He knew his history. As two of a party visiting Verdun he and I had heard about it firsthand.

Far across the plain a gun went off. For some reason this commonplace sound caught my attention. A dramatic silence followed until it was relieved by an extended *screech*, directly overhead. An instant later the shell exploded in a deep bang less than a hundred yards to our rear. That was far enough removed not to pose a danger, but close enough that I feared what a second might do.

'It's a good thing we're not on Hill 65, sir.'

Currie frowned.

'Apparently the enemy is using the reservoirs on the hill for target practice. Hopefully that wasn't an overshoot.'

Currie looked vaguely amused at this information. 'Are they indeed? For the first time that I can recall, MacPhail, I find myself wishing that their aim was true.'

As jokes go it wasn't much, but under the circumstances I found it amusing. Until the next shell fell, and both of us winced.

'The Boche appear to be doing their level best to put an end to our reconnaissance,' said Currie.

'Yes, sir. And it might worsen. Perhaps we should pull back?'

The shelling wasn't directed at us, and normally I wouldn't have been particularly concerned. However, were the Corps commander to be wounded, or worse… And whilst in my company…

Currie was to be knighted by the King any day now. Which would make the matter one for royal concern, especially if a burial ceremony were to intervene. On two continents two parliaments would be in an uproar. Not to mention the army. I shook my head. The last time I'd been in London I'd seen the famous Tower. For the life of me, though, I couldn't recall whether they still carried out beheadings at that location.

'Yes,' said Currie, nodding ever so slowly. 'It's been most illuminating, but I fear you're right. We should move back.'

With that we got to our feet. Hunched over so as not to present any German observers with too obvious a target – although a keen observer with good glasses would have had a fair chance of spotting us – we hastened down the hill to the rear.

'You'll be back in time for lunch, sir,' I said cheerily, as we neared the waiting cars.

The general's appearance, the paunch in particular, suggested he was someone who enjoyed his meals. In that he resembled Benoît. But at this innocent remark of mine the general took umbrage.

'Lunch is the very least of my concerns, Lieutenant.' While the physique of General Currie and Benoît DuBois shared a certain outward resemblance – there the similarity apparently ended. General Currie had made it very clear meals weren't high on his list of priorities. I wondered if he knew that other generals under his command saw this very differently.

Suddenly my thoughts wheeled off and went barrelling down a narrow sap of their own. Then it came to me. In my excitement I nearly cried out. Luckily I remembered where I was, and with whom.

When the general took his leave and climbed into the waiting staff car – a small anonymous Ford like mine – I felt the corners of my mouth turn up. I'd have to devote some thought to the details. There was undeniably an element of scheming and conniving involved I would have preferred to avoid. In certain circles, before the war, they might have described what I had in mind as being "dishonourable".

But after three long years of war, mores and values were changing. Not that changing mores and values would have changed anyone's mind about Long Archie's behaviour. Furthermore, I had to do something for Benoît. I'd already lost one good friend at the Somme. I wasn't about to lose him too, and most definitely not to our own side – even if that required a friendly casualty or two – metaphorically speaking.

CHAPTER 21

11th of July, 1917
The château, Château de la Haie, France

I'd already begun to tell Captain Ferguson the story when a minor commotion developed. I was counting upon it, and I'm not sure what I would have done had the minutes passed without one. But the clock on the wall indicated that it was nearly time. I'd already checked, fleetingly, several times. As punctuality was a virtue according to those who knew and cared about such things, I was reasonably confident.

Some of the chairs and tables in the officers' mess in the fine stone building of the Château de la Haie were being rearranged to make space for others. Which was not entirely surprising as the room was nearly full with those taking breakfast. The novelty of an officers' mess, in an actual room with high ceilings, a fireplace, windows with unbroken panes, and comfortable leather backed-chairs – located in a château no less – had the divisional staff in a state of high excitement. The dining room served up an excellent four-franc lunch. Fort George was long since forgotten.

I raised my voice, and pressed valiantly on, resisting the urge to turn to my side from where the noise emanated. For I knew very well Captain Ferguson's gaze would follow mine. I kept my eyes glued on him and hoped he would reciprocate. It wouldn't do if he started to gander.

'You should have seen him.' I said, cutting quickly to the crux of the tale. I was oddly conscious that my derisive laugh was a little too loud, a little too forced to be genuine. 'He was sitting there taking a piece out of his aide because his dinner was tardy. While at that very moment one of his battalions was getting tarred and feathered at Arleux. The worst of it was someone in his brigade headquarters had made a hash of the orders. So his battalion wasn't even where they ought to have been. But he hadn't noticed that. Actually it looked quite serious for a while. Yet there he was carping on about his dinner.' Wearily I shook my head.

Ferguson looked at me aghast. I'd picked him as I had a feeling he'd react that way. Ferguson had a strong sense of decency about him – I liked that – a man of the straight and the narrow. Appropriately he'd been a surveyor on the railway before the war. 'You can't be serious, Malcolm,' he muttered.

'Oh, but I am. I saw and heard the whole scene myself. Actually I was standing a few feet away. Saw the orders too, which was why I was there. The lines were out and it was important someone at brigade react. Unfortunately, other priorities got in the way.'

'That's simply awful,' said Ferguson. 'Somebody should hear about this. I hate to say it, but it makes one wonder if the man's fit for command.'

'Yeah, well, the problem with this brigadier is that he's a brigadier. Which makes it a little tricky when you're only a lieutenant, and not even from his division. I wish I could, but I can't exactly walk up to General Lipsett and say, "Sir, if you could spare a moment of your time, I've discovered a serious personality defect with the commander of the 5th Brigade. I think you need to take action."'

'No. No, I suppose you can't.'

Shaking his head, he glanced to his left, then turned a particularly pallid shade. If I didn't know better, he looked seasick.

It was some time before he spoke again. 'My God, Malcolm,' he whispered. 'Do you know who's sitting there?'

I stole a glance to my side.

'Perhaps we should move on?' I said softly.

He nodded fervently.

We left our coffee on the table; something I've never been known to do. It was only after the officers' mess was far behind us that Ferguson spoke again.

'I think the general heard everything.'

'Everything?'

He nodded. 'I'd watch my Ps and Qs if I were you, Malcolm. He didn't look pleased at all.'

'Yeah, well, the Nova Scotians at Arleux were even less pleased. And Lipsett is not the type to shoot the messenger – at least I hope he isn't. Besides, perhaps it's best he does know. You said so yourself.'

'Perhaps,' allowed Ferguson. 'I suppose we'll hear if something comes of it.' While he may not have been concerned about being shot, I do think he was worried about a posting to the trenches forthwith. 'We'll just have to wait and see,' he mumbled.

But with an invigorating, if not filling, breakfast behind me there was no question of waiting. In fact, time was pressing. His Majesty the King was visiting today.

Hill 145, Vimy Ridge, France

It was a fine clear day, and by 10.30 a.m. the Arras-Béthune road was already lined with thousands of soldiers, when a small group of us turned onto it driving fast in an open-top Crossley. A few of the men began cheering madly at the sight. Soon a bored battalion or two were playing along, while we each took our turn regally acknowledging the cheers and waving our caps as clouds of dust spiralled up in our wake.

After a spell we turned off the thoroughfare, climbing the plank road up the slope of Vimy Ridge, heading for its highest point. We'd been told explicitly that we should arrive well before the royal party. Only Fotheringham had forgotten his cap and helmet somewhere in the château, occasioning a long delay in proceedings and necessitating a faster drive than was likely prudent given that so many brass had descended on Vimy Ridge. Speaking personally, I hadn't had so much fun since I was ten attending the Dominion Exhibition parade.

From the observation post on Hill 145, the view was as beautiful as from the Bois de l'Hirondelle, the fall of shells into Lens less so.

In time for the King to see a little action, the midday hate was on and both sides were exchanging blows. It was several miles distant but through the field glasses you could almost feel the concussion as a shell went off between two rows of houses with a far-off thud, a pillar of oily black smoke billowing upwards before it slowly dissipated in the endless blue July sky. Ironically, had it been a gas shell, and there were plenty of those being doled out – we had new improved ones Benoît recently explained with a certain glee to his voice – it wouldn't have looked nearly so dramatic. Then one of theirs burst in our trenches near Avion.

George V arrived in a modest motorcade that nevertheless concealed an impressive column of brass: General Sir Henry Horne of the First Army; Lieutenant-General Currie from the Corps; Major-General Lipsett of the division; and a handful of lesser types, brigadier-generals and colonels mainly. I was wearing the white-blue-white ribbon, but not the cross that the King himself had pinned on me last December. It had been expressly noted that his visit today was not to be a formal one, His Majesty having expressed an interest in seeing the men in their ordinary daily routine.

Parades and formal dress were therefore dispensed with – attacks, too, I noted with interest. It was only because the OP was constructed by the 3rd Division engineers that a handful of the junior staff were invited. I suspect my inclusion owed everything to the fact I was the sole one in that crowd whom the King had awarded anything. The little bauble was finally proving of practical use.

The King's party – I could see General Currie leading the way, helmet firmly on his head, an arm thrown out expansively in explanation – was walking steadily towards the hill following the line of an old German trench, now little more than a duckboard walkway. Avoiding the peak, they made their way along the same communication trench I'd used earlier, to circle around to the other side where the carefully camouflaged concrete block was built into the hill facing north. Medal or not, I wasn't welcome there.

The group of us from the division, and a few other sightseers, were ushered on our way from the OP well before the monarch arrived. It wouldn't have done to draw Fritz's attention with an unseemly number of visitors. The King could gaze out in comparative safety towards the battlefield beyond, the historic one closer to hand, that of the present day several miles further. The present day battlefield was still helpfully marked by puffs of smoke as shells fell in Lens and environs. The army of his dominion held the ground for miles around. A squadron of aeroplanes circled warily in the skies above.

I left the others and went over to take a peek at the small hut that had been constructed near where the duckboards ended, and the plank road began. What with the hasty retreat at breakfast, my stomach was growling. I was hoping there might be the offer of a Royal Lunch – that would be something to remember. Unfortunately, I couldn't smell a thing. The only people milling around were drivers and staff officers – none of them the sort renowned for whipping up a midday repast fit for a king.

'Quite a scene, Lieutenant.'

A man, considerably older and shorter than myself and dressed in civilian clothes, and a hat to boot, came ambling up to my side.

His clothes and his manner were casual, and I confess to experiencing some puzzlement as to who he might be, when he spoke again.

'Were you involved in the battle?'

For a long moment I peered at him. I presumed he was asking about the capture of the ridge. Finally I said, 'Yes. Haven't missed a battle since early 1915.'

'Forgive me,' said the man in a rush, a charming smile lighting his face. 'I'm Roger Dickens.' He extended a hand. 'I write for the *Daily Mail*. It was a terrific battle I'm told… Lieutenant –'

'MacPhail,' I said, 'Lieutenant Malcolm MacPhail at your service, sir. Yes, it was quite a show. We spent some anxious hours because of this very hill you're standing upon.'

Dickens said nothing, nodding thoughtfully, encouraging me on with inquisitive brown eyes he held unwaveringly on mine. Nobody had been so interested in what I had to say since my first serious tumble from a bicycle, sometime about grade two. And her excuse was that she was my mother.

'I was on the right flank at the time,' I said. With the wave of an arm, I indicated the general direction down the slope off to our right. Dickens slipped out a notepad from his jacket and began to take notes. 'We didn't take the hill until the second day,' I continued, 'and it was a relief when we did. You see the Germans had the hill well-manned, with a whole warren of deep dug-outs on the cliff side beyond. Near the OP the King is now inspecting. We weren't able to dislodge them as quickly as we did elsewhere, and they had us under a regular hailstorm from this spot. Took a fearful toll, too. You can see what a view they had down the ridge. Of course, it's a little more pastoral looking at present.'

There was no need to add that back last April the ridge had been nothing but mud, and even some snow, pocked with endless shell holes. Today, for the occasion of the King's visit, nature had tidied up admirably; from the earthen fields the grass sprouted in abundance and, astonishingly, there were flowers visible, though the shell holes obstinately remained. There weren't many trees, either.

Dickens asked another question, and again I veered off into explanation. The man had a way with his inquiries. No wonder he was a correspondent. In this vein we continued until I lost track of the time.

Then, over his shoulder, twenty yards away and poking his way along with a cane, a familiar face hove into view.

'You wouldn't happen to know who *that* is?' I asked with a start. Dickens pivoted. 'There,' I said, pointing subtly. 'The officer walking towards the road.' It was the man I'd seen outside the bank in Paris.

He smiled. 'As a matter of fact, I do know. That's Major Smythe. He's on the staff of the First Army.'

Smythe!

I whistled. Suddenly there was a lot of clicking and whirring going on in the engine room upstairs. 'Any relation to Captain Smythe of the 5th Brigade?' I asked calmly, a tremor of excitement going through me. As to the question, I was reasonably confident I already knew the answer. It may have been coincidence that the two men shared an astonishing likeness. But to also share the same name… that was one coincidence too many.

Dickens shrugged. 'Can't say that I know a Smythe with you chaps,' he replied. 'But it's certainly possible. The Smythes are an extended family. A lot of cousins and nephews. They're very well connected in certain circles, and wealthy too. They own several factories up in Northampton.'

'You don't say.'

I stood there rubbing my chin. The coincidences were piling up. I would have rubbed it much longer were it not that Dickens coughed. I looked around and saw that King and entourage were approaching on the duckboards. General Horne was engaged in some sort of explanation for His Majesty. Strolling behind, Currie and Lipsett had struck up a conversation of their own. I wondered if the subject was the forthcoming operation against Lens and surrounding hills. I'd heard nothing in the past days, though it couldn't be long in coming.

'I'd love to talk more,' said Dickens, 'but it appears that duty calls. Your explanations and your time are most appreciated, Lieutenant MacPhail. Thank you so much.'

Inspired by our visitor I made a little bow with my head.

'Take my card,' said Dickens, pushing it into my hand. 'If ever you're in London, I'd love to hear from you. I'll be at the front for another week or two – should you have the time. You can contact First Army headquarters. Someone there will doubtless be able to point you the way.'

We shook hands. With that he left in the direction of a handful of other correspondents, one of whom was a uniformed photographer, camera and tripod poised in wait, and the King's party fixed in his sights. Tomorrow's papers would be full of this visit. The great victory at Vimy Ridge. There hadn't been many victories this war, great or otherwise, so the King's visit here would provide a welcome opportunity to relive one. I shuffled over to join the fellows from the division.

Major Smythe, I noticed, was standing on the road next to one of the staff cars, apparently instructing a driver on the intricacies of a Royal visit.

From a distance the King lifted a hand and waved in our general direction. Enthusiastically we waved back, which may or may not have been the correct protocol; I tend to suspect it wasn't. Not that it appeared to matter. He and the others were ducking their heads to slip into the waiting motorcars, whose engines were putting away in anticipation of a rapid departure – always a prudent policy on Vimy Ridge. The Royal Lunch, to my regret, had evidently been pencilled in for later.

Major Smythe slid into the car carrying General Horne and several high-ranking officers. Roger Dickens had known of what he spoke;

the Smythe family influence reached visibly into the very highest echelons of the army – probably far beyond it. I was going to have to tip toe across No-Man's-Land.

Whatever was going on, and something very clearly was, it seemed all but certain that the Smythes were heavily involved, with Captain Smythe of the 2nd Division in the fore. More to the point, I was convinced that Benoît had bumbled into the thick of the mire, and that left me no choice than to bumble ahead myself. Unfortunately, I didn't hold out much hope my morning performance for General Lipsett would lead to much. But for Benoît's sake I was going to have to take some risks. In a week's time he might be charged, tried and convicted.

On top of which the attack on Lens was surely imminent. When it occurred, Benoît would be on his own. Lipsett and Hayter would have me occupied day and night.

CHAPTER 22

12th of July, 1917
The château, Château de la Haie, France

In retrospect I blame myself that I wasn't more diplomatic. Not that diplomacy had achieved much these past few years.

'Look, all I'm saying is that I'm a little surprised you haven't been charged yet,' I said. 'It's going on two weeks since your run-in with Smythe. Granted he's not one for staff work, but I didn't expect it would take him this long to get a few papers in order.'

'Mac. You said you thought I'd already be in irons,' said Benoît, wearing his wounded puppy dog look. 'You sounded disappointed.'

We were strolling down the gravel lane from the stately château, with its yellow-grey stone exterior, and many elegant windows trimmed in neat white. Someone had told me the house belonged to Sarah Bernhardt, the famous French stage actress. It was fortunate she was no longer in residence for she would have been appalled at the state the army had left it in; even if to most of us it was a little piece of paradise compared to the front line. To either side ancient oaks lined the drive, full, tall, their foliage providing a welcome shade from the blazing sun. It was hard to believe that a mile away, two at most, there was barely a tree standing.

Dismissively I flapped a hand in the air. 'A figure of speech, that's all. You're going to have to learn these nuances of English sometime,

Benoît, and better from me than from someone else, don't you think?'

'Hmm.' Benoît looked sceptical. 'Tell me what you're so wound up about, Mac.'

'Wound up? *Moi?*'

He turned to me. The beaver pelts that did duty as his eyebrows rose in unison.

'Well, by chance there was something –' I mumbled, pausing for a reaction. When none came I carried on: 'You see I've discovered that Captain Smythe has a cousin with the Imperials. He's a well-connected major with the First Army, and he's a dead ringer for our man.'

'Half the army has a relation in England.'

'Yes, yes, I know. But I saw this man earlier in Paris, when I was on leave. At the time I was certain it was Smythe until I got right up to him. But then I happened to spot the same fellow the other day, hobnobbing with the King's party, and lo and behold – I discovered his family name was Smythe. You can imagine my surprise. So I asked around this morning. And do you know what I learned?'

'*Non.* But I have a suspicion you're going to tell me.'

'Captain Smythe's a cousin of the major! It's not just the major who is very influential. The whole family is. They're rich, too. Smythe's father has one brother, and that brother happens to own a substantial manufacturing concern. You'll never guess where his factories are located.'

'Canada?'

I sighed. 'No, no. Captain Smythe's branch of the family immigrated to Canada. But this is the interesting part. The rest of the clan all hail from Northampton. That's where the business is.'

'Northampton?' Benoît looked about as confused as if I'd asked him to share his thoughts on the historical significance of the 1846 repeal of the Corn Laws.

'C'mon, Benoît. Don't you know *any* English geography?'

'London. Does that count?'

'Northampton is the largest town in a region of England that happens to be known as the Midlands. Does *that* mean anything to you?'

'The Midlands, you say?'

'Yep.' I could see his face going through the same mental gymnastics I'd gone through earlier.

'*Mon dieu*,' replied Benoit, coming to a sudden halt. He turned round to face me. 'You don't think…?'

I hesitated. 'Benoît, I don't know what to think. But I too remember our visit to that *estaminet* in Cambligneul. If Smythe is a "benefactor" to half the divisional trains and supply depots, there has to be a very good reason. And let's be frank, most of what he could pilfer from army stores wouldn't be worth that kind of money. It's not as if there's much of a market outside the army for eighteen-pound shells –' A thought came to me. 'Or for boots, come to that. Certainly not if he intends on selling them to French children.'

Benoît nodded heartily. 'So what's his game then?'

'That, Benoît, is what we in the common parlance call a mystery.'

'*Un mystère*. Fascinating, Mac, but what does any of this have to do with me?'

'Isn't it obvious? If Smythe is up to nothing good all we need to do is discover what it is, reveal it to the proper authorities, and his credibility would be gone in a flash, and any charges against you along with it.' I could see from the creases in Benoît's brow I hadn't completely swung him over. 'Look. If the captain wants to play hardball with you and your career, we need to do the same with him and his. This is no moment to be gentlemanly, *mon ami*.'

'*Non*,' he said, shaking his head. I couldn't help noting he was rather tempered in his praise for my plan.

'Now that I think about it,' I said, 'the reason Smythe's let you be is probably because he's juggling too many things at once. He likely figures he has you running scared. So there's a good chance he's not watching his flank, which may provide us an opportunity. In addition to which there's always the remote chance he's preoccupied with his army duties. God knows, there's reason enough.' At this the crease in Benoît's brow cut as deep as the Regina Trench had at the Somme.

'I expect that they're going to send us against Lens soon,' I explained. 'It's a better than even bet the 2nd Division will be involved, so even the likes of Smythe and Long Archie will need to prepare. It won't be an easy slog.'

'Lens?' He smiled thinly, a knowing smile. 'You're surely right, Mac. But before we get to Lens, we're to attack Méricourt Trench.'

'We are? Where did you hear that?'

'Mac,' sighed Benoît, 'Who do you think is preparing the barrage?'

'Oh, yes, of course.' Camped out at headquarters all day, I was predisposed to thinking I heard all the news worth hearing. It wasn't the first time I'd forgotten there was often more news to be had from yesterday's newspaper.

'When's this attack to take place?' I asked.

'In ten days.'

I would have asked more, except, out of the corner of my eye, I noticed something peculiar happening in the group of cyclists at the end of the lane. They were awaiting orders, or new messages to deliver, loitering lazily under the trees with their bicycles strewn about on the grass, the soft buzz of their conversation and the smoke of their cigarettes carried our way by the gentle breeze. What caught my eye was a sight I'd seen several times already this summer. One I'd paid no heed to until now. A cyclist was leaning against the trunk of an oak with one arm extended to keep his balance, while the other pried at the sole of his boot, his leg folded up and across in the fashion of a stork.

'Your boot,' I shouted excitedly, staring over Benoît's shoulder.

Benoît might have been forgiven for thinking I was addressing him. That was very likely the case for he bore the shocked expression of a man who was a couple of thousand feet up having moments before spotted the Red Baron tearing down from a cloud above.

'Mac?'

I ignored him, and brushed past, opening my mouth to shout again. At the sight of an officer bearing down fast, waving his arms and yelling unintelligibly, the cyclists abandoned their casual routine. The two lazing on the ground sprang to their feet. All of them began fiddling self-consciously with their caps.

'Let me see it,' I cried out, as I approached the man by the tree.

By now his foot had made a safe and hasty return to solid ground and he was standing uneasily at attention. 'Sir?' The fellow could have been Benoît's dumbfounded co-pilot for all he understood.

'Your boot! Take it off.'

'Sir?'

'Hurry now.'

Flummoxed, he did as he was told. Impatiently I reached out an arm. When it was off, he handed it over and stood there with one leg in the air, again leaning against the oak. Benoît and the cyclists were examining me with unreserved astonishment.

Briefly I turned it around, examining it closer. It was of ankle height, in thick black leather with metal studs on the sole, a standard army boot were it not that the sole was coming loose. Then with my other hand I pulled out a perfectly decent, white, and reasonably clean handkerchief, turned the boot upside down and began rubbing at the mud and dirt on the arch. It took me a while. When the bulk of it was gone, I spat on it noisily. In the background there was a murmur, and what sounded like chuckles. Then I began rubbing again.

Finally I found what I was searching for. It was stamped indelibly in the hard leather, three short lines, encompassed in a small circle. It was a critical piece of the puzzle that had eluded me. Yet for all the questions it answered, it also raised one of its own. What the devil was Smythe up to? The stamped lettering read:

1917
Smythe & Company
Northampton

CHAPTER 23

22nd and 23rd of July, 1917
The château, Château de la Haie, France

I passed closely by Captain Ferguson at the field telephone as I entered the staff room. He glanced up from behind a curvy-legged, and highly lacquered side table in the corner where he and it were incongruously located. To my surprise, when he noticed who it was, the beginnings of a smile lit his face.

He raised an agitated finger in the air and began flicking it to and fro to indicate I should wait for him. Then he returned to his call. Ever since our breakfast encounter with General Lipsett I'd seen virtually nothing of Ferguson, and I dare say he intended it that way. Being seen around me was altogether too hazardous an activity for a staff man of good standing; on a par with manhandling open gas flasks into position; tap dancing in No-Man's-Land; or floating, untethered, in an observation balloon low over the Ypres Salient. Something must have changed his mind.

'Ah, Malcolm! The shout was hardly necessary. From five feet away there was little danger I wouldn't have heard. Even bearing in mind the absence of the general, Colonel Hayter, or even one of the majors in the staff room, this was positively exuberant behaviour on the part of the usually restrained Ferguson.

'Captain,' I replied cautiously.

'You'll never guess what I heard.'

'My promotion to field-marshal has finally come through?'

A sigh. 'Brigadier Macdonell has been relieved of his command!'

'Really?' Now that *was* interesting.

'Yes, Lieutenant-Colonel Ross is replacing him as of tomorrow. I just spoke with someone at 2nd Division. He heard General Burstall say something about his efficiency as a commander.'

'Efficiency as a commander?' I snorted. 'He means lack thereof. Well, Burstall had that right. Was it his idea?'

'I don't think so,' said Ferguson. 'My man says it came from General Currie. I think General Lipsett must have said something, don't you? Apparently Currie said the brigadier was feeling the "strain of war."'

I snorted again. 'Aren't we all? Currie's making excuses, of course, to make it all more palatable. No one likes to sack a general. So where are they sending him? Posthaste to an asylum?'

'No, he's off to England tomorrow at two. Then on to bigger and better. He's to command the military district of New Brunswick.'

This was enough to get even my eyebrows in motion. 'New Brunswick! The province?'

'Yep, that's it.'

'That'll be a harrowing command, I'm sure. By all accounts there's a terrific amount of action on the New Brunswick front these days. At least he won't need worry about three square meals a day.'

Straight-laced Ferguson managed a grin at this, but sensibly refrained from comment – it was a skill I'd never quite caught on to.

Meanwhile my thoughts were already leapfrogging ahead. By God, this meant Benoît was off the hook!

Before I could adequately think it through, Hayter reappeared in the company of two majors, and all minds, including mine, were then drawn to the evening's attack.

It seemed the main operation against Lens would indeed have to wait, precisely as Benoît told me. There were still preparatory objectives to be taken.

Near Fosse no. 4, southeast of Lens, France

Nestled between the hamlets of Avion and Méricourt, and altogether more imposing than them in size, although equally derelict, was the pit shaft, slag heap, and jumble of mining buildings and structures known as Fosse no. 4. The raid – for that is what this attack had also become – had as its objectives Metal Trench, and the dug-outs and trench mortar emplacements in the railway embankment that ran close alongside.

It was nearing midnight and I was anxious we wouldn't be late. ZERO Hour was to come at 1 a.m. and that didn't leave much of a margin. A guide from the 116th Battalion was leading us overland towards one of the jumping off posts close to where Meander Trench crosses Quebec Road. A few hundred yards north, the heart of the mining works loomed up darker than night, occasionally silhouetted by a shell burst or a flare going off somewhere. Metal Trench was not much farther than that, and a touch to the east. Of course, the trench was wholly invisible at this distance, with or without the pyrotechnics. I could still scarcely believe that I found myself here. It had all happened extremely quickly.

It began barely an hour before when Major McAvity bustled up with a frantic haste one doesn't see a great deal of at divisional headquarters. The intelligence section was thinned out as Captain Ferguson and Sergeant Neff had already left to a brigade or battalion headquarters – I wasn't sure which – closer to the front. If the raid was a success there would be prisoners, and potentially quite a number. Needless to say, with a much larger operation against Lens in the offing, the results of these initial interrogations would be anxiously awaited. Corps headquarters would have been quite insistent.

'MacPhail,' said McAvity. He was a little breathless for a man who always seemed so fit.

'Sir?'

'I've just spoken with someone in corps intelligence, and they tell me they believe the Germans may have one of their listening stations in a dug-out in the railway embankment. Perhaps even in the tunnel off the trench. If the 116th were able to capture it, it would be a huge coup if we could snatch their papers, and perhaps some equipment.'

'Yes, sir, I imagine it would be.'

'There won't be a lot of time to investigate properly, and I'm afraid we can't rely on the attackers; they'll have their hands full with the fighting. Captain Ferguson is already forward, and preoccupied with other matters, as you well know. So, you see, MacPhail…'

'Yes, sir, I think I see exactly,' I replied. You didn't have to be a whizz at crossword puzzles to complete his last sentence. Nevertheless, I didn't immediately throw up my hands and begin shouting *Kamerad*. 'You intend to send someone,' I said. 'What about Lieutenant Fotheringham, sir? He's ambitious. I expect he'll be keen to obtain some actual front line experience.'

'Fotheringham?' McAvity frowned. 'Oh, no. Besides, I think he's far too busy doing something for the colonel. However, I just spoke with Colonel Hayter. He agreed with my suggestion of sending you. Actually he was very amenable about it.'

'Was he now?' I groaned. *Fotheringham far too busy… that would be a first…*

'Oh, don't look like someone's sprinkled a dash of chloride of lime in your drinks flask, MacPhail. You've plenty of experience in such things. After all the stories you've told, I figured you'd find this a snap. On top of which I'm sending a man along to help out: Corporal Smith. He speaks German.'

'*Zehr gut*, sir,' I replied.

McAvity looked mildly amused, though he eyed me suspiciously as if he didn't really believe my answer. Then he glanced at his wrist, and thick clouds rolled in. 'Well… What are you waiting for? The raid begins in a couple of hours. If the battalion do capture the embankment there won't be much time, so you'll need to move up with them. You'd best get running.'

At this I was unsure whether he meant it literally – the running part. Accompanying the attack in was obviously non-negotiable. But fortunately alternative travel arrangements had already been made; that way I'd have a little breath left lest I did need to run.

'I've organised a car and driver for you,' he said. 'He'll be here any minute. Good luck.'

Then there was barely time to snatch my helmet and revolver; an undignified scramble down the front steps where Private Briers and

Corporal Smith already waited in the car; followed by a harrowing ride along narrow twisting lanes to the ridge. Once over it we took the arrow-straight but shell-pocked Arras-Lens road towards the front. All in the pitch dark. Right when the Hun would most likely shell the road. Finally, the driver slowed to a halt and told us this was La Coulotte, and that we should disembark. It was no little relief to hear it. Only that feeling soon disappeared.

We were greeted by one of the battalion officers: 'Your respirators, put them on,' he barked. As we did so, he introduced himself as Hutchinson – a nice enough fellow it soon proved, his first words of welcome notwithstanding. After an obligatory minute or two holding the newcomers' hands he apologized, citing demands on him elsewhere. He stepped quickly away in the direction of the jumping off lines and his platoon. Time pressed.

We also went to depart. The guide turned to me, bellowing through his mask: 'Fritz just began shelling us with gas, sir. Wouldn't you know it, eh? Bad luck for us.'

I'm never much for chit-chat on the eve of an operation, and even had I been so inclined, the canvas, rubber and sheer awkwardness of the mask didn't encourage loquaciousness. But it was bad news. The entire raid would need to be carried out wearing respirators. 'Yes,' I said simply. 'How far is it?'

'The jumping off line is almost exactly a mile from here, sir. Due east,' he replied.

We walked for almost thirty minutes. He deftly avoided the worst of the depressions, loose wire and other debris, carefully pointing out the worst obstacles to Smith and me as we followed in file.

I was staring at him as he stepped along at a good pace. He happened to glance around – no doubt to check on his gaggle behind – and caught my eye. He put up two fingers. Which was either two minutes or two hundred yards to go. I nodded and looked over my shoulder at Smith.

The corporal had his head bent down, and it was plain he was carefully watching his step, always a prudent policy at night near the front. I'd spoken with him briefly in the car. He was unfailingly proper, perhaps too proper for my taste. Although I hadn't really been able to make a fair assessment of him I had to admit. It did occur to me that

I might be searching for something in him that simply wasn't there.

Reaching the assigned line of trench not long after, we entered it. I introduced myself and Smith to the two lieutenants responsible and curtly explained our orders. They promised to pass the word along to the men, to keep an eye out for anything that might look like a listening post. As ZERO Hour was not long off we then moved out of their way.

The barrage opened with a fierce storm, Metal Trench immediately marked out by fiery bursts of whirling steel, accompanied by thunderous concussions. The men of A Company pulled themselves from the shallow trench and were off. 'Five minutes,' I roared in Smith's ear. 'We'll give them four minutes. Then we'll follow.' He nodded.

It was a calculated risk. If we left too soon we'd be in the leading wave of the action, and the chances of stumbling into an enemy signals dug-out by accident were negligible, assuming we survived to look. Alternatively, if we remained too long in the jumping-off trench the German barrage would surely catch us. Based on recent experience I figured it would take them between four and five minutes before their guns got into action. As Meander Trench wasn't a permanent line of ours we probably had several minutes more before they caught on. Four minutes should give us a margin of safety. I hoped the Germans would be as predictable tonight as they typically were.

Contrary to what our guide had said, luck was with us tonight. The enemy retaliation eventually came down, consisting mainly of a torrent of gas shells. But we were long gone. Sweating myself out in a gas mask was well worth it if we could escape both the barrage and the machine guns of the defenders.

Metal Trench fell surprisingly easily. By the time we reached it, passing around the south end of the slag heap of Fosse no. 4 first, it was firmly in our hands. I saw a dozen prisoners being lined up for the march to the rear. Ahead, however, there were rifle flashes, and once the extended burst of a MG.

In contrast to this crew, the garrison at the railway embankment were not giving up without a fight.

After roughly ten minutes, impatiently waiting, watching, and listening to the chaos – for despite the careful plans that is what all fights invariably become – I turned to Smith.

'I think we'll have to chance it. We don't have much time. There's a strong possibility they'll counter-attack at some point. We may even have to retreat. But I'd to like to find that *Ahrendtstation,* if we can. Do you have a weapon, Smith?' I couldn't recall seeing him with one earlier.

'Oh yes, sir,' he said. Seemingly out of nowhere he presented a bayoneted Lee-Enfield for my inspection. I could have sworn I hadn't seen it in the back seat between us – it's not the kind of thing one tends to miss.

'Good.' I yanked out my revolver.

At that very moment a young soldier approached.

'Lieutenant MacPhail, sir?'

'Yes.'

'You're to please follow me, sir. We think we've found something.'

'Something' revealed itself to be a wood-framed hole in the lateral communications trench close to where it intersected with the railway embankment. Smoke was curling out of the hole. Fifty feet away at the embankment there was a lot of shouting. There was a dull bang and a bomb went off. The fight there had yet to be decided.

'I'm afraid we bombed them,' said the waiting sergeant. 'They refused to come out, sir.'

'Wonderful. Having just blown them to smithereens, Sergeant, how can you be certain this was a listening post?'

'Oh, it was just the one bomb, sir. Although it did the trick. I checked myself. Which is how I happened to see all the gear.'

'Ah, so you did leave something to see. We'll have a look. Thanks.' I looked over at Smith, who true to form didn't appear daunted by the prospect of descending into a smoky, dark hole. Not that expressions are easy to read in the dead of night, and with a respirator sealing off your head.

'You may need this, sir,' said the sergeant. He passed me a trench torch.

'And any Boche that happen along. I trust you'll keep a good watch up here?'

'Yes, sir.'

With a boldness I didn't feel I edged down the steep staircase, one measured step at a time, the Webley extended and my finger uneasily

192

rubbing the trigger guard. Smith followed. The beams of the flashlight cut through the swirls of smoke, but not so well that I could see any further than ten feet ahead. Nor did the mask help. The one good thing about a small box respirator in a situation like this is that I wasn't keeling over from the fumes. Although with my senses so impaired, a new recruit from Bremerhaven, armed with a broom, could have caught me out.

I stepped down into a remarkably wide, but low ceilinged tunnel, of the sort built to provide ventilation and drainage for the principal mining tunnels further west. To my astonishment – it never ceased to astonish me seeing it in some hole in the ground in the middle of France – it was lit by yellow electric light. Though the light was not such that the flashlight was redundant. There wasn't a soul in sight. No, there were two souls, but they were lying on the floor and not likely to move anytime soon; the sergeant's Mills bomb had claimed them. Tables lined the walls. Signals equipment of various descriptions filled the tables and I spotted a set of headphones on one. The profusion of telephone wires fastened to the wall was truly extraordinary; half the telephones on the Western Front appeared to be routed through this tunnel. Thankfully, there was also less smoke than up top. Cautiously I edged off the mask, sniffed at the air, then pulled it off completely.

'Would you look at this, Smith,' I said with wonder, meaning it generally, until my attention was drawn to a couple of tables laden down with blue leather ring-bound books. I pointed. 'Let's start there.'

The books soon made even more of an impression than the equipment had. In fact it was mildly shocking to see page after page filled with the initials, abbreviations, units, and place names we referred to daily. How serious the interceptions had been could only be determined once someone examined the material more closely.

Smith cleared his throat. 'Sir? You should have a look at this one. I can't make heads or tails of it.'

'I was told you spoke German.'

'Yes, sir, I do. But this is in English.'

This left me to debate what the hell good it was being assigned a German speaker if I couldn't rely upon his English ability. On top of which, until now, everything I'd seen was in German. Then it dawned on me. The raw transcripts of the interceptions were naturally first meticulously transcribed in English. Only later would they be translated into German, for further analysis and diffusion to their commanders. That was what I'd been looking at. Smith had the raw material.

'Show me.'

Smith handed it over.

There was a single sheet, the type loosely spaced, and with room for comments in the margin. A date at the top, written in the European style with the cross through the 7, indicated it was intercepted approximately a week ago. There was no mention of where or how it had been intercepted.

Speaker number one (SP1): 'Relax, there's probably not more than a thousand left on the entire front.'

Speaker number two (SP2): 'Damn it. I'm paying you more than a general makes. There shouldn't be a single fucking pair in all of France. You know this. I can't bloody well do it all myself. People would notice.'

SP1: 'We've done our best [*unverständlich*]...'

SP2: 'Stop! Do you realize what would happen if word gets back to England there's a problem with them? Some righteous clown in the ministry will want a refund of every single, miserable penny. Worse, one of the other outfits will get the follow-up order. And, oh, how they'd dearly love that. Those orders will be worth millions. You may not have heard, but Crockett and Jones is doubling its production capacity. They're gearing up.'

SP1: 'Really?'

SP2: 'Yes, really. So get rid of the bloody things, and do it quickly. I don't really care how. Throw them in the Souchez for all I care. Just make sure they sink. It'll be written off as some army fuck up. But if there's one more pair of boots in army stores anywhere near Arras I'm going to [*unverständlich*].'

SP1: 'Consider it done.'

Abruptly the conversation ended. I flipped over the page to the reverse side. Empty. 'You sure there's no more?' I asked Smith. He shook his head. At the bottom of the page a short (by German standards) sentence was typed. I didn't really understand it, save that it was very obviously technical, and that was explanation enough.

'The bugger,' I cursed.

Smith stared, astonished at this outburst. It was the sort of family he came from, I think. 'You understand what that's all about, sir?' he asked, with surprise.

Grimly I nodded. There was no need to hear the voices on the transcript in order to put a name to them. I was convinced I knew who one of the speakers was, the one giving the orders. A court of law would necessarily see that differently. With the exception of his older cousin, there really was only one man it could be. Captain Smythe of the 5th Brigade was playing a treacherous high-stakes game.

A shout bellowed down the staircase: 'Sir! The lieutenant says you should hurry. In two minutes we're to pull back.'

I glanced at my watch. It was approaching 1.45 a.m. We'd been down here longer than I realized. Then I glanced at the sheet I was holding and hesitated. Smith was preoccupied taking stock of the stacks of reports in front of him. I folded the sheet in two, ran my fingers down the spine to sharpen the crease, and slipped it into my tunic pocket.

'We'll take the papers, Smith, all that we can. Shove them in here.' From my back I took the empty haversack, and held it open. It took a while to extract the sheets from the binders, and puzzle the stacks of paper in so that it held them all. With a grunt I pulled the haversack back over my shoulders.

Regretfully I looked round at the various pieces of equipment. 'We can't take all the gear I'm afraid. But it'd be a bloody shame if Fritz carts it off to use it again.'

'No, sir,' said Smith. 'We certainly can't take it. But we can't very well leave it either.'

'We could shoot them up a little,' I said, grasping the butt of the Webley.

'I've a better idea, sir.' Two Mills bombs appeared in his hand.

'Where did you get those?' He didn't immediately respond. 'Oh, never mind,' I said. Do you know how to use 'em?'

He nodded. 'Go ahead, sir, you get out. I'll position them in a suitable place. No sense both of us waiting around.'

I was about to quibble, but he was right. That was the sensible decision, especially as I felt as loaded down as Santa's sleigh on Christmas Eve, and considerably less nimble than the good man. 'Alright,' I said. 'Do your worst Smith. But don't take any chances. We already have the real trophies.' I reached back and patted the top of the haversack.

After a minute Smith bolted from the hole. The bombs detonated with two short bangs that I wouldn't have heard had I not been listening for them.

In the meantime the fighting had apparently ended. In the bright but tired eyes of the dirt-streaked faces passing I could see that Fritz had drawn the short end of the straw tonight. The battle of the railway embankment had been a stiff fight. Hand-to-hand fighting eventually cleared out the Germans who resisted. For those who chose to skulk in their dug-outs, the Mills bombs and explosive charges were employed liberally, I was told.

At battalion headquarters I debated using the telephone to report back to McAvity at the division. Then, remembering what I'd seen tonight, I waved off the offer. In an ironic twist the lines went down immediately after. 'We need to get this material back to headquarters as soon as possible,' I muttered to Smith.

Smith suggested we hike down the Arras-Lens road, with the intention of picking up a lift. While I'd forgotten to instruct him, our driver had lacked the foresight, or possibly the inclination, to wait around. At this hour I couldn't picture there being much demand for staff cars. Which made me wonder what the odds of a lift were. Nevertheless, I nodded.

The straps of the haversack were chafing something fierce on my shoulders – I'd neglected to employ the advantages of rank and pawn the whole mountain off on Smith – when the chug of a motor from behind overtook us.

I turned. As the car rattled into view in the darkness, I stepped into the middle of the road and began throwing my arms about.

The car slowed. A head poked out one side.

'MacPhail? Is that you? Hop in.'

Briefly I debated it. I'd have no time to think with Ferguson bantering endlessly away. I had a lot to think about. Then I considered the alternative. 'Thanks,' I said, and made quickly for the open door.

In the front seat behind the wheel, Private Briers looked away, avoiding my glance.

PART THREE

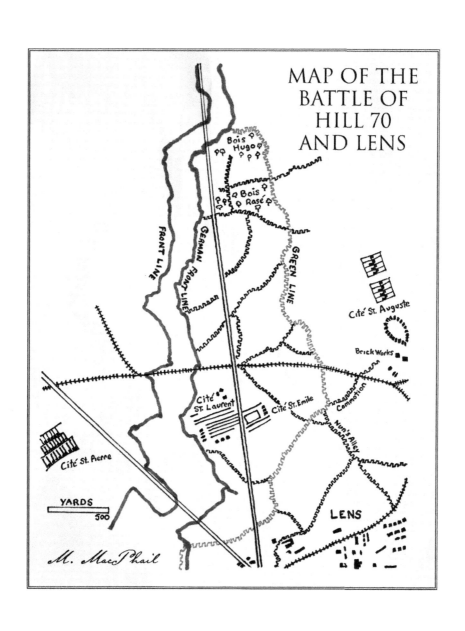

MAP OF THE
BATTLE OF
HILL 70
AND LENS

Bois Hugo

Bois Rasé

FRONT LINE

GERMAN FRONT LINE

GREEN LINE

Cité St. Auguste

Brick Works

Cité St. Laurent

Cité St. Emile

Commotion

Nun's Alley

Cité St. Pierre

YARDS
500

LENS

M. MacPhail

CHAPTER 24

23rd of July, 1917
The château, Château de la Haie, France

Shortly after breakfast the general and the colonel mysteriously disappeared.

There was a lot of speculation about what it could possibly mean. While both men were often away, regularly at the same time, a consensus had nevertheless formed that it must mean something as no one could put a finger on what exactly they were doing – inconceivable for a staff man accustomed to strict schedules and plans. So that left us to speculate. The transport staff didn't know anything we didn't know already – namely that they'd departed in the big Crossley. Then someone at corps headquarters called to inquire if there were further details from the raid of the 116th the past night, and let slip that the Corps commander, his right hand man, and a couple of others were away at a conference. When General Horne and the commander-in-chief himself, Sir Douglas Haig, were reported to have been spotted at 2nd Division headquarters the mystery appeared all but solved. Particularly as it soon emerged that not only Lipsett and Hayter were attending the conference, but the GOCs and GSO1s of every division in the Corps.

'Methinks it's something big. Lens probably,' said Fotheringham. 'We'll hear soon, lads.'

'Methinks, if it is Lens, it would be better if we didn't hear any-thing,' I grumbled loudly. Fotheringham looked confused, but others knowing well what an assault on the town implied caught my hint, and nodded vigorously. One thing was certain, Sir Douglas hadn't travelled to the down-at-heel mining village of Sains-en-Gohelle merely to discuss our next athletic championship, or the shaky state of the French coal industry.

The wind was still westerly and there was still a gas alert on when the general's car crunched up the long drive late that afternoon. It ground to a slow halt at the worn steps of grey marble that led into the château. Curious eyes peered circumspectly through the windows, whilst trying not to reveal to their superiors – those both indoors and out – what they were doing.

Several hours passed before the first details of the conference eventually made the rounds. Captain Ferguson, befitting his position, was the bearer of the important news. Colonel Hayter must have told him it was alright to tell us, for otherwise I'm sure we wouldn't have heard anything.

'So, it's to be Lens?' said Fotheringham.

'Lens?' said Ferguson, puzzled. 'No, Hill 70.'

'Hill 70?'

'Ha!' I slapped my hand on my thigh so hard everyone turned to me, expectant looks on their faces.

'What?' I said, defensively, throwing up my hands, conscious my cheeks felt warm. When I declined to explain myself they turned back to Ferguson. He never much liked being in the spotlight, so he likely rued the moment that he opened his mouth.

In the whirlwind that was my head, I was replaying the morning spent with General Currie reconnoitering Lens; in particular what I'd blurted out when he solicited my opinion. At the time it came as a relief when he appeared to share my scepticism about an attack on Lens. Apparently, I hadn't misread him. Perhaps he even valued hearing me put into words what he thought himself. But then again, Currie was no chump. He wasn't about to send us forward on some fool's errand, stumbling through the perilous built-up streets of Lens while German gunners on the surrounding heights picked us apart. No, Hill 70 was the sensible move. Evidently he'd even been able to convince the men who mattered of that: Haig and Horne.

There was no word yet what the division's role was to be. It may not have been Lens, but I had few illusions about the difficulty of the task assigned. This was not to be a quick in and out venture as the raids of late had been. We would be expected to hold the hill, no matter what the Germans threw our way; and as I'd also discussed with General Currie that was surely going to be a lot.

Major McAvity appeared before me. 'Have you heard anything from corps intelligence about the papers you and Corporal Smith brought in?'

'No, sir. Not a peep.'

'Well, there were a lot of them,' he said. He sounded almost apologetic, though it wasn't his doing; a despatch rider from corps headquarters had arrived almost immediately to collect them.

'I guess the damage is already done, so they probably don't feel much urgency,' I said.

'Yes,' agreed McAvity. 'That's true. But on the other hand it does point to the need to exercise a lot more caution with the field telephones, or any telephone near the front, come to that.'

'Yes, it certainly does, sir.' Ironically a reminder had made its rounds not so long back, although that was a communiqué Captain Smythe had either missed or ignored. It remained to be seen what, if any, the consequences would be.

Thinking of him, my next thought was of Benoît. I wondered if he'd heard of Long Archie's transfer to the trenches of New Brunswick. If he had, and especially if he hadn't, he'd be ecstatic that Damocles' mythical sword was sheathed. I was of two minds whether to tell him what I'd discovered about Smythe and his treacherous, nay, treasonous ways. Unfortunately I hadn't had much opportunity to think it through. None, to be honest. A 4 a.m. bedtime does little for my powers of concentration.

I took a look round the room. Men were sitting on the tables normally reserved for ordered stacks of paper, a few sharpened pencils, and perhaps a cap or a helmet. The telephone in the corner wasn't in use. As far as I could discern there was a lot of aimless chattering going on. Other than awaiting instructions concerning Hill 70 there was nothing to keep the staff occupied; the same battalions were holding the line; the enemy, whose nerves were badly frayed after our latest excursion into his trenches, shelled our front very heavily this morning; and two enemy aeroplanes were reported to have crossed over our sector. None of this constituted work in my book. Or anyone else's apparently.

When Fotheringham was summoned to Lt.-Col. Hayter, sourly I watched him leave. If after countless occasions in which to reconsider he was still the colonel's pet poodle, then Hayter deserved him. Disgruntledly, I snatched for my cap and headed to the door.

My destination was just down the hall. The hall of the Château de la Haie being more suitable to a marathon than the hundred-yard dash, I slowed my pace after exiting the staff room.

At the end of the hallway, and down two flights of stairs to what I presumed was the cellar, were the rooms assigned to the divisional artillery. With barely a glimmer of light escaping from the narrow barred windows, it mattered none that they were at the back of the building. The veterinary service was down the corridor, I guessed. Still, it beat a Nissen hut where they were normally bivouacked.

I was greeted very amiably by two officers, both of whom outranked me. There weren't a lot of unexpected visitors who popped by for the view, or to chat.

'DuBois?' said the first captain, when I enquired about Benoît's whereabouts. He sighed deeply.

The second captain grimaced, which set me to worrying. I knew Benoît and what he sometimes got up to, although honestly that didn't amount to much more than a few odd drinks. I hadn't met a man yet who spoke poorly of him.

'It's ridiculous if you ask me,' said the first officer. 'There's not a fella amongst us who will tell you differently. The OC thought so too, but he wasn't left any choice. We're all pretty chafed by it.'

'Any choice, sir?' It was a curious choice of words.

'Lieutenant DuBois has been confined to quarters, as of today,' said the second man.

There was silence. I don't think I breathed for the better part of thirty seconds.

The captain spoke again. 'He's confined there until his court martial.'

I chomped down so hard I bit my lip.

Eventually I found him in one of the little huts, four men to a hut, in Vancouver Camp, several hundred yards down the road. Normally I would have taken the time to look around a bit, enquire which battalion was billeted here at the moment. I might know a few men. But I didn't have time for that.

'What the hell, Benoît?' I said as I barged through the door of a simple square hut built in wood that had probably taken all of two hours to construct.

He looked terrible. There were bags under his red-streaked eyes the size of my haversack.

'What's this I hear? It can't be!'

'It's true, Mac,' he responded wearily. 'The charges were delivered to my brigadier this morning.'

'By whom?'

'By whom? The 5th Brigade, I suppose.'

'You suppose? Brigadier Macdonell – Long Archie – has been recalled to Canada. He's on a boat. I was coming to tell you that. He won't be any trouble anymore.'

'That's nice of you, Mac. But Macdonell must have signed the papers before he left. It's his signature at the bottom. They showed me.'

I clenched my fists. The blood in my forehead was pulsing. 'The buggers,' I spat out.

Benoît said nothing.

'What did they charge you with?'

'Drunkenness.'

'Oh, that's nothing,' I began, 'half the army is drunk. We'll have you cleared of that in no time.'

'And threatening a superior officer. Captain Smythe to be specific.'

My words died on my lips. After the lengthy list Smythe had rhymed off in Lièvin I suppose it could have been worse. 'That's a little more serious,' I finally said.

'Yes, Mac, I know,' said Benoît. 'It is what it is. *C'est la vie.*'

'I'm going to crucify that Smythe,' I whispered.

'Mac!' Benoît's face turned coldly serious. 'Promise me you won't do anything stupid. This is my own dumb fault.'

'No, Benoît, that's total codswallop. It wasn't your fault. And don't ever think it was.'

He shrugged. 'I'm relieved of my duties and confined here until they can arrange a court martial. Everyone thinks it may be a while before they do so. What with the attack coming and all.' He looked at me plaintively. 'I signed up to fight the square heads, Mac. Not rot in a hut.'

'Yes, I know,' I said. 'Your friends could well be right about the court martial being delayed, though. No one has any time for that nonsense now, at least I hope they don't. Besides, it's not as if you deserted. Look at it this way; it would give us more time to prepare.' Thoughtfully I rubbed my chin. 'Yes, a delay would be ideal. There may be a way out of this yet, Benoît.'

'If you say so. Thanks, Mac.' He didn't believe me. I almost didn't believe me. A new wave of anger swept through me. Benoît was my best friend in the army. He was the sort of soul who wouldn't harm a thing unless it happened to be Hun, which was rather the point of what we were doing here. There was one thing I could try. It would involve some risks, but few things at the front didn't. I had a feeling if I didn't do anything, this wasn't going to end well.

'A telephone. Do you know where I can find a telephone? I'll need to use it in private. They'll have my hide, and stuff it, if I use the one in the staff room. That's for critical calls only. Not to mention the whole staff room would be listening in.'

'Mac, what are you planning? I'll be fine. Don't get yourself into trouble on my account.'

'A telephone, Benoît, I need a telephone as soon as possible.'

'Try the artillery. We have several lines - for obvious reasons. You'll find the headquarters in the château, at the back.' He began to give me directions.

I held up a hand in the gesture familiar to policemen everywhere. 'Yes, I know it well. Where do you think I came from?'

At this I got to my feet. In my haste and my emotions, I made short shrift of the few feet to the door. Then I thought better of it and drew up. Turning I retraced my steps and thrust a hand in his. 'Keep up your guts, Benoît, I'm going to see what I can do. I'm going to be busy, but I'll try to come see you when I can.'

He nodded. He followed it up with a wink, which I'm positive I wouldn't have been able to muster in the circumstances.

The two captains were still there, along with a clutch of other ranks

I hadn't taken notice of the first time. The artillery office was more populated than I recalled.

'Back so soon, Lieutenant?' said the first of the captains.

'Yes, sir,' I said. 'I went to visit Lieutenant DuBois. I have an idea that may help him out.'

He turned to the other captain. I probably wouldn't have asked, otherwise, but they wore their sympathies on their faces.

'Is there's anything we can do?'

'As a matter of fact, there is, sir,' I said, and explained what I required.

Before long I was sitting in a chair warm from its previous occupant, a private who'd been sent on a sudden and inexplicably urgent mission to locate coffee. I was alone in a cubicle the average broom would have been ashamed to call home, addressing myself to the telephone on the table before me. It was to be hoped the forward observers would not call in any sudden barrage requests.

It required a number of attempts. I was beginning to fear I wouldn't have any luck when the operator at the other end said: 'One moment, sir. I'll put you through.'

The line crackled. 'Hello?'

I took a deep breath. If someone in the army hierarchy learned of this there'd be hell to pay. 'Mr. Dickens? Roger Dickens? Of the *Daily Mail?*'

'Yes, this is he.'

'Hello, sir. This is Lieutenant Malcolm MacPhail of the 3rd Canadian Division. We spoke at Vimy Ridge not so long ago –' I caught myself. I was speaking far too fast.

'Yes, of course, I remember,' came the smooth, easy tones. 'How are you Lieutenant? What a pleasant surprise to hear from you. You're lucky to have caught me, though. I'm scheduled to leave for the coast and England in a few hours.'

'I won't keep you long in that case, sir. But I didn't know who else to turn to.'

'Go on, I'm listening.'

'Do you have a notepad? I have something important to tell you.'

CHAPTER 25

27th of July, 1917
Marqueffles Farm, near Bouvigny-Boyeffles, France

The invitation had come as a surprise, but then again so had the
Scheme of Operations for Hill 70 that was issued two days before.
The division was to be in reserve; the 1st and 2nd Divisions were put
forward as the ones to carry the attack. Thinking about it, and unless
something extremely unforeseen happened, it would be the first and
only major battle I would miss since arriving on the Western Front in
that dreary spring of misbegotten enthusiasm of 1915. A lifetime had
passed in the interim. Scores of friends had come and gone – gone
mainly. Perhaps someone reckoned we needed the rest.

That was poppycock, of course, though I did feel a wave of relief
when I speedread the orders over Colonel Hayter's shoulder, while
he winced at the state of my general appearance. My relief was soon
tempered by the thought of friends whose prospects were decidedly
less rosy than mine. If that wasn't enough to dampen my spirits, there
was always Benoît and his mound of troubles.

This morning a handful of the divisional staff were on hand to
observe every unit of the 5th Brigade practising on the taped course
at Marqueffles Farm; our presence explained by the possibility the
division might be called up in support. Naturally, when I heard which
brigade was involved I had second thoughts about whether I should

go, thinking of Long Archie and consort. But the brigadier was long gone, hopefully leaning purposefully over the railings after a copious dinner somewhere on a choppy and stormy North Atlantic. Major Kennedy and his staff I knew, and had no qualms about meeting again. As to Smythe, I had absolutely no appetite in seeing him. In fact it was probably best if I didn't. Especially not now. But then, given the forecast for the crowds, I figured he wouldn't be too difficult to avoid; I might need to duck from time to time. Fortunately, if two years of war had taught me anything it was how to go about that.

We arrived very early to avoid the congestion expected later. Generals Horne and Currie, as well as Burstall and Ross of the 2nd Division, were attending, and such a weighty delegation inevitably brought with it a whole rearguard of pips, crowns and swords and their associated motorcades. Quietly I suggested we pick out a few spots ahead of time, in the hope the 3rd Division wouldn't be relegated to a position to the rear of some copse, and a hundred yards behind the action. It was a question of "bite and hold", I explained.

Marqueffles Farm was roughly seven miles east of our new headquarters at Barlin, where we'd moved only yesterday. Following a short drive, it was then a simple matter of traversing the hamlet of Bouvigny-Boyeffles, with its few nondescript houses – it took longer to spell the name of the place than to pass through it – and after a few hundred yards rolling downhill you arrived. The farm was in a shallow valley.

I'd never been to this specific spot, even though it was part of the great hinterland of the Corps, on the far side of Vimy Ridge and consequently far from the prying eyes of the enemy – full of headquarters, camps, batteries, training grounds, and everything else that sustained an army.

'It's rather pretty here,' said Major Lindsey of our party, referring to the green hillocks that rose up to the south and to the east, all covered by a scattering of trees. Even the mildly decrepit, low-slung farmhouse and its accompanying stalls had a certain pastoral charm to it.

'Wait a few moments, sir,' I said. 'The 5th Brigade isn't yet in action.'

Fotheringham lifted his head and appreciatively sniffed the air.

I turned to him. 'On that same note, enjoy it while you can. It won't stay fresh for long.'

By the time a few thousand soldiers massed to begin the assault on the precisely measured reproduction of a section of Hill 70, and its trenches, the air still smelled decent. But it was buzzing with voices. There must have been fifty observers of the well-clad variety, if not more. Most carried field glasses and an air of excited expectancy; there being nothing like playing guns in the unspoilt French countryside to bring out the boy in them. Compared to the real thing it had its advantages.

'A pleasure to see you, gentlemen,' Major-General Burstall said, as he swept past the 3rd Division's finest – no indication he remembered, or even saw me. Once back in 1915 I'd given him a personal tour of the Duck's Bill at Givenchy while he planned the pre-attack barrage. Admittedly, it was a small thing, and from a long time ago.

Someone in the host division had been deft in his arrangements. Contrary to my sombre predictions, the grassy field assigned as an observation point easily accommodated the assembled rabble, while also offering an excellent view of the slopes to be attacked. Predictably, the army, corps, division and brigade commanders stood together, slightly forward of the rest. Lieutenant-Colonel Ross (his appointment so sudden he hadn't yet been made brigadier) was explaining to Horne and Currie what they were about to see. Behind them, the division's senior officers were doing the same with their guests. Towards the back of the field little explanation was offered. Even if it had been I was too busy sipping at the mug of hot coffee a cook's assistant had thoughtfully given me. Besides, the whole operation seemed reasonably straight-forward. But then I hadn't been on the staff from the turn of the century; there being nothing like actual experience to hammer home the dos and don'ts of an attack on an enemy trench system.

'No rain,' said Fotheringham conversationally.

'No,' I acknowledged. 'But the ground's wet enough. It won't make the preparations easy.' For emphasis I dug the toe of my boot into the earth, effortlessly turning up a tuft of it.

Two days ago the weather had turned foul. From a dull and miserable sky rain poured down with abandon, the next shower already looming as the last shifted away. The following day it did the same. Eventually it would emerge that the warm, sunny days of summer were gone, ushering in one of the wettest Augusts on record. Today however it was fine.

'You know –' Fotheringham began to say, when a chorus of shouts and whistles interrupted. Men were leaping to their feet and streaming out of the practice ditches. The attack on Hill 70 – the meticulously photographed, measured, and taped approximation thereof – was on.

Small arms fire began shortly thereafter, and puffs of smoke appeared, the smell of it washing down the slopes towards us in the morning breeze. The hill crawled with men, seemingly a disordered swarm until one looked closer and saw that each group was moving methodically and with purpose. It was all over remarkably quickly. The brigade had reached its objectives. Would that the real operation proceed so smoothly.

Slowly, Major Lindsey let his glasses dip, nodding approvingly. 'They did well.'

While he hadn't addressed any particular one of us, surprisingly I was the first to respond. 'Yes they did, sir.' Usually I tried to leave the role of the sycophant to others. I'd always loathed the kid at school who waved an index finger around even before the teacher asked the question, in search of some modicum of glory or praise.

Lindsey glanced at me, then a curious look sailed onto his face. 'You must be pleased, MacPhail? Your haul at that tunnel made quite an impression. Even the colonel commented.'

'He did, sir?'

'Surely you must have seen the order?'

At this I belatedly stuffed my surprise away. I'd been thinking about corps operation order no. 140 all morning. If truth be told, it was the main reason I was feeling so garrulous – a pleasant morning in the French countryside, and a hot cup of coffee notwithstanding. 'Oh, yes, I did. Thank you, sir.'

The order he was referring to was signed by the corps Brigadier-General General Staff (BGGS), but it could have been written by General Currie himself, such was the impression it gave. And it might well have been. Certainly the whole point of the order was to draw attention to matters the Corps commander found wanting. Paragraph (e) under the heading "Secrecy" was what Lindsey meant: "It is beyond doubt that in some recent operations the enemy was informed as to the approximate time of attack. The most probable source of information is the improper use of the telephone..." The order went on to direct readers to an earlier letter warning about this very thing. There was no warning what would befall the reader should the warning be disregarded again. Nevertheless, coming from the Corps commander it made for an effective deterrent.

One of the 2nd Division officers now approached Major Lindsey. He excused himself.

'If I'm not careful you're going to snatch that promotion for yourself,' said Fotheringham, who'd been listening. His smile was well-meaning, although there were more sides to it than he let on.

'What makes you so certain there's a promotion to be had?'

'Ah. The sign of a true soldier. Oblivious to what's in front of his nose if it's not edible. Haven't you ever noticed the staff is short a captain?'

'No.'

'See. That's your problem, Malcolm. Opportunities are lost on the unprepared. It's a miracle you've made it this far.'

'True,' I replied. Which was quite truthful. It could indeed be considered a miracle. I was, however, eager for the responsibility and independence a higher rank would bring with it. Fotheringham, for all his quick wit and personable nature, was not exactly well equipped to lead men into battle – even from the confines of a divisional headquarters. 'I'm generally too busy keeping my head down,' I added. 'Personnel openings don't mean much at the front.'

'True enough,' he grinned, taking it on the chin. I don't think he really caught the innuendo though.

Then Major Clark-Kennedy came ambling towards me. He wore the glimmer of a smile. As he was a somewhat dour-looking man by nature, I took this to be a positive sign. Either he didn't know or didn't care about my altercation with his old brigadier. 'Hello, MacPhail,' he said, extending a hand.

'Hello, sir. The brigade did very well.'

'Yes. I thought so, too. More importantly our guests were satisfied.' He winked. 'We practiced yesterday.'

Practicing for the practice was an altogether new concept for me. Not that it wasn't sensible with the all the brass that had come to watch.

He looked over his shoulder. 'I don't believe you know our new commander. Come, I'll introduce you to him.'

Lieutenant-Colonel Ross, while missing the crossed baton and sabre on his shoulders, certainly looked the part of a brigade commander, with his neat soldier's moustache and greying hair, stout build, and a broad snow scoop of a chin that could have parted a line of enemy wire all by itself.

'Sir, let me present Lieutenant MacPhail of the 3rd Division,' said Clark-Kennedy. 'He was attached to the brigade during the Arleux attack as a liaison officer. It proved rather helpful.'

The colonel nodded politely. Given the company he was keeping, and the demands on his time, I noted with surprise how he took a moment to look me up and down. 'Pleased to meet you, Lieutenant. It was bad luck your division won't be involved. But should you miss the fight, know you're welcome to liaise with the brigade again!'

'Thank you, sir. Very kind of you.' I replied. I couldn't tell if he was joking or not. But *not* seemed a fair guess. He had that way about him.

Once he and Clark-Kennedy moved on to fresher pastures – ones more resplendent in gold braid – I returned to the others. But right before I reached them a couple of officers drew my attention. They were standing apart, deep in conversation. I stopped in my tracks and just stared.

'Do you know them? Who are they?' buzzed Fotheringham in my ear. The man had more eyes in his head than I had fingers on both hands. No wonder he knew we were short a captain.

'The Smythe family,' I growled. 'The major's something with the First Army, and the captain's on the staff of the 5th Brigade.'

'By Jove, they could be twins,' he marvelled. 'One's a little older. But other than that...'

'Yes.'

As we watched, the major brought a folded newspaper out from under his arm and thrust it – angrily it seemed to me – at the captain. Smythe said something and took it in his hands. Briefly he wrestled with the pages, and then stood there in the field studying what was written. Except for the smell of cordite and the predominance of olive green all around, he could have been reading the race scores at Ascot. After a moment he handed the paper back. The major refused it. With some violence he then threw it to the ground. He and the major suddenly cocked a head towards General Horne's party. Someone was beckoning to them. They moved off.

Fotheringham was droning on about something. He'd been talking for heaven knows how long, but I hadn't heard a word. 'Hang on,' I said, my stomach in my throat, and my heart pumping. As inconspicuously as I could I quick marched past the other little groups of officers to the spot in the grass where I'd seen the two of them standing. Yes! The newspaper was still there.

Furtively I glanced left and right. Not a soul was looking my way. The Smythes were gathered near General Horne, their attention focused on the high and the mighty. I bent over.

The paper was damp and badly creased. I guessed it was still open to the page Smythe had been reading. I saw one other thing; it was the *Daily Mail*! I began to read.

THE BOOTS SCANDAL: PROFITS BEFORE PATRIOTISM

For months thousands of our troops at the front have been supplied with defective footwear, our correspondent reports. The boots in question are manufactured by a major Northampton firm under government contract. Privately, officers in the field, who are familiar with the situation, describe themselves as appalled they haven't been recalled or replaced.

It is a matter of national shame that unscrupulous private interests are permitted to profit from selling sub-standard equipment while our soldiers suffer the consequences. This is precisely what the Munitions of War Act (1915) was designed to prevent...

The opinion piece went on for several more paragraphs, mentioning the need for an immediate investigation by the government and the army, while recalling the shells scandal of two years earlier. An opposition Member of Parliament was quoted as saying he intended to demand answers in the House of Commons. There was no mention of the Canadian Corps, or even Arras. But those details would surely not take long to emerge.

I reread the first few paragraphs and snorted a laugh. 'That'll get the buggers,' I said to myself, grinning broadly.

Some sixth sense made me look up. Smythe was standing beside his cousin, several paces from the First Army crowd, his entire being fixated on me. His face was a thundercloud. I'd looked down the barrels of *minenwerfers* that looked less threatening.

I gulped.

CHAPTER 26

29th of July, 1917
Barlin, France

There was a deafening crash above our heads. Everyone fell silent.

An angry wind howled out of nowhere savagely lashing the large French windows and brick façade of the Mairie. After a spell the wind ebbed away – deceptively – for moments later it returned with renewed fury, accompanied by rain pelting down in great torrents. It rattled furiously against the glass panes and beat down in an unrelenting roar upon the cobblestones outside. Moving to the window I watched as the rain transformed the *pavé* of the rue de l'Eglise into a veritable river racing in the direction of La Place and the tents of the field ambulance nearby. The horse lines of the divisional train with their wagons and animals, the latter shivering and frightened stiff by the thunder, were only a short distance to the north. All in all it was a miserable start to the day.

After a couple of days' respite the rains had returned with renewed fury. It was as well that new orders from the Corps arrived shortly before. The Hill 70 operation was delayed for forty-eight hours. Among other things, getting the heavy guns into position with the ground sodden from the earlier downpours was proving difficult. A peek at what the morning had brought suggested it was not going to become any easier. Even Fotheringham required no helping hand to conclude that the operation would need to be pushed back yet again. The weather was fit for neither man nor beast, let alone a temperamental heavy howitzer accustomed to a firm bed of solid planking, a half tonne of reasonably clean shells stacked neatly to the rear, and a dozen willing men at its every beck and call.

'No weather for a stroll in the village today, MacPhail,' murmured Major Bertram, coming to stand beside me at the window, his hands clasped behind his back.

I glanced at him. 'No, sir, no stroll today. No weather for being in the trenches, either, sir. I'm just thankful I'm here and not there.'

'As you should be,' he said. He said it with a faraway look which I took to mean he had some personal experience in such things – a characteristic I always appreciated in more senior officers, more so because of its relative rarity. 'This is no weather to be manning a trench,' he added.

Yet west of Lens extending along a front as far north as the Bois Hugo all the way south to the Souchez River, a distance of more than four miles, I knew that thousands of my countrymen were doing precisely that. With the objective finally fixed, dispositions had shifted. A British corps had moved out and the Canadian Corps moved in. Immediately to the east, the many lines of enemy trenches surrounding Lens and Hill 70 lay waiting. Inexorably, inevitably, the attack was coming. We were once again being ordered to get the job done.

Regardless, no one knew exactly when Z Day would be – even the generals were unsure about the precise details. But at least that ruled out Fritz knowing the date and the time, either. Perhaps not entirely trusting his own sternly worded instructions, that may have been General Currie's intent.

The Mairie at Barlin was no Château de la Haie. But it was commendably warm and dry, and free from shellfire. The village itself was an inconsequential dot on the map due west of Lens's northern suburbs and the 70-metre high hill that was the object of all our attentions. A few miles to the north were the delights of an undamaged and thriving Béthune, well known to any soldier with a day off. Bordering Barlin to the north ran the main Arras-Béthune line, and the proximity of that line and the existence of a station gave the place an importance otherwise not warranted by its dozen-odd streets, most of which were presently given over to various branches of the army.

There were the brigade schools that taught about varied methods of warfare (those both traditional and modern), the large hospital for the casualties that resulted from their implementation, and several YMCA venues of entertainment, as well as the officers' clubs, for those attempting to escape it altogether – if only for a night.

However, I wouldn't be in any real need of Barlin's facilities in the near future. The division was sitting it out in Corps reserve. Whatever the plans for Hill 70, and whenever they were to take place, were concerns of a decidedly abstract nature – as opposed to the kind that has you writing last letters home, just in case.

On that happy note I finished up the day's location report. As most units hadn't moved it didn't take me long. Around eleven I went in search of Benoît. Fortunately, the latest shower was sputtering to an end, and I found him exiting the church. I knew I'd find him either there, or at the mess. As the church was next door to the Mairie, I checked there first. A commanding officer wouldn't soon refuse a request to attend church service. Although listening to the chaplain drone on for an entire sixty minutes, the novelty of a dry roof overhead wearing thin in the first few minutes, wouldn't have been my first choice for a peaceful or productive Sunday morning. In DuBois's case, in urgent need of some divine intervention, I could understand why opinions might differ.

'Ah, there you are,' I said when I spotted him, rubbing my hands together. 'How about a little lunch? I won't say a word if you want seconds.'

He shook his head.

'You're confined to quarters, but you still have to eat, Benoît.'

Loudly he sighed. '*Non*,' he said simply.

After that I didn't dare ask the specifics.

Benoît didn't appear well. For a man who was the epitome of ruddy good health, and even better humour, Benoît looked about as deflated as an observation balloon after a *Jagdstaffel* painted in crimson had ripped past.

'Any news?' I asked.

He shook his head. 'Maybe the paperwork went astray. Do you think it's possible, Mac?'

It was my turn to shake my head. 'No, I'm afraid you shouldn't count on that. The army's ways grind slowly, but everything is in triplicate. It may go halfway round the Empire in the meanwhile, however, eventually something will surface.' Despite my words I was suddenly reminded of the occasion when a whole bundle of inconvenient paperwork of the 1st Division had ostensibly washed away in a flood up in the Salient. *That might be possible here, too!*

Then as quickly as the thought came I dismissed it. That had been in the first years of the war. Nowadays there were likely closer to a dozen copies, than the three I'd postulated, floating around.

I took an appraising look at the churchgoers. It had been a popular service evidently; sitting on a pew in a church beat standing for church parade on a muddy field in the streaming rain. The men were talking quite cheerfully, which reminded me of something I'd brought along to buoy Benoît's spirits.

'Have a drink,' I said, and pressed my canteen into his hands. For the occasion I'd filled it to the brim with rum, a little subterfuge I'd learned from him.

His eyes widened. 'Mac!'

'Oh, drink up,' I said sternly. 'They can't arrest you twice for drunkenness. Not even before noon.'

He brightened at that, although it was patently untrue. 'What you don't know can't kill you, dear,' my grandmother liked to assure me as young boy – blissfully unaware of the hazards I'd face on the Western Front in later years. So reassured, Benoît brought the bottle to his lips and drank deeply.

'*Merci*, Mac.'

'AND… I have this…' With a flourish I extracted a rolled-up *Daily Mail* from the inside of my coat and presented it to him like a field-marshal's baton.

He read it slowly, so slowly I was afraid he didn't grasp the English, or the significance. Until, finally, he spoke: 'You were right. No wonder Smythe was so excited about me seeing those kids in the boots.'

There was a long pause. I waited for him to say more.

'Of course, I was right,' I said eventually. I was a little disappointed he hadn't marvelled at how I'd discovered Smythe's rotten game, or how that game had miraculously come to grace the pages of one of England's largest newspapers. Naturally, I felt the need to elaborate.

'So you see, Benoît,' I concluded. 'Smythe stopped at nothing to get rid of that last shipment. What I didn't realize until recently was that when I spotted his twin cousin in Paris outside the bank, he wasn't depositing money, he was withdrawing it. Smythe needed those Francs. He was paying off men left and right simply to dump the boots. Although one was a little too eager when he made the mistake of trying to pawn a few dozen off on the local populace. Which is where you stumbled on the scene. It's also why Smythe reacted so strongly when he saw you. It had nothing to do with drink, and everything to do with what the kids were wearing.'

'But why, Mac? Paying off men to dump the boots. Why would he do that?'

'Why? Because if too many boots were issued, eventually there would have been complaints and someone would have started to ask questions about why the soles were all falling off. In no time the newspapers would have been full of it. That's just the kind of story they love. And then the family business would have been clobbered with a massive bill to replace every single pair, along with damages. This way, not only does the firm of Smythe & Co. get to keep its ill-gotten profits, it keeps its reputation. Actually, there's a very good chance they'll win new orders because of it. From what I gather there's not a boot to be had from here to Arras.'

'Bastards,' breathed Benoît.

I gritted my teeth. 'Yes, but they won't escape this,' I said, pointing at the newspaper. 'After the shell crisis Lloyd George is coming down hard on this kind of war profiteering. Smythe and cousin looked about as foul-tempered as that cloud behind you when last I saw them.' I wiggled a finger in the direction of the cloud. It was dark, rumbling ominously, and sailing across fast, almost on top of us. A wind was beginning to gust.

'You did well, *mon ami*. But this could take months to investigate. Longer.' He grimaced. 'I don't have months, Mac.'

I was about to respond (not that I had much of a rebuttal to hand) when the deluge began.

'*Merci*,' cried Benoît, pulling his collar up and his cap down. '*À bientôt.*' He threw a wave in my direction over his shoulder and began to walk rapidly down the street towards his billet.

'Keep your head up,' I shouted after him, and then clattered across the cobblestones to the Mairie.

'Lieutenant!'

I was standing in the vestibule, having just shaken the water off my cap, debating whether to even bother doing the same with the tunic. I was soaked. On the top of my mind was what Benoît had said, and the harsh truth it contained. I looked up at the sound of the voice, my face dripping.

Lt.-Col. Hayter was hailing me from twenty feet down the hall. Evidently he'd seen me slip in out of the gathering hurricane.

'Sir?' I put cap under my arm. Quickly I walked towards him – GSO1s aren't accustomed to waiting.

'I have some new orders for you, MacPhail.' A probing glance at me.

'Sir?'

'You're aware the Division will be in reserve during the forthcoming operation?'

'Of course, sir.'

He nodded. '2nd Division has suggested another exchange of officers. General Lipsett is favourably inclined to the idea, as am I. I don't need to explain to you that our role in reserve could well change depending on how the battle progresses. Having an officer in place, and aware of the details, could be invaluable. Either way, it'll be useful when we need to relieve them in the line when the time comes.' I nodded. 'There is one surprising aspect to this... 2nd Division have come up with a suggestion of their own who our man should be.'

I frowned. That was unusual.

'Come now. You must have charmed someone in that division, Lieutenant? More than I was led to believe.' He stared at me searchingly with those drooping, weary eyes of his. I blinked and then found myself having to wipe away the water that dribbled down my forehead. 'They asked for you, MacPhail. You should feel flattered, I suppose.'

'Me! They asked for me?' I felt the blood, if not the water, draining from my face. 'But what about... What about my duties with the division, sir?'

'Oh, Lieutenant Fotheringham will be able to assume those with little difficulty, I expect.' He may have meant it reassuringly. To me the effect was the opposite. It was bad enough that I was going to be involved in the battle after all, his conclusion that I could be effortlessly replaced – by Fotheringham no less – rankled. The only bright spot was that at least someone at 2nd Division held in me higher regard.

'When, sir?' I mumbled.

'Soon,' he replied. 'The operation could come any day. You'd best pack some dry socks.'

CHAPTER 27

8th of August, 1917
Sains-en-Gohelle, France

Regarding the extra socks, Colonel Hayter needn't have worried. While every day since I'd arrived at the 2nd Division it had rained, often quite heavily – Christ, it had done nothing else the past weeks – I had no reason for complaint about my surroundings. Being at a divisional headquarters was like that; seldom did irritating leaks spring into life overhead, hostile shells were few and far between, and it was unheard of for the divisional staff to work standing in a foot-high pond of foul water. It was one of the many reasons I appreciated being out of the trenches – though I was beginning to wonder if Hayter had plans for me in that regard. That being said, the other day I accompanied some of the staff to the trenches north of Cité St. Laurent and Cité St. Émile in order to reconnoitre the terrain. They would be crossing that ground during the assault, and the experience only confirmed everything I suspected. Hill 70 was going to be a very tough nut indeed. There was still no word when it was to happen.

Hayter's thoughts on the subject of Z Day hadn't panned out any better than his suggestions on socks. The operation had just been delayed for the fifth time by my count. At this rate, in a week, I wouldn't have any fingers left to keep track. Moreover, I understood General Burstall was hosting an important meeting here at headquarters later this afternoon. It couldn't be otherwise that Z Day would be discussed. Seeing an officer exit a room down the hall I hastened to catch up with him.

'Hello, sir. Is there any news?' I asked breathlessly.

Major Walker nodded. 'Hello, Lieutenant. The artillery was active all night on our front: theirs and ours. 4.1s and 77mms mainly. But that's about it.'

When I first arrived, Walker had been one of the first to greet me after I was deposited at the modest brick building in the distinctly unappealing village of Sains-en-Gohelle – the transition from coal mining to war having changed little aesthetics-wise. Both Walker and I were surprised to see each other. The last time I'd seen him was at Arleux. Then he'd been a captain and working for the 5th Brigade. In the interim he'd made quite a career.

He'd greeted me warmly enough, even if he was visibly puzzled as to what he should do with me. Others were equally welcoming. Even General Burstall himself exchanged a few pleasantries when he happened along. Mysteriously, no one had yet owned up to having put my name forward as the 3rd Division liaison. I suspected it must have the brigade major of the 5th Brigade, Clark-Kennedy. He'd been remarkably friendly when we met at the manoeuvres at Marqueffles Farm. Or even their new GOC, Ross. He was keen on reinforcements.

Walker now looked at me more closely. 'You look disappointed.'

I shook my head. 'It's the waiting, sir. I sometimes think it's worse than the battle itself. Although of course that's patent nonsense.'

'Nonsense or not, you're not the only one thinking that, MacPhail. But the battle will come soon enough.'

'Yes, sir, I suppose it will. In the meantime it'll give our artillery a little extra time to deal with the enemy wire and the batteries.'

'Yes,' he replied. 'Yes, it will. That could make all the difference.'

If there was one thing (or possibly two) that stopped an infantry charge in its tracks it was wire and the enemy artillery. Machine guns came a close third. Unfortunately, no one had yet devised a foolproof means of dealing with any of them before an attack, though our batteries were undeniably doing their best; Hill 70 and Lens were being deluged night and day. Not that the artillery's best was universally appreciated. Mean-spirited bureaucrats in the First Army were heard to grumble regularly about our daily expenditure of shells.

Then Walker caught my attention with a revelation of sorts. 'I should congratulate you on your new GSO1, MacPhail,' he said.

My eyes widened. 'You must know something I don't, sir.'

'Oh, you hadn't heard. Well, your Colonel Hayter has moved on to greener pastures. There's a new man come in his stead, by the name of Hore-Ruthven.'

'Really?' I was taken aback at this development. Hayter had been a decent staff officer as far as I could judge. On the other hand, his recent appreciation of my performance had not exactly been wholehearted, to put it mildly. So perhaps this was for the best. Fotheringham would certainly not be amused. I smiled wickedly at the thought. There was one other potential benefit; the new GSO1 would have his hands full, and I guessed a court martial for Benoît would not be top of his list of priorities.

'I must run,' said Walker, then mentioned the very thing I was thinking about: '5th Brigade is holding a Field General Court Martial here later this afternoon. Brigadier Ross has asked me to attend. He's acting as President.'

I went weak in the knees. Bile filled my throat and I felt as if I were about to faint. I reached a hand out to the wall to steady myself.

'A court martial, sir? Who is being tried?' I gasped.

'I don't rightly know,' he replied. 'A private charged with desertion is all I was told.' He looked at me with concern. 'Are you feeling all right, MacPhail? You look positively ashen.'

I nodded.

He hesitated, his eyes narrowing. I nodded again. 'Well, if you're sure, I'll be on my way then. Perhaps you should sit for a moment. You look faint.'

Deeply I breathed in, a wave of relief washing over me. It wasn't Benoît then, thank God. I should have known, but the double co-incidence of a court martial being held, and the mention of the 5th Brigade, was simply too overwhelming. As I stood there, my senses returning, I realized that Field General Court Martials were for offences that might result in the death penalty. Whatever charges Smythe had dreamt up they were more likely to be dealt with by a regimental or a district or, in the worst case, a general court martial. All those required more time to organize. In addition, it was quite possible it would be the 3rd Division's bailiwick, even if Smythe and Long Archie were 2nd Division.

I was still thinking about Benoît, and pondering what else I might do to help as I made my way to the staff room. He was literally a few short miles to the south of my present whereabouts. But hindered by my inability to use the telephone, or more specifically by the lack of requisite rank, position or urgency, and possessing neither runner nor pigeon to otherwise convey my messages, it was difficult to communicate anything. I would need to put my mind to it.

I stepped round the corner at a fair gait and slammed into a solid, but slightly pliable object.

Had I been that tiny bit more alert, less sunk in thought and worry, I would have noted the voices or felt the general air of commotion, and employed appropriate precautions. As it was, I was fortunate he wasn't on his back on the hardwood floor. In fact it was all I could do to avoid bumping heads with him, like two Bighorn Rams during rutting season. That would have truly put an end to my days on the staff.

'I beg your pardon, sir. I'm terribly sorry.'

The officer I'd run down was a head shorter than me, thin and impeccably turned out, moustache and hair generously trimmed in white. Somehow, there was something vaguely familiar about him. After the initial shock he fixed me with a steady gaze. I could see he was startled, which was not altogether surprising as I'd had the advantage of both momentum and surprise, and at least fifty pounds on him. What startled me most were the red tabs and the profusion of gold embossing I saw adorning his uniform. Then my gaze moved to his epaulettes, at the sight of which I winced. They my eyes shifted to his face and came into sharp focus.

'By Jove, Currie,' General Sir Henry Horne pronounced, the slightest hint of a Scottish accent emerging, 'you might have warned me. I would have worn my helmet today.'

Predictably there was a smattering of polite chuckles from the posse of red tabs and polished boots bringing up the rear. I recall smiling wanly myself.

Lt.-Gen. Currie lumbered forward. 'Afternoon, Lieutenant.' Then equally calmly he addressed General Horne: 'MacPhail here has seen a lot of action. You'll have to forgive him. Sometimes he forgets he's not still in the trenches.'

Horne looked at me appraisingly. 'Yes, of course. No harm done. But it would be reassuring if he were in the trenches.' Then to me, along with a measured smile: 'You pack quite a punch, Lieutenant. Put it to good use when the time comes.'

This last was surely an allusion to the timing of the attack. I understood GHQ was waiting impatiently for it to begin. General Horne was here in Sains-en-Gohelle to subtly remind Currie of that. He couldn't wait forever. As to the allusion I might be of more use in the trenches, I was hoping no one had heard.

Still breathing uneasily I shuffled to one side to make room, and stood to attention while the two generals slipped past. They were followed by Burstall and a half dozen others.

The last man in file was Major Smythe. He looked older than I remembered him.

I guessed that he both recognized and knew of me from the way his mouth clamped together when he caught my gaze, holding it for that telltale instant too long. There was no doubt at all after he spoke.

'Yes, indeed, a spell in the bloody trenches…,' he sneered in my general direction, his lips twisting into a frosty smile. Then the cold eyes darted away, towards the backs of the others. He lengthened his pace to catch up, and didn't look back.

I held my tongue and watched him go, strangely intimidated by this performance. No, what I felt was better likened to the sensation one has after narrowly ducking two Fish Tails in a row, only to hear a third on its way.

The next afternoon new orders from the Corps arrived. In the staff room I learned the essence if not the details of the weighty closed-door meeting. The results of the court martial weren't announced, and I made no effort to enquire, preferring to bury my head instead in the questionable supposition that the court had been merciful.

There was nothing equivocal about the orders. Z Day was to come "not before" the 15th read the curtly worded missive. Phrased otherwise, this meant it was to be the 15th. Which was less than a week away, and somehow I knew (prophetically?) that this was a date that was going to stick.

A number of days came to pass before Major Smythe's words would also, in their turn, appear prophetic.

CHAPTER 28

14th of August, 1917
Cité St. Pierre (1 mile northwest of Lens), France

Major Walker got the assignment. Or maybe he requested it. 'Ah, MacPhail, you're precisely the man I was looking for.' As I was demonstrably less important to the well-functioning of the 2nd Division than the fellow who chopped the vegetables each day – the role as liaison less onerous than several leaves of absence I could remember – his words put me on my guard. Especially as the operation was scheduled for tomorrow. By rights Walker ought to have had his hands too full to be searching every nook and cranny looking for me.

A few days earlier Z Day for the Hill 70 operation was confirmed for August 15th, pretty much as everyone expected. After which news the divisional staff promptly went out and were whipped 10 to 5 by the 5th Brigade during what was initially billed as a friendly baseball match. I'd offered to play on behalf of the staff. Somewhat unfairly they turned me down on account of my 'allegiance' to another division, although they were plenty happy to have me as umpire – at least before the game. Late in the first inning I became aware some were bewailing this decision, forcing me to race to my own defence. 'Who better to pass judgement on the 2nd Division than a man from the 3rd Division?' I pointed out. All too quickly this line of reasoning had run its course. Walker was still sore about my call in the seventh.

'You're a popular man in some parts,' he said presently. I shrugged, conscious the mood was apt to go downhill from here. 'Your friends in the 5th Brigade have asked for your assistance during the forthcoming operation. As you know, they'll be one of the first units that the 3rd Division will be asked to relieve so it could be useful. Come to that they were the ones who suggested your name in the first place – due to your skills as an umpire, no doubt. So, unless you have any pressing objections…' Impatiently he began drumming his fingers on a trouser leg. 'I was intending to give my blessing. Well?'

To no avail I tried to wipe away the sleep in my eyes. It was early still, and this was a most surprising development. I'd been assigned to keep the lines of communication open between our two divisions. I had no intention of repeating the mistake I'd made at Arleux. But evidently it had been the Brigade Major, Clark-Kennedy, who'd put in a good word for me; something few others had recently.

So I didn't feel I could let him down; even if a move forward meant I'd be virtually at the front itself. As a guest of the 5th Brigade there'd be no chance of avoiding Captain Smythe. Particularly now, I had no desire of seeing him. Nevertheless, common sense suggested that having Smythe at close quarters might throw up an opportunity to help out Benoît, assuming I could restrain myself from doing something rash. And when I considered it, I could as easily phone in a report to my superiors from the 5th Brigade HQ as from Sains-en-Gohelle. So be it. I'd faced down worse than Smythe and a few searching Boche shells. It was not as if there was much choice. In the army, polite requests are orders by any other name.

'No, sir,' I said to Major Walker. 'No pressing objections.'

'Good, that's settled then. Best of luck, MacPhail. I'm off to the coal mines, as it were. There's a lot to be done.' With that he turned away.

'When are they expecting me, sir?' I called after him. 'I mean down the shaft in the coal mines?'

'Immediately,' he replied. He was already halfway down the hallway. 'You know the schedule. If you hurry you might catch a lift. There are some lorries heading that way.'

The lorries were no idle rumour. I found a half dozen of them parked in a row, assembling before they headed out in the general direction of the company town of Cité St. Pierre, where I was reliably informed the 5th Brigade had planted its flag. Briefly I hesitated when I learned they were carrying shells, but soon ascertained the shells were of the H.E. and shrapnel varieties; 'No gas here, sir,' cried the private from the tailgate of a lorry, when I inquired. I clambered up into the back and sat beside him. It would have been easy to claim a proper seat in the cab next to the driver, but I felt a little safer keeping careful watch on the cargo.

'A lot of shells,' I remarked to the soldier, looking around.

He grinned. 'Yes, sir. We've been at this for days. And we don't mean to stop.'

'Then I expect the Boche are in for more of a licking than they've had already.'

'That's true, sir, but ole Fritz is giving us hell for our troubles. The boys at the guns say they're being smothered in gas.'

'Thank heavens for respirators.'

The soldier looked sceptical. 'Yes and no, sir. This new gas is something awful. It burns and blisters the skin. It's horrible stuff. Mustard they call it.'

I'd heard the name recently but it hadn't made much of an impression. One gas was as bad as the next, it always seemed to me. Only this mixture was apparently worse. At that a cold shiver ran down my spine. I endeavoured however to keep a straight face in front of the private. My experience in the Salient had taught me a healthy respect for gas. One good lungful and you tended to forget all the other hazards of life on the continent. By then you were retching your lungs out, and life itself if you were unlucky. Uneasily I reached to my side to double check. But I hadn't forgotten the canvas bag with mask.

It was late afternoon when I sprang down from the lorry. Shouting my thanks to the driver, I waved farewell to Briers, who'd talked my ear off the entire way.

As I gazed around, I couldn't help thinking Major Walker's casual coal mining references were a little too close to the mark. Of course, he knew precisely where I was being sent. In front of me were the tall remains of a mine shaft and what I took to be a water tower. Down the road that I was told to follow, were row upon row of low-slung miners' housing built in brick, none of which appeared inhabitable. Feeling very small and insignificant in this endless wasteland of destroyed industry, I began to walk; it seemed the fastest way to escape from where I didn't want to be.

It was only a short while before I reached the brigade. They were encamped in Cité St. Pierre near another coal pit, this one Fosse no. 11, on the west side of the settlement. Headquarters was located in what had once been a large H-shaped building (presumably belonging to the mine administration), now partly caved in. To my left (west) was the twin track of coal waste called the Double Crassier, two low mountain ranges of black culm that ran parallel for more than a thousand yards alongside the rail spur once used to ferry it there. The furthest end of the range was capped by two gigantic pyramids of slag. All the tangled and torn machinery and structures of the ruined pithead lay close at hand. Cité St. Pierre hadn't looked attractive in peace time, and war had not improved matters.

Once past the sentry at the door, I entered a high-ceilinged and remarkably (considering the exterior) well-preserved hallway. There I was delighted to spot Major Clark-Kennedy.

'Major!' I cried out.

Clark-Kennedy turned to face me. He looked harried. It was a natural reaction for a man whose brigade was going into action in less than a day. He hesitated momentarily before a flash of recognition brightened his features, then he walked briskly my way.

'*Whatever* are you doing here, Lieutenant?'

I explained. My explanation didn't appear to ring any bells.

'You say you were requested to come?' he said. I nodded. 'Not by me you weren't. Strange that I don't recall any of this.' Thoughtfully he rubbed at his chin. 'Well, it has been an exceptionally busy time... Welcome, nevertheless, Lieutenant. If you follow me I'll quickly show you what it is we're planning.'

The staff room was busy. The brigade GOC, Brigadier-General Ross – his promotion had come through a couple of weeks ago – was at the telephone. Clark-Kennedy led me to a table on which a sizeable map was displayed, several officers examining it. Politely they moved to one side to make room.

'1st Corps is carrying out a feint attack with dummy tanks today,' said Clark-Kennedy. 'Hopefully that'll throw the Boche off their game, but I'm afraid that's the best we can do in the circumstances; mislead them about the exact details.'

'They'll be expecting us, sir?'

'Oh yes, MacPhail, I'm afraid they will. I don't think there's any doubt about that. They'll have taken note of all the preparations.'

It was a shame – unavoidable some would say – but a shame nonetheless. Going on three weeks the back country was filled with the clamour of thousands of men and all manner of equipment on the move, taped trenches and well-trodden exercise areas everywhere that a slope might lend itself to become a temporary replica of Hill 70; unmistakeable as such for the aerial observers, or those studying the photographs afterwards. Had the enemy somehow missed all these signs, the growing artillery concentration was undeniable. Any Fritz in a trench in a broad radius round Lens could attest to that.

'4th Division will mount a diversionary attack on our right flank in the morning,' said Clark-Kennedy. 'That may draw off some fire.'

I peered at the map. 'And the attack itself, sir?' For someone who had hung around 2nd Division HQ for the better part of two weeks, and was furthermore expected to coordinate with my own division when the time came, I suddenly realized I had only the vaguest idea of what precisely was being planned.

'Three lines,' said Clark-Kennedy, dabbing a finger down on each in turn. 'They won't be holding the front line in any strength, of course, although the second line on the crest will be much stronger. However, the third line, that's the Green Line on the map, that will be a different matter altogether. On top of everything else it's on a reverse slope.'

I winced. A reverse slope. Military doctrine from time immemorial had dictated the primacy of high ground. Yet on the Western Front a wrinkle had emerged in that theory. At the battle of the Somme the Germans had demonstrated quite convincingly that the strongest-held trench was not that dug along the crest of a ridge or a hill, but rather the one a hundred yards or more down the far slope. The reason had mainly to do with the artillery; this was a war of big guns, and the high velocity field guns, in particular, shot straight. Plunging a shell into a trench on the far side of a hill without direct observation was a tricky business, even for the howitzers and trench mortars. All of this suggested that the German defences in the third line would be largely unscathed, no matter the barrage.

'1st Division is assigned the northern half of the hill,' Clark-Kennedy continued, '2000 yards from Bois Hugo south to the 2nd Division boundary near Cité St. Laurent. We'll take the right half from there to the Lens-Béthune road. The 4th Division's on our right flank.'

'The division's drawn a tough card, sir,' I said, studying the map. Most of the ground General Burstall's division was to cover consisted of a swath of built-up suburbs ringing Lens to the northwest. Although the highest point of the hill, the one that had given Hill 70 its name, was several hundred yards north of the divisional boundary.

'Yes,' he replied simply. '4th Brigade is on the right of the divisional frontage. We're to move beside them through Cité St. Laurent and Cité St. Émile. To reach the Green Line we'll need to cover roughly 1500 yards.'

In lieu of telling him what I really thought – that I didn't envy the 5th Brigade one bit – I clucked sympathetically. Sometimes a full tot of the truth is not what anyone wants or deserves to hear. A brigade is a sizeable force until you consider that an attack on a frontage of 1000 yards, penetrating 1500 yards deep, implies occupying 1.5 million square yards. Which is a figure large enough to raise any eyebrow. Even for 3000-odd men it was a lot of ground to conquer. Then there was the question of the terrain involved. The warren of ruins that were all that remained of the rows of mining housing would provide near endless possibilities for cover for the German defenders. Naturally, the artillery might have since transformed it all into ash, but that sort of false hope I'd given up on long ago.

'Assuming we reach the objectives,' he said, 'intelligence believes the Boche have three divisions in immediate reserve. We've been warned we're likely to face them in short order.'

'Three divisions, sir? In addition to the two already in the line on the hill?' Assuming my arithmetic was on the mark it was an intimidating number.

'Yes. That's right.'

'Hmm,' I replied.

An officer waved in our direction. 'Here.' Clark-Kennedy thrust an inch of paper into my hand. 'Take a look at the aerial photographs, MacPhail. I'm afraid I must run.'

Having thus explained the situation, Clark-Kennedy quite sensibly departed, leaving me to my own devices. He had more to do than shepherd a supernumerary lieutenant from another division through the various elements of the operation.

I examined the photographs with interest, and spent a considerable time studying the map again – that was invariably useful. The operations orders were particularly revealing. As was typical, the attack was expected to go in quickly. The unusual part of this operation was the focus on consolidation afterwards. That too had to be done quickly. I'd never seen such elaborate plans before, not even at Vimy. But then with three German divisions, including a Guards division, ready to be thrown in to regain the hill there was good reason.

No one of the staff appeared in the slightest interested in me. I was all but invisible; if not invisible then no more noteworthy than the tatty furniture that filled the place, with the further disadvantage I was not much to sit on. A typewriter was chattering away at a breakneck pace. The telephone was in continuous action. Every man in the room was engaged in pressing conversation.

'Lieutenant?'

Mildly relieved someone wished to speak with me, I turned to my questioner. 'Yes?'

Captain Smythe stood before me, flushed, his eyes coal black. It was an odd contrast with his eyebrows and moustache, which were as sun-bleached blond as ever. Earlier out the corner of an eye I'd noticed him flitting about, but studiously ignored him while I spoke with his superior. Suddenly he was standing in front of me. Perhaps for the first time ever I understood the wisdom of all the drill and discipline in the army.

'Sir,' I said, without thinking. I just said it. To a man with three pips on his shoulder, it was unquestionably the right thing to say, and almost certainly not what I would have said otherwise. Routine and rote had their advantages.

'You're to report immediately to the 24th Battalion,' he said officiously. There was a frost to his voice.

I frowned. 'The 24th Battalion?'

Until now I knew little of the 24th Battalion, except to know that they weren't the 25th Battalion with whom I *was* familiar, or the 22nd or 26th Battalions with whom I wasn't. Like all brigades the 5th Brigade consisted of only four battalions. Somehow I couldn't imagine this particular one was resting at some château in reserve. Only if it wasn't in reserve, that meant they were going over the top in – a quick flick of the wrist – a little more than twelve hours. I was being ordered to the trenches.

'Are you certain you have the right man?'

'Oh yes, MacPhail. Quite certain.'

Somewhat flustered I said: 'But, sir, I was expressly sent here in order to liaise with the 3nd Division, which I can't very well do at the front. This is most unusual.'

He chuckled, cruelly to my ears. 'Well, if you'd like to take up your orders with General Ross – by all means feel free, Lieutenant.'

The brigadier was in the corner with Clark-Kennedy and another officer. From their faces they appeared to be in the midst of something terribly important. Smythe's face was studiously neutral. However, there was something about this turn of events that was definitely not right. I looked again at the brigadier. No, that avenue was as firmly wired off as the approaches to Lens.

I scowled at Smythe but said nothing. There was really nothing further to say.

CHAPTER 29

14ᵗʰ and 15ᵗʰ of August, 1917
Cité St. Edouard (1500 yards northwest of Lens), France

Largely obscured by banks of cloud, an anemic sun was beginning to set as I moved down Cossack Trench. Small groups of soldiers were heading in the same direction I was, towards Cité St. Edouard and the assembly area. This was an "IN" trench. Heaven forbid that I'd chosen an "OUT" trench; the traffic control men had their strict orders and woe become a soldier, or even an officer, who disregarded the precise flow the brigade staff had so painstakingly arranged. A few hours from now, at 11 p.m., the crowded cellars of Cité St. Pierre would empty and the assaulting companies of at least two battalions would move forward, with the result that Cossack Trench would become far more crowded than it was currently. Those few arrows might indeed prevent unnecessary chaos.

From somewhere not far ahead there was the blast of a shell. My senses sharpened. I'd been conscious of the periodic booms ever since setting out, however this was the first that was so close as to require my immediate attention. Then the sharp crack of a gun firing beside me demanded it again. That sound I knew; it came from an 18-pounder. I darted a glance right and was in time to see a wisp of smoke curling from the muzzle of a barrel, the gun itself entirely hidden from view amidst the ruins of a house fifty feet away. Then a second gun next door went off. The field guns had been at it all day, pounding the German wire and trenches. In return, the enemy was lacing this area with shells in an attempt to silence them. It must be said there was little evidence their gunners had achieved much. The men were thankfully still underground, keeping their heads down. But the German bombardment sounded as if it was increasing.

Not being underground only reinforced my resolve to keep my own head down. This resulted in a wrong turn or two, but finally I located battalion headquarters in a spur off Martyr's Alley – a dozen men working in tight quarters in a small dug-out. I remember thinking the air didn't smell too fresh after I'd gone down a few steps. Another shell went off nearby and I tumbled down the remaining steps with alacrity, almost landing in the arms of an officer from the Victoria Rifles (that was how the 24th Battalion preferred to describe themselves).

'I'm Lieutenant MacPhail of the 3rd Division staff,' I proclaimed, a little awkwardly, to the assembled faces.

'I was told we were being sent an extra man,' responded a voice. 'Even if you aren't quite what I imagined, Lieutenant.' The voice belonged to a lieutenant-colonel, surprisingly youthful for his rank, who'd cleared a way past the others and stood perusing what had dropped down his staircase.

'I know exactly what you mean, sir. That's how I feel most mornings when I spy myself in the mirror.'

The stern expression he wore slipped. It had probably only been an attempt to lend gravity to his modest age; I learned later he was a mere captain a few months before. But then he gathered himself, crossed his arms, and solemnly introduced himself and the rest of the staff. Majors Hall and Bales, the second in command and the adjutant, looked on.

Colonel Ritchie carried himself with a natural dash, and with his piercing eyes, and a long forehead capped by thin, neat hair that he parted to one side in a modern fashion, made me think he was an intelligent man. It was a novel enough trait in the senior ranks of the British Expeditionary Force that I took note.

However I couldn't help thinking about what Ritchie had first said to me. It was a curious turn of phrase he'd employed, about an 'extra man' being sent to them. There wasn't a word devoted to the importance of cooperating with another division, or how I would be invaluable in maintaining links with battalions that might be called upon to reinforce his in the heat of battle. But as his next sentence revealed the colonel hadn't misspoken.

'You're very welcome here, Lieutenant, whatever unit you hail from. I have a feeling I'll need every officer I can lay my hands on in the next few hours.'

Cannon fodder, I grumbled to myself. That's how he saw me.

With that everyone went back to their affairs. And I came to rue the moment I hadn't protested more forcibly to Captain Smythe when I had the chance. Not that I entertained any illusions protest would have helped.

Fortunately, I wasn't left to stew in these dark thoughts. Major Hall approached and kindly offered to show me their plans – an offer I gratefully accepted. Neither the Victoria Rifles nor its sister 26th Battalion were to lead the Brigade's advance; they were to leapfrog through the other two battalions at the first objective and advance to the final one. However, in order to avoid the German counter-barrage on our lines it had been decided that they should go forward on the very heels of the others.

'Excellent, sir,' I said excitedly. Many a follow-up unit had met its demise by waiting too long.

The whole world exploded above our heads. The timbers that held up twenty feet of earth or more swayed and shook, and seemed as if they might buckle completely. Dust and dirt tumbled down. I feared for a desperate moment that we might be buried alive. The candles flickered briefly under the onslaught, then went out. In the darkness someone began to cough. The air was heavy with thick dust, but the roof held. I closed my eyes, my heart galloping wildly.

When I reopened them, someone had found a match and had it going, and soon others followed. Then a candle was lit. Blinking, as my eyes adjusted, the central chamber of the dug-out looked as if it were cloaked by a thick fog. Through the fog I heard voices and saw the forms of men getting to their feet.

'A direct hit,' someone muttered.

'Was it, now?' said another. A pause. 'He'll have to try better than that.'

All in all I found it a chillingly decent effort by Fritz. Any better and there would have been few wise noses around to comment. Of course, this banter was part of the game. At one time or another we all played it. If you weren't afraid, the fellow next to you couldn't very well be either, and vice-versa. No one had any patience for the man who fell to his knees and began sobbing at every turn. If anyone had, a lot of us might have been tempted to join him.

After a spell outside to clear the lungs and the mind, and allow one of the staff to pronounce the dug-out roof sound – though I questioned his expertise in such matters – most returned below. Some like the chaplain and Major Hall disappeared in the direction of the assembly area to await the companies coming up. If given the choice I would have joined them. Dug-outs were fine and well, and an excellent place to be provided they didn't cave in on your head as I was unconvinced this one wouldn't. When in doubt better to take my chances against a Maxim. With the exception of a small slip up at Regina Trench with a trigger-hungry Fritz, I'd been pretty lucky in that regard.

But no one gave me the option, and I stayed put in the dug-out all through the assembly, as the falling gas shells forced the troops to don their box respirators. By a quarter to three in the morning it was reported that all four companies were formed up and prepared for the attack.

Then entirely of its own accord the sky rumbled, and it stormed, the gas blown to the four corners of the Artois in sharp gusts of wind and rain. The waiting resumed. Everything that could be done had been done: one hoped.

At 4 a.m. there was a scare when the Germans began to heavily bombard our lines. Was the enemy aware of the plans? My next thought was of the *Arendtstation* that Corporal Smith and I had seen, and the pile of transcripts from intercepted calls we'd found there. But after five minutes the shelling died away. Creased brows were mopped in relief. A pregnant stillness reigned. Someone cleared his throat. A lone rifle fired in the distance.

Finally, a roll as of thunder filled the air. The roar neither wavered nor receded in volume, the earth shaking in weary commiseration, while the sky flashed brightly. The field guns were firing a creeping barrage. The medium guns and the Vickers machine guns were aimed at the trenches and strongpoints that were the day's objectives, while the heaviest howitzers and naval guns were reserved for assembly areas and gun positions far to the enemy's rear. For those who wished to consult their wristwatches, it was 4.25 a.m. The long-delayed attack against Hill 70 had begun.

To the east a line of flame appeared as if marking out the Gates of Hades. In addition to the fury of the barrage a special company of the Royal Engineers was projecting drums of blazing oil onto the German lines at several points along the line. They would be most effective for their shock effect, and the dense black smoke that billowed forth when the flames died away – less so as a weapon. Dawn was an hour and a half distant but already the sky was a slate grey, and the violence of the shellfire risked lighting up the advancing platoons as they hastened forward. Many had worried beforehand about enfilade fire from the south. The smoke was a godsend.

Flurries of S.O.Ss went up along the German line; green bursting into two green. The OC and a few of the staff were topside watching the spectacle, but fled to the dug-out when the German bombardment began a couple of minutes later. It hadn't taken the Boche gunners long; Cité St. Edouard was being pummeled.

It was some while before the first word from the advance was received. I was as anxious as the rest.

'Brigade reports the Blue Line has been captured,' announced the man at the telephone. But this positive development was soon overshadowed by the arrival of a runner ten minutes later with other news. While the bulk of the battalion had successfully jumped ahead of the German bombardment, two platoons of the last company, D Company, were caught navigating the ruins of Cité St. Edouard heading towards the enemy front line. Losses were heavy. The company commander and two platoon commanders were reported to be amongst them. Furthermore, from the sparse details, it appeared the survivors had since veered off course.

Then sometime before 6 a.m. it was confirmed that the rest of the battalion had passed through the 25th Battalion at the Blue Line. The report was timed 5.21 a.m., almost exactly an hour since it began.

The battalion was through Cité St. Laurent, and were fighting their way into Cité St. Émile. Moving house to house, enemy soldiers hidden in fortified cellars, B Company reported the opposition as "stiff". A Lieutenant Matheson of the company was wounded in a duel with a German officer. Beyond that Matheson was said to have had the better of the duel, it was unclear whether the attack was being ground down in the ruins of the suburb.

After a little less than an hour came the answer. Major Lamb and the rest of B Company had fought its way through St. Émile and were mopping up. This news was closely followed by other messages that stated that both A and C Companies had passed through and gained a precious foothold in the final objective, Nun's Alley. However, C Company was reduced to 30 men, and A to 20. They'd lost nearly every officer they had at the hands of "concentrated" machine-gun fire.

Lt.-Col. Ritchie appeared caught between two conflicting emotions. On hearing that the Green Line was taken he slammed the fist of one hand ebulliently into the palm of the other. No one had thought it would be easy, but his battalion had done it. His elation ebbed quickly when he heard the present state it was in. He turned now to Major Bales. 'Two companies. Between them they're barely a full strength platoon,' I heard him sigh. It was an aside not meant for general consumption, although in a dug-out this size it was hard to hiccup without the entire chamber hearing. 'We have to scrounge every man we can and send them forward to reinforce,' he muttered. The worry was etched on his face. There were far too few men to hold the line when the enemy counter-attacks came. No one doubted they would.

As he finished saying this a private tumbled down the stairs in much the same manner I had.

'Private Grant, sir,' said the soldier, panting, presenting himself to the colonel. 'Major Hall sent me. He's found what he thinks is a suitable dug-out for a headquarters in City St. Laurent.' He made no pretense at saying it the French way, but then few did. No one misunderstood him as a result. Which might have given me reason for reflection. He handed the colonel the folded message he'd brought from the second in command.

Ritchie scanned it quickly before looking up; every man in the dug-out was watching. 'Major Hall says he's had two runners killed, but Grant here knows the situation and can guide some men forward. Bales, you'll remain here with me. We'll keep a couple of men to assist. All the rest of you I'm sending forward.'

He caught me frowning.

'You came at a fortuitous time, Lieutenant MacPhail. It appears we need you more than I could ever have imagined.'

When I thought about it, it was nice of him to say; I couldn't have imagined them needing me either. Nevertheless, it was meagre compensation for what was being asked of me. As far as my superiors in the 3rd Division were concerned, I was already missing in action, and the odds of being added to the real casualty list were increasing with every step. Particularly as every step was away from the dug-out and heading east towards Cité St. Laurent and the front line.

There were only seven in our party, hardly the stiff reinforcements required. On the other hand, the boys presently holding the line numbered only fifty. It sounded more impressive to think of our contribution in terms of percentages.

Private Grant led us down a trench, and up and across what had been No-Man's-Land. Then we crossed another trench so blown in as to be unrecognizable as such, and went into what the dawn's early rays revealed to be a graveyard of timbers, brick and plaster. The men who'd gone this way earlier had practiced every step in the preceding weeks, even down to learning the street names and the location of individual houses. I would have benefited from the practice, too, even if my first impression was that neither streets, houses, nor landmarks remained – the place had been badly thrown about by the barrage: first ours, then theirs. Every so often I spotted a doorway or a trapdoor leading below. All were marked with staked signs: CONSIDERED SAFE. As the alternative was MINED – DANGEROUS this was positive; they'd all been checked and found free of traps. With the indomitable Private Grant in the lead, we threaded our way through the rubble.

Arriving at the advanced headquarters I noted it too was considered safe. It was a deep cellar since tidied up and rid of inert bodies by four German prisoners of war. There we were granted a pause for a drink of water before Major Hall hustled us off in the direction of the front line. He appeared as concerned as Lt.-Col. Ritchie about the situation. He was most insistent we hurry.

Where Cité St. Laurent ended, Cité St. Émile began, a demarcation that was clearer on the maps than on the ground where, once past one demolished house, another loomed. Out of the built-up suburbs the ground turned flat and featureless, the scenes of recent fighting more vivid in consequence. We marched in file past three of our men lying face down. They too had been in file. A machine gun had caught them. Then a thought came to me, and I fell out and doubled back.

'I may be needing this,' I said in response to the questioning looks, brandishing the Lee-Enfield and the extra clips I'd scavenged.

At the Green Line (on a reverse slope as promised) we piled into the trench and were greeted with considerable enthusiasm by another major, Amphlett. He told us that not thirty minutes before he and the remnants of his company fended off a whole swarm of Germans approaching at the double from the south and the north. They had a Lewis gun set up to cover the immediate approaches down slope, and he'd hoped we might have brought another, which we hadn't.

The men were busy with picks and shovels reversing the parapet. For the moment there were no complicated strategies or brilliant tactics required here – an extra pair of hands at most. The Poor Bloody Infantry was doing what needed to be done. I picked up a shovel and began to fill sandbags.

My sweat was up and I had my tunic thrown to one side, the sleeves of my shirt rolled up to well past the elbows when two men dropped precipitously into the narrow confines of the trench beside me. Startled I pivoted towards them, raising the rounded point of the spade high, poised to thrust in an instant. They outnumbered me, but I wasn't about to go peacefully.

'Easy on, soldier,' shouted the older of the two in English. The red veil lifted. Then I recognized him and his weary, sagging eyes, and he recognized me and mine. 'MacPhail! What on God's green earth are you doing here?' asked Major Clark-Kennedy.

Wearily I let the spade fall and leaned upon it. 'Well, sir, it's like this. After Captain Smythe told me I was ordered to the Victoria Rifles, one thing led to another, and now I'm here. It appears on top of everything else we're in desperate need of men to fill sandbags at the moment.'

The man beside Clark-Kenny shook his head in what looked like amazement. It was Major Walker. The two of them stood there, dishevelled, white chalk staining their trouser legs, a tired air about them I could relate to. They seemed oddly pleased to see me.

'The major and I were reconnoitering,' said Walker. 'It's reassuring that you have everything under control in this section, MacPhail.' Walker had never been particularly charmed by me and my opinions, although he seemed to be warming recently. Evidently it didn't hurt that they'd come upon me digging trenches for the brigade.

Our attention was caught by two red lights going up, one after the other. They were to the north of us, near the divisional boundary.

The flares were barely extinguished when an explosion of shellfire erupted in our rear, followed immediately by a string of sharp blasts. It continued for the better part of five minutes. Plumes of smoke could be seen rising.

'A Boche counter-attack,' murmured Clark-Kennedy. 'The artillery seem to have them.'

'They're fast off the mark,' I said, referring to the Germans.

'They're well prepared. Everything is planned. We'll surely need them again soon,' he replied, referring to the artillery. 'Keep it up, Lieutenant.' He motioned at the shovel – it was a gesture revealing in its own way, though I may have been mistaken about that. 'This isn't over by a long stretch.'

CHAPTER 30

August 15ᵗʰ, 1917
Commotion Trench, Hill 70, France

The battalion was holding a 250-yard section of Nun's Alley, from the railway line south to the junction with Commotion Trench, and 250 yards more along that trench. On the map, the line held by the battalion resembled the left half of the letter X where the two trenches crossed each other; everything to the east being German – a common enough situation on the Western Front. As to numbers: with sixty-odd men, a major, and three lieutenants (including the orphaned one from the 3ʳᵈ Division staff), it didn't take much arithmetic to make the sum that the Victoria Rifles would be hard pressed to hold it – even if it was only half a letter.

When a platoon turned up from the hard-hit D Company at around 10.45 a.m. under the command of Sergeant Dunwoody – there wasn't an officer of his company left standing – I wasn't the only one glad to see them. But even with the arrival of Dunwoody's crowd the numbers still didn't add up to what they needed to be. Furthermore, despite repeated messages sent by runner there was no sign of the requested Lewis guns. I suspect that had more to do with the deadly perils of snipers and shellfire than recalcitrance on the part of the battalion or the brigade. To the rear, two strongpoints with heavy Vickers machine guns had been established, one near St. Laurent, and the other at the southeast corner of the yard of Fosse no. 14. That was well and good, but the front line had as many uncovered holes as the roof of my first dug-out in the Salient.

By afternoon every last man of the Victoria Rifles seemed to be rushing forward – signallers, runners, cooks and batmen appeared – as well as a considerable number of soldiers who'd lost their way at some stage and found it since. All in all, our ranks grew to 140 men and officers.

'They're massing, sir,' said Private Hillhurst, lying on his stomach and peering cautiously over the newly placed sandbags. There was an excited urgency to his voice. Major Amphlett had assigned me and a dozen soldiers to a 75-yard length of the trench south from the intersection with Nun's Alley. It was my first front-line command since 1916. He didn't know this, although he did know I came from the staff, and if that wasn't enough to dissuade him I felt it only fair I not let him down.

At Hillhurst's shout, I immediately scrambled up the stony incline of the trench to join him and reached for the field glasses. It was the sole pair we possessed.

The enemy soldiers were 800-900 yards distant. They were clustered together near the Brick Works, which was considered in the pre-battle intelligence reports to be one of the spots where Fritz would assemble his reserves. From this position we had an unencumbered view. I felt a lump in my throat. It was a sizeable force, even when viewed from a distance – at least a company, and possibly more. Their officers were forming the men into ordered ranks before moving forward.

'We'd better hope the artillery isn't napping,' I said brusquely, a coolness in my voice I didn't feel. I glanced down at the map that Major Amphlett had given me. I studied it briefly, then sighed. 'Damn. The problem is they're not in our sector. There's no point sending up a flare to alert the gunners. All we'd end up doing is having them bombard the wrong quadrant of the S.O.S. line.'

'But, sir, those Fritzs will be heading in our direction at any moment. I'm sure of it.'

'If you're so sure about it, Hillhurst, stop gabbing and go alert the others. Tell them to stand to. And bring the Very gun on the way back – just in case.'

'Yes, sir.'

'Be quick about it!' I shouted after him.

While I may not have let on, Hillhurst's assessment was entirely correct. I too thought the direction of the German advance would be towards us, down the shallow, blown-out ditch known as Commotion Trench. Nor was it simply a question of what my eyes saw; it was precisely what I would have done had I been in the German commander's boots. The alternative was considerably shorter, from the Brick Works due west to Nun's Alley, but across that ground there wasn't as much as a blade of grass for cover. Commotion Trench to the southwest was the only sensible move.

But how to warn the artillery?

I turned to resume my study of their preparations, the question digging at me. The glasses were halfway to my face when a brief flash caught my attention and it was then I noticed the Royal Flying Corps in the skies. A duo of contact aeroplanes was banking over the Brick Works, one final turn before heading towards our lines. Surely they must have spotted them! Many of the contact planes were equipped with the new-fangled wireless sets. Through the glasses I tracked their progress as they buzzed away over Hill 70, the squadron aerodrome a short flight to the rear.

There was movement now in the German ranks. A double file had detached itself from the others, a line of figures that inched methodically forward in our general direction. Appearances deceived for I was certain their pace was more rapid than what observation suggested. Before long that file, followed by several others, would enter the trench and be largely hidden from sight for a period. When they did re-emerge; we'd have ten minutes – if we were lucky – before they reached the trench we were in. Less than that in an overland charge.

'Flare gun, sir,' said Hillhurst in a rush, standing behind me. His hand was extended, holding the pistol by its barrel. He was gulping in air. Obviously he'd taken my orders quite literally.

A field gun cracked and I cocked an ear. 'Hang on to that thing for just a minute,' I mumbled.

The aeroplanes had indeed been equipped with wireless. With the guns loaded and targeted on a pre-assigned grid they took no time to come into action when the report arrived. The barrage whistled overhead in a perfectly magnificent orchestra of noise, the fall of the shells plain to see from our vantage point, a relentless *crump, crump, crump* following it up. Both the double line and the dense formation of soldiers disappeared behind a curtain of bursting shells, plumes of white smoke everywhere, the smoke already curling up and away in the gentle wind.

From afar the bombardment had a surreal quality to it. The blast of the explosions was clear to the ear, though one grew inured to that sound surprisingly quickly on the front. Yet the scene of spewing earth, and puffy white mid-air bursts of shrapnel, drew the eye as a magnet will metal. A spectacle to draw gasps of appreciative awe. Until one remembered what it was like to be in a bombardment like that. I shuddered at the thought. I kept shuddering until I remembered what it was those soldiers in field grey intended, and then a smile of satisfaction and relief came.

Once more that afternoon the guns banged out. And once more the presumptive attack wilted under a furious hail of shrapnel and high explosive. It couldn't be otherwise that their casualties were enormous. Yet nothing seemed to deter them. That was what was most worrisome.

When Lieutenant Fisher of the 25th Battalion turned up out of the blue, with an entire company of Nova Scotians in tow, I could have kissed him. In fact, I might have done so had he not recoiled at the sight of me.

'Mac? Is that you? I can barely see you under all that chalk.'

I assured him it was. For his part he looked nearly identical to that day in the Arleux Loop when he and B Company had so admirably plugged the gap. That was a mere three months previous. That I'd aged prematurely in the meanwhile, to the point of being unrecognizable, couldn't be helped.

My inducements for them to stay in the front line he politely declined. With an apologetic shake of his head he referred to his orders that they dig in "in close support". 'What could possibly be closer support than right here?' I countered loudly. To which he again shook his head. An extra few tins of bully beef and a handful of soggy *Red Ruby* Havanas were not sufficient to tip the scales.

'Good luck, Mac,' he shouted, when he went off to establish the company's positions. 'We'll be here if you need us.'

He was probably thinking about holding the line, although for me the help might well come too late. I thought then of Kathryn, my late wife. Memories of her popped up at unexpected moments, still startlingly vivid. But I'd faced down death before. Until now I'd scraped through every time. And I would do so again, I told myself sternly.

To underscore my resolve I took out the Webley and flipped open the cylinder to confirm that it was fully loaded. The water bottle was essentially unloaded, and there was nothing I could do about that but wait for Fisher's men to come forward with fresh supplies. I clean forgot to check the rifle.

I am increasingly of an opinion that there is no man quite so predictable as a German. Yet for all the absurdness of shelling a trench at a particular hour every day without fail, whilst his foe is in possession of both a time piece and a certain presence of mind that must inevitably result in precautions being taken, there is an undeniable cunning about the Boche. Given all that had happened this day, it could be no surprise that General von Below would again send forth his men. There was a mad and frustrated desperation to the actions of the enemy. The loss of Hill 70, so unforeseen, had driven the German High Command into a dark rage. Their guns roared and the reserve battalions were flung profligately into the breach. There would be no rest until we were driven from this hill.

It shouldn't have surprised me, therefore, when the next German foray came several hours later – most conveniently after dinner time, and most inconveniently not presaged by an assembly on flat ground in full sight of our lines. On this occasion, as the evening sun slowly set, they slipped down Commotion Trench and Nun's Alley undetected. Until they were 200 yards distant. Then the alarm went up.

Red flares ripped skywards, officers held the empty Very pistols in their hands and felt relieved their duty was done. The more experienced amongst them realizing it was only just beginning. As it had been on every other occasion this long day, the response from our guns was both immediate and devastating.

But, impossibly, stepping through the hurricane of noise and the rolling clouds of smoke and dust and flashes of flame, came the stumbling ranks. Perhaps not so ordered as they had been, and certainly not so numerous, but nevertheless a sight every soldier could respect for their bravery and discipline.

I was concentrated on something altogether different. 'Shoot for Christ's sake! They're all lined up like ducks in a bloody shooting gallery. What the hell are you waiting for?'

There were a lot of them, well more than a company. That was what worried me most. Barrage aside there were scant yards between us. They were pouring down the trench and now also rushing across the open ground in a headlong charge towards our position. Their haste had as much to do with the bombardment at their backs as any real eagerness to fulfill their orders. They couldn't have fallen back if they'd wanted to. The Lewis gun was chattering non-stop. But we desperately needed the extra firepower from the rifles.

Under my firm but steady command – no one seemed to have noticed the shrillness to my voice – the men to either side began shooting like madmen. I stepped over to join them and raised the Lee-Enfield. Every rifle was required.

The short Lee-Enfield is a good weapon. Sturdy and reliable, seldom prone to stoppages, and with a powerful kick to it – at both ends – yet manageable in the cramped confines of a trench or a dugout. Nevertheless, it suffered from the same inadequacies as any other rifle in the field. By the time I discovered *that* I already had a Fritz in my sights.

CLICK. Again I pulled at the trigger. *CLICK* came the unyielding response. I cursed myself for not having checked the magazine. Fear shot through me.

And then it was a scramble every bit as mad as the Fritzs were experiencing before I'd rammed the 5-round stripper clip down into the magazine, thrown the bolt back and forth, and raised the rifle to my shoulder, bayonet fixed. And looked for a target.

He wasn't hard to find. In fact he was heading dead at me, not ten feet from the parapet and screaming like a banshee. It was a target even I couldn't miss, not even with an ungainly 17-inch steel blade protruding from the bottom-end of the muzzle. I fired and he fell. The casing whizzed past my ear when I yanked back the bolt. I rammed it forward and down, and was rewarded with a satisfying click as it locked, my movements oiled by a certain desperation. I fired again. This time the Fritz was so close he catapulted forward and landed with a clatter between Hillhurst and me in the trench behind. Neither of us could be bothered to check. We were firing as fast as we could. The Boche were falling in droves.

'Sir!'

The first shout I'd ignored, what with the desperate scene in front of me and the ruckus all around. But in the meanwhile, someone had thrown a well-placed bomb that cleared up the situation in front. The ground was carpeted with bodies. Smoke was thick in the air.

'They're in the trench, sir.'

At that the blood drained from my head. If they gained a hold in the trench they'd fill it to brimming with men. It would be a sore in the entire line. No, it could better be described as a hole in the dyke, and it didn't take much to imagine how that might turn out.

'Where?' I managed to shout.

'At the junction, sir.'

In many ways it was the most predictable of answers, and also the very worst. The battalion's frontage was centred at the intersection where Commotion Trench and Nun's Alley crossed. Of all the positions to lose that was the most serious because of the ease it afforded the Germans to reinforce, with not one but two trenches funneling into it. If the junction were lost it couldn't be long before the entire 500 yards the brigade held were lost. The 2nd Division's hold on the left half of Hill 70 would be in grave jeopardy. If that didn't hold… well… I shook my head.

'Hillhurst, go and round up some others,' I roared.

'Sir?'

'You heard me. If they capture the junction we're done for. Nothing else matters. We have to put things right, Hillhurst. Find as many as you can.'

Fortunately, Hillhurst was a soldier after my own heart, preferring action to inaction, and not inclined to sink deeper into his slit trench while the furies of the war played out around him. He reappeared within minutes, the fruits of his manhunt trailing behind.

'Six! Six men! Is that all you could find?'

'Yes, sir, including myself. You see it's like this this, sir. Harris and

Clements are on the wire,' he began. Then he checked himself. 'They –'

Impatiently I waved him quiet. 'They fell. Yes, I understand. You mistake me for someone who's sat at a desk this entire bloody war, Hillhurst. And the others?'

'Well there's the fellas on the Lewis gun. We can't very well take them, sir, can we? We'll need to leave a few others behind to hold the trench.' He looked at me dubiously.

'Pfff. Yes… Yes, you're probably right.' Behind him a line of nervous but grim faces stood in file, grasping their rifles, with a wary eye on me.

There was a risk to this I realized. If the Germans didn't capture the junction I might very well be called a fool for rushing off to help, and a fool wouldn't begin to describe it if the junction held and the Boche pressed through the very line we'd just exited. But if there was any chance they did take the junction... I stared back at the men.

'We'll use bombs first. Make sure every man has at least one. Then depending on what we find we'll try a charge. So fix your bayonets if you haven't already.' I frowned menacingly. 'My experience is that Fritz doesn't much like cold steel,' I growled. Brave smiles answered back. My act met their act, and by then all were mutually convinced it would work out fine.

The Lewis gun twenty feet away took up its frantic rattle.

Then we were off. Running.

I insisted on going first, though this was neither customary, nor particularly smart should we unexpectedly encounter the enemy. Having the commanding officer put out of action in the first clash was not a tactic recommended in any manual I'd ever read. However, I needed to determine the situation with my own eyes. There'd be very little time, and decisions would need to be made in a flash. I couldn't permit a bomb being thrown into a melee with our own men. In addition to which, while I may have been a little rusty, I had more experience in the trenches than half these boys combined. Even Hillhurst was slowly cottoning onto that. Most of all, I didn't want them to see my fear, and that was a lot easier done when the only thing showing was my back. I remembered all too well General Lipsett's views on officers who let down their guard on that score.

Approaching the junction with Nun's Alley it was the absence of gunfire that caught me by surprise, for I was expecting a fierce fight. Not more than five minutes could have passed since I first learned the enemy was in our line. While the counter-attack was audibly still underway, I had the impression the tide had turned in our favour. For one thing the artillery barrage was all but silent, and the rifle fire markedly less. But to not hear a single rifle shot ahead?

Motioning to the others to hold fast, I crept forward down the trench. It had been pounded by the artillery into not much more than a deep ditch at this point. I was bent over low so as not to present a profile for a sniper, a loud pounding in my ears, although it could as easily have been my pulse. I wasn't more than ten feet away when I heard the man speak. His comrade responded. Cautiously I retraced my steps.

Only twenty yards measured the stretch of the junction between where first, Nun's Alley, and then Commotion Trench joined our own lines. We hit it running.

This time I wasn't in the van for the very simple reason I'd discovered that, despite my admonitions, MacPhail was the only man without a bomb. In other circumstances it was the sort of dereliction of duty that would have led to a stern dressing down.

'The first two of you throw your bombs. Then push forward until you spot more of them. When you do, hold up for the boys behind you. We'll take it step by step.'

It was a tactic that worked perfectly for the first number of yards. Until we ran out of bombs.

'Damn it to hell,' I cursed. 'Is there no one who has a bomb left?' Heads were shaken. 'Alright, we'll roust the fox with a taste of Sheffield steel instead. *D'ye Ken John Peel* and all.'

They nodded. The march song was one all were familiar with. Vaguely it had something to do with a fox hunt I knew, but mainly it was just rousing.

'Hillhurst, you lead.'

'Yes, sir.'

Which he did with verve until he stopped one with his head at the third traverse. He went down in a bloodied heap, and my heart sank when I saw him lying there, crumpled in the chalk. But rather than dispirit the others it gave them a pluck and a fire in the gut, and all I could do was follow.

A shot to one side, a jab with the bayonet to the other, the Fritzs couldn't have known what hit them. First the exhilaration of taking the trench, the taste of victory on their lips, and then a band of death-dealing intruders descending out of nowhere, wielding half the weapons known to man: bombs, rifles, bayonets, knuckledusters and more.

We rounded the next traverse and came face-to-face with three Germans, all of whom had their weapons pointed and ready. There was little hope for surprise anymore. Even a lightning charge wasn't up to it. Their rifles cracked and our two front men went down. There was nothing for it, but for the handful of us remaining to scream like men possessed and storm down upon them.

I was the third man, an unfortunate coincidence. It was widely held that the third man was the one to tempt fate; the third one to use the match to light his cigarette, or the third one to go over the top; he was the one that went down. There was little I could do except follow the others.

Our first man speared his opponent through the chest, and was attempting to extricate the rifle, while the second shot from the hip, before also using the bayonet. The Fritz facing me stood poised, his helmet down low over his eyes so I barely saw his face, his feet apart, and his rifle held firmly across his body with two hands. With that extra second's grace, he'd accurately assessed the odds. He hadn't attempted to reload. Instead, he batted away my extended bayonet and rifle barrel with a savage swing of his rifle, the sound of it like two bucks clashing horns. I let it fall. And reached for the Webley. But we were far too close together. The German reached forward with both arms, and grasped me firmly by the neck, and began to squeeze.

He was of medium height, but stocky and strong. I started to gasp, my breath coming in short puffs. I felt dizzy. I clenched the hand at my side into a fist and in one quick, violent jerk of the forearm brought it up under his chin. His head shot back and his grip loosened. With my left hand I pulled out the pen in my tunic pocket, and with a desperate thrust I stuck it in him with all my strength. He jerked backward. I shoved him roughly to the ground, and stomped a boot down on his chest, pulling out the revolver.

Suddenly there were sounds of rifle fire at close range. A section of men in olive green stormed into view from ahead. They were led by a lieutenant.

He approached me. 'Morgan. C Company.' He glanced down at the soldier underfoot, the pen still protruding absurdly from him. 'I'm guessing you must be the staff guy from 3rd Division,' he said slowly.

I nodded. 'MacPhail.'

He looked at me curiously, then slowly shook his head. 'You know, until now I never really believed that old adage about the pen and the sword –'

It had been a long day.

The only problem I now foresaw was that night was beginning.

CHAPTER 31

16th to 18th of July, 1917
Front line, Hill 70, France

That night we buried the dead – theirs, and ours. There weren't any burial parties made available by the brigade so Major Amphlett insisted we do it ourselves. Those in the trench were easiest, but during the moments when the shelling rolled on to the north and the glow from the flares receded, a few men would slip out into No-Man's-Land to retrieve another body. Later, others would carry him a few feet to the rear for burial in a hole hastily dug in the chalk. That theirs outnumbered ours by a wide margin didn't make it any easier.

The hole for Private Hillhurst I insisted on digging myself. A penance I suppose. Certainly it was the only thing left that I might do for him after peremptorily sending him forth to his final battle. When we were finished with the whole sobering task, I consumed some iron rations without thought or appetite, and crawled into a corner in the trench where the stones weren't overly large, and made an attempt at sleep. I was dead tired. The ground was cold and hard without a greatcoat, or even duckboards, to lie on. The dark skies flashed incessantly, rumbling and cracking with every shell fired – of which there were many that night.

The walking wounded, by whom I mean anyone capable of standing – there not being sufficient stretcher-bearers – were sent to the casualty stations as soon as practicable. The prisoners went with them, under a cursory escort, for they too were almost all wounded. I relieved the Fritz, the one who had come within a breath of strangulating me, of my pen before he joined them. It was the only one I had. His war had ended. All things considered he was little worse for wear for the experience. As I drifted off, the thought occurred to me he would probably also see a better bed than mine tonight.

I woke an hour later, startled into consciousness by a salvo of 5.9s noisily straddling the trench. It was a wonder they were only straddling it, for the location the Germans knew all too well. A few more desultory shells and the barrage rumbled off towards our support line at Catapult Trench, 800 yards behind in St. Laurent. I went to lie down again but a comfortable position was difficult to find. My side hurt, my feet ached and a confusing procession of visions swirled round in my head. Sleep came, eventually, when like the barrage the procession of visions moved off. Only to be wakened by more shells not long after. And so it went that entire night.

By morning I was shattered.

'Coffee, sir?'

Gratefully I accepted the battered tin mug. It was a contender for the worst coffee I'd ever tasted, but at that moment it was nothing short of perfect. And hot. It was certainly a cup I would remember. Which was a bit like life in that it sometimes takes something brutish to grab you by the neck, in order for you to sit up and take note that things aren't half bad. I sipped more hurriedly than I should have and burnt my tongue. Then I looked round.

The trenches at Hill 70 were unlike any I'd ever seen. If anything they resembled a burlap sack of grain sliced down the middle with a sharp knife, the contents pouring out to either side leaving a narrow path with bulging banks. This trench certainly wasn't the deep, well-built work I was accustomed to from our foe, with its neat willow branch revetting or timber planking along each wall, elaborate dug-outs with electric lighting, plus all the other appurtenances and amenities Joey Blagstock would have approved of and a German abroad required. While it may not have seemed so, the trenches were deep enough that the chalk close underneath the topsoil was amply revealed. It showed up as startlingly white lines on the aerial photographs. I had a startling white about me, too; every inch was either caked in chalk or dusted in chalk. It was as if I was back at the classroom blackboard writing "I promise I shall not throw snowballs in the schoolyard at recess" a hundred times, and making a mess of it.

Early in the afternoon a heavy barrage came down on the junction and we scrambled for such cover as there was. Naturally everyone's first thought was that this was a precursor to another counter-attack. And this proved accurate.

Advancing in long columns four abreast they came, a tactic from another age. The enemy was wantonly flinging battalion after battalion into the struggle. Summoned by the flares, our heavy machine guns started up first, firing long arcing streams of bullets at the distant targets, but to effect. Before long the artillery's mailed fist crashed down in the Germans' midst. Whirling clouds of shrapnel cut swathes in the neat ranks, and by the time the survivors had closed to within rifle range there was little for the rifles to do but pick them off one by one. Then they dispersed entirely.

I sighed in relief. The thought of another mixed battle at close quarters was almost too much to contemplate.

'Thank heavens for the artillery,' sighed Major Amphlett, appearing beside me, setting to words my own sentiments. From his appearance he'd slept as little as I had. Not that any of the men in my little section looked well rested. 'Any casualties here, Lieutenant?' he asked.

'No, sir,' I replied. 'We got off lucky.'

'We were fortunate, then. It appears the company didn't lose a single man. However, our Boche friends show few signs of giving up.'

'No, sir,' I snorted. 'I've kept track of their insignia, and so far I count five different battalions. In a day and a half! You'd think we'd encamped next to the Kaiser's summer home. We've taken the hill, but it's not at all clear if we're going to keep it.' I glanced over at a couple of the men who were sitting with their backs to the wall, their legs splayed out in front, chins on their chests, too tired even to talk.

'I hope the men are up to it,' I added. I said 'the men', although I may have meant me.

'There is *some* good news,' Amphlett said, with a wry grin. 'We're to be relieved tonight.'

I whistled. 'Finally!' I believe I also grinned back.

As events transpired, it was fortunate I didn't get carried away with my exultations.

'Sir?'

Blinking furiously, I looked up. The usual morning haze was affecting my sight. Then I remembered I'd sat down for a bit after dinner. I blinked again. It wasn't dawn at all.

Private Pellow stood over me, staring down. 'There's a S.O.S. gone up, sir. You told me to tell you if there was anything.'

'Yes, I did. Thanks. I must have dozed off. What time is it?'

'7.45 p.m., sir.'

Quickly I discovered the S.O.S. hadn't originated from our section, or even from the two flanks. By then the artillery was already in action, lambasting the interdiction line along a broad frontage.

Tremors shook the ground and a series of bangs reverberated all around. A large black plume of smoke rose from the vicinity of Catapult Trench to our rear. A glance to the left also revealed smoke only a few hundred yards distant, where the 26th Battalion held the line. At the risk of life and limb I climbed the gravel slope to the parapet to get a better view.

'Is Fritz attacking again, sir?' one of the men asked, crawling up beside me.

I'd been pondering that very question. 'I'm not sure. He could be.' Then I took another look. There was a shell falling every twenty or thirty seconds. To my way of thinking that was an intense strafe. The scene to both flanks revealed they were dropping mainly to the left, the north. The rear was getting it as well. If there *was* an attack coming that would make sense; there'd be no possibility to send up reinforcements.

'If Fritz is attacking, I'm quite certain it won't be here,' I said evenly. The man nodded, seemingly reassured. If our boots were switched (or better yet our rank insignia) I would have quizzed him 'til his ears fell off. But apparently my credentials as a staff man who must know such things were finally of some use; which showed how little the poor fellow knew about the staff. In any event it would have been premature mentioning that if the 26th Battalion was under attack, the 25th would

260

be next in line. There was no sense in getting his blood up prematurely. After twenty minutes the ground was still being rocked by shellfire, with no signs of relenting. In the turmoil it was hard to tell which side was getting the better of this battle of the guns. The Green Line to the north was clearly receiving the brunt of the German shells.

It was tempting to keep my head down and hope a shell didn't find its way into our trench. But if the 26th was indeed under attack, or threat of attack, surely it was better to be in the know? That way we could fashion a response ourselves before it was too late. I resolved to go find Morgan of C Company to see if he knew more. They held the 26th's right flank. Locating the sergeant, I detailed him to take command in my absence and tore off towards Nun's Alley.

Morgan shook his head 'No, they haven't been attacked,' he replied. 'Not up 'til now. But they're being peppered alright. I have the impression it's tailing off, however. Our guns are letting them have it.'

'I have a few men I could send should they need assistance. Better to beat them off before they're breathing down our own parapet. That is, if you think they need it?'

Morgan smiled. 'They don't. Not for the moment. But I hope you realize someone may take you up on that, MacPhail. Brigade just sent a message; B Company is at the disposal of the 26th Battalion. If you get an urgent summons from them for men, don't forget you were the one to volunteer.'

I retreated to Commotion Trench feeling a little silly, though later I realized I shouldn't have, and especially not after Morgan told me he thought 2nd Brigade on the other side of the divisional boundary *was* being attacked. On the dominoes theory, the 26th would not be far behind. Then every man would count, including the half-dozen I could scrape up.

The shelling showed no signs of diminishing. By now it was 8.45 p.m. and it had drummed on for an entire hour. Yet no officer turned up with orders for me, or even a runner with news or orders. I instructed the men to keep their heads down (a common sense sort of advice, even if that wasn't something they taught at law school, or even cadet school), and to rest if they could, but to keep their rifles within close reach. I insisted the sergeant do a rifle check of the section. To set an example I did one myself. I'd followed the example of the 5th Brigade and done a practice run beforehand so I wouldn't mess it up in front of the men.

At 9.45 p.m. darkness had fallen, and still the guns roared. Now instead of merely the endless and soul-destroying crump and crash in my head, there was also an accompanying lightshow. The clouds above flashed and flared menacingly each time a gun fired, and again when the shell found its mark.

By 10 p.m. I could restrain myself no longer. I was going bugs from the shelling and the helpless feeling of simply not knowing what was going on. Four men from C Company were just reported hit. I went looking for Major Amphlett, the senior officer of the battalion in the line. Though the chance seemed slight given the severity of the shelling, I hoped he was in communication with headquarters.

Amphlett appeared pleased to see me, and he did have some news. Warmly he shook my hand, when I approached. Then in response to my question he said: 'The telephone is down again, but a runner managed to get through. Our orders are to stand fast, MacPhail. The relief has been cancelled.'

'Cancelled?'

'Yes. The shelling is far too heavy for the 22nd to come forward. Or for us to go back, for that matter.'

'What about the Boche, sir? Are they counter-attacking?'

'The 26th drove them off earlier. But the 2nd Brigade appear to be under attack again at the moment. Other than that I'm afraid I don't know much.'

Barring the sporadic illumination from the shellfire, we were in the dark, speaking literally. Figuratively speaking the situation was not much better.

However, the line of the Victoria Rifles was not yet under attack. With the exception of the occasional stray and the maddening noise and shaking, my section was also having little real trouble on account of the bombardment. That was not true for others.

'We lost a man and had another wounded in the trench, and the same on one of the Stokes,' said Amphlett.

'It was that bloody 4.2 firing at long range, I suppose?'

'Yes. The frustrating thing is I don't think we were even the target.'

'No signs of any gas, sir?'

'No. That's one small mercy.'

I hadn't yet encountered any gas here on Hill 70, even if many had on the way to the assembly area. But respirators like rifles were best held close at a hand. My own experience, with lungs burning and gasping for breath, left me with few illusions, and I'd seen too many men on the battlefield, in the casualty stations and in hospital beds, wheezing and hacking from the effects. But it was the story recently heard of the man from the divisional train in his mask, listening helplessly while his horses shrieked and screamed as they inhaled the poison, which truly twisted the dagger. I hoped I wouldn't be needing that respirator tonight.

'So,' said Amplett. He'd apparently been giving me his final thoughts. 'You'll just have to tell your boys to keep their heads down for another night. With any luck the relief will be tomorrow.'

'Yes, sir,' I replied. That was a turn of speech I was quite sure they *had* taught at cadet school, though admittedly not at law school. It was often useful when you didn't know what else to say. I returned to the men.

It took until 11 p.m., three hours after it began, before the artillery was turned off and I was at last able to order the men to stand down.

Just before midnight another red flare went up.

I muttered a succession of words my mother wouldn't have approved of, and stared apprehensively through the glasses at the ground to the east. Further away fires were burning in Lens – the town was taking quite a basting the past several days. But look as I might there was no sign of enemy activity in the vicinity. To all intents Hill 70 was at rest – inconceivable though that might be.

However, when I thought about it, I could have sworn the flare going up hadn't come from our lines at all. It was too far to the east. I was groggy, but I was quite sure about what I'd seen. Not having seen what I saw, the artillery and the MGs dutifully started up on the S.O.S line with renewed fury.

The men – they'd only just lain down thirty minutes before – dragged themselves again to their feet. They'd been on those feet for two days running: fighting, standing guard, toiling on the trench works. One of them held out an arm and rested it for support on the shoulders of another. They both nearly toppled over. They were dead on their feet.

'I'm going to see the major,' I announced. 'Sergeant!' The sergeant nodded wearily.

Amphlett was also on his feet, pacing nervously back and forth. He was staring intermittently at the plunging barrage a couple of hundred yards from his position.

'Sir,' I said as I approached. 'You didn't send up that Very light, did you?'

'It was not called for by us,' replied Amphlett.

'That's what I thought,' I said, a conclusion already forming in my mind. 'I was watching and I'm convinced that flare didn't come from our lines. I think it's a ruse.'

'A ruse?'

'Yes, the Boche have been seeing S.O.Ss every hour since we've taken the hill, so they must have caught on about the colours and whatnot. I think they're toying with us, sir. Not only will the gunners get no rest, neither will we.'

'I'll send a runner,' he said.

Sooner than I would have expected the guns went quiet. Others must have agreed with my assessment. With that the men settled down to catch some sleep, and I made a stab at it as well.

When at 4.30 a.m. another S.O.S. went up, the whole dreary routine repeated itself. Later I heard that it, too, had been a false alarm. By then dawn was approaching. With the coming of dawn, a new menace appeared.

The Lewis gun near the junction with Nun's Alley suddenly started rattling furiously. There were rifle shots. I grabbed my glasses and rushed to the parapet, only to see the same bleak, shell-mottled slope in front, not an enemy soldier to be seen.

'Sir, get down!' shouted a man. Contrary to my usual inclination to first ask why, I did as I was told. It was his tone, I think. The aeroplane buzzed over low, making a terrible racket and stitching a neat seam down the parapet. Chalk dust permeated the air.

'Thanks,' I mumbled to the soldier, my heart pumping. Richthofen had spawned a whole stable of impersonators it would seem, although this one hadn't painted himself in red to rub it in. Since Vimy I had a grouse on about red aeroplanes. We watched the biplane briefly waggle its wings, climb, and bank off to the east.

For the battalion the day progressed quietly, albeit anxiously, awaiting what the enemy might attempt next, and never sure whether the attempt would involve us. Nor was the quiet particularly quiet. The artillery was at it continuously, dispersing small parties of Boche who had unwisely ventured into the open, or were attempting to move through the shell-torn streets of Lens.

The 1st Division had it tougher I gathered. They fended off at least two strong attacks. The bitter memory of their advances a day earlier resulted in the Germans abandoning their attempts with waves of men, in favour of attacks in small groups. To their dismay the new tactic hadn't worked either.

If my small band was any indication, there wasn't a tactic in the history of warfare the Germans might use that would bump us off this hill.

Except perhaps a scheduled relief. But for all his wiles, that was a tactic not in Fritz's hands.

That night, at an hour past midnight, while our foe played boisterous accompaniment on a whole ensemble of guns, the Victoria Rifles finally moved to the rear. After three days in the front, and for all the weary bones and blood-streaked eyes, and many score of casualties, morale was good. For my part I was even able to manage a relieved smile at the sight of the cellars of St. Pierre. Until I realized I needed to report to the division.

They hadn't heard from me in days. There was some chance that in the absence of any credible evidence to the contrary I'd been marked down as missing-in-action.

So, in the dark, I bumbled through the ruins of St. Pierre and found my way to the brigade headquarters. There I asked for some water and a typewriter, and was obliged with both. If questioned, I wouldn't have been able to say which day it was. Day had passed into night and back to day, and through it all the guns roared and the Germans threw themselves madly at the hill. Fortunately, my report was to be in chronological order.

'Lieutenant MacPhail?'

Wearily I sighed at this interruption and glanced over my shoulder.

265

Brig.-Gen. Ross and Major Clark-Kennedy were assembled, peering down at me. I made an attempt to push the chair back in order to stand.

'Stay where you are,' said Clark-Kennedy gently, a hand on my shoulder.

'Are you quite alright, Lieutenant?' asked the general, frowning.

'Oh yes, sir. I'm just writing my report to the division.'

He screwed up his face in an odd fashion. 'Well, we'd best leave you to it then.' He turned away, then looked back at me. 'Thank you, Lieutenant. And try to get some sleep. This battle's not over by a long stretch.'

It was only the next morning after I saw myself in the better half of a cracked mirror that I began to realize what the fuss was all about. For all the chalk, dirt and smears of blood, I barely recognized the grizzled, hollow-eyed apparition staring at me.

CHAPTER 32

18th of August, 1917
Cité St. Pierre (1 mile northwest of Lens), France

The staff of the 5th Brigade greeted me as one of their own when finally I was able to tidy myself up, put on the fresh socks I was now pleased Colonel Hayter suggested I bring, and eat something other than hardtack and bully beef.

While much had changed in the past several days, not least my standing with the others, the staff room had changed little in the interval. Its thick stone walls and the steel beams of the high ceiling still held the rubble of the floor above from tumbling down, while the cracked tile floor was even muddier than it had been. There was a full complement present, with one notable exception – although I didn't notice that immediately.

Lieutenant Jameson saw me first and made his way over, vigorously pumping my hand and welcoming me back with genuine enthusiasm. The others soon grouped around. Until a soft clearing-of-the-throat sounded, and a passage opened for the brigade major.

'Lieutenant, a moment of your time, please.' Then Major Clark-Kennedy took me aside. Uneasily he glanced around. There were nearly a dozen others in the room. 'Come. We'll take a short walk.'

'I'm afraid I must apologize,' he said, once we were outside in the corridor. Apologies were not something one heard a lot in the army, and from senior ranks to junior ranks not at all, so I was all ears.

'Sir?'

'It's come to my attention the real reason for you being here with the brigade. It puzzled me when you arrived, but it pains me to say that I've since discovered that one of my staff has taken certain...' He paused, clearly searching for the appropriate word. 'Liberties, shall we say. You should never have been sent to us, MacPhail.'

My eyes widened. 'But how is that possible, sir?'

'There was a request sent from the brigade to division alright. In fact, it even appears that I signed it myself. But while the request was in my name, I certainly didn't order it, nor did Brigadier Ross.'

'One of your staff made the request?'

'Yes. It appears that way.' Clark-Kennedy gritted his teeth. 'Well, not entirely on his own. He must have included it in a stack of papers along with other orders for my signature. Why he'd do so, I still don't understand. He refused to say anything when I confronted him.'

The blood rushed to my head. Angrily I clenched my fists. Of course. Smythe. Little wonder I hadn't seen him. This whole charade wasn't meant to be a liaison at all. He'd conspired to get me here, and then sent me to what he probably calculated was the most dangerous spot on the entire brigade front. In that he hadn't miscalculated. And he'd done it with a single purpose in mind; to be rid of me – permanently rid of me. Were it not for a considerable dosage of good luck on my part, he'd very nearly succeeded. With me gone there would have been no chance to reveal what I knew of the entire rotten business with the boots, and his role in it. The bastard! I was conscious I was breathing heavily. 'Where is he?' I mumbled.

'I relieved him of his duties and he's been sent to divisional headquarters.'

At the look on my face, which Clark-Kennedy must have mistakenly taken for concern at my own role in these developments, he continued: 'Oh, don't worry, MacPhail. Your hands are entirely clean in this affair. I'll be certain to inform your division of that.'

'Thank you, sir. However, what shall I do now?'

'That rather depends on what orders you receive from your division, Lieutenant. We'd be most pleased if you remained with us.

'That's twenty one by my reckoning,' I overheard Brigadier Ross exclaim to Clark-Kennedy when the news of the latest counter-attack was reported. 'In four days, twenty one counter-attacks. It boggles the mind.'

Clark-Kennedy, of a similar mind, simply shook his head in amazement.

The following morning the two miles of Hill 70 were still in our hands, and the intensity of the fighting had waned markedly. There were worried discussions about how secure the front was at the boundary of the 1ˢᵗ and 2ⁿᵈ Divisions, where a gap had existed. But fortunately the enemy was licking his wounds – to all appearances. Heavy shelling aside that happy state of affairs endured into the next day.

All of which made my most important task of the day considerably easier. I was to accompany a couple of very important gentlemen to the front line to reconnoitre. Outside of Field-Marshal Haig requiring my immediate assistance these two came near the top of the pecking order. Maj.-Gen. Lipsett and the new GOC of the 7ᵗʰ Brigade, Brig.-Gen. Dyer, arrived at the old mining administration building in Cité St. Pierre at the crack of dawn.

I was prepared for their arrival. Lipsett raised an eyebrow when he saw me, though he must surely have expected my presence. He and Dyer took my hand and shook it, a friendly gesture I hadn't anticipated. 'We were rather beginning to think you'd been lost in action, Lieutenant,' he said.

'I was rather beginning to fear that myself, sir.'

'Well, thankfully, you look in fine fettle.' Diplomatically he refrained from commenting on the state of my tattered uniform; several days of buffing by Major Clark-Kennedy's personal batman had not yet succeeded in removing all the chalk and other stains.

Typically, a patrol such as this to the front-line trenches would be led by an officer from one of the units to be relieved. In this case, all concerned agreed that seeing as it was not only my GOC who was visiting, and I knew the ground as well anyone else, it might as well be me doing the honours – a most convenient solution. Although they were indeed short-handed.

I took the generals by way of the route through Cité St. Edouard, followed by St. Émile and down Carfax Trench to Commotion, virtually to the very spot I'd spent three days and four nights. I attempted to show them the trench itself, the rebuilt parapet and traverses, the two Lewis gun positions situated strategically as had been carefully planned beforehand, but the thing they were most interested in was the view. Therefore, I had them lie on their bellies on the crumbled chalk and stone and peer down the slope towards Lens. The town centre was almost precisely a mile south – I'd measured it on the map in a moment of distraction – the outskirts roughly 1200 yards distant.

'We've had some trouble from those first rows of brick houses that you can see,' I said. 'Snipers.'

The two generals flattened themselves even further.

'I don't expect it'll be a problem today. We're a little too far north here. But follow this trench down to St. Elizabeth – then they're only 700 to 800 yards away – and you'd be advised to keep your heads very low indeed.'

Brigadier Dyer grunted. He didn't seem impressed. A little stoic gruffness for the benefit of the divisional commander, I expect. He'd commanded his brigade for little more than a month.

Lipsett went off on his own tangent. 'You've seen it, MacPhail,' he said. 'What do you think?'

I paused, gathering my thoughts. There could be only one thing he was referring to. I was hoping very much it wouldn't come to that. 'Lens is a veritable Sevastopol, sir,' I replied. 'It may not look like much, but many of those ruins you see are fortified with reinforced concrete, and if they don't have a sniper in them, they have a machine gun. The whole town is connected by tunnels, allowing the enemy to move when and where they please. The artillery would have to turn the entire town to dust.'

'Come now. Surely it can't be that bad?' protested Brigadier Dyer.

'Worse, sir. Even if the whole town was dust they'd simply climb up from their caves and their tunnels when the barrage was done.'

'I see,' he said.

Lipsett began fidgeting with his field glasses. He refrained from further questions.

Later I took them up Commotion to Nun's Alley, and even further to the junction with Norman. They thanked me politely when the reconnaissance was done, but said little further. So little that I wondered if I'd somehow said something I shouldn't have. It had been known to happen. Perhaps Brigadier Ross would have me.

Very early the next day, on the 21st, the 6th Brigade of the 2nd Division, and the 4th Division in concert further south, accompanied by a thundering barrage, began to push the line forward. Down the modest slope of the hill in a southeasterly direction lay the objectives of Cinnabar and Combat Trenches, a scant 500 yards away. So close to Lens were the objectives that the men in those trenches could probably smell breakfast being prepared each morning. Although by dawn this morning the battlefield was a smoking, bloody mess, and breaking the fast was the least of anyone's concerns.

The Boche were quite finished with licking their wounds and had construed plans of their own. In some bizarre coincidence they counter-attacked in force at precisely the same moment as our attack went in. Two locomotives collided head-on in No-Man's-Land; a barrage to front and to back to keep the contestants in the ring. They fought it out with the bayonet and the fist. A battle royal.

There was little question the enemy had again brought forward new divisions; music to the ears of our commander-in-chief, whose very design was to draw the enemy away from his precious offensive in the Salient. Locally, this development was received with less enthusiasm. As the prisoners were questioned and identified, it was confirmed that the flower of the German army was being sent against us: the 1st Guards Reserve newly arrived, to reinforce the battered 4th Guards and the others. There was a palpable sense of relief as first evening, and then night came. The fighting subsided. A costly and futile day behind them, most of the troops who survived were back at the Green Line by sunset.

For me the evening was only beginning. My division was to relieve the 2nd Division this night.

Brig.-Gen. Dyer and staff arrived around nine to establish their advanced headquarters. This allowed Brig.-Gen. Ross and his staff to pack their bags, which consisted mainly of countless boxes and large leather valises filled with paper.

With a few others I remained behind to ensure there was no

confusion about the entry routes or the final destination. Reliefs are generally routine affairs; only, one brigade relieving another in the front line in the middle of the night is never routine. This relief was no different.

Fritz pounded the back areas with his guns. For a time, all feared the worst. Nevertheless, word eventually came that the 7th Brigade was forward; the 5th had suffered only lightly on the way back.

By 6 a.m. the next morning the relief was reported as complete. Benoît's old regiment, the Royal Canadian Regiment – I had paused, my thoughts of him when I first heard which unit it was to be – relieved the 25th in the line and the 22nd in immediate support. The other battalions went into reserve.

Shortly thereafter I hitched a ride with the remaining 5th Brigade staff as far as Sains-en-Gohelle. The 2nd Division HQ had moved a couple of days before, on account of the frequent shelling from heavy howitzers and naval guns. So I didn't linger. With the sun at my back I walked the four-odd miles to Barlin, the next village over, in roughly an hour.

I spent most of the walk wondering what would come next. Then I got to thinking of Benoît again. Part of me was worried he'd been tried, convicted and was waiting in a military gaol at the coast to be transported to England. But the other part of me could barely wait to tell him about Smythe's downfall at the hands of Clark-Kennedy.

CHAPTER 33

22nd to 25th of August, 1917
Barlin, France

'Look who Fritz gobbled up and spat out,' said Fotheringham, by way of greeting when he spotted me entering the familiar first-floor office at the Mairie – otherwise known as the staff room. He was wearing a big grin making it difficult to take him too seriously. Still, given my druthers, I would have removed it for him in a flash.

Instead, to chuckles from the others, I merely clenched my fingers into a ball and jabbed playfully in the direction of his nose. It was an inviting target it must be said. He sniffed, then smiled tepidly, perhaps guessing at my thoughts. Uncharacteristically, he said little as several of the others questioned me about my experiences in the line. Eventually he couldn't help himself.

'While you were off rolling around in the chalk you missed meeting our new GSO1,' he said sprightly.

'Colonel Hore-Ruthven? Yes, I heard. What's he like?'

There were grunts of approval, or the nearest wary staff men might come to a full-fledged endorsement at this early stage. Fotheringham had no such reservations. 'He's a very engaging man when you get to know him.'

At this I rolled my eyes. 'And you do, I take it… *know* him?'

'Don't be such a spoilsport, MacPhail. If you hadn't taken it upon yourself to disregard all your orders and disappear for a week on end, you might know him, too.'

Which though I hesitated to say it aloud, was more or less precisely what I was worried about. Good intentions and convoluted explanations aside, I had virtually disappeared for several days – if not exactly the week Fotheringham suggested. The new GSO1 might indeed have something to say about that.

As the gathering broke up, Fotheringham had one other thing to add. 'Now that we're back in the line, and with a new number one, it appears that the position on the staff will be filled shortly.'

'Position?'

'Don't be coy, Malcolm.'

I rubbed at my chin and pretended to reflect. 'Ah. That one,' I said, finally.

'Yes, well, good luck and all that.'

'Yes, and all that,' I repeated. I don't think he so much wanted to wish me luck as to hear me say it to him, and I wasn't going to give him the pleasure. As far as Fotheringham was concerned his promotion was as good as a done deal. He may have been right.

As soon as I was able – it proved to be the next morning – I went in search of Benoît. I first walked over to the same little street, and to the same little house where he'd been billeted. I pulled at the little brass door bell. Inside I could hear the chimes ring.

A little old, grey lady answered the doorbell. '*Oui?*'

I explained in my best French that I had come for Benoît DuBois, a lieutenant in the army, who was billeted there only a couple weeks before, and that I was a friend –

'*Ah, monsieur DuBois,*' she interrupted, her eyes sparkling. '*Entrez, monsieur. Entrez. Entrez s'il vous plait!*'

Benoît was seated in the sitting room on a chesterfield whose origins must have predated the little old lady. He sprang to his feet when he saw me. 'Mac! *Enfin!* There you are,' he boomed, grasping me in a firm bear of a hug, and smiling from ear to ear. 'I was worried something had happened.' A lot *had* happened since I'd seen him last, but it had only been two weeks.

The old lady was beaming at the sight. Suddenly she put an index finger to the air as if some thought had descended from on high, and she rushed off. We both looked at each other. Benoît shrugged. She reappeared with a gleaming silver tray, and perched on it a bottle of Champagne and two crystal glasses. '*Et voilà, messieurs.*' Leaning forward she carefully lowered the tray onto a round wooden table of a similar vintage to the chesterfield, and began to peel back the gold foil from the neck of the bottle.

Volubly protesting Benoît stepped over and took her place. He grasped the bottle with one hand, and with the other he helped her find a seat. The foil went flying. With a *crack* the cork popped and I nearly jumped out of my skin. The old lady laughed deliriously at this. Then he poured a glass and handed it to her. She sipped seriously before nodding her approval. Benoît filled the other glass foaming to the brim, thrust it in my hands, and disappeared still holding the bottle.

Moments later he reappeared with another glass: a water glass, this time – she probably only had two of the real thing. We laughed, drank our champagne, and spoke exuberantly of nothing at all, though it seemed at the time like much more. When the glasses were empty the little old lady turned solemnly to Benoît and explained that she would leave now so that he might be able to speak with his friend in private. He thanked her gravely.

Then when we were alone, he refilled both glasses with what remained of the wine. His face was now of a grey seriousness.

'A date has been set,' he said.

'For when?'

'Next Monday.'

Today was Thursday, so that made it... 'The 27th?' I asked.

He nodded.

'Do you know who's presiding?'

He shook his head.

Then I told him of Smythe being relieved of his duties and sent to headquarters. 'That must surely help,' I said. 'In fact I was hoping it might have already. Perhaps if I speak with Brigadier Ross and connect the dots for him. It is his brigade, after all. And I did help him out –'

Wearily Benoît shook his head. 'Thanks, Mac, but it's far too late for that.'

I assured him that I didn't think that it was, but deep down I also had my doubts. Once the army started marching it wasn't easy to call a halt, or even change direction. If the worst came to the worst, I did have some things to say in his defence; I'd devote some careful thought to how best to do it.

Benoît wore a stiff upper lip, though his eyes woefully betrayed him as he and the old lady stood together in the narrow doorway and waved good-bye while I ambled off down the street.

Back at the Mairie, sunk in my thoughts, and somewhat lightheaded from the wine – even for my doing it was on the early side, especially after days imbibing nothing more intoxicating than petrol-infused water – I went to climb the white marble steps to the door. Someone else was doing the same. It was a lean, middle-aged man with thick dark eyebrows and matching moustache, a triangular face, pensive eyes, clad in the uniform of a lieutenant-colonel. Little guesswork was required to establish his identity.

Smartly I saluted. He returned it rather more casually as befit the disparity in rank.

'I'm Hore-Ruthven, and I'm presuming you must be the elusive Lieutenant MacPhail?'

I hadn't realized it before, but our new GSO1 was an Englishman. I should have known with a double-barreled name like that. 'Yes, sir,' I replied.

'I've heard rather a lot about you,' he said. I observed him closely hoping to garner some clue what that might imply, but to no avail. It was a problem I'd encountered before with English gentlemen, especially those of a military bent, who can be infuriatingly inscrutable. On the other hand, he didn't ream me out as some officers might have done, along the lines of: "what the hell were you thinking, you fool," or "I think you'd be more in your element in the trenches, MacPhail." Or worse.

'I'm certain we'll have another opportunity to speak soon,' he said. 'However, with the 4th Division operation on...'

'It's on, sir?'

'Oh, you didn't know. Yes, they went after the Fosse St. Louis and the Green Crassier very early this morning. With a little luck we'll hem Lens in from three sides.' He turned away.

The abandoned pithead installation of Fosse St. Louis, with the Green Crassier to its right – the latter so named because of the grass and weed that had taken root on the towering mound of slag – dominated the southern approaches to the town. The rail yards and the station were immediately behind, the town centre only a few hundred yards further. 'Damn,' I said, thinking of the many soldiers and machine-gun posts I'd spotted amongst Lens' houses.

Hore-Ruthven turned very nearly 180 degrees to face me again. I'd seldom seen a senior officer change course so drastically. If he'd been in the navy the boat would have sunk in its own wake. 'Do you happen to know something I don't, Lieutenant?'

I felt my cheeks reddening. 'Oh, I don't think so, sir. Only that both those objectives are almost in Lens. And Lens is as good as unconquerable, sir. At least from what I've seen of it.'

'Yes, well, I'm sure General Watson and Colonel Ironside have taken that into account.'

However, by the end of the day it appeared they hadn't. Or not such as their men noticed.

'The Fosse's changed hands several times today,' said Captain Ferguson. He was naturally the first man I'd gone to, looking to hear how it was progressing. 'It appears it's more heavily manned than anticipated.'

'I could have told them that,' I grumbled. 'And I've only seen it on a map. I thought your colleagues in intelligence would be on top of these things, sir.'

Ferguson ignored me. He was good that way. 'They've scaled the Crassier, however. But the whole thing's a little up in the air at the moment.'

By dawn the next day there was little in the air, least of all hope. The puits no. 14, Fosse St. Louis, was again in enemy hands. The last of the 44th Battalion were still clinging to the sides of the mountain of culm known as the Green Crassier. By afternoon they were killed or captured. Or so we assumed after many hours passed and there was no word from them. It had been a pointless slaughter. And entirely predictable.

I blamed the GSO1, Colonel Ironside. He was the height of arrogant superiority at the best of times, hence it seemed only fair to blame him at the worst. But General Watson shared the blame, as did the brigade commander, Hilliam, all of whom must have known the fool's errand they were embarking upon. If only they'd considered it more carefully. Many more attacks like the last few and the hard-won victory at Hill 70 risked becoming a defeat.

The next day Lt.-Col. Hore-Ruthven took me aside. 'It appears your scepticism about the attack on Lens was well-founded, Lieutenant.'

'It's a shame if you ask me, sir. We have the hill, and even a toehold in the town itself. The Boche are surrounded on three sides. Why don't we just let them stew in their cellars? With all the gas and H.E. coming down on their heads they may eventually decide Lens is not worth the bother.'

He sighed. 'Before you jump to conclusions, Lieutenant, you must realize there's a great deal of pressure for the Corps to capture Lens.'

That he'd condescended to explain was remarkable. His explanation no less so, though I'd suspected as much. Dreaming up schemes of conquest was always easiest when staring at a map in a quiet locale, with birds in the trees, and nothing more dangerous than a cup of hot tea to hand. Field-marshals didn't drink anything stronger I was told.

'Yes, sir,' I replied. Which was not really a reply at all, but it hadn't been Hore-Ruthven's fault. Besides, he wasn't interested in my views. That a lot of men were dead, wounded or prisoner due to bad judgement, was nothing new this war. Likely not in any war.

'You may be interested to hear the good news, however.'

'Oh yes, sir.'

'The 50th Battalion took Aloof Trench this morning. It cost them only seven wounded.'

The German position in Aloof Trench had allowed our foe to retain a nasty salient around the suburb of Cité St. Théodore on the western side of Lens. On the map its form resembled the bubble a schoolyard bully from the east was blowing in some kid's face to the west, not realizing General Watson's boys intended to burst it in his. They'd tried without success on the 21st. But today's encore was more successful.

'That is good news, sir.'

I hesitated, wondering if I should ask. I barely knew the colonel. But he seemed to know me, or at least *of* me, so there seemed little reason not to. It was definitely a question of acute interest to me. Having relieved both the 1st and 2nd Divisions we were now holding all of Hill 70. Any fresh attack from the north or west of Lens would be the 3rd Division's show. I wasn't sure I was up for another show.

'Do you think there'll be new plans for us, sir? Will we be expected to take Lens?'

Then, decisively, he shook his head and told me the best news of all. 'No. There aren't any new plans,' he said, 'least of all regarding Lens. We're to hold the hill until further notice. The offensive has come to an end, Lieutenant.'

I grinned, a smile that could have stretched from sea to sea. The average Very light shone dimly by comparison. Hore-Ruthven couldn't help himself. At the sight of me glowing thus, he too began smiling. If he hadn't been a colonel I would have slapped him good-naturedly on the back. The two of us must have looked a sight standing there; the trim, neatly-dressed colonel and the tall, less neatly-dressed subaltern sharing a private joke. But then anyone who'd heard what I heard would have completely understood.

No more plans. No more attempts to wrest Lens from the enemy. For his part, with the passing of each day, a weary resignation came over the enemy and increasingly he seemed to accept his lot. To appearances Crown Prince Rupprecht had abandoned any further designs of reclaiming the ground lost. No wonder. He was probably short of men.

It hadn't exactly been Sir Douglas's intent – his concern was that more Germans not turn up in the Salient – but General Currie had thrown the enemy's plans for relief in the north into violent disarray, and transformed Hill 70 into a vast cemetery for the enemy. Our casualties were not light. They ran into the many thousands, nearly half in the past several days – maybe 9,000 all told. But in return we'd gone up against some fifty battalions. Five German divisions were mauled, a couple badly enough they had to be pulled from the line. No one knew for certain but total German casualties were said to be 12,000 to 15,000. I found it a cautious estimate. One figure was absolutely certain; nearly 1,400 of them were prisoners. For the attacker to suffer fewer casualties than the defender was unheard of this war. Almost equally unheard of was an instance where Sir Douglas's strategy of attrition resulted in fewer losses to our side than to theirs.

It felt good to have carried the day. But most of all I was relieved it was over.

CHAPTER 34

26th of August, 1917
Barlin, France

Some days you waken and shortly thereafter something happens that makes you almost certain the day ahead is going to turn out all right. I hadn't had many of those days since the war began. But I hadn't forgotten they existed.

After what was probably the best sleep I'd had in months, partly due to a proper bed, but above all because of yesterday's news that further attacks were off the table, I had a spring to my step. Then came breakfast, which invariably lends a further spring I find, particularly if generous portions of bacon are on offer. Eating my bacon and sipping my tea I was reading the morning papers, dated yesterday. First came my new favourite the *Daily Mail*, which had some lines about our progress here at Hill 70, but was mainly devoted to events in the Salient. However, buried in the back pages, I came upon a notice that made me jerk straight upright. I very nearly spilt the tea over my bacon, newspapers and clean shirt. All of which would have been a great shame. "In the matter of the bankruptcy of Smythe and Company..." it began. I read to the end.

Quickly I flipped to the front page and began anew. At the bottom of page five on the left there was a small column I'd missed earlier. My eyes flitted over the text.

NORTHAMPTON MANUFACTURER BANKRUPT

One of the nation's largest suppliers of boots to the army filed yesterday for bankruptcy… Embroiled in a growing controversy about the supply of deficient footwear to the army the venerable firm of Smythe & Company has entered into voluntary insolvency. Sources inform the Daily Mail that since the suspension of government contracts the company's finances had deteriorated rapidly… Investigations continue into the company's role in the "Boots Crisis", which some, including this newspaper, have likened to the Shell Crisis of 1915…

I raised my cup in salute. The Smythe clan had reaped their just deserts. Cold or not, tea had never tasted better. I drained the last of it, rolled up the paper with the intention of showing it to Benoît later today – he'd enjoy this I knew – and jumped to my feet. Only at the thought of Benoît my whole feeling of well-being evaporated in a flash.

I would go see him as soon as possible, I decided. His trial was tomorrow and I still knew nothing of the details.

'Ah, Lieutenant MacPhail. A moment of your time, if you please.' Startled I looked round.

General Lipsett and Colonel Hore-Ruthven were standing in conversation a few feet away. Since returning to headquarters I'd seen almost nothing of the general. In fact the last time we'd spoken was during the reconnaissance with Brigadier Dyer.

I went to them, stiffly self-conscious, pulling at the creases on my trousers.

'We haven't seen a great deal of you the past month, Lieutenant,' said Lipsett casually. 'There were moments I almost forgot you were still on the staff.'

'Sir –' I began to sputter.

Lipsett held up a hand. 'I spoke yesterday with Brigadier Ross of the 5th Brigade about you. As a matter of fact, you were the reason for his call. I understand that there was a mix-up with your duties. The brigadier explained there'd been a staff error, but he also said that he was very glad for it. From what he described it sounds like it was a real scrap those first few days. He wished to tell me that several of his officers mentioned your name in their reports – in rather glowing terms, according to him. Fearless was one of the words I recall he used. Not that I've ever doubted that.' The glimmer of a smile appeared on the general's face.

I looked at my feet. 'I – '

'Good staff work is crucial,' continued Lipsett. 'But no good staff officer is a one-trick pony. That's the expression, is it not?' A pause. 'You did the division proud, MacPhail.'

He turned to Hore-Ruthven. 'Colonel, you've rather a lot to do. Perhaps the captain might be able to assist?'

'Yes. Yes, he might very well, General,' replied Hore-Ruthven. My head was spinning.

No, there was no mistaking the smile now. 'You heard correctly,' said Lipsett. 'I'm promoting you, MacPhail.'

'You are, sir?'

'You seem surprised?'

'Well,' I bumbled, 'Fotheringham just seemed...'

'Fotheringham?' The general's eyebrows furrowed together. He shook his head. 'No, I'm very certain the orders I signed had your name on them. It's not a name I'm apt to forget.'

'I don't quite know what to say, sir.'

Lipsett glanced at me, then at Hore-Ruthven. 'For posterity's sake, remember this day, Colonel. Young MacPhail is seldom at a loss for words.' Then he looked me back to me.

'"Yes, sir," is always an excellent response I've always thought,' he said sternly.

I nodded. 'Yes, sir.'

It was hard to concentrate on the chores Hore-Ruthven came up with. I suppose it was the colonel's way of letting me know that, captain or not, I was on his staff. After the report on the disposition changes, orders for reliefs both planned and provisional, and having fielded a dozen calls from various units on every topic imaginable, it was evening.

I went outside to get some fresh air. Barlin wasn't much. But it did have the advantage of being out of range, or out of mind of the Germans, maybe both. The air was definitely plenty fresh. There was also something refreshing about not having to flinch at every bang or crash, calculating whether the next one might be coming my way. The skies however had darkened. What had been a fine day until past noon, was showing the signs of an impending storm. Thus forewarned I made it as far as the white marble steps before concluding there couldn't be a finer place in the entire village to have a seat.

'Mac!'

Suddenly there he was. Striding down the street, an arm held high in greeting. The voice was unmistakeable. To anyone other than the blind, the sight was too; there were few silhouettes on the front less obvious than his.

I stood. 'What the devil, Benoît? You're confined to quarters! I'm not sure this is the best moment to be out and about, not with your trial tomorrow.'

'There's no trial, Mac!' he beamed. 'It's been cancelled.'

'Cancelled?' I repeated cautiously, suddenly worried he'd misunderstood someone's English.

'Yes, I'm a free man! There's to be no court martial.'

It was only after I heard every last detail that I believed him. Captain Smythe had been arrested, his visitors from the provost marshal had explained. There were no details, and no word of any charges related to Smythe's involvement in the boot fraud. Not that they would have told Benoît even if there had been. So I didn't enquire further. But I knew Clark-Kennedy was livid about the orders drawn up in his name. That would be more than enough. It was a serious charge.

'With Smythe under arrest there was no case anymore, Mac.'

'Ha!' I cried, finally catching the clue. 'No. Of course not. They couldn't very well take Smythe's word against yours when they've just locked him up. And with Long Archie guarding the gates to New Brunswick... How perfect!'

I'd never before thought the army administration pragmatic. But someone had intervened at the appropriate moment. Which was a miracle in its own right. Ironically it was Smythe himself, in his panic, who sealed his fate. If he hadn't been so dead set on seeing me at the receiving end of a Moaning Minnie, Benoît would have been tried. There was a good chance he would have been convicted, too, though I would have made an unholy ruckus of it.

Benoît looked at me with that terribly earnest look that I knew foreshadowed something serious he wished to say. 'I owe you, Mac.'

'Of course you do,' I said breezily. 'I'll add it to your tab.'

'No. I'm serious.'

'So am I. How about dinner? *La Tour d'Argent* in Paris? I hear it's a decent feed. You pay, I eat?'

'Mac!'

'What about your water bottle then? You did bring that, I hope?'

He shook his head of a fashion, and handed it to me without further ado.

Then the rain started coming down. In great buckets. But it didn't matter. He was smiling and I was smiling. And it didn't matter one little bit.

AUTHOR'S NOTE AND ACKNOWLEDGEMENTS

As the spring of 1917 gave way to summer, the disastrous French offensive at the Chemin des Dames under General Nivelles was coming to a bitter end, the French army in near mutiny. Further north, along the banks of the Scarpe River, the Battle of Arras stuttered from battle to battle to finally reach an inconclusive and costly close by mid-May. The first days' gains, and particularly the capture of Vimy Ridge, the only significant successes achieved in five weeks of battle. Soon Field-Marshal Haig would begin the offensive in Belgium (the 3rd Battle of Ypres), better known today as the Battle of Passchendaele. It began well, with a spectacular attack in June at Messines Ridge, but the fruits of that victory were left to rot on the tree. It would not be until August that the attack began in earnest. By then the worst rains in a generation were transforming the ground of the Salient into a morass. The campaign quickly devolved into a bloody grind, with heavy casualties on both sides. And from that grew the idea of a diversion, a distraction – something to draw the Germans away. It was to come at Lens. All summer, from across the Douai Plain, and from the west, the Canadians and the British had pricked and probed at their opponent, pressing the line steadily closer.

Lens was a modest enough town, its only real strategic value due to its position at the southern approaches of the city of Lille, and as the centre of the French coal industry. As the many references in the book attest, mines and installations littered the countryside in this area, and still mark it even today. Making one's way to the Hill 70 memorial (east of Loos, and close to Cité St. Pierre and the trenches the 5th Brigade would have used to move to the front) the pyramids of slag are inescapable. The siege of Lens, however, would become the battle for Hill 70.

The fight for the hill was not an easy or a costless one, but a fight for the town would have surely been far worse. What was a rare and decisive victory for the Allies could have ended much differently had the objectives not changed, the result of a timely intervention by the new Canadian Corps commander, Lt.-Gen. Currie. While Lens was to remain a thorn in the Allied side until the war's end, its sharpest point was clipped, and the well-laid plans of the Germans to relieve their forces in the Salient disrupted. Despite this, Hill 70 has sometimes been called the forgotten battle of the First World War, and there is a certain truth to that. I find it a shame.

Malcolm's story (whilst fictional) hews closely to the actual events of that summer. The battles, units, places, and the majority of the characters described were real. One of the unexpected joys of researching this book (and the others in the series) was encountering some of these men at different times and in different places during the course of the war. Every so often I could place one of them in Malcolm's path.

An example is Major Clark-Kennedy, whom Malcom first met at the railway dug-outs near Vimy, and who eventually (to my surprise) became a recurring character in the story. Later in the war he was promoted to command the 24th Battalion, and would win the Victoria Cross in 1918 at the Fresnes-Rouvroy Line.

Other men are more controversial. Brigadier-General "Long Archie" Macdonell is one of these. His fiery reaction to his tardy dinner (Chapter 3) whilst his brigade fought their way forward through the wire and the trenches at Arleux did not happen. Yet the story is inspired by a similar (and true) event in September of 1916 at the Somme while his brigade was in action at Courcelette. As far as I am aware, no historian has yet bitten his teeth on the details surrounding his brigade's confusion during the attack at Arleux, nor the circumstances of his curious transfer home on the eve of the Hill 70 battle.

Another figure who I had hoped to have Malcolm cross paths with was Ernst Jünger, of *Storm of Steel* fame; unfortunately the facts didn't lend themselves. Tantalizingly, during the second of the Arras offensives, he and his battalion of the 73rd Fusilier Regiment were stationed in Fresnoy, only 1000 yards from the attack at Arleux. In fact, they were amongst the first to be thrown in to hold back the tide. Sensibly (and frustratingly for me), Jünger was in a cellar much of the time, and emerged unscathed – unlike the men from the other two battalions of his regiment, one of which was all but destroyed.

Where the historical details didn't always cooperate in my favour, sometimes they did; revealing illuminating details such as the on-off fear of a German general withdrawal that kept staffs busy, contradictory evidence arriving almost daily. In my take, Malcolm was ultimately put on the wrong foot. However, I suspect even the Germans were not of a fixed mind. What is cut and dried in the history books of today was anything but that summer, and I hope to have conveyed the very real uncertainty the Allies felt as they sought to tighten the noose around Lens.

The sub-plot revolving around the interception of telephone communications arose from reading various intelligence summaries and orders. The date and approximate time of the attack of 28 June towards Avion was indeed known to the Germans. Furthermore, an *Ahrendtstation* was captured sometime later, although no intercepts regarding boots would have been found at the scene - the "Boots Crisis" being entirely of my making.

Once again I owe thanks to my stalwart platoon of Dexter Petley, Diann Duthie, Dr. Gary Grothman and Ian Forsdike for their time, efforts and good counsel, which saved me from my worst mistakes and unquestionably improved the final result.

I hope you enjoyed *A Summer for War*. If you did, I would be thankful if you were able to leave a few words of review online at the retailer where you purchased it.

Should you be interested in receiving early notice of future publications, I encourage you to sign up for my email list at www.darrellduthie.com/email-enlistment. You may also be interested in browsing the rest of the site to see details of all my books, as well maps, a glossary and other information related to the Great War. There's a contact page as well, should you want to get in touch.

Many thanks for reading!

Darrell Duthie
Amersfoort, the Netherlands

BOOKS IN THE MALCOLM MACPHAIL WW1 SERIES

The books are numbered in the order in which they were written. Each can also be read on its own, or in chronological order.

Also available as e-books, and some titles in hardcover and as audiobooks.

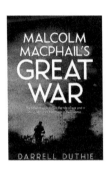   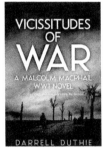

WRITING ORDER

Malcolm MacPhail's Great War – (1917-1918)

My Hundred Days of War – (1918)

A War for King and Empire – (1915-1916)

Vicissitudes of War – (1916-1917)

A Summer for War – (1917)

CHRONOLOGICAL ORDER

A War for King and Empire – (1915-1916)

Vicissitudes of War – (1916-1917)

A Summer for War – (1917)

Malcolm MacPhail's Great War – (1917-1918)

My Hundred Days of War – (1918)

Printed in Great Britain
by Amazon

36204060R00169